Desires
and
Darker Knights

Wendy Ruocco

To Marie + Roy with much love Wendy x

Torbay Books
7 Torquay Road   Paignton   Devon TQ3 3DU

By the same author

Dark Knights of Compton Berry

Dedicated to my husband Michele,
our three children, my Mum and Dad.
With thanks also to friends whose support
has encouraged me to continue.

ISBN: 978-0-9551857-5-5

First published 2009 Torbay Books

Torbay Books
7 Torquay Road, Paignton, Devon TQ3 3DU

Printed and bound by CPI Antony Rowe, Eastbourne

Chapter 1
Leonora

An overpowering pungency of wild garlic permeated the still air trapped beneath the canopy of trees in summer growth as the gentle eyed little palfrey picked her way along the path; unseen birds chattered their disapproval at the intrusion. With hauteur unsuited to her youth the lovely young woman perched side saddle stared ahead, oblivious to the beauty of the woodland around her. Sunlight formed a halo around the lustrous brown curls tumbling down her back, as if glad to be free of the jaunty little riding cap that sat slightly askew on her head. Stooping she patted the horse's neck and spoke tenderly

"Well my pretty it seems that the wealth of Sir Ciabhan of Compton Berry doesn't extend to welcomes!" At the bottom of the slope and rounding the large elm that stood sentinel she found herself facing a small castle whose limestone fortifications contrasted starkly with the green of the surrounding forest; tangles of bramble and overgrown shrubbery encroached almost to the walls. High handedly she called to a man walking beside an elderly woman towards the arched gateway, Leonora wasn't certain but he had appeared to hasten his step on seeing her

"Good fellow," she called, "pray tell where I may find your master of Compton Berry?" A sound behind her made the young woman turn irritably in the saddle; a man stood close to the horses' flanks, "Do you not know it dangerous to approach a horse and rider from behind sir?"

His features were hidden by a straw hat, one worn by those who toiled in summer sun, she didn't see his smile as he replied, "And do you not know it is equally as dangerous for a woman to approach where she is neither invited nor welcome!" Her cheeks coloured and the blood pounded her temples, how dare a common villein …. For that was what he appeared to be….. Address her so! She had merely stated a fact. She dismounted and smoothed her skirts before straightening to her full five foot. Raising her head she found herself looking into a pair of bemused sapphire eyes, they glinted beneath the brim and for a fleeting moment she was reminded of the sea on a blue and flawless summers day, slightly higher than usual her voice cut through the silence, "Dangerous certainly that your master considers it fitting to address visitors in such contemptuous terms, invited or not!" Now In the shadow of the entrance and almost out of sight, the woman leaned closer to her companion and whispered, "Well there's no mistaking who that young madam is!" without looking back Ciabhans response was terse, "but without one ounce of her mothers charm or grace; beauty sits ill on one so proud!"Mati smiled tolerantly, "like her father I meant my dear."

1

Alain waited for the girl to speak again; slightly ill at ease in the company of one so confident he remained inscrutable.

She continued, "Allow me to start again sir, the decrepit over there seems unable to hear! Let alone reply!" she nodded in their direction but the archway was clear, making her feel rather foolish.

She brushed at invisible specks on her skirts, "Maybe you will afford me the courtesy of a reply?" she added.

Alain pushed his hat back and wiped his brow revealing a tanned and youthful face, his voice had a slight accent, taking care to avoid further offence, he asked, "And what exactly is it that mademoiselle requires of us?"

Mallow nudged towards some inviting grass, Alain held on to the reins tightly.

Leonora without appearing too familiar edged closer hoping for an invite into the castle …but the young man was far from the naive she supposed! and blocked her path …. Ending any hopes she had of going further; seeing her plans foiled she reverted to petulance.

"Is it true the great Sir Ciabhan is so detested he lives in constant fear of the retribution he so deserves?" her words were ill chosen and Alains reply curt. He was beginning to dislike this trespasser, never easily goaded he replied civilly, "You are mistaken Miss! Sir Ciabhan is not detested, that is an honour held by one much closer to yourself."

Of whom he spoke puzzled her. Alain bent to her stirrup, "Having found your way here, I presume you in no need of an escort back!"

Sweeping aside his cupped hands she hoisted her skirts and mounted neatly, "you presume rightly Sir!"

She jerked on the reins; Alain backed away, "I wish you a safe journey mademoiselle." He said bowing slightly.

Ignoring him she prodded Mallow back the way she had come.

Offering no escort to a lady was insulting, and unchivalrous, Leonora fumed as she rode; the day had been wasted, her plans come to nothing. Pagonston was in view when she recalled his parting words…..'Back to Pagons Ton' he had said, but how did he know from whence she came? She had never set foot near accursed Compton Berry before this day… the young man certainly was odd but a warlock? It was said they could see the future and were possessed of strange powers; a simple farm labourer could no more see the future than she could. She smiled at her foolishness; magic existed only in the mind, a realm of fancy…. but his words continued to puzzle her.

Never would it have occurred to Leonora that resemblance to her father made her familial ties obvious, she was fixated only on the slight to her person, and her failure to claim her mothers emerald ring.

Distinctly chill an easterly wind whipped from the sea, jamming the cap firmly over her ears, she hunched low over Mallows neck hoping no one would stop her as she headed home. Passing a tavern popular with apprentices she tolerated their taunts, "Hey sweeting care for some company?" the whistles rang in her ears, drunkenly they slammed tankards on trestles. Leonora ignored them. One cockier than the others hollered, "Us could do wonders for a little beaut like you! You don know what you be missing maid!" from lowered lids she saw their lewd gestures and heard the laughter, she spurred Mallow on soon the voices faded but the sickly sweet stench of cider lodged in her nostrils, the all too familiar smell she loathed.

As she passed the woodcutters' cottage smoke stung her eyes, in the sandstone quarry the ringing of axes echoed, chipping and hewing at the soft stone, in summer the forest trees swallowed the toiling men completely. But in winter the red quarry cliffs stark against watery skies could clearly be seen, when young she'd played in the dangerous quarry even though forbidden; too carefree to realise the red dust had been an obvious giveaway.

How long gone were the Golden days of her childhood thought Leonora bitterly.

Skirting marshy flats she turned into the narrow street where Pagons Ton started, stalls did a brisk trade serving locals, the slayer of livestock revolted her and she pulled her cloak across her nose, shutting out the smell of blood , likewise the butchers where bloody carcasses hung; the very air seemed tainted by flesh.

Her father still mocked those sensitivities, he had been gentler when she was a child, holding her tight he'd carry her pass the noisome fowl, and squealing beasts.

As she neared home Leonora wondered what awaited, for in truth little of that once warm childhood remained. Her parents' sandstone manor had once been a haven of love, she and her siblings adored, as first born she was always her fathers' favourite; a cynical smile trembled her lips, how times had changed!

Late afternoon when her father took a nap was usually peaceful, maybe she could slip in without being noticed, but today it seemed that was not to be,

Indicating the chaos that waited the noise shattered the silence,

Disbelieving she surveyed the scene in front of her, with revulsion she watched the figure staggering drunkenly in the centre of the confusion.

"Father what in Gods name is happening? Have you taken leave of your senses?" about him chickens and ducks flapped and scrabbled in clouds of feathers in their bid to be free of the confinement, unbelievably the fat

3

sow normally found wallowing in her mud pen slid past in a squealing mass almost taking Leonora with her.

"Gods blood" she gasped regaining her balance, "this truly is a madhouse!"

From the mayhem her Father staggered, jug of cider clutched in his hand, it slopped on the soiled floor as he kicked wildly at the squawking hens. Confronted by his daughter he slipped on the fouled slabs, and landed on his backside.....disgusted Leonora looked at him.

"So I share my home with two pigs now!" she spat.

Slowly Leon recognised her through the alcoholic haze and attempted to rise, scrabbling in the filth, he mumbled, "No home of yours this child you made your bed with the 'milksop' Now sleep on it!"

Leonora bristled, her father always used the same insulting term to describe her husband and she hated it; especially as he was right!

Leon laughed; a drunken guffaw that showed up the yellowing broken teeth in his drink mottled features, his once proud Gascon face ravaged by neglect. Leonora shook her head in despair; how she wished she were a son then she could have beaten him, or used the sword to bring sanity to the monster before her. Dear God what had become of the bright eyes and easy charm of her once adored Father, this wretch was a disgrace!

"You disgust me," she hissed as he rolled in the dirt, "have you no shame? How can you taint our family name ....and my mothers' memory!"

Seizing a pitcher of water from the table she hurled the contents over him, and followed it with lead pitcher for good measure, it flew from her hands to land inches from his lolling head, how she wished it had hit him! For a moment he remained silent, almost reflective, had she humiliated him? Suddenly he tried to strike her, flailing around like an idiot.

"Your mother, that bitch, that Templars whore, and you! I should slit your throat, like I should have slit your mothers! Lucifer's bitches...both of you!" he spluttered, "get from my sight or by God I'll do it!" She'd heard it all before, "Believe me father, I would rather be Lucifer's daughter! Believe me leaving will be a pleasure, maybe I'll take my chances with The Templar dog!" She knew those words would hurt.

"What point a useless daughter anyway?" he screamed.

That night exhausted and scared of her fathers' wrath she was unable to close her eyes for any length of time .It may have been of some comfort if she known that but a few miles away the man she unkindly thought of as a 'farm labourer' found sleep as elusive as she did.

4

Alain Rousseau was no fool, and well aware of whom the day's uninvited guest had been. On first appearance the visitor possessed none of the renowned beauty of Faye. The haughty young woman was the image of her father, a man Alain knew well, yet there was about her person a subtle aura, the way she sat her little horse, the proud turn of her head, and the tumbling tresses, all bore more than a passing resemblance to her mothers' loveliness; the intangible essence that had been Faye.

However the defining moment for Alain, the actual proof that Faye's Daughter stood before him were the girl's eyes, sincere yet defiant…and somehow innocent! Faye's had been pure hazel, the colour of autumn forests, whereas her daughters were green, almost the green of the emerald Ciabhan wore! Unusual eyes but with Similarities to her mothers that were inescapable, hazel or green the warning flash of anger when the pupils darkened were identical,...... never would he forget the girls' eyes.

What kept Alain awake that night was that he knew Ciabhan had noticed those similarities to, even from a distance; probably the reason he hastened his step, unwilling to face the moment.

Hours passed, night birds quieted and the tallow burned low, Alain struggled to sleep, finally as a fox barked in the valley slumber descended silencing his sighs.

On the highest part of the parapet overlooking the valley Ciabhan also had heard the fox, alone with the memories that haunted him nightly.

The heavens draped their beauty around him as they did Night after night. Ever since Faye's death when the castle slept was when his soul ached most to hold her, to smell once again her perfume, In the terrible days after her death he wanted to follow her, thoughts of flinging himself from the walls filled his mind, but now they seemed selfish, traitorous to her memory, and embarrassing…she was worthy of so much more.

Peering into the darkness he saw in his minds eye the curving path that led to the silent clearing where she lay, alone; beneath the mossy mound under the high beech and oaks, with his mind far from reality he allowed his eyes to imagine the path ways...

He could even feel the stinging branches as they whipped against his skin, he felt the dew damp and cold beneath his feet, with every step the illusion became his reality and he trod the familiar path closer and closer to his love, praying that death would hasten for his soul. Filling his head was one thought only, the absolute need to lie within her embrace, for eternity to grant in death that which had been denied them in life.

Morning light silvered the little glass bird; it had sat on the window ledge as long as Leonora could remember, in this her parent's bed chamber. When young she and her siblings slept in the inner chamber that led from the main room, always warm the snug inner chamber projected over the screen passage and hall below, and benefited from its fire, many were the times as a child that she listened excitedly to the comings and goings of visitors. She remembered how the chill draughts gusted from one open end of the screen passage to the other; particularly so when the house was full of guests and doors were open...she could still hear their footsteps grating on the pitched pebble floor. Eyes sticky with sleep she lay quietly enjoying the moments before her father and his unpredictability stirred. She supposed him laying semi conscious wherever he had dropped the night before, any sympathy she felt for his predicament was long exhausted. With an effort she pushed thoughts of him from her mind concentrating instead on the glass birds glowing colours. She heard the town waking, without servants to help with every day tasks she prepared to rise. Leon had seen to it that those once happy to be part of their household no longer wished to work under such a master; particularly one of whom it was whispered was a murderer. She listened, beyond her door the timber gallery was quiet; no footsteps sounded on its wooden floor or on the circle of steps that led down to the parlour. By the light of the tiny window that lit the stairway she tiptoed downstairs, through the outshut and into what remained of the garden. The charred pear tree once so proud looked sad, its growth never recovering from the fire that swept through house and outbuildings; still it struggled valiantly with little shoots from season to season.

Even though she had tried to be quiet her father had heard, "Daughter?" he called from the parlour. Pulling her shawl around her shoulders, she made her way in, "And who do you think it might be, God and all his saints?" For a moment she thought him about to apologize, she even opened her mouth in readiness to forgive him. "Did you get it then?" he enquired. "Get what Father?" she stammered back. Deliberately as if talking to a child, he slowly spoke the words, "Don't play games with me girl, or has marriage to the milksop weakened your little brain!" frustrated he continued "The emerald? Or has it already slipped your empty head? You went to Compton Berry yesterday, why?" suddenly Leonora remembered, but remained silent. Leon raised his voice, "Curse you girl! Did you or did you not bring back the end to all our troubles? God in heaven don't tell me you returned empty handed, that the black dog still has what is rightfully ours!" Her fathers' French accent was thick and pronounced, ugly even, how could such a rough tongue ever have been thought attractive? according to her mother his broken English made

6

young maids go weak at the knees.

Now it repulsed her and she pushed him away, anger transformed her green eyes to daggers, as loosing the demons of her hatred she screamed, "You are the only reason for our wretchedness Father, your obsessive jealousy, blaming any but yourself for our misery, you alone have bought us to ruin. Mother has lain cold in her grave these past five years yet still you look for excuses! You sicken me, your and pathetic ramblings, in fact I no longer believe anything you say, as for the ring I don't believe there was such a thing, just a figment of your imagination! Another facet of hate!"

Leon stared at her his cheeks a florid infusion of temper and cider, choking with emotion the words stuck in her throat and she struggled to continue, "You think the town has sympathy for the wronged husband, but let me tell you, they whisper of your dark heart, how you abandoned mother even though she begged you to take her home, to the little she had left! Look around you!" waving her arms in the direction of the east gable where daylight shone through charred rafters, "You couldn't even rebuild her home properly, the home you knew she loved, that's how much you loved her!" Tears stung her eyes and she turned in disgust from him, "you killed the man responsible for her murder, you avenged her death so let that be an end to it, you were no longer even her husband!"

That even his daughter accepted the divorce he considered illegal bought Leon to boiling point and he exploded "Yes I killed the monster who took her life, but not the man who stole her soul, mark my words daughter I will have the blood of that dog of Compton Berry!"

Physically spent, Leonora gathered her shawl from the ground where it had fallen amongst the feathers and dirt, wearily she replied "Call me no more daughter, from this moment I am fatherless, kill the dog of Compton Berry if you must, and seek out the elusive emerald, but do it alone for I would rather return to the milksop!"

Within the hour Leonora had collected and packed all she possessed into a leather saddle bag, together with a few coins. Within the folds of a spare woollen cloak nestled the little Venetian glass bird, the only object she possessed of her mothers, she smiled ironically, the emerald would have to wait!

In a repeat of the night Faye rode from the sad little sandstone manor so many years before, her daughter now left, with her fathers' curses ringing in her ears.

Chapter 2
Trey

The Cornish landscape stretched before him; its golden fields shimmering their heavy crop as far as the eye could see.

Treys pig like eyes shone with satisfaction, all this bounty represented his hard work; his alone. A dead father untimely taken and a mother over the border in Devon, neither had helped him; five years of sweat had been his, and the toil of one relative, his father's sister Ida whose small holding it had been. From humble beginnings Trey now possessed wealth, and power over others. Although only eighteen years of age he looked older, bullish he resembled his father Torr, a name that would have sat upon him well, but Trey, short for Trefor it was.

Little about his appearance or personality could be considered attractive, short and bowed of leg from years in the saddle his gait was hefty and forward leaning, a threatening posture used to intimidate, something that came naturally to Trey, it compounded his air of menace. His thickset frame was topped by a thatch of coarse sandy hair making his Saxon ancestry obvious; no one could mistake him for a Norman. Any unfortunate enough to incur the wrath of Trey would recall his bizarre eyes, yellowish in colour, primeval and hostile to pity darting slyly beneath heavy brows missing nothing. What passed for communication was primitive also, consisting of guttural one word commands and replies. Manners and etiquette were foreign to this ignoramus, for tutored only by Aunt Ida who little by little had undone any of the good learned from his simple but worthy mother; not one saving grace remained.

"Harvest looks good master, plenty for the winter and some to spare" said the thin lipped man beside him scanning the horizon "we'll be needing more help with the cutting"

Barely moving his lips Trey replied, "No more, let them earn their keep!" Used to his masters' morose nature the reeve nodded agreeing.

"That they'll do."

Trey watched the reeve trot down into the barley, shouting orders, when only the top of his head showed and his yells had died away, Trey turned his face towards Devon, "Eighteen! Time to settle the score, murdering Templar dog."

Trey ate as Ida bustled, she placed in front of him potatoes in pastry with beef and turnip, meat juice ran down his chin as he slurped his tongue around sticky lips. Again and again he asked about Devon and the night he had come to Ida all those years ago………

"Bleddy miserable little thing you was, I never saw nothing like it
before; nothing! Skin and bones, not like now you bleddy great ox you!
God knows what they bleddy fed you on buy? Theys good for nothing in
Debn' just a load of bleddy milking maids, tried making you one an all, If
you asks I!"
Open-mouthed Trey listened, he liked it when Ida talked about the night
he arrived with his father and how she lay into her brother, "Tell us again
aunt what did you do to e?"
Ida placed a crock of steaming apples bubbling under even more pastry
before him, "Well buy I tells e, es' a shameful fethur an dun deserve a
son, if e dun wan im then I'll ave im for working the land, then e tells me
all what 'appened an how you wus both thrown owt by that there sir
Kevan, Well I tells Torr the thick fool, that I can't be feeding two mouths
but I would take you buy and look after e till e came back, but as you
knows well as I, e never came back again!"
For years Trey had heard this story, it always finished the same, when
with ale soaked breath Ida would whisper,
 "When yous eighteen buy an a lot bigger, thens the time for revenge, for
your fether was murdered , by that Sir Kevan sure as I's a Cornish
woman!" throwing her head back she would cackle, "Come on buy eat up
them teddies afore you wastes away, you'ms got to get them bones strong
if you wants revenge!"
Trey could remember happy days spent with his parents Mati and Torr in
the sandstone manor by the sea, he recalled their Master Leon, who
always gave him coins, and his wife the pretty lady Faye who smelled so
sweet. His only friend was the fair lady's daughter, Leonora... older than
him by a few years she had cared when others hadn't; taking his hand as
they collected mussels from the shore, occasionally he thought of her.
  A sallow youth called Edmund would come visiting, and then Leonora
would ignore Trey and had eyes only for the skinny stranger.
  One day the house was busier than usual, Leonora kissed Trey on the
cheek, embraced her mother and Father, and waved goodbye to everyone.
Trey recalled his mother and Lady Faye weeping in each others arms
while Torr and Leon escorted the young couple from the house. Much
later he understood the celebrations had been marriage, that the boy
Edmund had taken away his Leonora, from that moment Trey hated a
man he hardly knew with a passion .....Such was his ignorance.
None since made him feel as special as Leonora, the wenches of Pagons
ton scoffed and called him names, they would point and snigger. His
father told him to stop his girls' blubbing and take the taunts like a man,
Mati cuddled him close and kissed his tears away, while the lady Faye fed
him comfits and sweet lemon water.....

9

Those far off days had ended in a haze of fear, with wailing and fire and fights between his parents, locked deep in his mind were the memories of a convent where girls of gentle spirit had treated him kindly, then yet another move, back to the house in Pagons Ton, but it was never the same for the confused young boy. With no Leonora and the Lady of the house often in tears together with his mother, the little manor became a depressing place for a child especially after the fire. He became stronger when facing the teasing but still suffered; with no one to protect him, Trey grew morose and solitary.

How he became resident at Compton Berry was blurred, a night journey with his sobbing mother and his father's reluctance in accompanying them, for all his childish fears, once there it had been the start of a happy sojourn, slowly his mother began to smile again but his fathers moods while at Compton Berry became blacker. At Compton Berry Trey started his path to manhood, learning to use a sword, and shoot a straight arrow, lessons learned as play....he enjoyed them. A dark knight dressed in black with even blacker eyes and hair had held his hand while scything sword blades through the air, applauding when Trey thrust and cut with youthful enthusiasm. Watching from the walls his mother and Lady Faye clapped their approval.... sometimes an imposing bearded knight joined them, but in his presence Trey found himself shy, especially when he lifted Lady Faye's hand to his mouth.

Ida's voice cut through his dreaming and brought him back to the present, "After that night your fether left you with me and went back to Devon, to settle a score so e says......I heard no more until word of his murder."

Trey rose hurling his dagger into the trestle, it quivered in the wood. He was well aware that the wily old crone had been provoking him to avenge his fathers death for years, well the time had come; sly eyes flicked to his aunt, she had prepared the ground well. Trey like his Aunt never thought to question why his father had been killed, believing blindly what he had been told by Ida and she always assumed rumour to be truth. Cruel rumour bought to her ears news that the murderer of her brother Torr was a Devonian Knight, 'Sir Kea'van' of Compton Berry, she believed it absolutely. From the seed of a lie planted in Treys ignorant mind, grew a festering obsession to kill an unknown man, innocent or guilty was one and the same to him. "Enough of your goading woman, Fether will be avenged." In the fields Fires glowed as labourers toiled, smoke rose to meet the gathering storm clouds. After fleeing Devon his arrival at the farm had been on such a night, acrid smoke blocking nostrils and stinging eyes; torn from his mother's bed with no time for goodbyes, he had been dumped in her dubious care, sacrificed to the mercy of his strange aunt, how he had cried for his mother.

"Tomorrow woman make ready for my leaving, I'll take only the reeve, see to the harvest! Waste none!"

Ida nodded, at last the years of moulding this great lummox had paid off, the chances of him gaining a wife and bringing her back were slim if not nigh on impossible, chances were he'd fall prey to footpads and be killed in some petty squabble. Physically powerful he may be but his experience of the outside world was very small, and as for brain? Well she had the money well and truly safe.... for the great fool wouldn't last five minutes pitted against clever men!

Years of planning to gain the farm and the wealth he had created for herself had paid off, she had laboured and tilled the soil but it was his greed and brute strength that stole profits from the idiot workers too scared to protest, now all was theirs; and in the not too distant future just hers! Presuming the devil kept his side of the bargain.

Her brother Torr had been born a fool, died a fool and his son was following true to form. Trey glanced slyly at his aunt, resembling a witch she poked over the ashes in the grate, nodding her head and making strange noises in her throat, through red rimmed eyes she squinted back, "You watch your back buy, they Devonians is slippy as adders, don' want any arm' coming to you, do us."

"You'm an old witch." Trey mumbled under his breath.

"What'd say buy?" she cackled

"Nought aunt! Your ears be addled as your body!"

Neither love nor respect clouded their relationship but he would never see her destitute, Ida had provided for the nephew her brother had sired, and they were blood, liking each other was of no consequence.

"I'll be back! don't e' forget it!" he growled.

She heaved her skinny bones upright, "Oh for sure you will buy, for sure you will."

Thunder rattled the heavens and rain pattered the fields, steam rose from hot ground as little puddles dried on the hot earth, Trey concerned that the harvest gathering may falter in the inclement weather, emphasised his last words to Ida, "Rain or not, tis harvest comes first, any slackers, flog them!"

"Don be feared lad, not a bleddy thieving mouse will escape me!"

Rain ran down his leather hood and dripped from the end of his nose as he and Walter Trewin turned their mounts towards Devon, in the sky a slither of blue like ice upon a lake broke the grey, Ida's mouth twisted into what passed for a smile as she raised a saggy arm.

"You take your time lad, all the time you needs."

11

Chapter 3
Alain

Once again Leonora found herself on the road to Totnes; the second time in as many days.

On passing the sign post to Compton Berry she shuddered, the memory of that ill fated trip still fresh, she spurred Mallow into a trot.

If her leaving had not been in such haste a rouncey would have pulled a cart, and an escort would have accompanied her so far, but this had been denied by the manner of her leaving, Mallow laboured slightly, so when possible Leonora walked leading her at a gentle pace, and talking in soft whispers.

Mounds of decaying Leaves lay damp on the track making the going at times difficult, thunder storms had left deep muddy ruts.

Tired and muddy they finally descended the steep hill into Totnes, and crossed the bridge spanning the fast flowing Dart.

A staging post and inn busy with travellers sat back from the rivers edge, Leonora had enough small coins to stable Mallow and rent herself a pallet for the night; offered a tiny stall at the back of the inn she took it gladly.

Trying to be inconspicuous she pulled her hood and covered her face before pushing through the throng, with her head down she was unable to see the curious stares a lone woman attracted.

Suddenly a touch on her shoulder made her jump, and she caught her breath, feeling for the dagger concealed beneath her cloak she heard a familiar voice, "Forgive me mademoiselle, I meant not to alarm you."

She recognised the French accent, and turned to find the 'labourer' from Compton Berry at her shoulder.

"Pardon my intrusion but I saw you arrive, do you need assistance?"

Seconds passed until his hand dropped from her shoulder, then Leonora answered, "I Thank you, but no."

but he persisted, "it is late for a lady to be on the road."

"You presume sir that I travel alone," her green eyes locked with his own, "pray let me pass," she said coldly.

But he continued calmly, "I would consider it an honour if you would partake of some wine with me," then with a disarming smile he added, "but not offended should you decline." She hesitated; wine would be very welcome, I, I," she stammered as if in doubt, taking her hesitation as a 'yes' he gestured towards a secluded area, gallantly he cleared a path, "To the left mademoiselle," he said standing aside. Wall flares showed the chestnut and golden lights in her hair as she passed.

"Here," he said stopping at a settle by the roaring fire, "this will warm us both."

After settling her he called for mulled wine; he remained silent as she sipped the warming liquid, and ,she watched as he drank deeply from his own tankard, For a while they sat a little uneasily in silence.

When at length their eyes did lock and she decided to speak, he was ready for her scolding, "Well sir, I am waiting for your apology, or did you think a simple cup of wine would be enough to forgive your insult to my person?" she said teasingly, "I do not forget so easily!"

He made no excuses, "Mademoiselle, you are right to be angry, my conduct was ungallant, I have nothing to say in my defence, will you accept a tardy apology?"

Leonora wiped her mouth, and stared into her cup, she frowned before answering, quite enjoying his discomfort.

"Sir, you have been kind, and I am loathe to say it but," She savoured the moment making it last as long as she dare...... "This wine is so good I could possibly forgive you anything Sir!"

His blue eyes crinkled with relief and throwing back his head he laughed showing strong white teeth.

"I swear on all the saints it was never my intention to offend." he said. They laughed together. "Is Compton Berry your home Sir?"

"Yes although my birthplace is Aquitaine," he replied.

"Oh! You are a long way from home then."

The smoky room gradually emptied, and the fire burned low, flushed with wine Leonora asked "How did you know I had ridden from Pagons Ton Sir?"

Alain smiled, "It was obvious"

"Obvious?" she queried

"Very, for you look much like your parents."

She grimaced at the thought but knew it true, "that is far from complimentary sir if you are talking of my father, and God forbid I should behave like him?"

"You did on the day you came to Compton Berry," he replied.

Reminded of her behaviour she was shamed and listened as he continued, "For that reason alone you were not made welcome! You failed to show any of your mother's charm."

The truth hurt, "so rude sir that even for my mother's sake you would not receive me?" Leonora challenged

"We sometimes make decisions that later we regret!" replied Alain.

His azure eyes were so direct, as if expecting an apology. But if he thought to humiliate her further he was making a mistake; neatly she evaded a reply, and asked mockingly,

"So you make decisions for your master?"

There was the same haughty voice! Alain answered a patient, "No mademoiselle.... but from respect I choose to protect him."

It was his turn to be cold now, "tell me, why exactly you came to Compton Berry?"

Leonora hesitated; guiltily she thought of the emerald and her father's foul temper at her empty handed return, so she lied,

"I wished to see for myself the man who stole my mothers' soul and broke my father's heart, the man who bought us to penury!"

She flushed as the words tumbled out.

Alain disliked her misguided pride, how it soured her beauty! She knew nothing of his master!

"And what pray would you have my Lord of Compton Berry do? Taint Faye's memory by humbling himself on bended knee to beg your forgiveness for loving? Or God forbid, Leon's?"

Though she recoiled Alain saw no reason to go easy on her, and continued, "Of one thing I am sure; The Knight I choose to serve is a man of honour, all but destroyed by the hand fate dealt him, it is he who should be seeking retribution Madam!"

Leonora considered her fathers whining self pity, it angered her still as she asked, "you know my father sir?"

"Yes," Alain said curtly after draining his tankard, "I had the honour of riding with Leon when he joined us as a mercenary; I recall an effective fighter, your Father and Sir Ciabhan were friends, on and off the battlefield."

Pin pricks of orange from the fire lit his pupils dangerously and the blue darkened, Leonora thought with anger, and she looked away.

Was it wine or weariness that dulled her senses? For the flash of anger had made him rather attractive, God forbid! Was she so shallow?

It was time to take her leave, lowering her voice she whispered,

"Did you know my father is considered a murderer by some?"

Alain looked unsurprised, "Killing is Leon's business."

She must be aware of her father's trade.

"Yes, a mercenary sir, I know what that entails, killing for money by any overlord who seeks his help in making war! But I know also that he is no common murderer who kills for pleasure!" emotional now she continued, "It is whispered that my father killed my mother, then murdered our reeve Torr to make it seem he had honourably avenged her death." she looked to him for reassurance, "but I won't believe that!" Suddenly he felt some sympathy, leaning across the trestle he spoke kindly. "Take comfort, it was not your father who killed your mother, yes he intimidated and threatened, as was Leon's way but," here he hesitated picking his words

14

carefully, "Torr was indeed Faye's killer, but by accident I believe, even one as ignorant as Torr would not have killed a defenceless woman, though it seems he had his own reasons for wishing Ciabhan dead."
Leonora gasped, "Then my father was telling the truth!"
"It seems for once he was, Torr the man who cared for the manor in Pagons ton , your father's right hand man murdered your mother with a shaft intended for Ciabhan of Compton Berry, a dreadful mishap!"
Leonora stifled a sob, Alain touched her hand gently, "Torr paid the ultimate price for taking Faye's life, Leon saw to that."
"So he did avenge her death? As he said." She sniffed.
"Of that I am sure," replied Alain, "I have been witness to Leon's handiwork, Torrs death bore the mark of Leon's hand, a professional killing, throat cleanly cut, and body slung from a gibbet, a declaration of his revenge for all to see." Alain knew she listened, "believe me he took his vengeance in the only way he knew, the ravens fed mightily at the crossroads to Compton Berry!" Leonora shuddered at the awful vision it conjured in her mind.
"Leon was very satisfied with his handiwork," added Alain, "but even in that selfish action he denied my Lord the right to avenge his dead wife! Think you not that Ciabhan would rather Torr had died by his hand? And Leon would have known that! Your fathers loathing for Ciabhan is unjustified, rather it is he who should hate the very ground Leon walks upon." Leonora shifted position, the wooden seat had become as uncomfortable as the words she was hearing, "How do I know you tell the truth sir? Is not a stolen wife the perfect reason for a man to hate?"
"Not stolen mistress, Faye's heart was not stolen like some inconsequential trinket" said Alain bluntly, "love requires two hearts Faye made a courageous choice, and never once did she falter in her resolve to be with Ciabahn, theirs was a unique love guided by divine fate." A lovely speech she thought meanly. "You seem to know much about my Mothers state of mind sir, and very little if I may say of my Fathers heartbreak!"
Exasperated Alain bit back, "the truth is this Mademoiselle, all involved in the saga are heartbroken! We cannot change that which is done, the past is the past!" A log dislodged and fell into the hearth, sparks spat onto the tiled floor and glowed briefly before dying. Alain continued, "It was I who when Ciabhan had forbidden any to touch the carcass, cut Torr down and buried him beneath the gallows for Matis sake, she loathed her husband and was not sad to see the bully's passing, but it distressed her to think of her son witnessing the ghastly sight. Ciabhan on the other hand would have taken him to see it for himself, Mati was spared that."

Alains features changed during the conversation, one moment soft and caring, to casually talking of brutal death! Well acquainted with the arts of war, she realised that death held no shocks for him

"I see no saving grace in your Sir Ciabhan sir! You describe a cruel and arrogant man," Said Leonora studying the Young man's changing expressions.

"The arrow that struck Faye, I've no doubt was intended for Sir Ciabhan, even Mati his wife agrees, he harboured grudges against both Ciabhan and Faye, but like a bully he was cowardly and sly, and too scared to strike on his own ; he was after all a lout, with brawn, no brain and certainly no archer."

Leonora listened intently as Alain related events leading to her mother's murder, dazed she heard him tell of the mischief Torr had caused at Compton Berry, setting friend against friend, fed up Ciabhan finally ran the trouble maker off his land at the point of a sword vowing to kill him on sight if he dared come near again.

"Ciabhan kept his son as hostage, God knows how but Torr got word to his son that Ciabhan intended to murder him! Somehow in the dead of night the lad Trey crept from his bed and disappeared, to this day poor Mati has no idea if the child lives. Torrs vindictiveness would have her believe Ciabhan carried out his threat!"

Leonora recalled Mati and her son; "I remember Trefor," she said, "he was younger than me and ill at ease with others because of his churlishness, when children teased him he used me to protect him, we were left to amuse ourselves, when guests demanded Mothers attention."

Alain tried to imagine this feisty young woman as a carefree child. "I doubt you remember the day I was one of those guests?" he said.

"I don't think so sir, many visitors passed through our gates," her brow puckered as she recalled past faces, "I was much younger then and guests merely took mothers time away from me, all knights looked the same."

Alain could almost see her stamping a delicate foot.

"If you had been there, I'm sure you would have remembered Ciabhan, for then he was a Templar Knight, " Try as she may she could not recall this young man, his blue eyes, or the Templar Knight he spoke of. "The Templar knight being the same Sir Ciabhan? No sir I cannot recall this man, and besides I would find it hurtful to think of him partaking of my fathers' hospitality, only to betray him later with treachery!" Leonora was in no mood to pardon her mothers weakness. Leon's daughter would prove an unforgiving adversary, Alain sighed, but at least the truth had been told, he could do no more. Ciabhan was no opportunist wife stealer but an honourable man; however this young woman would need a lot more convincing.

"Forgive me mademoiselle I have talked for far too long and kept you from your bed," tentatively he added, "may I escort you?"

Trying to stifle a yawn she rose from the bench, "I need no escort Sir," Only a day ago an 'escort' was what he had denied her and besides pride wouldn't let him know she was to sleep in a stall.

French he may have been but English sarcasm was not lost on him, the meaning in her reply was only too obvious, ignoring it he added diplomatically, "An inside room has been arranged."

God forbid! Was he suggesting she retire with him! Eyes ablaze she turned to scold, did he think her some common strumpet?

Before she could speak he raised his hand, "you see insult where none was intended madam! a room more benefiting your status is now available."

He gestured towards the narrow stairs that creaked with every step, from the small landing a door opened onto a pleasant chamber, warm with the smells of the kitchen; Alain bade her enter but remained himself at the threshold. "I shall be comfortable here Sir....my thanks."

Before taking his leave he bowed in a very French way, low with his cap in hand.

"Sleep well Leonora, my apologies for the way I behaved on our first meeting, maybe fate will cross our paths again in the not so distant future."

"Tis no chance I pass this way sir, I am bound for Plymouth.... a decision not of my choosing."

Her smile was strained. "Sir.....I return to my home and husband, I have been too long from both"

Alains demeanour changed, suddenly he was mindful of a married woman and became serious, he did not trespass on another's wife.

In that moment she knew him to be as honourable as he said the master he served was and she gave him her hand.

"Thank you Sir for your company and your kindness."

He raised her hand to his lips, "May God protect you on your journey mademoiselle and may he grant you all your heart desires, buon nuit."

Then placing his cap back on his dark curls he turned and left, she stood on the landing until his footsteps faded before closing the door on dark stairs.

Leonora woke with the cockcrow; memories of the previous night replaced by an urgency to be away.

Welcoming early risers, flames crept around cauldrons of bubbling oats as a serving girl sullenly ladled portions into earthenware bowls.

Leonora found a place at the trestle where a bowl was placed in front of her. Pushing her spoon into the hot sops the thought crossed Leonora's mind that the unwashed girl had probably slept on a pallet of straw in a chilly stall, not on soft goose down as she had, she smiled kindly then but received no smile back.

Leonora followed the hot food with milk and delicious honey, when finished she beckoned the maid; "I would like to speak with your master, the inn keeper?"

The girl seemed not to understand and stood slack mouthed until Leonora repeated herself, then hurried off.

Wiping his hands on a greasy apron the round little inn keeper was all smiles and declared brightly, "Tis settled, all taken care of miss, your companion saw to everything, is there more you desire?" in a state of disbelief Leonora shook her head.

"Oh, I nearly forgot lady" he said, "when you goes to collect your 'orse from the stabling, e' paid for another, a strong backed rouncey as an extra, in case the little mare bain't up to the journey, it'll be waiting with the groom." he wobbled away with a cursory wave of his hand.

Leonora left the inn with more than when she arrived, two horses were better than one and though her baggage was meagre it allowed little Mallow a rest.

Well fed and rested Leonora left leading two horses, with a bounce in her step that hid a heavy heart, in such a short time she had learned much from Alain, Some of the mystery surrounding her mother's death had been explained, more than her father had ever bothered to do.

Alain was surely her link to the emerald if it did exist and if ever she were inclined to claim it, a pity they would never know each other better for unlike him she had no reason to believe their paths would ever cross again, so reluctantly she put the memory of Monsieur Alain Rousseau's handsome face and clever tongue as far from her mind as she could.

Chapter 4
Edmund

Edmund Morton gasped through cracked painful lips, his hands of
blackened brittle charcoal stiffened over his stomach; barely conscious he
hung between heaven and earth, survival doubtful. Human shapes
suspended in yellow fog drifted in and out of his narrowed vision, but
none came near, concerned as they were only in aiding the saveable, he
spluttered a cough and nature kindly closed his eyes.

For the last miles of her journey strange colours lit the skies freakishly
above Plymouth Town, thinking it some natural occurrence Leonora paid
scant attention until the acrid smell became too strong to ignore. Concern
seemed to grip the travellers heading that way; until without further
warning concern became panic, a tide of humanity trying to reach their
destination.
As the crowd surged forward, Leonora fought to stay on Mallows back,
while the rouncey being led threw up its head and snorted in terror at the
pushing shoving mob, Leonora shortened the lead rein hoping the animal
would not rear.
This was the familiar route to her marital home but swept along by the
mob it pushed her in another direction completely, she bent to speak to a
woman struggling along beside her, "Pray mistress can you say what is
happening?"
Red rimmed eyes looked up fearfully, "I dunno miss, but it don't look
good, three little'uns is waiting at home for I! God above, I hopes they be
safe!"
The throng broke briefly when town marshals pushed through shouting at
the crowds to turn back, most though were in no mood to be kept from
their homes and refused to budge, pressing forward again, drawn swords
above their heads did nothing to deter them. Alarmed at the melee
Leonora fought to free herself from the crush, her mind was in turmoil
and she needed to think. The smoke was unbearable, clogging and
clouding the air, and it was obvious that the way to her home would be
closed. A different tactic was needed, before covering her raw throat and
mouth she hailed one of the marshals trying to clear a path as he drew
level, "Sir! Pray tell what is happening? I must get to Plymouth Town, I
must continue?" Another bloody stupid traveller, he thought! A fool who
wouldn't listen and a female probably lost her spouse in the crush!
He looked her over before answering, "Every one on this 'ere road wants
to get to Plymouth mistress, but the place burns, you must go back!
Nothins to get through, they is the orders, mine not to question!"

He reined his mount around and was about to ride on but hesitated, the slightly built young woman spoke and carried herself well, nothing like a commonplace wench....maybe a reward could be gained in helping her, a rich husband, lover even!

"Be you headed for city parts, or one of the manors?" he coughed.

She certainly didn't look as if for the stews! And he thought it the better part of honour to not suggest such; a reward was what he sought ...not the wrath of a jealous paramour.

Leonora guessed rightly that he was motivated by avarice, taking advantage of his ignorance she straightened her back and replied in her best tones, hoping she sounded like the chatelaine of a rich manor,

"For the barbican area sir, I know I am close for even in this foulness I smell the closeness of the sea, there must be some way?"

"Tis the barbican that burns madam, ablaze like a tinderbox" he spluttered.

"But man its imperative I be allowed to pass, my husband shall be much displeased at the delay, fire or not!" after the arrogant outburst she feigned tears, lowered her eyes and dabbed at them daintily, while smoke threatened to choke her.

Women were such stupid creatures he mused; irritably he beckoned her to follow, still thinking of the reward his efforts may bring. "Keep close lady for I can't come back if you gets stuck or lags behind." he growled.

Turning left he headed for a quieter path, fighting for a way forward and avoiding as much as he could the billowing smoke, but by a fork in the path marked by a huge oak the path was blocked again.

Ordering him back a group of marshals shouted above the roar, "no way through here man, nothings left beyond this point, back! Back now!"

"But I must get through sir, a matter of urgency," Leonora screamed.

"No miss, the barbicans an inferno,nothing left! Turn back afore you're trapped." Before she could object the marshal grabbed the reins spun her around and whacked Mallows rear, "now! Get back before it's too late!" Debris fluttered like black snow and bright sparks fizzed, leaving little black holes in her skirts, scalding the tender skin beneath. "ride towards the water, quick as you can...don't stop!" he shouted, I hopes you find your husband." Peeved at a missed opportunity he joined the others.

Leonora could smell the sea; even under the sooty flakes that she constantly brushed off her lips she tasted salt. Mallow tossed her mane and flared her nostrils unnerving the other horses, both were troubled by bits of debris irritating the soft pink tissue of their noses.

20

Danger gave Leonora no choices, it forced her from her home and Edmund, an overpowering feeling of guilt descended on her along with the black depression of impending loss.

Following the wretched crowds, she eventually found herself where the river meets the sea.

The harbour area known as the Barbican was closed to all and still burned fiercely, overhead the darkening sky danced with great tongues of orange, and red, she wondered if hells inferno blazed with such terrible beauty and shuddered.

The priests who gave the most frightening sermons assured sinners that it did indeed burn so!

While his wife struggled to reach his side Edmund had been dragged to a safe distance, as far from the firestorm as his terrible injuries would allow, but if the conflagration had spared his life, the rough hands that manhandled him from its path had all but finished him off.

Swamped by pains relentless ferocity he prayed for death, death however ideas of its own had and ignored his pleas, Edmunds suffering was total.

Like a dying animal he moaned and whimpered, screaming only prolonged his torture.

The Colour filling his head was red, and only changed to bellowing blackness as consciousness deserted him, .then he tumbled down, down and around into blessed oblivion.

Pain knifed through every fibre of his being as in a final desperate struggle for breath he prayed, he prayed only for death to come speedily for him.

The two storey wooden house on the dockside, Edmund and Leonora's home collapsed in a fury of smashed and burned timber while the fire continued to roar unstoppably through the town.

Perversely the stone dwellings either side of their marital home were still standing, but theirs being wood stood no chance when the fire swept through, the space acted like a funnel for the wind, the emptiness proclaiming bleakly, 'And that's the end of that!'

Not one timber building remained and the devastated area smouldered for days, even die hard scavengers, human and animal avoided the bleak misery that once had housed so many. On the fringes of such desolation the dispossessed could only stare blank eyed from blackened faces unable to grasp the horror they saw, most scurried away like insects vanishing in the scorched terrain.

Some used initiatives and constructed small shelters, like boils sprouting on a pocked landscape; little havens of family hope. Tacked together from whatever could be found or begged in the outlying areas, these sorry hovels offered small cover to a desperate people.

In one of these improvised shelters Edmund had been placed by kindly hands, nuns from a charitable convent found him apparently dead on the wharf side. A sharp eyed young novice saw signs of life in the barely recognisable creature, the laboured rise of his chest and a faint wheeze, proof that what passed for human did actually draw breath.

The same nuns separated what remained of Edmunds hands from his blackened arms, beyond saving, the stumps were amputated cleanly and bandaged; all the sisters could do was pray for his quick release, and his soul, survival did not appear to be an option.

Together they begged God the Almighty for Edmunds salvation.

Briefly during this awful time he woke to see Leonora bending over him, Blood fever made him hallucinate; at the sight of the wife who had left him a noise bubbled deep in his throat; something between a howl and a curse.

Agonizingly clear the words came forth, "So sweetness you return to the milksop, not so bad after all, at least not when compared to your father!"

An attempt to smile turned his face into a grotesque mask as excruciating pain assaulted his frail body.

The young nun tending him so carefully staggered backwards unprepared for the venom that spewed from the delirious Edmund, all consuming in its hate, "You she wolf you!" he screamed into Domenicas face,

Hell! Ever present opened wide its jaws and he plunged in.

"Sweet mother of God," gasped Sister Domenica,I do believe he thought I was the devil himself!"

Shaken she gathered her wits and looked closely at the now unconscious man, only the twitching of his face muscles moved; she considered how a man could hate so much.

Sister Domenica had taken it upon herself to care for the badly injured man, since the removal of his hands the other nuns had continued with the business of saving, leaving her to work some youthful miracle, for a miracle was all that would cure his suffering.

She had nursed him for weeks convinced her prayers had been heard by God as slowly he gained strength, whether he would live or not was up to his will power, as far as sister Domenica was concerned her saintly duty had been discharged, the essence of her calling.

Amongst the ruins Edmund grew stronger, succour was never in short supply.

Tenderly like a babe he was fed by whoever was in charge of him, his scorched cheeks remained blistered but beneath they healed, sometimes a grunt would pass for thanks, or so sister Domenica liked to suppose.

Through unrelenting pain, Edmund endured the changes of his linen, unable to look at the mangled stumps that had once been his hands.

On occasions he fell into blessed unconsciousness, for seconds before it came he would feel his being enfolded in softest feather down, he wished often for that sweet embrace, but the hold hell had on him was merciless.

With the gradual healing of his body came the horrors of memory, brightly coloured flash backs; his last lucid memory was of being lifted and carried outside still clutching the precious implements of his trade.

On the ends of his arms he watched the flames lick at his wrists, just before his hands exploded. Oil, rags, parchment quills and ink clutched in his hands suddenly were as two flares on the ends of his arms! He had wondered where the screaming was coming from, as his hands with a mind of their own danced, then the sizzle as they were doused in sea water and covered in wet rags.

He recalled they looked at odds to the bright flames of a moment before; mercifully at this point he lost his grip on reality and passed out.

"Edmund," the gossamer voice of Sister Domenica broke through his torment, "Please take more soup, it will help."

The face was not that of Leonora, but one of an angel and he panicked, unready for eternity after all; so this is heaven! fearful he whimpered, "my wife, I need my wife! Not your charity." he grimaced as his bandaged stumps knocked the bowl from the young nun's hands.

23

Chapter 5
Meryn

Tirelessly Leonora searched amongst the scattered and homeless for Edmund, refusing to believe he had perished, nighttimes she slept for comfort with the horses and as close as possible to any normal looking family, but still she was unable to reach her home. Peasants and merchants alike torn apart by the devastation approached each other hopefully in their search, offering what little news they had of families and friends. Meryn the inn keepers wife first spotted Leonora in the crowds as the barbican burned, her stone built inn survived the blaze, blackened it stood still, unlike Edmund and Leonora's home.

Clutching two of her offspring she pushed through the throng, gripping Leonora's arm she stammered, "Mistress Start 'ow be e' my dear? I didn't know you'm be back 'ere!"

Leonora wrapped her arms around the plump body, so glad to see a friendly face, even if it was more apple red than usual, "Good dame what has become of Edmund? Pray tell me you know of his whereabouts?" she sobbed, clinging to Meryns shoulders.

Leonora's pleas saddened Meryn, for so many had suffered, and although she didn't wish to be the bearer of bad news, one more hardly mattered. Maybe mistress Start should know what she had seen.

"Come with me my dear, you needs to sit down for what I 'ave's to say, 'baint good, though, come."

She led Leonora to a quiet place, the child at her breast started to grizzle, his little boys face a picture of misery. "now, now me little lamb," she soothed, "tears bain't good for e'now you be a big boy like your brother here," Clinging for dear life to his mothers torn skirts the five year old seemed petrified and close to tears, his huge eyes gazed up at his mother and the pretty lady by her side; when Leonora took his little hand in hers he grinned timidly. Through tattered trees the river twinkled as it ran to the sea, the sun shone burnishing autumn's gold with warmth, how strange that in the midst of death life went on. Leonora wondered why she was sitting in sunbeams to be told bad news, she tried to concentrate on Meryns words, but her head spun with confusion, "I saw Edmund carried from the house my dear, sure as I is here I knew it was e' in the arms of a great big fellow e' was!" Meryn hesitated, "being carried to safety." Leonora's head started to spin and she felt faint. God forbid young mistress Startmor was about to swoon! The maid was not strong enough to bear the truth, the awful truth; Meryn had seen Edmund Starts terrible injuries and was convinced that by now he must be dead.

She did not know what made her lie but she did, blurting out,

"He lives my dear! I as seen e' with my own eyes."

In truth she prayed the Almighty had taken him, for she had never seen a human form so disfigured, the sight still disturbed her nights.

What the good dame could not know was that Edmund did indeed live! God for some reason had seen fit to save him, though in what condition was questionable,

On hearing the words Leonora sank to her knees in what Meryn thought was a faint, "oh merciful God he lives?" Leonora gasped, Meryn grabbed at her shoulders, she hadn't passed out but looked fit to do so any minute, "God in heaven what have I done?" she exclaimed, gently slapping the pale cheeks, "come now maid, tis good news surely."

The poor lamb looked awful; a far cry from the lovely young bride who flushed with marriage had come to live next door with her new husband Edmund, in retrospect Meryn wished she'd kept her mouth shut!

Mistress Start had been sleeping in the open from her appearance; Leonora was a strikingly pretty young thing and usually well groomed; Meryn had always thought her far too spirited for the sour faced Edmund Start. She called a couple of strong looking lads, " oi' over ere, you two' the Lady there needs your help, strong lads like you should have no trouble carrying 'er a few yards!" The 'few yards' were actually a good quarter mile, over difficult and scrubby terrain; however the lads did as Meryn asked and carried their charge uncomplainingly. Once at the small inn they fidgeted while Meryn fussed over Leonora, seeing to her comfort before thanking them, "ere you are lads take this, tis all I have for now, when I's up and running you come by an have you some victuals," she dropped a note of promise into the grateful hands, "now I thank ye both! I've work to do."

Resting on what felt like a hard pile of rags Leonora slowly recovered her senses, one of Meryns boys crawled among the dirt, on seeing her move he shouted excitedly, "Ma! Ma, quick, lady open eyes!"

Meryn wiped perspiration from Leonora's brow, and her eyes flickered, "tis alright miss, youm's safe ere," Meryn whispered, "don't be a feared now." Leonora smiled feebly and gazed around the room, Meryn took her hand, "you do remember me don't e?" Leonora bewildered lied, "yes, yes of course!" On tiptoes two dirty little faces watched Leonora intently, one trilled, "we watch Lady Ma!" in the enclosed hovel that passed for a room the stale stench of alcohol suddenly reached her nostrils making her think of the house in Pagonston, she recalled her drunken father. Barely controlling the urge to vomit She clutched a rag over her mouth. Dame Jenkin soothed her, "Now, now my dear, don't fret just rest a while an then we'll talk some more." shooing the boys from the pallet, she patted their scrawny behinds, "away with you two, let the lady rest now."

All humanity passed by or begged outside the inn, a steady stream of desperation searching for some thing or someone to remind them of a life they had once known.

Ale, food, whatever was wanted Dame Jenkin sold. She cobbled together soups, stodgy dumplings scraps of meat and offal and all were gratefully devoured by those who called.

Always a popular haven, the Inn and Dame Meryn were well liked, without a man in her life now she was pleased to have Leonora's company. Desperate times meant desperate men, prowling the devastation there were those who would not think twice about violence, and two fit women would at least have a fighting chance.

Fog clammy and grey shrouded everything, stealing in from the sea it fused with the Smokey air.

With her head and body muffled against the damp in an old woollen shawl Leonora decided to see for her the remains of the home her and Edmund had shared, picking her way over fallen timbers in the swirling mist she was glad none could see her tears. What had once comprised her home, between the stark and flame assaulted walls of the inn, and the Chandlers on the other side had vanished; nothing remained of her life with Edmund, not a trace to remind her of the two storey dwelling that had stood there. As she staggered through what had been the little back garden, debris and thick soggy ash dragged at her feet, hindering her path. Meryn patted her arm, "come now, I think you as seen enough." Leonora steadied herself on the wall of the inn, too lost in misery to notice the sooty black staining her palms. The garden was unrecognisable, where once other buildings had stood only the odd wall or stone building survived, anything wooden had disappeared changing the scene completely, unnatural and pungent a thick yellow light pervaded the air, deadening everything even birdsong But of course thought Leonora there was none! "Where are the ducks and the hens," she stammered, "think you they flew away?"Meryns heart was heavy for her, "Oh for sure miss" she comforted, "they would have known what be coming, the good lord protects they for sure, why you do suppose he gave them wings!" she had seen quite enough and turned to go, "boys be alone," she said, "I must go."

Poking around in the debris Leonora was too preoccupied to hear Meryns departure, by the time Meryn had picked her way back, Leonora's emotions had boiled over. Great tears coursed down grimy cheeks and she sank to the ground overwhelmed by the reality of her predicament wringing her hands together she sobbed;

"Dear God above, another fire? Another home destroyed in flames? Why? Oh God, Why

Dejected and bitter she could find not one reason to forgive God for her loss, another house destroyed by fire, lives ruined once again, Even now the house in Pagons Ton stood unfinished and neglected by her drunken father, the story was well known by now..

While Leon was away in the pay of local landowner Sir Ralf of Boscombe Valle, his son Halbert having always desired Leon's wife Faye had in a fit of madness abducted her and fled to his manor in the process he fired her home as well! Not satisfied with just taking Faye he had set fire to her family home in Pagonston, all but destroying it!

Now To the grief stricken Leonora It appeared the Almighty conspired once more against her family, could this be divine justice for the sins of her mother and her tarnished lover? Would Leonora always suffer the backlash of the selfish lovers?

She thought how like her father she was; maybe bitterness would gnaw away at her as it had him?

Returning to the inn Leonora barely noticed Meryn scrubbing the tiles, but was very aware the bulky form blocking her way.

He made no effort to move and she was not inclined to squeeze pass; on raising her head her head to ask him to move she found herself staring into the face of the ugliest man she had ever set eyes on involuntarily she shuddered, this revulsion did not go unnoticed by Trefor.

Meryn dropped the soap into the bucket and bustled over, "oh my dear girl such good news our visitor brings, Edmund lives, tis definite my dear, your dear husband lives!" Meryn clapped her hands with such joy that it seemed the world was exploding with glee!

Leonora felt no such elation, "and Pray how do you know this good dame?" she asked.

"Tis the gent there my love, there in front of you, the very man what saved your husband with his own hands, he swears Edmund lives still, all us needs is to find e' Oh I's so happy for you my sweet!"

Trefor had melted into the background; a dark shape somewhere in the murky interior.

Meryn stroked Leonora's face, brushing away the sooty hair that stuck to her wet cheek, "there's my girl love, tis a shock I know, but tis good news to be sure! Come, this ere gent will tell you all about it," Meryn looked round for Trefor. Too shocked to speak Leonora's shattered mind raced, Alive Edmund was alive! Dread filled the space where she should be feeling joy; but no joy came with the thought of her husband, rather

27

a heaviness of heart, she had accepted the real possibility that Edmund had perished in the fire, and no great grief tore her soul, rather a deep sadness that death should have ended that which she had started, the day she made the decision to leave her tedious husband behind in Plymouth Town and return alone to Pagonston.

Of course she had lied, letting him believe it was to support her father, suffering still from his wife's death, but in reality she longed to flee from Edmund and their dreary life, a life she had grown to loathe.

Colour flushed the cheeks so pallid a moment ago, and her thumping heart threatened to burst, she wanted to flee, disappear, be anywhere but here, and she certainly had no wish to meet the stranger who had so accurately read disappointment on her beautiful face.

News of the disaster travelled quickly, within hours Compton Berry was fully aware of Plymouths tragedy.

Enjoying an evening cup of wine Alain and Ciabhan discussed the events; dying embers lit the empty dining hall, and tallow candles dripped the hours away. For a change Ciabhan opened the conversation, "the fire swept through the harbour area and much has been destroyed." kicking back a log that had rolled from the cinders, he added, "There was loss of life... inevitable when so many dwellings are made from wood."

He saw the flicker of alarm that crossed Alains features, clouding his eyes, the young man he thought of as a son seemed preoccupied, "Alain is something amiss?" he asked.

Alain never mentioned his chance meeting with Leonora, there was no reason to mention one who was so dismissive of his master.

"An acquaintance Sir, someone I passed the time of day with in Totnes recently, he replied, "was travelling to Plymouth."

Making light of his meeting with Leon's daughter felt like betrayal, but he could hardly admit that the beautiful 'acquaintance' filled his thoughts night and day.

Thinking of the proud young woman, Alains vitals churned with fear for her safety; fanciful of thought he imagined himself a knight in shining armour, riding forward to pluck her from the jaws of certain death!

But here in front of the man he revered as a father he couldn't even bring himself to mention her, shame made him sick to the pit of his stomach.

He agonized over her safety, the young married woman whose fate he dared not guess at; the muscles of his face tensed and twitched.

Ciabhan studying his young companions' expressions, "Come sir! Share your thoughts, maybe I can be of help?"

Staring at the grey ash in the grate, Alain mumbled in reply, "no Sir, it, it's just that fire reminds me always of the Manor in Pagonston, that terrible night."

Then wishing he hadn't mentioned the fire, he added quickly, "I'm sorry! forgive me?"

Ciabhan stood, and placed a reassuring hand on Alains shoulder, "don't apologise," he said, "we all know that life isn't always a joy, it seems the greater the love or happiness then the worse will be our nightmares!"

He must have been thinking of the flight from Pagonston, for he added unexpectedly, "my nightmares were yet to come!"

Just remembering Faye's murder must have hurt because he changed the subject completely, "maybe it time you took a wife Alain?" he said tossing the dregs of his cup into the grate where they fizzed in the cinders.

Alain remained silent, thinking still of Leonora.

Ciabhan stood, placing a reassuring hand on Alains shoulder he said, "Good night, my son, think on what I said."

Alain watched Ciabhan cross the hall, he leant slightly these days due to a wound, a legacy of the crusades. The sword cut to his upper thigh had been serious, but not life threatening, whereas the deep stomach wound and its subsequent effects had very nearly claimed his life.

Ciabhans footsteps faded into echoing distance and Alain considered their adventures in the Holy Land facing daily the rigors and dangers of campaign. They had retreated to Sicily the five comrades, Alain, Ciabhan, Ivan, and their two Turkish retainers, had licked their wounds in the peace of a Templar monastery. Alain Rousseau had been hungry for excitement, and eager to join the great Templar knights who protected pilgrims visiting Jerusalem. Alains dream had come true when Sir Ciabhan, a well respected Templar Knight, visited Aquitaine, Alains birthplace.

Alain had begged his father to let him accompany the Templar until the elderly Henri Rousseau indulgent of his only son eventually conceded to his pleas.

The old man first extracted an oath from Sir Ciabhan to protect his precious son with his own life; a promise Sir Ciabhan gave gladly.

Alain sighed; his beloved father passed away but two years ago knowing Ciabhan had taken on the mantle and responsibilities of Father to his son. From page Alain had risen to Knights squire, progressing to personal bodyguard. Now as friend, confidante and surrogate son he had over the last five years partly filled the emptiness left by the departure of his masters' greatest friend, the enigmatic Ivan dei Romani Scuri.

Ivan. Comrade and Man of God.

His abrupt departure has been shrouded in secrecy, leaving as he did the day after officiating at the marriage of Ciabhan and Faye.

True to his priestly duties and the promise he had made to the couple.

Gossip had it that dark, mysterious Ivan had cuckolded his friend with Faye, a deed Alain refused to contemplate, for the bond of friendship between Ciabhan and Ivan was one that lesser mortals could only dream of. Alain held both men in the highest regard, and he missed Ivan today as much as the day he left, he missed his wisdom, his wit and his intellect; their discussions had taught him so much.

the villagers had named Ivan 'the Raven' for his long glossy hair and his habit of wearing black, a pang of nostalgia for what had gone forever stung Alains tired eyes, how he wished Ivan here again.

It was Torr, Matis husband who put evil between the two friends, no one knew quite what had happened but Ciabhan in fury had Torr run off the estate keeping his son Trefor as hostage for his good behaviour; to Ciabhans fury Trefor with no word to Mati had crept away in the night and joined his father in banishment.

Finally Alain slept as the dying embers glowed garnet, and then old Lupo padded through the archway to lie sighing at his feet.

Dawn came and Mati tiptoed into the dining hall, Alain snored slightly, his head slumped to one side and the woollen cloak now dragged on the cold stones.

Lupo blinked up and tried to rise. "Shh, boy" whispered Mati, fingers on lips "stay!"

Mati knew what troubled Alain, the reason he stayed sullenly behind in the hall.

Ever Since the day Faye's daughter had arrived unannounced at Compton Berry he'd been elsewhere, 'twas only natural a red blooded young man would be disturbed by such beauty, ruddy faced village lasses could not compare in fairness to Faye's daughter.

Alain seemed oblivious to their charms; and maidens a plenty would like to know monsieur Rousseau better!

Beyond a few trysts with the farriers'pretty daughter the enigmatic young man had shown little inclination to wed any of the ripe wenches, who like birds fluttered across his path; If any had found their way into his bed, Mati certainly knew nought of it!

Like Alain, Mati had chosen to remain at Compton Berry with Sir Ciabhan. After Trefor disappeared Mati spoke rarely of her child referring still to him as 'little Trey,' though he was nearly of age. Inwardly she missed his presence achingly, sleepless nights were spent fretting over his whereabouts and safety.

Over the years her hate for her morose husband had grown, the more she despised him, the more she loved her protector, Ciabhan.

From the day fate exacted its terrible revenge with the horror of Faye's murder, she had vowed to remain like Alain at Compton Berry, and close by the side of the man she had long loved in silence.

Like a crutch she supported him, absorbing his grief as day by terrible day he sank deeper into the jaws of hell, with unwavering strength she and Alain willed the broken Knights daily existence.

Constant and resolute their every act and decision was for his good alone. And it was during those dark days that Matis admiration for Alain grew.

It was Alain who'd bravely agreed to cut down and bury her hanged husband, even when Ciabhan on learning of his actions had questioned the knights loyalty with spiteful words , "did you not stop to think ," he had spat, "that I might enjoy seeing the dog hang? That I would have enjoyed watching the crows feed boy!"

With a face as black as hell he had spat, "the devil take you both!"

Only when alone in the solace of her room did Matis tears flow for the loss of her beloved mistress Faye.

They soaked through already damp pillows leaving her spent and exhausted.

Chapter 6
Mati

Mati put down a bowl of water for Lupo hoping he wouldn't disturb Alain, "here," she whispered, as he heaved his shaggy old body towards the bowl.

Mati watched him slurping around the earthenware bowl, "drink up boy; cook'll kill me if he sees you drinking from his best!"

Lupo snarled as the cloak was pulled from beneath his paws and the bowl clattered away onto the stone flags; Alain yawned, and stared blearily around the hall, Lupo padded to Mati and flopped down at her feet.

"Sir," whispered Mati, "I was just thinking to wake you, the household stirs, masters already at prayer"

Alain stretched stiff limbs, he'd slept soundly, and dreams had fled quickly with waking. "Already at prayer? Is it so late?" he yawned again. "No, but he was about before dawn, another night of sleeplessness I suspect." Mati replied. She pulled her shawl tight and shivered, "Brr! It's a chilly morning," she said before disappearing into the kitchen.

Within minutes Alains peace was shattered, although mostly uncommon in households, here at Compton Berry breaking fast was a ritual observed long by Ciabhan, a habit he maintained as benefiting his household, Mati continued to embrace the routine.

Kitchen boys scampered in and out with armfuls of fresh kindling, fires soon roared and pots clanked, shattering the early morning peace.

Trestles were dragged into place, steaming bowls of oats placed on them next to serving dishes of cream, jugs of hot milk and baskets of bread were accompanied by mounds of butter.

Above the dairy smells, a tangy sweetness permeated all as willow baskets full of apples were hauled across the hall.

Alains unexpected presence invited coy glances from the wenches; the boldest amongst them even managed a "morning young Sir!" then giggled together.

The modest Alain gathered his cloak and made his way from the hall if he noticed the blushes at all he gave no indication of it.

Mornings pale radiance lit the chapel as Ciabhan finished his morning prayers, just a little sun settling on his head gave him the familiar godlike appearance and highlighted his mostly chestnut hair streaked now by threads of grey, likewise his beard though still dark contained slivers of silver contrasting starkly with the brown.

Spectacular in his prime the Templar Knight remained a handsome man, though sorrow rested heavily on his features. Golden skin had dulled and the beautiful brown eyes, his most dramatic feature had lost their lustre, their magnetism. Deep creases ran from nose to mouth, hardening his face, and giving the lips a slightly cruel down turn. Advancing years and war wounds had to some extent stooped his shoulders, but his overall bearing was still that of a warrior, hard muscle and a strong back marked this Knight as a force still to be reckoned with.

Illuminated by the shafts of topaz that spliced the dull interior and with his scarred forearms resting limply on the bar in front of him Ciabhan resembled today a man at peace, not a soul tormented. On his finger the flawless emerald glinted, deep in thought he toyed with the gem, the ring had once adorned Faye's own finger, such a short time!

Sewn into his tunic near his heart was the miniature portrait of Faye, a tiny painting on plaster he had commissioned from Brother Alfonso. Skilfully the Spanish artist had followed Ciabhans instructions, producing finally an exquisite likeness of Faye, catching her very essence.

Around Ciabhans waist the remains of the belt Faye had woven irritated him with its bits of frayed linen as it slowly disintegrated; this piece with its stronger flax backing had hardly left his body, the rest lay in the sandalwood chest. He welcomed the discomfort as a constant reminder of the love which had been lost!

Easing himself upright he reached inside his tunic, taking the little picture his eyes lingered on the image, then before placing it upon the altar cloth he kissed it. The wall above hung with the accoutrements of his calling, a templar banner draped above his battle shield; dented and slashed it had saved his life countless times. Stealthily the suns amber blush reached Faye's face as she stared from the little frame; great calm settled on him as he watched its progress.

"A fine morning, I trust you slept well my lord?"

Alains voice broke the chapel's peace.

Ciabhan turned, looking the dishevelled Alain up and down, he replied, "far better than you it would seem my friend!"

Unable to stifle a yawn Alain lied, "I did until Mati and that hound woke me Sir, I was sleeping like a baby!"

Ciabhans smile was warm, "if you say so Alain" he said.

33

"I have been thinking," said Ciabhan, "the days are shortening, and Christmas will soon be upon us, methinks this mantle of sadness has lain on Compton Berry too long, what say you my friend to celebrating our Lords birth with joy this year."

Alain studied the older mans face, for a moment an enthusiasm long lost had flashed across the features lighting shadowed brown eyes, but for a split second in the muddy depths, a little flame had flickered and just as quickly died ,but it had been there!

"An excellent idea, my lord," Alain agreed, "This house will be greatly pleased to celebrate."

Ciabhan agreed and added, "Faye would have wanted it so, her birth date also! When May comes."

Alain grinned, "Methinks Faye she would have insisted on it!" he replied. Ciabhan smiled a secret smile, standing on the chapels steps he raised his face and let the autumn sun warm his skin; then rubbing his hands together he called back over his shoulder, "then so be it."

Alain heard his boots crunch on gravel as he stepped from the chapel, suddenly Ciabhans voice sounded again, "It's a fine day my friend, Bella Donna needs to stretch her wings, will you join me?"

Alain called back, "I'd like to see you leave without me!"

A day in the high meadows was what Alain needed, fresh air to blow away his fears, and besides his own new peregrine would give the monstrous Bella Donna a run for her money!

He knelt in the ripple of sun light, slowly it became a stream, crossing himself he saw the rays had fallen on a little portrait of Faye, sure the picture had not been there before he squinted at the luminous colours, and there was no doubting the painted beauty's identity as it shimmered with life.

Alain kissed the tips of his fingers and pressed them to the picture, a tender gesture of respect for the departed.

Remembering his first encounter with Leonora he thought her the image of Leon, now studying the tiny portrait the similarities between Faye and her daughter were as clear as the sunlight puddling the pristine cloth on which it stood.

In the last few days Red breasted robins had appeared, a sure sign of winter's imminence, and although bright the suns heat was waning fast; summers furnace was fading fast into a memory. In fields turning slowly russet, early risers laboured gathering in the harvest, muffled voices, the clank of carts and of snorting horses carried through the trees. Alain mused on his masters' good humour, how quickly a day could change; Christmas would now be a time to look forward to, a small beacon of hope in the dark winter days to come.

Ciabhan strode across the bailey and took the stairs to the bedchamber that had been his and Faye's.

Only under cover of night did he venture there, entering the room only occasionally. Sometimes he would stand as motionless and lifeless as an effigy in front of the small window and look across the valley to where she lay, only the all seeing moon with her train of attendants, Orion, Cassiopeia; Ursa Major, and Minor were his companions, like old friends. Transfixed by their celestial beauty he would track their path across the heavens from the dubious comfort of an ancient settle; many a night he had fallen into fitful sleep only to wake when dawn passed damp fingers over his stiffening joints.

There was no obvious reason for today to feel any different but somehow it did! A feeling of sanguinimity settled on him at prayer this morning, now Faye's chamber drew him, he hastened towards the steps.

With barely a squeak the door swung inwards, his boots made more noise on the stone flags. The chamber was his refuge and still so special, sacrosanct almost.

Mati had been taking care of the room; nothing ever changed, he looked vaguely at the furnishings and artefacts that had been Faye's, his fingertips brushed familiar objects, nervously, fearful that any intrusion might taint or change the way it was when Faye left laughing, never to return.

Catching sight of his face in the mirror above her escritoire he forced himself to look back at the man facing him. Set in stunning turquoise inlay, the frame should have complimented the reflection, but for this haggard, haunted face it failed. Ciabhan smiled in irony, Faye had begged the mirror from him for this very room, loving the fact that he had borne such an elaborate object all the way from Acre; she said it showed 'his gentleness of soul.' Would she love the man reflected in it now he wondered? He feared she would not!

Birdsong filled the room, even though the window remained closed. The unforgiving mirror was too unkind and he forced his attention away from it. Satiated after passion they would lie content in each others arms with the window open, the wolf skin cover warming their nakedness as they listened to the silence. Faye loved the sounds of night equally as much as the dawn chorus. Only this last week Orion the hunter had reappeared in the night sky, as he had just before she died. Teasingly she had called Ciabhan her 'Orion, her protector' he had laughingly threatened to stalk her even into eternity! After giggling at such childishness they had made love, tears pricked his eyes, threatening to shame him, the memories were still raw, he crossed to the window alcove.

Beneath the coloured glass of the window Faye's sandalwood chest remained locked, its metal clasp reflecting the windows colours. Anguish lay in its scented interior but he still unlocked it. Fragrance, exotic and intoxicating wafted from the heart of the treasured chest.

After her burial Ciabhan had placed Faye's wedding dress inside, the golden cloth shimmered beneath his bronzed hands as he caressed the folds; he had bought the precious fabric back from Rome with their marriage in mind.

For burial he draped her in pale green, the colour of the velvet gown she was wearing when first he set eyes on her.

Within the folds, nestled a glistening row of pearls, and beneath them in stark contrast to their milky purity lay the stained fragments of his embroidered belt. Even sandalwood and spice could not mask the bitter odour of stale blood, his blood; he blanched at the memory.

Carefully he moved the treasured pieces aside until he found Faye's manuscript protected by soft felt padding; he untied the cord with trembling fingers.

Settling himself on the footstool he spread the parchment across his lap and began to read.

He had no idea how long he had been in that scented room, it had not mattered, for as with everything now, the passing of time had no relevance to his present existence.

Minutes passed as Hours, drifting into lonely days, inexplicably months lengthened into years with the words Faye had written while at Compton Berry.

In places blobs made the neat script almost unreadable, the smudged ink had been her tears when recounting certain events had been painful, Ciabhan imagined her alone in her solar filling the lonely days in his absence with memories, memories of their love, 'their story' she called it; but it remained unfinished!

On their wedding day as a gift she presented him with the manuscript, pleased with her efforts she promised to finish 'their story.'

To that pledge she had made up a little verse; the verse carved into her grave stone:

> Our story, far from being done,
> Will live each day, my Love, my Sun.
> And when death calls for us to part,
> You'll live forever in my heart.

He was reading when Mati came into the room.

Irritated by the intrusion Ciabhan snapped, "In Gods name can't you knock woman!"

Mati knew of the manuscript, she was witness to its conception and near completion, it was she who had wiped Faye's tears when the recollections became too much, and she who supported Faye in the dark days after Ciabhan left for Rome; when Faye's mental state became a cause for concern, when even 'the raven' struggled to cope!

"Come sir, you know I care for this room."

Having just been told by Alain of Ciabhans plans to celebrate Christmas she added,

"Do you wish to use this chamber sir?"

She thought he hadn't heard her and watched quietly as with great care he rolled the parchment and retied the cord, with a heavy sigh he replaced the manuscript, taking care not to damage anything within the chest.

Ciabhans heart thumped in his chest and pulsed in his throat as he looked around the chamber, emotion threatened to choke him in front of Mati as an unbearable aching for Faye dragged at his soul.

Finally he answered Mati, "no never! I will never use this chamber, never!"

Mati pitied the man before her and understood exactly, a lifelong passion for battle, a constant quest for honour, his body and blood a sacrifice for God alone, how ill equipped he was to deal with lost love! Until meeting Faye desire for a mere woman had been an unknown emotion.

At night he could feel her soft body wrapped in his arms, he longed so for her embrace, he ran his hands over the wolfskin and inhaled, sure her perfume lingered still, wanted her essence to enter him, how he hated such a cruel God! Fury boiled within him!

He turned to face Mati, "Gods blood woman is there no end to this torment!"

She did not want to see him lose control, he despised weakness.

"No my Lord there is not!"

All his life had been about strength of character, time and time again she had tried to convince him that loving Faye was no weakness, rather an act of incredible strength, the greatest test that God ever sent to this devoted Knight, even she had begun to wonder if it was a pitiless and vengeful God that tested him so? Would a compassionate God have sent such torment of the flesh? to a disciple who had dedicated his life to Christ? Destiny obviously had other ideas and schemed to unite the two of them at every turn, tempting and testing their loyalties, until fate joined with destiny and drew the threads together with a vengeance; binding them forever with the knots of love.

37

For a short time the Templar enjoyed such love he had not known existed; just why Treachery decided to take that love as surely as fate had given it, he would never know;

Breaking the mornings still, a bird hammered at the glass, he tried to open the window, but rusty from disuse the latch had become bonded to metal. He pounded on the fragile glass unsure whether his wish was to push the bird away or capture it. From its glossy wings and beady eye he knew the bird to be a raven, a creature of mystery. At sight of its great beak, Images of another long lost raven slowly filled his vision, until from the depths of his subconscious stepped Ivan; so clear and tangible.

Ciabhan struggled to escape the advancing image, staggering back away from the vision he screwed his eyes shut, while yet another part of him desperately wished to clasp the visitor to his chest.

Scared by his sudden reaction Mati asked, "My lord what ails you?" somehow she found strength to fling open the window! "Look, Tis only a bird, there! It has flown!! Taken flight in fear I should think!"

Deathly pale Ciabhan faced the apparition; floating as on air Ivan came towards him, hands in supplication, soon Ciabhan would grasp his friend's hand, oh how he wanted to embrace him; he reached out, smiled and mouthed the words, "well timed my friend!"

Thinking him possessed Matis voice cracked, "My lord!" his expression frightened her, "my lord! What troubles you?"

From behind a woman's voice interrupted, irritating him, why would she not stay her noise; another step my friend and we're united again but Ciabhans feet suddenly were rooted in clay, he plunged forward almost falling, as Ivan retreated; ever further away his outline blurred and faded, but his hands still extended. Another step and Ciabhan fell clawing at nothingness.

"Ciabhan!" hysterical Mati shouted but her terror went unheard as Ciabhans vision of Ivan vanished; Mati tried grabbing at Ciabhan as he crashed to the ground.

Slowly his mind cleared, why had Ivan appeared now? Here in this room, why pleading? For forgiveness? For treachery? Oh! Ivan he thought, if you only knew, there is nothing to forgive my friend! Surely he knew nothing mattered any more, nothing at all!

Ciabhan pushed Mati away; roughly he grabbed her arms nearly lifting her from her feet.

"He was here, here in this room! Your wailing drove him away woman. Another lost!" his maddened eyes frightened her, "my lord I swear no one was here, she spluttered, "just you and I, no one else has ever, ever been here!"

Such a look of hate bore into Mati that she imagined how an enemy would feel on the end of his sword, one whose life he was about to take. He pushed his face so close to hers that she felt his breath in little puffs on her cheek. Scrabbling for some support and fearful of falling she clutched at the door frame.

"Never enter this room again, not you or any other ever!" Ciabhan spat, "Do you understand? No one! "

His hard warriors body threatened to crush her as he demanded, "your word Mistress, do I have your word?"

She bobbed her head in agreement, unable to answer.

It felt like an eternity before he let go, a look of disgust crossed his features as he left.

Though Well aware of her masters' short temper she could not understand why this happened, always he treated her with respect and quiet appreciation, and he knew she was the only person caring for the bedchamber he and Faye had shared, no other had ever set foot in that room since Faye's death.

In a moment's madness Ciabhan had lost his mind, what or who in Gods name had been in that room? She shivered, had he seen Faye?

A presence there certainly was in the room, but not a malevolent one, many times Faye's spirit had come to her, the perfume of roses wafting through the chamber, sometimes in the depths of winter, and roses were always Faye's favourite. Ciabhans senses had been momentarily overcome.

With relief Mati shut the door and listened as his footsteps faded on the stairs, but once in her own small room she sobbed like a baby ,she cried until sleep overcame her, so much that the raven tapping now on her window went unheard, she wept for the man who had dismissed her so pitilessly,

She cried so much that even her dreams found such misery impossible to defeat.

Ciabhans brainstorm was never mentioned again, but the days passed miserably.

When his apology did come it was in the form of the tapestry stool which had stood at the foot of the bed in their bedchamber. Woven by Faye in Ciabhans absence, the design of blood red Templar cross on a white background had been softened by Faye's playful introduction of dark mulberries and golden acorns. Though no message accompanied it, the stool appeared as if by magic in Matis room.

She thought of the times of gossip and laughter with Faye sitting straight backed on the stool while Mati brushed her hair; the gift was very personal and such a gesture surprised Mati, her hurt at Ciabhans anger softened, she made an effort to find him.

The limp plaguing his mobility lessened as the day progressed, now striding through the great hall he came fresh from the stables, smelling of horse sweat and leather; she breathed him in.

Nervously she approached, "A moment of your time my lord?" she prayed he would not notice her trembling; "the footstool is greatly pleasing to me." A smile flicked the corners of his mouth; she dared not look into his eyes. "I am glad mistress that the gift makes you happy." "Very much so," she replied. "Good." He said brushing away strands of hair that had stuck to his cheeks, their exchange of words over, he swirled his short cape over his shoulders, "good," he said again and strode on. Mati detected the faintest hint of rose amid the stable smells.

Humming softly, a spring returned to her step as she headed to the kitchen; friends again she thought contentedly.

Chapter 7
Changes

Christmas slunk in bringing mild, muggy days, curtains of cheerless grey cloaked the castle and moisture dripped from walls and stair wells. Coughs, sniffles and aching joints affected everyone in some way as the clammy dampness stole into bone and muscle.

"Keep all fires burning?" Ciabhan demanded, "night and day let them blaze!"

Compton Berry glittered under December's finery, not since Ciabhan and Faye's wedding day had it been so garlanded. Candlelight flickered and danced on the holly and ivy adorning walls and window embrasures. Hearth fires roared and wall flares blazed, banishing dark corners with leaping shadows. The gloomy larch woods beyond the walls were illuminated as the castles silhouette shimmered over the tranquil valley.

Through leafless trees, its brilliance burnished the silent slopes and sparkled over the tumbling stream, its path ending as jewels upon the waters of the lake, ruby, amber, and moonstone danced on the ripples beneath the willows.

December's celebrations filled the household with renewed hope, their gaiety proclaimed the dark days of mourning over; the Master of Compton Berry lived again!

Travellers and vendors who previously found the castle gloomy and hostile once more were welcomed with generous hospitality.

Wrapped in fur Ciabhan and Alain rode to the high meadows and flew the hawks; Bella Donna not to be outdone still proved superior to Alains new peregrine, much to Ciabhans delight. Gradually the mantle of sorrow dropped from his masters' shoulders and the Ciabhan of old shone through.

On the days of a rare hunt fire returned to his eyes and the thrill of a hunting chance filled him with renewed vigour, never a man for idle frivolity a glimmer of humour would at times surface, and take the same course; Ciabhan making suggestions of a wife for his friend.

"Alain!" he would say, "what say you to the farriers' daughter, a fair wench if ever I saw!"

The more Alain avoided the subject the more Ciabhan would tease.

"Gods blood man! Methinks you a cautious soul, do tell," he would whisper close to Alains ear, "Which maid is it causes you such secrecy? Or must it fall to me to find a wife for you?"

Always Alains reply would be the same, "Patience sir, be assured you'll be the first to know."

Christmas proved a short respite for the whole of Devon.

January's blizzards swept in rapidly, scything mild air before its easterly onslaught. In sheltered valleys complacent villagers lethargic with Decembers indulgence, were jolted into frenzies of gathering, with an urgency to fuel not only the fires but their own vulnerable bodies.

While Alain roamed the countryside organising food and supplies, Ciabhan responded quickly to the cold crisis, opening the castle to any unable to fend for themselves, the frail and the needy.

Those too sick were availed of the castle infirmary, a small charity started in the days of Ciabhans absence by Faye and Ivan; and their needs administered to, always at Ciabhans expense. Kindly villagers, particularly widows put their skills to good use by treating simple ailments, glad to escape the drudgery of daily life, grateful of their custodian's benevolence.

Mati accepted Ciabhans decree that she not go near the chamber again, but it pained her, quietly she went about her duties making everything as comfortable as she could for her Master.

He only spoke when necessary; never appearing to notice the little kindnesses she took so much trouble over.

Until one evening at dinner, as the end of a bitingly cold day froze the castle stones into ice blocks, he leant across Dickon the castle reeve, acknowledged her place at table and raised his cup to thank her for the coddled eggs and honeyed mead she had sent up to his bedchamber that morning.

Matis head pounded so she barely heard his words; though his lips moved.

She noticed only his eyes; the first time ever they were focussed on her alone.

Chapter 8
Leon

Coastal Pagons Ton fared worse than inland shelter; vicious winds like banshees howled over the bay and hurled blizzards onto pasture, burying fertile soil under ice. For days the sandstone settlement of Pagons Ton was invisible, as snow piled ever higher against red walls, leaving in some cases only sodden thatched roofs as evidence of the town's existence. Muffled by the blanket of snow the bells of Pagons Ton parish church rang timidly, inviting the faithful to prayer, it was imagined that for those plucky or foolish enough to brave the conditions, God would end their plight.

Visual comfort to those trapped were the red walls of the church, although not completed the church could be seen for miles; close by the tower of the Bishops Palace rose equally proudly, unbeaten by natures fury.

Braziers, flares and fires, maintained by committed parishioners shone a message of hope from the tops of church and tower, flames lept and fire glowed day and night into greying skies; red, orange and yellow flushed the glittering waste.

Leon, warmed and probably kept alive by the alcohol that coursed still through his veins, stirred beneath a pile of stinking rags, "Gods blood !" he cursed, " someone give me light for Christ's sake! It's as black as the arse of Lucifer in here!" he scrabbled at the barred window of the tiny jail house with numb fingers. "By Christ it's so cold!" his teeth chattered so much he could barely speak.

He swiped his hand between the bars, not knowing what the blinding whiteness outside was, "What the hell?" he drew his arm back quickly, slicing his wrist on rusting iron. "Gods Blood!" he cursed before screaming out again. Gradually his eyes adjusted to the milky light and he looked around trying to recall where he was, icicles hanging from ceiling and window ledge dripped with monotonous plops, and little freezing puddles were slippery on the freezing floor.

"Is anyone out there?" he shouted, blue and battered his hands hurt like hell so he kicked at the cell door with what little energy he had left.

"Will someone free me from this hell hole? By God I'll have blood if not! Sweet Jesus Christ is anyone left in this God forsaken town?"

The more he yelled the hoarser and rawer his throat, From beyond the door a feeble voice sounded. "aye, aye, holler as much as you like, these legs can go no faster, t'would be easier to leave e' to rot, making all that row!" Leon yelled again, "Christ man do you know who I am?"

A key rattled in the lock.

"Oh to be sure I knows who ye be, sir, that I do," muttering under his breath he added, "An' Leon the mercenary you can perish for all I cares." It took forever before the door scraped open.

Greeted by a wild eyed Leon, old Alcock the 'make do' jailer slipped on doddery heels trying to flee, quivering he paled as Leon grabbed his scrawny neck, "in hells name you old fool what took you? I should break your neck here and now!"

Alcock almost peeing himself with fear garbled, "I baint no jailer sir, just the keeper of the keys, Wills the real jailer be trapped somewhere like t'others, wont be no use beating me sir, you bin lucky any how's if you asks I, by rights you should be stiff as they poor goats," he flapped his arms towards a huddle of goats. Resembling some gruesome ice sculpture the bodies had become frozen solid, feet from the orchards safety.

"Can't figure how you baint dead!" Alcock stammered.

Irritated by the fools gibbering Leon stared at the landscape trying to think where he was, he gripped Alcocks arm, "How long? How long like this and why? Who put me here?"

Leon remembered nothing and was suddenly fearful...he shook the feeble jailor, "What foul play put me here, Christ knows I'm no common felon!" Wily Alcock guessed rightly that Leon was scared as a child, scared of the unknown! And had no recollection of the crime he had committed.

So Leon, this fearless mercenary was not quite so tough after all; in fact Alcocks ancient mother had more backbone!

"Two night's sir you've been in there, not I that put you there, no sir! Tis said you killed a man in a brawl, over some gambling debt?" he smacked his lips enjoying Leon's discomfort, "They says you lost every thing sir, even your house!"

He then changed his tune, "I says that can't be true sir, not such as you, you's not daft, us all knows how much you loves that house o' yours, fact all Pagonston knows don' um?"

Like an assassins blow the truth hit Leon.

Shoving Alcock roughly aside he looked towards his precious little manor. The snow was so deep the orchard short cut was impassable, and he laboured up to his knees in the stuff just to reach his home.

As he passed the frozen goats and their sightless eyes he looked the other way.

He'd fought his way past three cottages almost hidden from view when fresh snow began to fall, clogging his brows and lashes and reddening his nose, little icicles formed at the ends of his nostrils as relentless cold turned his body to ice.

Slowly the realisation of his own stupidity dawned, Christ, had he really lost his home in a card game? With every step he became more sober than a judge.

At his gate a path had been roughly cleared through the courtyard to the house. No dogs, no noise, and no snaffling swine rutted in the sodden straw, were they frozen too? Like a man twice his age, Leon wheezed and clutched his chest, the only comfort of sorts was the white stream of breath; proof of life, that he didn't dream!

He fumbled for a key, to no avail; of course the door would be unlocked. The solid oak wouldn't budge as his icy fingers wrestled the iron latch, "Gods fish!" he cursed.

Without warning the door swung inwards nearly dragging him with it! To reveal of all people, Oxton Napier, crook and occasional church warden! Contemptuously he looked Leon up and down; grinning through grimy stumps of what once had passed for teeth.

"Well, well, well" he said in mock surprise, "Good Master Leon, pray what brings you here?"

Leon barged forward trying to shoulder past Oxton, but like the bullock he resembled Oxton stood his ground, an immoveable hulk, while reedy laughter echoed from behind him.

"What takes thee Oxton, who be at our door?" the faceless voice enquired, "Run they through boy, there's nought here for any what calls!" more laughter crackled along the empty hall.

"Quiet man tis a nithing, no more than a big puff of wind!" Oxton sneered, "or maybe a little puff of wind now is it sir?"

Leon erupted, "out of my way merde, you trespass in my home."

These were hollow threats and useless words, without sword or men at his back Leon was as ineffective as an ant against such men.

The plotters had seen to it that their victim had been left with nothing to defend himself; utterly powerless Leon was at boiling point.

Oxton mocked, "Don't do them fancy French words on me sir, rant as you will but you don't belong here, now just bugger off! Or freeze to death!" with a mighty shove he pushed Leon back and tried slamming shut the door, fury made Leon quick and as the door flung back he grabbed Oxtons throat and pinned him to the ground. Spluttering the bulky Oxton tried rising but Leon's heel ground hard into his chest, inches from his face. "Dog merde!" spat Leon, "you are dog merde! here taste it!" he ground the sole of his boot into the writhing mans lips."

Leon still possessed enough muscle and cunning to take the blubbering lump of lard apart with his bare hands, but against three pairs of arms even his strength was useless. Oxtons accomplices had hurried to his aid

45

and held Leon firm, as he cursed the collaborators mocked Oxton, " us told e' to finish the French bastard off, Ox! T'was a mistake to spare the fool."

Grunting Oxton heaved himself upright and faced the grinning Leon, with all his force he smashed his fist into Leon's face, cracking his nose. "That'll teach you Frenchman, as I said, you as no place ere." Blood poured from Leons nose spraying his neck and shirt and Watkin the self proclaimed 'judge.'

Watkin thrust a yellowing parchment into Leon's face, "Tis all legal and binding Master Leon, this be the deeds an see ere," he pointed a filthy finger at some scrawl, "you as signed it!"

Leon blinded by blood and half dead with pain slumped forward onto the bloodied parchment, choking.

Watkin continued, "fair an square its, you signed this house over you bain't got a leg to stand on, tis all ere' Twas your wager!"

Watkin shook the parchment blood dripped from its corner, then stabbing his finger into Leon's chest he smiled, "strange you don't remember any of this, a man of honour like you!"

Turning to his accomplices he sniggered, "even though you be's a Froggy man!" pressing his mouth close to Leon's ear he snarled , "now just you listen ere' Leon of Pagons Ton, we put you in the clink for your own good, for your own safety, you ad killed two men in your temper! us put e' there from the goodness of our hearts an' this is ow you repays us?"

Leon kicked out catching Watkins shin, Watkin replied with a chop to Leon's neck, "stinking French bastard! Us should ave' left e to rot!" with those words he sealed his own death warrant.

Attracted by the fracas a crowd of onlookers had gathered, cold numbed they spilled from cottages into the Manors yard, jostling for the best view. Those most vocal even offered opinions, Kate Truscott wife of the Coach Inn keeper was the loudest, her sharp voice rang out, "tis true Leon le mercenaire, first your wife, now the house she loved, you've lost them all, shame on you!" hands on broad hips she worked the mob, goading them to react, excitement shivered the mob as they watched one mans humiliation!

As surely as alcohol had destroyed Leon's body and mind, his reputation had suffered most. Some still suspected him of being a wife murderer, for many townsfolk he was no longer the handsome and charismatic French mercenary, once an admirable member of the tight knit community. Now the pitiful foreigner was an outcast of his own making. Leon The brave fighter whose eyes had twinkled with good humour, a fortunate man who had loved his beautiful wife, and cherished home and family, had succumbed to the evil demons of excess. Now he Wallowed in self pity and under the influence had even disowned the daughter who had returned to save him, driving her from her family home.

Kate's voice rang out again, "I doubts you even remember your lovely Leonora, God knows what's become of the poor maid now , what with that fire an all in Plymouth Town!"

The crowd muttered en masse confusing Leon; he struggled to be free, kicking wildly as Watkin still flaunted the deeds in front of his face.

Suddenly as if from nowhere a command rang out, over the heads of the baying mob, carrying the tone of authority the haughty voice demanded "what in Gods name goes on here? If you lot have nothing better to do than taunt a defenceless man then make way for the bishop"

The voice belonged to Bertram the Bishops attendant in chief.

The oft absent Bishop remained the crowds' least favourite person, at mention of his name they broke apart, belligerent no longer; like rats down a privy outlet they vanished.

Only Kate spoke out once more, "that's precisely what us was doing sir! Plenty folk round here still be trapped, us was helping they!"

"That's right sir, helping us was," piped up her spindly husband.

"That'll be all of you then?" the attendant said sniffing in disgust.

One face was familiar to Bertram, that of the Frenchman Leon, "Ah, Master Leon, a friendly if somewhat battered face at last! No problem I hope my friend? All in order here?"

Bertram studied his fingers nonchalantly, but he'd missed nothing. Leon's tormenters meanwhile had scurried back inside and slammed the barricade back in place. Another squabble, more lawlessness, a curse on these peasant fools, thought Bertram impatiently.

"A question Sir," he addressed Leon, "unless you've more pressing business at this moment?"

Leon straightened; this could be an opportunity? Though the pain was furious he casually checked his ruined nose, dabbing at it with a grubby shirt sleeve, and winced, then with a shrug of his shoulders as if a broken nose were nothing he replied as best he could, "nothing that won't wait!"

"Good," said Bertram," our bishop languishes some leagues from here in a most inappropriate abode, sickly and ill at ease he grows daily more inpatient; it would appear God makes no concessions even for the reverential!" Bertram smirked, his even white teeth chattering through blue lips. "As usual it's fallen to me to smooth Gods chosen ones passage and temper!

Contemptuously he swept his arm over the now empty yard, "I can see it would be easier to tempt St Peter himself than raise a hand around here!" Though swathed in fur and wolf skin Bertram was colder than he'd ever been in his life, so how the man in front of him felt he couldn't imagine. Badly wounded, unarmed, and dressed for summer Leon's lack of outer clothing started Bertram shuddering.

Chamois breeches that had seen better days were overhung by a loosely woven tunic, long sleeved and open at the neck; he had neither cape or covering for head or hands, and a pair of knee length boots were sodden to their tops, his feet must have been paddling in water.

Ragged and filthy he resembled one of the louse ridden beggars who squatted daily by the walls of Exeter Cathedral; yet this was the respected and usually suave Leon who never failed to pay court when the Bishop was in residency.

True he was a mercenary and had managed to acquire an unsavoury reputation of late but he was always respectful of mother church and his religious obligations.

Bertram dismounted with a groan, "God's blood, I'm stiffer than Lucifer's fork! And not where it matters my friend!" he laughed.

With his arm loosely about Leon's shoulder he bent close, "any assistance at this time would not go unnoticed or unrewarded my friend. The Bishop can be generous, what say we take some ale; discuss the possibilities of your help?" He looked Leon over, and added, "Hardly dressed for the weather are you sir?"

Grimly Leon smiled his pain obvious as he limped alongside the man who had become his saviour, the two mounted assistants to Bertram followed; in the white stillness their hushed voices still seemed strangely intrusive.

Leon glanced over his shoulder as they left his courtyard, Watkins face drew back from the leaded window.

"Bastard" hissed Leon under his breath, "laugh while you can for I will have my revenge."

Bertram smiled, but kept his counsel, more pressing worries sat on his weary shoulders than those of feuding peasants. "My belly aches with hunger, you sir look as if you might die from it!"

Bathed, rested and nourished all courtesy of the Bishop a very different Leon exited the Palaces guest rooms some time later.

Full of pain killing opium and with his shattered nose protected by swathes of dressing, he rode beside Bertram; accompanied by nine tough volunteers, they left Pagonston and headed north.

The nine had joined willingly, better to ingratiate themselves with a view to reward than freeze by a barren hearth.

Sturdy Rounceys Laden with tools, saddle bags and equipment rattled along, heads down against the cold they quickly settled into a steady rhythm.

With a wolf skin cloak draped about his shoulders and a new quilted gambeson Leon was comfortable now his feet were at last snug in new boots, he patted the borrowed sword and smiled wryly, Lady luck was once more at his side, how soon the wheel of fortune changes!

The villains who thought him beat could wait, time aplenty for Leon to take revenge.

Well used to hard rides and adverse conditions Leon made sure the others understood, "Stay close at all times" he'd said, "take care the whiteness for it will blind and play tricks on you!"

Weaponry and harness glinted as the horsemen rode, tinkling and jangling with the movement, for a while they talked and joked, excited by their mission.

But gradually one by one they quieted, preferring the warmth of their fur lined hoods, and silence.

North to Exeter they headed, quickly fading into the white as the landscape absorbed and muffled all signs of their passing.

Chapter 9
The Bishop

On a horsehair mattress with a coarse pillow beneath his pin head, the Bishop reclined awkwardly, his flaccid features colourless as the white fur cloak draped over his corpulent body.

Dribbles of spit like those which soil the swaddling of an infant stained the fur where his germ laden sneezes had missed the linen laid under his chin for the purpose. The Bishops podgy ring burdened fingers fluttered as he waved a cotton remnant beneath his great nose, wheezing he dabbed the drips.

To the confused wife of the merchant in whose house he lay the Bishop was a nuisance, his attempts at communication pitiful, she turned away in disgust, silently cursing this man of God; the last thing she needed was another wretched mouth to feed. She cursed also her soft and charitable husband who had taken it upon himself to offer shelter to the Bishop, their supplies were all but exhausted, and the Bishops entourage were eating like locusts, much longer and God knew there'd be nothing left. Trying to ignore the quivering figure she blew on her numb fingers and threw the last log onto the fire, it fizzed with sparks, from the bed the heaving lump of lard panted his thanks, "you're a good woman Mistress Cobley, God will reward your charity."

He sneezed loud enough to wake the dead then feigned the vapours, letting his head drop back onto the prickly pillow, "Pray dear lady is there more of your delicious mead?"

Tight lipped she poured the last drop of honey liquid from the flagon, first warming it, in purpled hands the Bishop clasped the cup slurping the contents greedily while Mistress Cobley looked on coldly, by God her husband would feel her tongue when this was over! Suddenly Cobley appeared in the low doorway, she nearly collapsed with relief, anger she promised herself would come later.

"Good news at last Wife," he said, "the Bishop's men have broken through and cleared a path, God be praised! And you'll never guess who brought them?"

Cobley didn't get to tell her for the Bishop interrupted, with mead dribbling down his chin he croaked, "did I hear right master Cobley? Did you say there was passage at last?"

"Tis true my lord," Cobley answered, your men have broken through, the way to Pagonston is clear!"

"God be praised," the Bishop rasped, "let us pray the good Lord grants this poor body the strength it needs to proceed! Eh! Mistress Cobley." Wide with innocence the actor in him demanded her agreement.

50

She glared at her husband warming his ample backside at the fire, but he looked away as an exhausted Leon burst through the door in a flurry of powdered snow.

"Leon of Pagonston!" Cobley stuttered, holding his arms wide in surprise, "of all the people I least expected to see! On such a night as even Demons would be loathe to face!"

Leon scowled beneath thunderous brows; if the Bishop were not present he would have had the merchant's tongue from his head!

"Merchant Cobley it takes a man to work as I have this night, not a lactating dormouse!"

The Bishop raised himself, speaking between sneezes, "tis no surprise to me though Master Leon, you always were a good friend of Mother church! Come sit awhile, warm yourself."

To Cobleys wife he almost begged, "I expect Mistress you will find a little more of this excellent mead for our guest!"

With a thin lipped smile she gathered up the flask. Scuttling past Leon she almost ran into Bertram who had just entered, "careful mistress you will come a cropper," he said steadying her.

Blushing she extricated herself, "I'll see what's left in the kitchen."

The Bishop watched her go, "those two fine people have inconvenienced themselves greatly." he told the newcomers, nonchalantly examining his soft hands.

Nearly as hot as the fire Cobley simmered over Leon's words,

As if to truculent children the Bishop spoke, "now, now gentlemen tis not the time nor the place for hostilities! My thanks are extended to you all!"

A bout of coughing shook his body, red in the face he spluttered,

"Leon it is good to know the rumours of your disgrace and ruins are unfounded!"

Smirking Leon answered, "Rumour like Icarus my Lord flies too close to the truth, then falls apart from lack of substance!" he looked witheringly at Cobley who huffed with irritation, but the Bishop raised his eyebrows in a warning glance .

"The truth was ever safe in your hands Master Leon, but a straight yea or nay would have sufficed; we need no intellectual wit in this room!"

Sighing with exasperation he leant heavily back on the pillows.

Mistress Cobley returned clutching more mead, and poured for the visitors. To lessen the tension Bertram who had watched the stand off with amusement chuckled, "think you my lord that women could be right regarding their men folk, they believe we are no more than green lads clutching our mother's skirts?" he smiled mischievously at Cobleys wife and her already pink face suffused bright red.

Leon glowered through blackened eyes while Cobley shuffled uneasily from foot to foot.

"Bah! Enough of this foolishness now help me up for I swear this mattress is stuffed with all the bones of hell!"

Throughout the night all was made ready for the Bishops departure, at Leon's commands they loaded wagons, packed chests and baggage and fed and watered the horses, only then did they find time for a short sleep. Leon dozed as fitfully as his shattered nose would allow until the watery dawn.

a groaning staircase threatened to collapse as the Bishop was carried down and settled with much fuss on the strongest beast, impatient to be away the horse stamped and snorted, steaming breath mingled with that of the riders in the icy air.

Against sentinel black trees shook their barren tops while leafless saplings bent and twisted in the horizontal blasts.

Bertram miserable with fatigue rubbed sleepy eyes, Leon was out of sight, but his voice carried above the wind, Bertram didn't know how the man got his energy especially wounded. However this was Bertram's second journey, and he was sick to death of overseeing the comfort of the finicky 'Man of God.' He would rather be anywhere then here, even Leon's grating mixture of French and English irritated him; God! It worsens by the hour! He was however well aware that without the Frenchman's help they would not have made it this far and God knew what retribution Holy Church would have taken then!

Even Criminals whether he liked it or not, have their uses he mused. Hunching his tall frame as low into the horse's neck as possible Bertram sulked, his nose dribbled and eyes watered continuously; courtesy of you my friend he fumed, his eyes boring into the Bishop's lumpy back.

Not once did the Bishop glance back at Bertram, maybe he knew the resentment his attendant felt. Bertram meanwhile imagined the Bishop as a lump of ice, imagined the great block tumbling and smashing into thousands of pieces of ice!

Chatter ceased, luckily the same gentle chink of harness that kept Bertram awake on the previous journey, now saved him from falling from the saddle. Leon energetic as always laboured back along the column, Bertram's tunic flashed red beneath his wolf skin; crimson and gold the colour made a gash like blood in the white bleakness.

"How does my lord?" queried Leon, through the bloodied bandages, his nose throbbed like hell, and he struggled to be heard above the wind. He nodded towards the Bishop, "the Bishop will be twice the size by the time we arrive sir, snows sticks like honey to his bulk!"

Leon's poor English, jolted Bertram from his misery, for a moment he feared he'd been on the verge of unconsciousness. "Be mindful of what you say sir! The man has the hearing of a hare!"

Leon's customary swagger showed itself even from the saddle, "tis freezing fast, the distance will test us all, watch out for the Bishop, should he topple, I fear none will have strength to lift him!"

Leon peered beneath Bertram's hood; hoping for a sign of humour, he looked a little too closely it seemed to Bertram!

"No need to peer so sir!" he snapped, "I breathe still!"

Leon smirked, "Well you could have fooled me Sir, 'twas a terrible sight, like a corpse my friend!" he said wickedly.

Witheringly Bertram looked back, before falling once more into the isolation of his hood.

Leon ploughed his horse towards the front chuckling to himself, no humour at all these haughty Parisians! The superior Bertram's discomposure was well worth the agony a smile bought to his raw face; well satisfied Leon's eyes twinkled roguishly for the first time in weeks.

Chapter 10
Sister Domenica

Sister Domenica retreated to an isolated valley on the edge of the moor.
She found Sanctuary in an isolated Convent where she nursed Edmund in
a place of safety. Slowly the horrors of the past months paled.
Sisters gave their time willingly, supporting the young novice in every
way.
Once settled she put Edmunds recovery and comfort above everything,
her own well being came secondary to his, however for some of the
sisters the pitiful Edmund seemed not quite deserving of such devotion,
especially as Domenicas Godly duties were at times neglected.
Four serene months had passed since her arrival, now spring draped
hedgerows with May blossom, and bluebells swayed in a smoky haze
through shadowy copses.
Domenica rested against the buttery's cooling stonework, warm even for
a spring day, she welcomed the chance to work in its cool interior, the
churning and patting of butter was calming work. Day dreaming in the
fragrant air, she had not heard her Mother Superiors approach until the
older nun spoke, "my dear I would talk with you, come."
Naturally compassionate, rather than cultivated kind, the elder woman
liked to be called simply 'Pia' plain and simple. Of gentle manner she
fussed over her novices like a mother hen. Probably in her middle fifties,
Pia sought the Sisterhood after a series of personal tragedies; stemming
from a violent male dominated family background.
Escape came in the guise of betrothal when a respected and landed knight
begged her hand in marriage, foolishly she dreamt of happier times. Her
happiness was short lived, on the wedding eve, a vicious argument
erupted between her affianced and one of her brothers; it ended in the
horror of the Knights slaying. Heartbroken she vowed never to love
again and sought an isolated order, surrendering herself to Gods service,
now devoted solely to prayer and piety she had found tranquillity. The
fire in Plymouth meant the convent had more than its share of the injured
passing through its benevolent doors, most recovered as best they could
and moved on, all except Edmund, he remained the lone male in a female
only convent. It was agreed by all that a miracle had brought young
sister Domenica and her burned companion to the convent, it gave Pia
her greatest challenge, and for the last months the sisters had gladly
nursed Edmund, they did it not only to see his recovery but for love of
the dedicated novice. Pias liking did not quite extend to Edmund, his
black moods and spitefulness had not gone unnoticed, pique that blighted
his mending.

Pias feelings of anger towards Edmund caused her such remorse at times that often she ended the day in prayers for forgiveness.

Gently guided Domenica to a bench beneath the wall. Early jasmine promised heady perfume, not yet rampant it crept over the back of the seat.

Domenica asked, "mother, is something wrong, have I angered you?"

Pia smiled at the young woman and shook her head, "no child of course not, I am concerned for you alone, nothing else," she patted the seat, "here sit beside me," she took Sister Domenica's hand and asked, "I believe Edmund is greatly recovered"

"he will never recover, but Yes mother he is coming to terms with his fate, but for your kindness he would not have survived, it is you who must be thanked." her eyes shone at the mention of his name just as Pia feared, this was going to be very hard, she did not want to see this lovely young nun distressed, but it was her duty to say what she had come to say. "Child," she faltered as Domenica fixed her with clear grey eyes, "yes Mother Superior?"

"Sister you are aware of our rules? That it is my sworn duty to observe those rules?" Domenica nodded.

"Well" Pia continued, "Our benefactor's charity depends on our pledge to run a woman only order, you do understand my dear?"

Domenica suddenly understood, looked away and pressed her hands across her mouth, "No, please don't send him away, he's too ill, he will die!"

Great tears spilled down her cheeks, some plopped onto Pias habit, Pia grasped her shaking hands, "I have no choice sweeting; others notice his stay is overdue, it is time to make a choice."

Sister Domenica shook herself free and stood with her back to Pia, "I will not see him sent away Mother." She said defiantly.

Pia shifted uncomfortably, "A place of safety can be found for him child; I know of a male order that take the sickly, they are kind and understanding, they will care for him."

Domenica would not be moved, "No," she said, "if Edmund cannot remain here then neither will I!"

Pia tried to reason with her, "You cannot mean that child, will you renounce your vows to travel the highways with one so maimed, you will be so vulnerable, the world outside our gates is a dangerous place, God knows what could become of you, it is madness!"

Domenica remained adamant, "I promised God to look after Edmund. and I will continue to do so, even at the risk to myself I will care for him, Mother you do me dishonour to think I would change my mind." Pia knew in her heart not to challenge such determination, but still she tried.

On her knees she clasped Domenica around her middle, "I beg of you change your mind."

Domenica closed her eyes shook her head from side to side.

Wearily Pia rose. "Then so be it child, I will continue to pray you will change your mind," she couldn't help but remind the stubborn young thing, "and Forget not that Edmund is a married man!"

Hurt at Pias suggestion, Domenica replied, "I need no reminding Mother Pia that Edmund is married, it is the reason we head for Pagonston, that they may be reunited; if not Edmund assures me her family will shelter him."

Her grey eyes even if holding a secret were direct as she added, "And as for God Mother? Why would he change my mind when he is with us?"

It was with heavy heart that Pia reported Domenicas decision to leave the convents safety with Edmund, and her prayers were in vain.

Within the week Edmund was ready for departure, Domenica fussed as her patient fretted. In the convents safety Edmund had become accustomed to tenderness, believing he was the focus of all attention, it never occurred to him they nursed from charity, that the future of their order depended on the woman only rule.

He fidgeted, and tried to raise himself on weakened elbows groaning as he did so with pain, Domenica tried to explain, "Do not blame Mother Pia Edmund, she has no option, our stay was always temporary, we knew that, now do not fret so, we must put our trust in the Lord, he is our protector."

Edmunds breath hissed between his teeth, he wanted to stay. He did not believe the mother superior had to let him go; she was being over cautious, worried at her benefactors reaction indeed! More likely because she was a bitter dried up old spinster and jealous of a man being cared for by one younger than her.

"She wants me gone because I am useless, if I could work she would be glad of my labour," he carped, "I should have died, far better for everyone methinks!"

Domenica wept, "You are too harsh sir!"

Insultingly he added, "Not you of course, nuns are not real women!"

He cared not how much his words hurt.

"When we are to be thrown out then?" he resembled a petulant infant.

"The Sisters are trying to fine a guide" she whispered, "one who will give of his time, someone who owes the Almighty a debt."

Sullenly Edmund nodded, then pointed to a blanket on a stool beside his pallet, "cover my shoulders Sister, it turns decidedly chill in here."

A strong volunteer soon showed up willing to escort a young nun and a cripple to Pagons ton, the man who came forward seemed sincere, and certainly strong, his muscle bound physique would hopefully prove a deterrent to footpads. A wrestler the man entertained in the only way he knew, Pia unconvinced that he was the best man for the job very reluctantly agreed to accept his services.

Edmund lay in a small covered cart, strapped to the horses saddle bags bulged with supplies and medications, plus a fresh change of garment for Domenica; this was most important, Pia had said, "remember child, first and foremost you are a bride of Christ, therein lies your safety."

Promising the Mother Superior that his charges would be delivered safely, the wrestler set forth for Pagonston; safely sewn into her robe Domenica carried an introduction to the Brothers of the Abbey of Buckfast, explaining the circumstances that bought Sister Domenica and Edmund to ask for their protection. Pia had insisted they carry papers, for she was aware the Abbey of Buck fast sat on their route, that knowledge gave her confidence; for if they made it there the brothers would be sympathetic to Edmunds plight; providing Domenica was not too proud to ask for it!

Embracing the young nun, Pia was uneasy; she felt she was abandoning a young woman and helpless man from sanctuary, once more she beseeched, "my dear child, it is not too late to change your mind!"

Convinced what she was doing was right Domenica replied, "Mother you torment yourself needlessly, It is my choice alone, I would rather die than desert Edmund! Bless me and give me strength, not your doubts." She smiled her angelic smile, as tears filled Pias eyes.

From the cart Edmund scowled, defenceless and weak, but still he would not meet the eyes of the woman who had taken him in, preferring to grumble at his young companion.

On this beautiful day in May as sounds of rebirth filled their senses the sisters gathered for the sad farewell, they watched with pity one of their own start into the unknown; but one and all agreed; if this was freedom not one of them envied her!

Chapter 11
The Escape

Plymouths conflagration left such misery in its wake that simple folk questioned Gods very existence, Meryn was no exception, she wondered if life would ever be the same again, and doubted spring would return.
 However it did return, dressed in glory; not early, neither late, but on time as usual, blossom dressed trees the flames had spared, and froths of pink and white protected the minute apples that would appear from their centres. Green shoots returned, punching through scorched earth, where many thought life had died forever. Lime green Ferns unfurled snake-like in dank places like puddles of bright green; tough little bluebells waved defiant azure heads.
Life burst forth, daily the orb of life lifted its golden head above the horizon, until mother moon replaced it; lighting mans way through darkness. Nature's continuity seemed to announce, nothing altered, nothing changed! But in truth it was a cruel pretence, nature's beauty merely a vacant image, for everything had changed, human Lives and society had transformed beyond recognition, those who suffered would not easily be placated by gilded dawns and violet sunsets! The march of destruction had left humiliation and misery and stolen all human dignity.
Leonora searched tirelessly or Edmund, the fruitless hunts finally numbing into indifference, then she immersed herself in menial tasks, volunteering anything to shut the unthinkable out of her mind.
Besides she had another concern now! Trey.
Edmunds supposed rescuer had developed an interest in her, how was she to deter him? His intentions were so obvious, and Leonora was far from comfortable. Meryn laughed and made light of Leonora's concerns, occupied as she was with the fight for survival, not with trivia.
Together on their knees they scrubbed the pantry floor, chatting idly, usually flawless Leonora's skin was flushed with the efforts of her labour, and little beads of perspiration ran into her eyes, she rubbed them impatiently, "I know not how to discourage him further," she sighed, "in truth he knows I am a married woman, does the man have no pride?"
Meryns own bones ached as she straightened; Leonora was so lovely, strange how God never balanced his gifts of beauty, for her young friend seemed to have more than a fair share! 'Twas no wonder men looked.
"my dear the great ox is no more than a love sick puppy dog," she chuckled, "the whole inn be laughing at 'im, why don't e' just be friendly an take what e offers" she whispered, "ain't no time to be picky, an' e's a man of means! You can always rid yourself of e later!
 If you knows what I mean!" Meryn winked.

Leonora feigned shock, "My you are a wicked woman Meryn Jenkin! May the lord look sideways at you!" The thought of riches untold did however cross her mind, but guilt soon pushed them out.

Rich, Trey certainly seemed when casually he mentioned lands in Cornwall; or rather his companion had.

She recalled the weasel like Trewin, and his sneaky aside, "it be a wife my masters looking for missy! And you'm be a pretty piece!"

Too closely he'd studied her body, remembering the little beady ferret eyes on her breasts she shuddered.

Edmund had bored and stifled her with his childish possessiveness, his constant carping had nearly driven her mad, but she had made her bed as her father had reminded often enough, and must lie on it. She was a married woman, shame on Trey who should know better.

How strange coincidence? That her childhood companion, the son of her mothers housemaid Mati, someone she never imagined meeting again, had broken his journey here and was the rescuer of her husband.

Had he no honour? Trying to muscle in on her, Leonora's tolerance of him was based on nothing more than gratitude for saving Edmund, and old time's sake. At first their shared memories had entertained, one so closely linked to her past was a novelty.

That was until he became a nuisance, appearing unexpectedly from nowhere, when she was alone or his friend at every opportunity speaking for him, always lurking, so much so that Meryn found outside tasks for her.

One morning as she counted swedes Trey came and stood in the storeroom doorway, his bulk blocking what little light there was, fear of being trapped made her freeze.

"That's no job for the likes of you girl," he mumbled, "Mother Jenkin cheapens e."

Leonora snapped back, "I am No girl, but a married woman and well used to labour, move so my task is no more difficult then!"

She held her breath as his peculiar eyes narrowed, but with just a grunt he turned on his heels and was gone; Leonora breathed a sigh of relief.

Little did she know that her rudeness was a challenge, her beauty and coldness of manner only served to inflame his passion.

The time had come for Leonora to think of herself, it could be that Edmund lived, in what state or where she had no idea, deep inside neither did she care too much! Her choices were bleak, remain here with Meryn and share the struggles, or take her chances in a harsh world? Servitude was no choice; she wished to be once more mistress of her own destiny.

Let Fate determine her path, if she and Edmund were to be together then it would surely happen.

Strong and determined the Leonora of old suddenly returned, her mind was made up and nothing would change it.

She would leave Plymouth and return to Pagonston, once there she must challenge her Father and demand her inheritance.

Maybe he had confronted the Lord of Compton Berry, possessed at last her Mothers emerald, the precious ring he spoke of so often and desired so passionately.

She smiled wryly at the thought of inheritance! By now her father had probably lost what remained of her childhood home; if his actions on the last night she saw him were anything to go by.

Telling Meryn of her decision would be hard; she so hoped the dame wouldn't cry and try to change her mind.

But of course Meryn wailed and wept a sea of tears, enough to fill Plymouth sound two times over so Leonora teased.

"Oh my pretty what is I to do without e' what with they thieves an robbers all over the place?"

Her two little ones, snotty nosed Arthur and Ambrose dragged at their distraught mothers' skirts, eyes wide.

"Oh lord above!" she wailed, wiping her nose on her sleeve, as she clung to Leonora's neck, her body shuddering.

"Shh, mistress you'll wake the dead" scolded Leonora, "I want to do this in secret, none must become suspicious or I'll have the 'Ox' on my tail, he is the reason I must go, come now I need you to make my plan work!

The perfect day had come when Trey and Trewin announced they had business on the far side of the river, that two or three days may pass before their return, in two days Leonora could be well on her way to Pagonston and she had seized the moment, barely able to disguise her excitement.

"Now remember Meryn, no weeping I beg you, see me off as if I am merely gathering the days kindling, come Dame be brave."

Daily Leonora's outside task had been to rope 'Mallow' and the rouncey together with empty panniers at their sides.

It was not unusual for her to be seen miles away searching for firewood, today though the panniers were full with what Leonora needed for her journey, a warm blanket, a change of clothes and what little food could be spared.

Had Trey seen her departure on this balmy morning he would not have been suspicious, since the fire women foraged along with their men folk.

Meryn kissed Leonora's cheek wetly, "Remember my sweet there's always a place for e' ere, if that there father of yours is as you says then you'll be back ere' sure as I's a woman!"

Leonora grinned. "Woman? Meryn, why you're an old witch! You'll survive as you always have."

Seriously she added, "Meryn you have been so good to me, like a Mother, I will never, ever forget your kindness, God willing we will meet again, now kiss me and let that be an end to it, witch!"

Their laughter tinkled, as Leonora stepped out of the shadows and into bright spring sunshine.

61

Meryn whispered in Arthur's ear, "lets hope Missy brings back plenty, now be off with you and watch your brother for me," she pointed to, Ambrose climbing upon the bench, his skinny arms were just about to topple the yellow contents of a cream jug.

Meryn made the day as normal as possible, neighbours she knew from experience were aware of the tiniest changes.

The plan went better than expected, delayed by a fight the two men found themselves stranded when their boat was seized as recompense for damages, so it was an evil tempered Trey who returned later than expected.

For a time his anger blinded him to any thoughts of Leonora's whereabouts, cleverly Meryn kept out of his way, busying herself with the children, both victims of a sneaky fever.

Meryns work load was never ending but she still found time to make her way to a little makeshift altar where she prayed for her friend's safety.

Luckily the weather held fair, the roads out of Plymouth busy and Leonora's progress easy, she slept in the open always choosing a sheltering hedge to hide behind.

On one starlit night when dew lay damp on her cover, she'd woken suddenly, alarmed at the sound of horsemen, with only the hedge between her and the riders she hardly dared draw breath, the clink of mail gave them away as Knights. She wondered at their mission riding so hard at night, finally the thump of hooves passed, but unable to settle she spent the hours until daylight jumping at every rustle.

Discovering Leonora gone Trey seemed to believe Meryn when she told him of Leonora's news, that her husband had been sighted! "er' took off sir, soon as er' knew, just went, no by your leave, no nothing! Towards the moor, where er'husband lived afore."

"To the moor you say?" Trey glanced at Trewin.

"Oh for sure sir, Master Edmund Start was born an' bred up there, Mistress Leonora was pretty sure t'was e what had been seen, I was a bit peeved to say the least sir!" Meryns ruddy cheeks burned almost scarlet with lying, her cheeks itched beneath their blush.

"I 'opes she finds 'er 'usband then," he muttered to Trewin, "Us'll leave in the morn man, make ready for cock crow."

As Trey lumbered away Meryn considered his strange eyes, almost yellow, not at all nice, a most peculiar face for a young man.

After breaking their fast Trewin paid for their stay and thanked Dame Jenkin for her care, "tis a shame we had no chance to bid the young lady farewell mistress, maybe us'll catch up with er' on the road." He smirked slyly before pulling on the reins and trotting after his master.

Such an odd pair thought Meryn, as she watched them, Trey hunched in his saddle, bulky and brooding, and Trewin, skinny and rodent like.

Meryns heart raced as she saw them turn not towards the dark moor but along the river, the direction Leonora had taken.

Uneasy she chewed her lip and wrung her hands, oblivious to the newly arrived traveller until he spoke.

"Pray mistress, do there be any chance of a bed for the night? Only the one night mind, I be moving on tomorrow like."

"God love us sir!" Meryn said turning to the elderly stranger, "You made I jump fit to die! Course I as room."

Chapter   12
Totnes

On the approach to Totnes Leonora had doubts, without her husband,
homeless, and penniless she was a girl on the verge of beggary,
undistinguishable from the destitute who trudged the well worn highway.
One difference however was Leonora's appearance; pride did not allow
her to neglect it, when possible she cleansed her person and untangled her
hair, to lessen the signs of rough sleeping.

 Some however knew as soon as they saw a lone female in stained
clothes, tugging two weary horses behind her; 'Mallow' now lame was
unrideable while the rouncey laboured due to old age.

 Glorious weather warm and dry heralded summers heat, in other
circumstances she would have enjoyed such balmy days, strawberries not
yet red peeped from hedgerows alive with birdsong, tiny Jenny wrens
skittered between oak saplings and hazel trunks, their sharp twittering
bold from the ivy covered bark. Myth had it that the wren was evil and
some still beat the hedgerows with sticks to drive them out, but not so for
Leonora, she loved its habit of building decoy nests, something so
beautiful could not be evil; not even the buzzard with its plaintive call
soaring high on lazy wings.

Concerned for Mallow she soothed the brave little palfrey, "not long now
my sweet girl, rest is near and you shall eat the sweetest hay I can find, oh
I promise you my pretty we shall fare well, I will steal if I have to for
you."

And steal she might just have to, especially as the last of her food she had
given to a sad looking young thing crouching by the track in a shabby
Novices habit. Under the shelter of an oak a horse pulled at spindly grass,
and a cart rested on its broken shafts. Leonora stopped out of concern on
seeing a woman alone, but conversation was far from easy.

On the cart under a pile of rags something moved, with his head covered
and his face turned away from them lay a man, shadows, dark and light
danced over his form.

 "Pray sister what ails thy burden?" Leonora spoke gently and gestured
towards the cart, the shape groaned.

The Novice responded, but a veil over her mouth made hearing difficult,
"We are bound for Pagonston," she said weakly.

Leonora smiled, "A coincidence for I am for there also," maybe I can
help? Does he need aid?" She made towards the cart.

Putting out her hand the Novice stopped her, "No! We do not beg
mistress; sadly we have been robbed, it is sanctuary we seek now!"

Again Leonora turned to the cart, "then I will help, please let me!"
The nuns reply was adamant, "no! He is better left to rest; being seen would only worsen his distress! The visions hurt his mind."
The Novice pulled the veil tighter over her mouth.
"Our guide betrayed us, and the good Sisters who trusted him!"
A terrifying thought suddenly occurred to Leonora,
The creature on the cart could be leprous! Had not the girl kept her own mouth covered?
"Is the Abbey of Buckfast far distant?" the Novice asked, "I carry a letter of introduction, I believe the brothers better suited to cope with his needs."
So it was true! Leonora knew a leper colony existed somewhere near Totnes town, the Brothers would be bound to know.
She stepped back and pointed over the fields to her left, "A few hours ride," she said.
Guilt overwhelmed her and she added, "I will come with you, f you wish?"
If the Novice smiled, she knew not.
"You are most kind Miss, but tis better you look to yourself, your circumstances seem little better than our own."
How right she was and observant for mallow was in truth suffering greatly.
"Apprehensive about touch Leonora placed the crusty bread and cheese on the ground in front of the girl.
"Then take this, if not for yourself then for your sick companion, please take it!"
Hesitantly Domenica picked it up, "it is not charity we seek miss, but I thank you." Her hands and arm were pale and smooth.
"Tis no charity." said Leonora, "it pleases me to give."
It shamed Leonora to leave the vulnerable couple, at last sight of them the novice was bent over her charge offering the food.
That night Leonora slept uneasily, shuddering with the chill she fought with her conscience over whether she had been right to leave them? She decided it had been for the best.
Without warning Edmund s face flashed across her mind, she hoped if he did live that an Angel was with him, please God do not let him be lying abandoned somewhere?

Domenica gave silent thanks to God; the almighty had sent an Angel in their moment of need as surely as the devil had tempted the guide to steal from them, Domenica would remember both.

65

At least by taking the food and rejecting help the Novice kept her pride, a powerful yet sometimes misguided sentiment.

Leonora prayed hard for them both.

Just outside of Totnes the river babbled along beside her, and the highway became busier, food sellers shouted the merits of their wares, pies, cold meats, candies and sweetmeats, Hawkers traded trinkets for self adornment and gifts, and jostled for space with painted wagons and stalls. Beggars, some limbless others able bodied bellowed the merits of certain taverns and stabling, humanity that great unwashed made Leonora aware of her own body; she needed a change of clothes and a wash, rose water and fresh linen she could only dream of.

Having come this far she was allowed to dream!

One bold young knave approached, bobbing up and down at her stirrup he babbled almost as much as the river, "fine lady, that there horse needs rest, I knows of a good place."

"Really" said Leonora patiently. She had decided to stay at the same coaching inn on the riverside as before, "Thank you but I have stabling already."

The child was persistent, "but miss, where I will send e' is the best known for miles, knights and ladies just like you use it."

Of one thing Leonora was sure, she resembled no lady and his pushiness was beginning to annoy, "thank you, but as I said, my lodging is booked and I am expected, now if you please,"

A group of approaching riders kicked up a swirl of red dust as they approached, it clogged her nostrils; pulling her scarf tight over her mouth she backed into a gateway; the boy darted across their path, and fattened himself into the hedge beside her.

Mutterings and curses filled the air as other road users ran for safety, their frustration obvious. "Bloody Knights" swore a pockmarked fellow squashed to her other side, "They thinks theys above the law, pushing folk out of the way, women an all," his contempt was clear. "Whenever theys on the road, like tis only for they!" he spat with no regard for her skirts. "Bloody knights!" he cursed. Leonora backed away.

How glad she was for the scarf over her face, for it was with horror she watched Alain the young Frenchman approach, Alain, the last person on earth she would have wanted to see her so.

To the grumbling villain, she said, "Are they so hated sir?"

He looked her up and down before replying, "Nay miss, not really, tis the master of Compton Berry and his men at arms, not seen often is he these days, off to Buckfast I should think, nothing else o'er that way." He spat again, Leonora glared.

"And the tall Knight at the front, would he have been this Master of Compton Berry?" she asked.

"Aye miss that 'twas e'alright, an if I's 'onest not so bad as far as their like go, if you knows what I mean."

She nodded sagely as the man brushed himself down and disappeared back into the crowd.

She had guessed rightly that Alains companion was Ciabhan of Compton Berry, she glimpsed him only briefly but would remember for a long time his remarkable eyes, the mirrors of his soul were dark as the peaty moor, but amazingly luminous against a bearded, swarthy complexion, they were also the saddest eyes she had ever seen.

By far the tallest of the riders, he was proud of countenance and arrow straight in the saddle, he neither looked to right or left, but ahead as if nothing would stay him from his purpose, totally detached from those milling around the track, as if they were of no consequence, It convinced Leonora that he was almost certainly extremely arrogant.

In the short time it took for them to pass by she noticed how his hair swung shoulder length over his dull grey cloak and curled over a green and yellow kerchief, knotted at his neck; a leather helmet bobbed from his harness.

A sudden bright spark of colour bounced from his hand where it rested lightly on his thigh; in his right he held the reins slackly on the horses' neck.

Like that of the kingfisher as it whirs unexpectedly past the watcher the flash of green made her gasp, against his tanned skin the emerald sparked, proclaiming its existence, as if purely for her benefit!

'Well' she thought to herself, if that were the dog of Compton Berry, he was a passing handsome man! Could it be her Fathers jealousy was well founded after all?

Almost overcome with emotion, she could hardly believe that upon his finger for all to see, her Mothers lover, and now widower still wore for all to see, the emerald ring; the gem so coveted by her Father.

She watched until the riders disappeared from view then brushed the dust from her clothes, there was little chance of bumping into Alain now, and once more the young knight had ridden from her life!

He was she decided a very attractive young man so fine looking,
With a pang of regret she remembered his company.

The inn keeper at the 'Seven Stars' recognised her,

"A room miss as before, an stabling?" he frowned at the state of the horses and bent to examine mallows feet, "this littl'un baint good miss, been like this some time as err?" Leonora looked away, she knew 'Mallow' suffered, also the rouncey, their resilience bought this far. Choices had to be made, one of the horses must go, with no means of paying for lodging, it was the only way.

Long hours tramping rutted roads had began her thinking of alternative ways, a relaxing trip down river seemed an easier way of getting to Pagonston, but how could she pay for passage?

When Master Dawks had finished fussing over Mallow Leonora spoke, "sir, to pay for Mallows needs I will sell the rouncey,"

Leonora hadn't noticed as the innkeepers' daughter sidled up; on tiptoe the child stroked Mallows nose and whispered softly.

Looking indulgently at the pretty child Dawks said, "tell you what miss, I'll take the lame'un off your hands, even though er will cost me, seems the little maid as fallen in love with her."

Leonora shook her head, "No sir, you are mistaken, I couldn't possibly part with Mallow, we have been through much it would seem a betrayal, tis the other horse I wish to sell."

The flaxen haired child clinging to Mallow fixed her father with periwinkle eyes while the inn keeper chewed hard on his bottom lip; he walked over to the rouncey, free of burden the horse pulled greedily at fresh hay, running chubby hands over twitching flanks and legs the inn keeper muttered, "tell e' what Miss for the two I'll give e' two nights free lodging, what say e' to that miss?

"No sir, I am bound for Pagonston, too long on the road has made me wish to take the river route," she hesitated, "I need to pay for passage." The inn keeper rubbed his chin, "The rouncey is nearly done for miss, I wont get much out of her, but the palfrey is another matter, tis only er whats worth owt, little Freda has fallen in love I thinks,"

He watched his daughter clinging to Mallows mane, and was lost!

"Look miss you knows I's a man of honour from last time," he smiled, "what say you to this then, free lodging, an passage soon as tides right? That's a more than fair deal though I say so myself." as an after thought he added, "Always been soft round women as I!"

Leonora never imagined parting from Mallow, not now, nor in the future, Mallow had been her constant friend through many years, her chin trembled and tears stung her eyes as she made the choice, nodding sadly she swallowed a sob.

"Tis hard miss I know but she as come to a good home, an little Freda will love er, don weep miss, shame to puff up they lovely eyes."
He called the child. "Er's all yours my sweet, but afore you loves er'clean away, help this nice lady to the top room what over looks the street."
Her fair curls bobbed as obeying her father the child skipped to Leonora's side, slipping her tiny hand into Leonora's she led her through the inn and upstairs.
 "You will take care of Mallow, and love her?" Leonora asked the child. Freda's head tilted backwards and she fixed Leonora with an innocent stare, "pretty lady, you won't take my horse away will you?" Leonora squeezed the little hand, "of course not sweeting, she is yours now!"

During the night clouds covered the moon and hot dry days of the last few weeks ended in fearsome thunder claps and the devils own lightening. Snuggled beneath her covers Leonora was content; just in time she had reached Totnes.
She wasn't sure why she had thought of the boat to Pagonston, maybe it was inspired by her guardian Angel.
Closing her eyes tightly as thunder chased lightening around the room she considered recent events; Alain in particular she thought of , if she were honest with herself she would very much have liked to meet him again, but his world was a far different one to her own.
When she shut her eyes she saw the stunning emerald and imagined it upon her Mothers finger, she felt she should hate the man who had stolen her, but try as she may all she recalled were his dark sad eyes.

Thinking of the young Novice and her grim charge she crossed herself, clasped her hands together, and prayed hard that they rested safe at their destination.

She prayed also for Edmund, if dead for his salvation, and if living? For his well being, beyond that the Almighty himself would know best.

As for her Father and the odious Trey they could both go to hell! She would not plea for their deliverance from sin, let the devil they served look out for them!

69

God alone knew how Domenica travelled as far as she did, and God alone knew why he placed her in the path of Trey and Trewin.

Trewin dismounted when he saw the lone girl, Novice or not she was alone on a deserted road, and there for the taking, Trey remained in the saddle, indifferent as Trewin harassed the girl. "Be e' alone then maid, or is yon baggage family?" he nodded to the cart.

Innocently she replied, "We are victims' sir of the fire, and cruel robbery! We seek the Brothers of Buck fast." wary of the men she remembered Pia's letter and added quickly, "We are overdue sir; they probably ride to meet us at this very moment."

Trewin leered at the fresh face beneath the grubby wimple, and lifted a corner with his grubby finger, "oh do they really?" he mocked.

"Tis a pretty piece walks alone sir," he looked over at Trey and winked, "methinks she be no nun! Lets see what er' scraggy beast hides shall us?" Trey not bothered in the girl looked though with interest at the cart, heaving his bulk from the saddle he replied, "Likely it'll be bastard brats."

Trewin shook his head and pushed his face into that of Domenica, "Nay friend", he leered at Domenica, "more like a thieving whore making off with some poor sods goods!"

Terrified for Edmunds safety Domenica appealed to Trey as he padded towards the cart, "Sir I beg you, your friend is wrong, in truth we are sent by the Sisters at Brent Priory, we are promised sanctuary, my patient is sorely injured!" Domenica backed against a tree winced as bark dug into her skin; his cold hands were upon her bare thigh Trewin grinned as he pushed against her blowing foul breath in her face; through revolting brown teeth he hissed, "not bad my sweet, not bad at all!"

On the verge of fainting she begged, "For mercy's sake Sir! I beseech you do me no harm?" she looked pleadingly at Trey, but her calls were in vain it was as if he were deaf, she saw as he peered beneath the pile of rags, She alone heard Treys sharp intake of breath, along with her own as Trewin tore her habit and pushed his bony groin against her body, she heard the almost gleeful gulp of surprise; and in that moment knew they were lost. Wrenching her face from Trewins fetid breath, she begged one last time, "please stop this violation, I am sworn to God , would you violate a bride of Christ, would you burn in hell for this?" For an answer he forced his disgusting mouth wetly onto her own, and fumbled with his breeches,

With vomit rising in the back of her throat she raked his face with her finger nails, and his howling was the last sound she recalled, just before he struck her full across the side of her head; like a rag doll she collapsed in his flailing arms.

Looking up at Trey by the cart he moaned, "ers' fiery as hell, that's for sure! 'Er as scratched I well and proper! The little cow! Er needs teaching a lesson!"

Domenicas squealing had irritated Trey, his eyes never left those of Edmund as he hissed,

"Do what you like with her man but in Gods name shut the bitch up!"

Edmund, cowering in the cart knew he looked death in the face, as his life flashed before him he pitifully raised what were once hands in a useless gesture of defence.

Trey immune to compassion showed no mercy, a smile parted his lips with satisfaction; unbelievably the devil had delivered into his hands the husband of the woman Trey wanted!

Leonora's doomed husband opened his mouth to scream but no sound came; it took seconds only for one of Treys massive hands to squeeze the life from Edmunds frail body; sending him to eternity with no more resistance than a stifled gasp and a shudder.

The way was clear, Faye's husband now a limp corpse lay sightless, Trey threw a rag contemptuously over the face and exhaled; pleased by his handy work, his only emotion a shiver of anticipation thinking of Leonora.

Fate in the devils murderous guise had played Trey a good hand this night. He sneered to Trewin,

"You'ms right man, Tis nought but junk and a dead man, 'appens you chose to 'ave your way with a madwoman! Fool," he snorted, "er could be carrying anything!"

Trewin still struggling with the limp Domenica paled, trying to hold her slight body upright he thought of leprosy.

"Leave er' man" sneered Trey, "er's good as dead out ere' man, there be lusty maids a plenty in town, an you won't ave to wrestle no poxy whore for it!"

Disgusted Trewin dropped her as if she were contaminated, totally unconcerned when her head struck a raised root; brushing himself down he fastened his breeches,

"Bleddy whore, devil take you!" he spat.

Over his shoulder Trey sneered, "More like to be dogs and foxes, what'll finish er' off!"

Massing across the watery moon, clouds thickened threatening a storm, darkness slowly hid any sign of the sinister deed.

Domenicas world ended that night; left to die near the murdered man she had fought so hard to save!

She could not know that throughout her ordeal God had been all present, protecting her.

Edmund was the sacrificial lamb, Sacrificed for her virtue and her life.

God sent blessed unconsciousness to numb mind and body, holding back the rain he let instead a sneaky little wind rustle leaves from the trees, until they settled over the girls' childlike form like a coverlet.

Good and evil fought a hard battle that night, good was the victor!

As for evil? It could have, but chose not save Edmund!

Had Trey not discovered the helpless Edmund his animal instincts would have driven him, goaded by his accomplice to brutalize the girl, but taking the life of Leonora's husband satisfied his needs, at least for the moment!

Next would be the dog of Compton Berry.

Trey could not rest; his unfounded hatred for the man he believed had taken his fathers life consumed every waking moment. Nothing else would have bought him so far into the detested county of Devon, with its treacherous peasantry!

If not for the fire, his sojourn in Plymouth would have been shorter; then Leonora had crossed his path, he supposed she would eventually make her way to Pagonston.

The earlier he gained the woman he desired!

The sooner he ended the life of his fathers' murderer!

And the quicker he could return to his lands in Cornwall!

Eerily an owl hooted, rain drops spattered onto Trewins hood, "us'll see rain afore nights done," he called to Trey.

Already Ten paces in front Trey ignored him, and the owls mate returned the call from somewhere in the darkness.

Chapter 14
Buckfast

Water filled clouds emptied themselves of warm rain, on ground parched by weeks of hot dry weather it lay in little puddles before disappearing into the thirsty earth.

Ciabhans intention had been to spend one night at Buckfast, he preferred being close to Compton Berry, but the heavy rainstorms made immediate return impossible; At the Brothers insistence he agreed to stay.

Glad for intelligent visitors from beyond their cloisters the hospitable Brothers of BuckFast enjoyed any opportunity to talk, particularly so with Ciabhan of Compton Berry.

Ciabhan was a favourite of the Brothers, a regular visitor and benefactor along together with his delightful spouse Faye of Pagonston, on her visits they had spoiled her with gifts of medicines and parchment.

One of the eldest brother Jaime joined Ciabhan when dinner had finished, after years at Buckfast his Spanish accent had hardly changed, Ciabhan still struggled to understand him, "young man," he said, "these old bones no longer can resist your English weather, may I join you by the fire?" Ciabhan stood, "here take mine!" then he laughed, "Young man is stretching the imagination somewhat is it not!"

Brother Jaime smiled and instead lowered his creaking frame onto a footstool beside the Knight. "No son, if I sit comfortably I will never rise, this suits me fine," Ciabhan settled back in the chair.

Brother Jaime fixed Ciabhan with eyes still bright in a face weathered by years spent in the open, the lines as furrowed as the soil he tilled. "Its good to see your smile my son," said Jaime, "too long you have been absent, we pray still for you." Ciabhan replied, "Then God has been inundated with prayers these past years, Brother Jaime patted Ciabhans hand, "he hears every one! my Son." Relaxed in each others company they sipped wine and talked, rain and wind rattled glass and sputtered candles, flapping the tapestries. "A ferocious night" said Jaime, "pity any unfortunate enough to be out," Ciabhan nodded, heavy eyed he thought of Alain who'd chosen to sleep with the horses, "My young companion will be having a rough night, on the other hand maybe he won't remember much of it!" He smiled to himself, Alain had imbibed more than enough Buckfast wine and unsteadily had staggered to bed; Medicinal he had called it jokingly. Alains company had as always lifted him, what would he have done without the young knights wit and understanding, he and Mati had saved his sanity.

Just before retiring Brother Jaime leant close, his scrawny hand on Ciabhans shoulder, "Listen well Sir Ciabhan of Compton Berry, It may seem that fate deals you a callous hand, tis true your troubles are not yet done, but doubt not for a moment that your beloved Faye is with you, her spirit at your side, forever watching; her presence may not be felt but believe me she lives on!"

A shiver rippled Ciabhans skin but he humoured the old monk and smiled,

"Aye Brother, how I wish you spoke the truth!"

"Oh I do not lie not my friend, but mark my words, now I must bid you goodnight."

Ciabhan tried to help him, but the feisty old brother shrugged him off, "The almighty takes his time in calling me home." He said.

Ciabhan escorted Jaime to the hallway, they paused by the door,

"Tell me," Jaime said, "did the Lady Faye finish her writing? It was for you she said, the Brothers would give her anything; even my finest parchment."

Ciabhan answered, his voice trailing off as he remembered the verse she left, "no Brother she never did finish it."

In the middle of the night those Brothers who slept closest to the infirmary were wakened by an unholy commotion, three hours past midnight brought them running to the dispensary; sandals flapping noisily on the stone flags.

Alain in his alcove close to the stables woke to thunder and lightning and the restless snorts of horses, throwing a cape over his shoulders he went outside, straining to hear above the rain; without warning a Brother rounded the corner nearly colliding with him, Alain started,

"Good God man you scared the devil out of me!" he gasped,

"The same devil that has been at work tonight I hope sir!" came the Monks reply.

Alain followed the Monk; above the storm he shouted, "What is this talk of the Devil? What has happened?"

The monk mumbled something but Alain did not hear, just past the stables they entered what Alain supposed to be the infirmary, judging by the smell. As his eyes adjusted to the flickering candlelight he looked to his companion for explanation, but the Brother had gone

Alain found himself watching a bizarre scene, it filled the centre of the room where four Brothers administered quietly to a deathlike figure, stretched upon what resembled a bier, and reminiscent of a scene so many years ago, Alain for a moment thought he was dreaming, believed the horror of past remembrances had returned to haunt him?

To see better the form upon the pallet he pushed forward; monks tut tutted as he shoved them from his path, on reaching the patient he stared open mouthed, the figure was draped in a tattered Nuns habit, not night attire!

"Thank God, oh merciful God thank you." he croaked.

A senior Monk shocked by such disrespect, took him aside,

"Pray sir your words are ill judged, before you lies a young woman fighting for her life, she needs your prayers!"

Alain shamed said, "Forgive me; my words are thoughtless, for a moment the past returned! A moment of fear, May I be of help?"

"No! She is in the hands of the Lord, what will be, will be." he nodded in the direction of those around her, "be assured we will do all we can for this bride of Christ!"

How a lone girl came to be here, curious Alain asked, "Who is she brother?"

A tall Monk who had been overseeing her wiped his hands and answered, "Brother Dru returning late because of the storm stopped to relieve himself and literally stumbled across her, like a corpse she was! A little longer and she would have been!"

He smiled as the patient whimpered.

"You see, Miracles do happen!" Dawn brought calm and a fresh breeze, unable to settle properly after the night's tension Alain sat alone on a bench, his eyes closed.

Earlier the tall monk had sought him out to say their prayers had been answered, the novice would survive her ordeal.

A familiar voice interrupted Alains peace.

"Well my friend time to return to Compton Berry now, or maybe a Monks life would suit you better?"

Ciabhans body blocked the sun, he was dressed for travel and in a teasing mood, "Ah I remember it well, a life of prayer and hard toil and certainly no women."

Alain stretched long legs and rested his arms behind his head,

"Well seeing as you mention it my Lord, t'was a woman who diverted my attention this night, I have not slept a wink!"

Alain didn't see the flicker of a frown cross Ciabhans forehead, only noticed a subtle change in his friend's stance, as if embarrassed , he took advantage of Ciabhans discomfort a moment longer before adding, "tis the truth I speak Sir, you really should see the maid yourself, come."
Ciabhan began to object and huffed with impatience but at Alains insistence he followed him to the small cell where Domenica lay.
The fragrance of rose unexpectedly reached Ciabhans senses as they stooped beneath the entrance, he paused breathing deeply for the scent of England's loveliest flower reminded him ever of Faye.
"Here my Lord lays the 'woman' who kept me from my bed! He grinned watching Ciabhans expression as the truth slowly dawned on him.
The sleeping Domenica lay still as a corpse, beneath pale lids her eyes flicked rapidly, the old Brother beside her put a finger to his lips, "SSH!" he hissed.
Ciabhan stammered, "A nun man! A Nun?"
"SSH." Another warning look shot in their direction.
"Yes, a Nun!" said Alain his eyes twinkling, "what on earth were you thinking, Shame on you my Lord!"
Both men bent over her, as if checking she actually breathed until her over zealous guardian croaked, "She lives, but is best left alone."
The inference was obvious, as the Monk waved them out.
"How and from whence came the maid?" asked Ciabhan, When did this happen, I heard nothing, did you?"
"And there you have it sir! You were sleeping like a baby, safe from the elements! I unfortunately witnessed the drama, It seems she was waylaid, attacked and left for dead, God only knows what horrors the girl has endured, "Her survival," say the Brothers, "is a miracle."
Ciabhans mouth hardened, and his eyes clouded with anger, the light heartedness of a moment ago gone, "there live those who would treat a woman so, but to commit ill on a bride of Christ is unforgivable!"
"And that's not all my Lord," continued Alain, "Her only company was a corpse, A man, a pitiful creature!"Alain kicked at a loose stone, "without hands! Just bandaged stumps, he should have been long dead, he could not have helped the Maid, Brother Dru said it was a most   gruesome sight, Can you imagine the poor girls' terror? No wonder she has lost her mind!"
"We know too well the horrors of war, the suffering of the wounded," said Ciabhan, "for some the mind never fully recovers."
"The girl had on her a letter from the Mother Superior at Brent Priory, it begged the Brothers of Buckfast to grant them sanctuary." said Alain.

"Brother Dru read the letter," said Alain, "it upset him so that he and his companion decided to bring her themselves to the Abbey, that's how she came to be here. Is it not strange my Lord to think of a Novice, barely out of childhood herself, violated and abandoned with such callousness? That she came this far is a miracle!" Alain ran his hands through his hair and sighed at the enormity of the task.

"Stranger things happen my friend," added Ciabhan, "acts of bravery born out of desperation, a mystery yes, but not our problem; she is in good hands now, do not torment yourself Alain."

Alain didn't reply, instead he gazed sulkily at a puddle scuffing his boots around the edge.

"I wish to be away by noon," said Ciabhan" Is something wrong Alain?" surely the fool wasn't enamoured, he thought, and was about to say so, when Alain spoke, "The Abbey will not let a woman, even a nun, stay longer than is necessary."

Impatient Ciabhan snapped back, "every one knows that! When fit they will escort her to the convent from whence she came, that's the way it is." Alain looked pleadingly at Ciabhan, his eyes bluer than ever, "I thought we could offer sanctuary at Compton Berry?"

"Oh No!" exclaimed Ciabhan, and who do you suggest cares for the maid? What use a nun who has lost her mind? Any suggestions? he demanded.

Alain answered sheepishly, "Mati could help."

"Mati help!" Ciabhan laughed, "Have you not noticed how she struggles these days? Methinks she would rather work less Sir!"

He avoided the beseeching eyes, "in fact Alain I was rather hoping you would provide a bride of your own to run Compton Berry, Maudie for example ; Not a bride of Christ!"

Alain angered by Ciabhans refusal to help snapped back, "Surely you do not think my concern for her is one of desire?" Have you forgotten how we rode from Faye my lord, she was sorely wounded and in the care of the Sisters of Mercy! Would you not have changed your decision knowing now the hand that fate dealt you?"

As soon as the words were out Alain knew he had misjudged his friends' tolerance, Ciabhan exploded.

"How dare you talk so of Faye Sir? She was no whimsical dalliance, I had no option! You forget she was another's wife!" his eyes blazed, "Gods blood, there is no comparison!"

"My Lord I meant no disrespect," Alain struggled to explain, "I understand honour kept you from her, I meant only that, if you knew then what fate had planned?"

77

With the speed of a cat on its prey Ciabhan seized Alains throat, "You cross the line Sir! Another like comment and honour won't stop me from rendering you senseless!"

Alains muscles strained against the older man's superior strength, inches from each others faces they snarled, spitting like leopards, if any of the monks witnessed the show they stayed well away, only Dominica's guard hobbled out to see what caused such commotion, Alain saw the old man approach, saw him stop to view their childishness, as they glared at each other; neither willing to back down.

"We have an audience!" Alain hissed into Ciabhans ear, with a flick of his hands Ciabhan pushed Alain away; Alain stumbled but quickly gathered his balance

"Then have it your way!" Ciabhan said morosely, Alain not surprised grinned and rubbed his bruised throat, sidestepping the puddle he bowed flamboyantly, "Thank you my lord, merci bien."

Ciabhan glowered beneath dark brows, fuming at defeat but the greater part of his rage had passed, within minutes all was forgotten.

Alain was no fool, well aware that Ciabhans quick temper was at the end of a very short fuse, it flamed, burned intensely for a while then just as quickly sputtered and died.

"Your damn 'do Gooding' would try the patience of a saint!" Ciabhan growled as he stalked off, "we leave, now!"

Within the hour, laden with gifts of wine and food they were on the road, all earlier tensions forgotten; they chatted easily, Ciabhan even found the grace to ask, "So when should we expect this newest member of our household?"

Alain replied, matter of factly.

"When the Brothers see fit for her to travel I would imagine my Lord." Ciabhan followed it with quick sarcasm, assuming of course it's what the maid wants! You have of course considered that?"

Alain smiled and remained silent.

Avoiding the well used paths and waterlogged meadows they made heavy going on the journey home, tracks previously bone hard were as rivers of sludge and debris, when the mud spattered group finally reached the castle of Compton Berry atop its wooded hill night had well and truly fallen, the riders whooped at sight of it.

Flares had been lit casting shadows over the walls, in the upper chambers candles flickered, and a blue haze wreathed along the ramparts, curling upwards and over the tree tops.

"Ah! What a smell messires!" a rider pushed from behind, "if my nose serves me right tis venison on our table tonight, what say I claim the first chunk?" A challenge went up.

Jostling for position, like children rushing for a treat the company of men spurred their sweating mounts up the steep incline.

Chapter   15
Master Dawks

True to his word Master Dawks arranged Leonora's passage, "Twas good you chose the river maid, road is still bad from top to bottom." He smiled, "times right now; river runs high and now be a good time to take ship."

Jolly and caring, Dawks the landlord of 'the Severn stars' had looked out for her; in truth she would miss his cheery nature.

Often he would joke when placing food in front of her, "Best fatten e up miss, you looks not much bigger than young Freda there! Don't want your family thinking us starves us guests now do we?"

From the tiny latticed window Leonora could see the pig pen near the guests stabling. "Not much chance of that master Dawks, any longer here and I would resemble one of those fat sows you love so much!" she said patting her stomach, or look like yourself she thought, wickedly.

"Did I hear you say the road is still fit only for the mounted?" she tried opening the window in an effort to see the steep hill that led from the town.

"Aye miss," he replied, "us had two riders turn up late last night, in a right state they were, Aryl saw to them, wanted food an' drink, an' bed for the night, ridden 'ard they 'ad from Plymouth, Two fine great 'orses though, they's!" he never finished the sentence for Leonora stepped back from the window so fast that she nearly knocked him from his feet.

"Gods bones miss!" he wheezed steadying himself, "you looks like you 'ave seen the devil!"

Leonora's face turned white as a sheet. "Yes master Dawks, the devil is here! He walks in your yard!"

Dawks peered through the dusty panes; Freda was dancing across the yard and into focus, "but I only sees Freda Miss! Surely you don' mean er?" standing by the stabling he recognised the travellers from last night. At his shoulder Faye caught her breath, "oh sweet mother of God! Freda will give me away; he will remember Mallow, oh! Master Dawks I am lost!"

Dawks waddled to the door, "tis they what came in last night, I don' know what you is on about but don't fret, our Freda's no fool, you can tell us later!" and he was gone.

Leonora wiped at the grime, there was no mistaking Treys bulk. Peering through the lattice she held her breath as Dawks approached them, deftly he placed his body between Freda and the horseman, just as Trey appeared to notice the scruffy little girl tripping gaily across the yard. With one arm Dawks caught the child, whispered in her ear, and pushed her gently away, Freda nodded and with a wave disappeared into Mallows stall, closing the door behind her.

Leonora's hands were clammy and her skin damp from tension, with her mind racing she dipped back from the window as muffled voices drifted from below. She prayed the inn keeper would not betray her, after all she was nothing to him he owed her no loyalty, they on the other hand had ways of paying for information if they so wished.

Leonora half expected Trey to appear at any moment, but it was Dawks who came in grinning widely, "well miss, nought to fear now, they's gone an' in quite a hurry mind, never suspected anything! Now how's about you tell I what's goin' on?"

Leonora made a mental note to repay his kindness sometime.

Dawks studied the lovely face, thinking her the most perfect creature he had ever seen, certainly since the death of his dear Morwena, Freda's mother, God rest her soul; he dabbed at his eyes.

In between long pauses Leonora explained all that had happened in the months since last she had passed this way, She told of the fire that destroyed her home in Plymouth Town, of meeting Trey, a figure from her childhood past. She told how Trey said he had rescued her husband Edmund, and then never saw him again after placing him on the quayside. "Oh Master Dawks I searched for Edmund, but to no avail, I must presume him dead, For it was said his injuries were so terrible that only a miracle would have saved him!" She lowered her voice in embarrassment when telling of Treys pestering, how she feared his obvious obsession for her. "This is the real reason I left Plymouth for Pagonston, Master Dawks, the man in the yard scares me, and he mistook my kindness for interest, though he knows me a married woman."

Dawks listened intently, hardly taking his eyes from her face as she continued. With the help of Meryn Jenkin I left her lodging and fled Plymouth; we concocted a story that I'd been informed of a definite sighting of Edmund that I had gone in search of him.

In truth I know not if he lives or is dead!" She fell quiet, and dropped her face into her hands, "Master Dawks I am so scared of what the future holds, my father is become a drunkard, and our once lovely family home is in disrepair, but I have nowhere else to go. Speaking of Pagonston she realised how much she grieved still for her mother, she missed also her brother and sister, both far away in different parts of England each with lives of their own, in a strange way she even missed her father, or at least the strong man he once had been! Strangely for all her soul searching the one person she missed not at all was Edmund.

Rather where she should have felt at least some love she felt instead a heavy guilt, as if she were abandoning him!

Was it really Edmund she was fleeing once more running from him?

Or was it from the odious Trey?

Suddenly confused great tears spilled from her eyes, unable to stop or hide them she let them plop onto her gown, where they left dark green splodges against the lighter shade; Dawks squirmed with discomfort, he had long forgotten how to respond to female angst.

"You can stay ere' miss if e wishes!" the words were out before he had time to think, she would probably think him just another man after her skirts! He fiddled with his apron strings as she sobbed,

"Master Dawks you must think me such a fool," she sniffed, "forgive me for embarrassing you so!" Dawks would have forgiven her anything.

"Best if I leaves till you's more yourself miss, I'll send Freda up with some honey mead."

By the time Freda arrived Leonora had composed herself, "Have the two men left now sweeting?" she asked, "Did they say where they were headed?"

The child put the jug down, clumsily slopping golden liquid over the rim. Pointing through the lattice she said, "Up the hill, they went up the hill, Papa wouldn't let me show them my new horse, are you getting a new horse now?"

Leonora nodded absent mindedly, "maybe."

So Trewin and Trey had left, Leonora puzzled over where they could be headed.

Compton Berry was close; could it be Trey had murder on his mind? Often enough he'd spoken of his hate for the 'dog' of Compton Berry, The man he held responsible for his Fathers death.

Leonora had kept quiet, letting Trey believe what he wanted, for all her resentment towards Leon she could hardly condemn her own father to certain death.

Neither did she hold any affection for Ciabhan of Compton Berry; she did however think often of his blue eyed friend, the charming Frenchman who explained so patiently the events of the past years; the loyal friend who defended his master Ciabhan of Compton Berry so passionately. She hoped Trey was not headed to Compton Berry, where Alain could possibly be in danger.

Maybe Trey was headed to Pagonston, God forbid! She would hate to meet him in her home town, maybe it was safer to remain in Totnes; she could throw herself on her Brother Adrian's mercy, surely he would help, even though he thought her far too independent for a woman! but she had no means of reaching either him or her married sister.

No she must stick with her first plan, For the last time she would attempt peace with her father, offer the hand of truce, assuming of course that he was still capable, and hadn't drank himself into a cidery grave.

And the emerald, the glorious gem he was so obsessed with? It certainly existed for she'd seen it for herself, in fact been nearly blinded from the flash, as it sat on the hand of her Fathers mortal enemy.

Leonora thought of the jewel, her mothers while she lived, surely after her death it should pass to her daughter.

The possession of such a valued jewel would have lifted Leonora from the mire into which she had been brought!

At the moment without any means of her own she was without bargaining power, at the mercy of fate.

More and more she found herself thinking of the emerald, wanting it! God in Heaven she was becoming her greedy father!

She closed her eyes and murmured softly under her breath, "It seems my Lady Fate that I am in your hands, so do as you will with me! But an emerald would be nice!" she giggled out loud at her own silliness.

Freda kneeling on the stool by the window turned, her pretty little face puzzled, "is funny lady?"

Leonora nodded, "oh yes sweeting it's very, very funny!"

Serving as a landing stage for the town of Totnes the little jetty buzzed with activity; two boats were moored one behind the other, the first a fast passenger vessel.

Merchants sending their wool cargo by water used the second and slower, anxiously they watched porters stacking the precious bales.

Paying travellers boarded the faster vessel, the first on taking prime sheltered positions, others of lesser standing followed, jostling for room.

Fascinated Leonora watched the colourful scene, roughly pushed aside she watched two highly strung destriers arrive, wild eyed they tossed magnificent groomed heads as slithering they negotiated the planks of wood, disdainful of the greasy conditions. Grooms risked life and limb placing straw beneath the flailing hooves, as they coaxed the temperamental charges into the onboard stalls; almost as disdainful as their destriers two expensively clothed Knights strode by in the space created for them, Father and son judging by their similarity.

Exquisite in dark green velvet, buckles and baldrics glinted like gold beneath thick woollen cloaks, deep in conversation they acknowledged no one. Once aboard the elder of the two dropped a purse into the captain's hand and took their place in the prow, without talking Father and son stood side by side, cloaks tight around their bodies.

With a bellow the ships captain gave command, the rowers in unison
lifted the oars and dipped with hardly a splash; to the grunts of oarsmen
and the creaking decks the boat little by little slid away.

Fluttering gaily from the mast, a jade and white flag proudly displayed its
Devon ownership as the painted prow nosed into midstream with the
caution of a baby taking its very first steps.

Leonora signalled towards the worn and tired vessel that would carry
herself and sighed, "Somewhat different my transport is it not master
Dawks?" he bent and picked up her small bundle of possessions, "Tis still
better than the road miss! Come now let's get you aboard."

He shouldered the light load easily.

Leonora left Pagonston with very little, and returned with even less,
Wrapped in felt the glass bird was still the most prized, she felt for its
reassuring shape in the bundle, then lifting her skirts she mounted the
slimy plank.

Choosing the stern she claimed a space beside some thick bales, before
beginning her farewells; Dawks eyed the gangplank uncomfortably.

Taking his fleshy hand Leonora began, "Master Dawks I can't thank you
enough for your kindness, you have been more than generous in your care
of me."

He looked at her with pale eyes, "Twas nothing miss, the young'un liked
you, an' my good wife would ave' done same!" he hesitated as if wanting
to say more, then continued, " I'm sure that father of yours will be glad to
ave e' back miss, I would if e' were mine!"

Even a kiss on the cheek would have been too familiar so instead he gave
her a friendly pat on the shoulder, and then turning on his heels he
wobbled down the gangplank, helping hands grabbed him at the bottom.

"You will take care of mallow?" she shouted after him.

"Of course us will," he waved back, then because he wanted her to know
she would be missed he added, " an you knows where us be if e' needs us
miss don't e'

"That I do master Dawks that I do."

Ropes twanged and boards creaked as the boat swung into midstream,
pressed against the side she hoped the wind hadn't stolen her shout of
thanks; she stayed thus for a while watching Totnes slowly fade from
view.

For a while the painted ship carrying the knights could be seen ahead, but
after the first bend it disappeared from sight.

Glad of the warmth from the linen bales at her back, she lifted her face to
the Midday sun, it shone hotly, but the wind cut chill in mid river, she
snuggled deep as she could into her thin cloak. Finally lulled by the water
sounds her lids drooped and she succumbed to much needed sleep.

Chapter 16
Amber Man

Like the hollow rasping sound that pebbles make when the sea drags at them, a strange voice broke into her slumber, its harshness grated on her senses, slowly she opened sticky eyes.

A mixed bag of passengers clustered in little groups, minding their business, again the strange voice sounded, closer now.

"You No more sleep pretty lady, water is stop."

Resembling a performing monkey the strangest creature crouched in front of her, his long skinny arms rested on even bonier knees; Leonora sat upright, what on earth was he saying, the words made no sense at all, to discourage him she turned away.

Nimbly he scampered to her other side, crouching again and fixed her with little black eyes; like smooth pieces of jet they were set deeply in a face as rough as weathered hide.

Leonora looked imploringly at fellow travellers, could they not see the uninvited guest embarrassed her? No one seemed interested except a mother and her small son, most were watching as the boat approached Dartmouth Town.

Flailing sinewy arms the man threw back his head and laughed showing surprisingly healthy teeth, somewhere between a cackle and giggle the laugh wrinkled his face even more and shook his puny frame.

The orange piece of cloth that passed for a garment barely covered him when he started rummaging in its folds Leonora looked away, nervous at what he may produce; she prepared for shock.

The child pushed aside his mothers restraining arms struggling for a better look, while the woman pretended not to! Wide eyed he sniggered at the mans antics.

"Sshh Jago!" his mother scolded, "bain't right to mock at the afflicted!"
The child too fascinated by the funny man to look at her asked, "What's afflicted ma?"

His mother nodded towards the man,

"That's afflicted son, now shut up an' keeps still afore I cuffs you one!"

Leonora jumped when the man touched her arm, he backed away making
a sign of peace, "I no hurt miss, I show you this, you see?"
In his palm a large piece of amber lay, Leonora caught her breath at its
beauty. "You take" he said, offering it.
"No," she shook her head, I couldn't, it is of too much value."
His face creased with rejection, bewilderment shadowed his eyes, "you
no like?" he asked.
Leonora smiled, she had no bargaining power, and no means of
purchasing an object purely for its beauty.
"Of course I like, it is very beautiful, no money see!" She gestured to the
bundle of possessions and spread her hands.
"Then you take, here!" before she could say anything more he dropped
the piece of amber into her hand and curled her fingers around its warmth.
"You keep lady," he said.
Entranced by its beauty she gazed at the moss and tiny insects suspended
in the golden resin, muttering nonsensically he watched her.
"You have face of another, many moons ago a lady buy my lovely amber,
and you like her! I see now in my mind!" he pointed to his head then
to his eyes before closing them and lifting his face to the sun; rocking
gently back and forth he hummed.
Unsure what to make of the odd little man, she took the amber so as not
to offend him, "You are very kind, thank you," she said graciously.
He appeared not to hear and remained still, Leonora thought he dozed.
All of a sudden he began making strange clicking sounds with his tongue
and fumbled again in the folds of cloth.
Leonora gasped, this time he produced a necklace, a strand of amber
beads as smooth as fat golden beans, each the colour of Devon honey.
"For you" he said, gesturing for her to put them on, it seemed pointless to
argue so Leonora took the string of beads, and lifting her hair from her
neck fastened the clasp, self consciously she let him admire it.
"Oh tres bon!" he clapped his hands, "You so lovely lady, you like?"
Spontaneously she answered in French, "Oh ma oui, magnifique!"
They were still laughing as the boat bumped the side of the landing stage.

Ready to disembark the amber man hoisted a leather sack onto his back;
neatly it fitted neatly across his bony shoulders. Glad to stretch her legs
Leonora stood, and for the first time saw him clearly, the orange fabric
draping   his body was in fact a clever piece of design covering all it

should with surplus enough to swathe even the head. Small and lithe he wriggled effortlessly into a lightweight cloak that covered him from shoulder to ankle, effectively hiding the outlandish wear beneath.

Only his smooth brown ankles and sandal glad feet showed , when a gust of wind caught the greying strands of hair she noticed a gold hooped earring in one ear; He really did cut a peculiar but strangely exotic figure. He stood patiently waiting to disembark, Leonora beside fingered the beads at her neck.

Making eye contact with her he spoke clearly, seriously with no trace of his funny accent! In circumstances other than these his words might have been prophetic.

"Hearts will break for love of you lady, men will compete for your favour," he hesitated, "You will know great Happiness but at a high price, Allah! The all merciful, the all seeing guards such beauty jealously."

He raised his hand in salutation, "you are the mirror of one gone taken before her time, her flawlessness is destined to live on in you Lady," his next words were issued like a warning, "let not men destroy it!"

His verbal skill surprised her, but the significance of his words were not lost on her, their intensity however she found discomforting, and he appeared weakened by his efforts. She bent to hoist her bundle, when she looked up to thank him he had scampered off, vanished into the dockside bustle; she looked for him in vain.

The boy Jago giggled still, within the safety of his mothers arms he stuck his tongue out at Leonora, she responded with the same gesture! And he began to grizzle; despairingly his mother yanked him up the gangway, as Leonora followed.

While the boat bumped at its mooring, porters heaved baggage and made ready for fresh passengers to come aboard.

Glad of exercise before the next part of her journey Leonora strolled along the river path before doubling back through a small cluster of houses, a trader selling cockles tempted her, a few paltry coins purchased a portion, she delighted in their salty sea taste, licking her fingers when she thought no one was watching!

She set the chunk of amber beside her and ran her fingers along the smooth sides, it had been cut to create a peak, the bottom left flat so it could stand freely, and the whole resembled a little golden mountain? At its heart the debris of the past hung forever suspended, mesmerised by its mysterious depths Leonora's spirits suddenly lifted; so high they soared!

The words spoken by the strange man however puzzled her, beautiful she was not and as for wealth or future, she had neither!

What man would look twice at her? And a Knight? What nonsense!

More likely Inn keepers and knucklchcads would be her suitors! Leonora sighed, the monkey like man was just another crazy old fool and she had been the one to cross his path, for no reason she shivered as if someone walked upon her grave, a picture of Edmund and his suffering flashed into her mind, guilt descended heavily on her for thinking so frivolously of suitors!

What had become of him did he live? If so he would get word to her somehow, or seek her out, of that she was sure, Edmund had always been determined, but for now, realistically she must presume her husband dead! She tucked the amber into her cloak and walked back to the boat.

She might not look like one but the necklace of beautiful beads at her throat made her feel like a princess.

Chapter 17
Corentyn

Leon yawned and clawed at his unshaven face; across the green swathe stretching between the palace dwellings and the encircling wall, a lone guard raised his hand in salute from the tower. Above his head streamed the pennant of England, until yesterday the banner that proclaimed the bishop in residence had hung limply in humid air.

Leon breathed the fresh sea air nipping at his nakedness, late rising he was irritable, "Damn boy" he muttered "letting me oversleep, I like to rise with the dawn!"

Today he had an account to settle.

Since the rescue of the Bishop, Leon's rise to favour had been dramatic; for the lethargic 'Man of God' the excellent Knight Leon could do no wrong. Empowering him the Bishop gave Leon custodianship of everything in his absence. Providing the all important Church and Palace ran smoothly Leon could do as he wished! Allowing him carte blanche!

Wily and devious Leon was now invaluable to the Bishop; every ounce of cunning he used had paid off to his advantage, at their peril let any call him common criminal again! For he sought and took vengeance on those who crossed him

"Corentyn?" Leon hollered for his young servant, "Gods blood boy, do they not move quicker than snails in your God forsaken Cornvall?"

Leon struggled with w's and he knew the boy would appear with a grin on his face, laughing at him, "what sort of name is Corentyn anyway he spluttered, "girls name and girls face I say, dress me, tis nearly noon!"

Corentyn did as told, his master was always an angry man, but Corentyn didn't mind, even when drunk he was miles better than the flabby Bishop.

"And take that stupid look off your face boy or I'll send you back to Corn...vall!" Corentyn bent to lace Leon's boots, "Food and apple juice is on the table Master, and your arms are polished."

"The stiletto boy? You've done as I said?" Leon leant menacingly towards the boy. Corentyn nodded, dark curls bobbing on his shoulders, hair far too beautiful for a boy!

"Just like you said master, tis done." He replied solemnly.

He recalled how when drawing the stiletto across his hand it sliced two fingers, he'd tried to keep them hidden from Leon.

For the Bishops return to Exeter, Corentyn was not needed as personal steward this time, but was to stay behind with Leon in Pagonston.

The boy could hardly contain his joy for there was nothing he wanted more than to be rid of the wheezing Bishop and his boring predictability. Overjoyed to be assigned to the flamboyant Leon 'le mercenaire'

Corentyn served his new exciting master with devotion.

One person however was far from happy with Leon's elevation; the present church warden. Oxton Napier knew that when the post he had enjoyed under the watchful but now absent Bishop was given to Leon his days were numbered.

This would be the last time he locked the Church, his wife had packed all he needed for his journey, in an hour he would leave Pagonston.

"Cut yourself boy?" Leon laughed, grabbing Corentyns fingers; the boy hung his head in embarrassment.

"So you know it to be no toy! Today you will see its consequences, learn what it is to be a man!"

Leon kicked the footstool away cursing under his breath for the laces of his tunic seemed like cotton thread in his gnarled fingers.

"Boy!" He barked, "These laces are short!"

They weren't, but Corentyn scrambled to his masters aid, deftly fastening them while Leon stamped impatiently. From under his lashes Corentyn studied the blotched cheeks and pitted nose of his master, with the callowness of youth Corentyn wondered how any woman could find this man pleasing. Sun light was a brutal mirror, it emphasized Leon's straggly greying hair, he had used grease, and it stuck to his head, even the strengthening breeze failed to move it.

Leon studied the sky from the doorway, seagulls shrieked on currents of air, filling the sky they circled ever higher above the sandstone church, almost disappearing into the blue. Pointless creatures thought Leon, no use whatsoever, the same couldn't be said of the Church for it never failed to overwhelm him with wonder.

Started with money from the coffers of Pagonston and still unfinished it was a stark reminder to the townsfolk of Pagonston that an all powerful God kept saw their every move.

Voices drifted over the walls where a pathway ran between the narrows of Palace and the church, alert Leon listened as workers pattered towards the Coach House Inn, some voices he recognised, sometimes he memorised their words, one never knew what one might hear!

He turned to Corentyn, "Stay close boy! I may need you."

At Midday the Church and its surroundings became silent, for an hour, maybe two, services and duties ceased, Warden and Priest, altar boys and bell ringers ate and rested, even the ever present stone masons put down their tools and the chipping stopped, as they made for the nearest inn..

Only the homeless, sad or lonely might linger; or the very devout, but the general rabble, those who liked to be noticed by the bishop drifted away from Mother Church at his leaving. Until the Bishop graced Pagonston again the church would see no overcrowding!

The churchyard was peaceful and luckily today free of people, even the tower guard had left his post.

Alive with birds the ancient yew cast its shadow over the sacred ground, beneath the lower branches Leon passed stealthily, somewhere a woodpecker hammered; its resonance eerie in the noon quiet.

Sparrows chattered, arguing in gutters and stonework, feathered witnesses to silent paths and shadowy corners.

Oxton Napier was a frightened man, with a quick look over his shoulder he breathed a sigh of relief, pulled closed the door and rattled the key from its hanging; not long now he thought! The sooner he was on his way the better; the murderous Leon could strike at any time!

Oxton still smarted from the Bishop's refusal to take him back to Exeter, he recalled the Bishops words.

"Certainly not man!" the Bishop had said, "Our new Palace Guardian needs reliable helpers, and you are the longest serving, find another to take your place, then join me in Exeter!"

No amount of pleading had budged the bishop so Oxton had contrived this plan of his own, only minutes now and he would be safely on the road........

Footsteps crunched gravel and he looked up, blood drained from his face and his heart thumped almost choking him.

Leon's eyes were chilling, cold and determined, but his voice was cheery, "Well met Napier," he said, "It would seem I am just in time!"

Dead before he hit the ground Oxtons mouth remained open in surprise as he lay crumpled on the paving, the keys clattered to the ground momentarily stopping the birds, within seconds their chorus started again. Corentyn held his breath frightened to exhale while Leon wiped the stiletto indifferently on a cotton kerchief, nodding to the body he callously whispered in the stunned boys' ear, "Think you he wanted to say something Boy?" he didn't listen for a reply but hawked and spat on the body before turning on his heels, Corentyn stumbling after him stole a look back. He saw only the blood, dark against the slab of limestone, it snaked across the step before disappearing into the gravel.

A minute later he stumbled into Palace grounds on Leons heels Leon, tossed the murder weapon on the table and laughed, "Clean it well boy, blood if left discolours a fine blade!" then as if nothing had happened he swigged warm cider from the mornings flagon before going upstairs.

Mistress Napier's wailing was enough to wake the dead in the churchyard and ended the afternoon's peace. Bursting from sleepy cottages townsfolk sounded the alarm as news spread; running hither and dither they screamed outrage at murder on the Church path.

Deathly pale but calm Corentyn opened the door to Father Loveday, he begged an audience with the new custodian, "foul murder has been committed dear boy," he gasped pushing into the hallway, "foul, cowardly murder!"

Corentyn remained silent, watching as the priest staggered and clutched at his head.

"Who could have committed this foul deed, the Bishop must be told! Oh! Merciful God help us!"

"Can I get you something Father?" stammered Corentyn.

"Yes, yes my child, your Master, Leon the custodian, he must be informed, oh mercy that this should happen so soon after his appointment! And Pagonston still without a justice!"

His whole body shook and the red blubbery lips worked over-time, mouthing words to himself, what a fool thought Corentyn, weak as a woman.

above Leon stirred and stretched on his feathered bed in the pleasant chamber, the clamour coming from below had woken him from deep slumber, Gods fish! It came to something when a man couldn't get a moments rest under his own roof; he had barely managed an hours sleep, he stomped down the stairs.

Red eyed and disagreeable he faced the quivering Priest, "well man, speak, it had better be worth my time, I am not of a mind for time wasting!" he frowned. "God in Heaven what's that noise?" he pushed past the Priest and flung wide the window.

Father Loveday wringing his hands attempted to speak, "it's, it's the warden, Master Oxton, he…he's been, been…!" the words stuck in his throat and he faltered.

"For Christ's sake man" snapped Leon "speak! Or go!"

"Murdered, on Church ground, murdered in cold blood!" he blurted out spraying Corentyn with spittle, Corentyn backed away in disgust.

The Priest seemed near to collapse but if expecting sympathy he received none from Leon or his young servant.

"Ahhhh" Leon let out a long sigh, followed by a dramatic pause, "So someone got to him at last then?"

Beneath his mop of girlish curls Corentyn smiled, what guile! Such a fine actor was Leon he mused, such calm! such control, so this is what makes a man, a man like Leon. Today Corentyn learned something, lessons he would never forget.

"My son," the Priest cut in sharply, "I can't believe you would condone such a deed?"

Leon shrugged, "How did he die Father? In fair fight or a knife the back?"

Leons lack of sympathy snapped the Priests patience, "murder is murder, you speak harsh words of the dead, he was one of us!"

Leon thrust his face into the Priests own, "Harsh words man? He was not one of us as far as I am concerned! The ox got his just desserts."

With a stabbing motion Leon added, "In truth I wish it was me who dealt the blow!" Father Loveday visibly blanched.

Corentyn stunned at such blatant disregard for the truth listened as Leon ranted, "Your memory is short Priest, where were you when I needed help against Oxton and his cronies? Skulking behind doors if my memory serves me well, no Sir! Sympathy I do not have, the dog deserved to die, justice has been done! And a good job too! Now if you don't mind Father, I'd rather like to continue my siesta, the boy will show you out!"

Leon's face and neck was redder than normal; anger or guilt? Corentyn really couldn't tell.

All he saw was the wicked smile curling the corners of Leons mouth as he turned his back on the furious Priest.

Corentyn barely had time to open the door before father Loveday rushed past without even a nod, it crossed Corentyns mind that maybe he should have been more polite to the Father after all he didn't wish to jeopardise his mortal soul.

Upon his comfortable bed Leon lay arms behind his head, thinking over the day's work, strange how the death of Oxton Napier had provoked such a reaction by the townsfolk?

Only a few weeks had passed since the hanging of Pagonstons 'judge Watkin' and that had gone almost unnoticed! The townsfolk seemed to accept Watkins death by his own hand as divine retribution! Pay back for all the hangings he had overseen in his vile and corrupt court!

No one knew that Leon and Leon alone had been witness to Watkins terror, had delighted in watching him beg for mercy as the noose was tightened around his neck!

When he was discovered hanging in his own court simple folk were convinced it was because the so called 'judge' could no longer live with the blood of innocents on his evil hands.

Only Oxton Napier guessed the truth, for as surely as waves broke daily on Pagonstons shores, Oxton knew that 'Leon le mercenaire' would come for his blood.

93

Nestling in its sheltered hollow at the orchards edge the little manor long neglected, was now firmly back where it belonged, in Leon's hands.
Leon shielded his eyes from the sun as he watched work men repairing the timbers of the fire damaged house; their voices rose and fell with banter.
Timbers and plaster had been replaced and the new Cornish slate roof glinted, the place was finally weatherproof; no more would the damp be a source of irritation.
In the walled garden a young pear tree had been planted next to a blackened and scarred stump, all that remained of the original tree, Leon almost could hear the happy laughter of his children playing in its shade.
Well pleased with the rebuilding he moved on to the mews tucked away in the orchard, run down and empty, it was hard to believe the place had once echoed with the sounds of birds of prey, how Faye had enjoyed riding out with 'Bella Donna' upon her wrist.
He remembered his 'gift' to her; he wondered did the bird still live?
He tried shaking off the memories.
The mews must go! He had no use for it now; he would demolish it, just as his errant wife had demolished his love for her!
Wherever he looked memories lingered of Faye, trees bowed with blossom seemed filled with her fragrance, and the soft soughing in the branches surely whispered her name , 'Faye' Faye, the rustling canopy sighed, sweet wife Faye. "Oh Christ Faye! Why did you leave me?"

Leon clutched his head and whirled around expecting her to step from the shadows into his arms, filling his head, her laughter tinkled as she ran excitedly to the mews to welcome her new peregrine.
Round and back again Leon spun in turmoil to face the mews, was that her? Did she return to him?
But only the door of the empty mews rattled on its rusty hinges! revealing the dark interior, Leon reached for the catch, that soft cry was surely Bella Donna? A call so distinctive, did she fret for Faye? Leon's head pounded fit to burst with thoughts of Faye, curling his fingers around the broken wood he pulled at the door but a sudden gust of wind ripped it from his grasp and banged it shut.
Confused he staggered towards his young servant, but instead of Corentyn, two figures watched him, Leon's blood ran cold.
perched side-saddle on 'Mallow' clad in her favourite moss green an apparition of Faye floated just above the ground, upon her wrist Bella Donna flicked malevolent eyes in his direction, panting through a half opened beak, struggling to comprehend the vision Leon shivered as a

horseman drifted from nowhere to float at her side, even before it
materialised he knew it to be Ciabhan of Compton Berry!
Leon shrieked, wildly indicating the emptiness around him.
"There! See there the dog, the wife stealer!" clearly Leon saw them,
smiling into each others eyes, mocking him!
 Their love was suffocating, he felt sick and trembled violently,
his reason ebbing away, now his end approached, so this was how death
felt! Clutching his chest he moaned.

Corentyn steadied him in strong arms, "master! What in Gods name ails
thee?" Leon collapsed to his knees, gasping, "Get from me you traitorous
pair."
Corentyn waved his hands desperately in the empty space in around Leon,
"nothing is here Master, look!" he shouted, leaping into the emptiness,
"Sir you are unwell, could it be the cider was tainted!"
 Leon stared vacantly about him, save the sighing breeze the orchard was
quiet, an easterly breeze straight from the sea shivered the blossom heads,
and the rush of waves roared unnaturally loud in his ears.
Strange how he could not hear any birds of prey, no screeching hawks
could be heard, even though he listened hard.

Slowly, very slowly the fog in his head cleared.... unlike the sea mist that
crept over his feet, dampening the grass beneath the apple trees.
 Where only moments ago workmen's voices had carried cheerfully on
the breeze they were now muffled and indistinct, panic rose again in
Leons throat he clutched at Corentyn, "my dagger boy where's my
dagger?" his hand flew to his side.
 "Tis there master where it always is, there's nothing to be a feared of you
walk your own land Sir!"
With his dagger Leon lunged and twisted from the images in his mind,
"Demons boy, demons methinks!"
Corentyn stood well away from his master, shivering as tendrils of mist
wreathed about his legs, "this way Sir," he soothed, coaxing Leon
towards the gate, "no demons dwell here, tis the mist only, it quickly
cools the air, come." He said.
Cautiously Corentyn looked back over his shoulder, the orchard moments
ago in sunlight had darkened, Corentyns nerve endings tingled with talk
of demons, his young mind believed they and evil were good bed
fellows; but as yet wasn't convinced his master was really possessed by
any of them.!

"You as eard bout' Oxton, then?" Kate Truscott's sarcasm was aimed at the two men heading towards her.

"Aye woman that we have," said Leon, "tis known that the devil takes care of his own! No more than the fool deserved!"

"Strange," she said, "so soon after Watkins' hanging, and just after the Bishop up an leaves...quite a coincidence don' e' say?"

Leon looked Kate Truscott up and down, "No mistress I don't say, best you mind that prattling tongue though!"

Kate put down the pails, greasy slops spilt over the sides, "an what would e' do about that then, Master Leon?"

Damned Kate Truscott was beginning to get under his skin, because of her vindictive tongue all Pagonston now blamed him for Faye's death.

"Have it removed mistress! should it stay still long enough!"

Corentyn whispered, "come Sir, the woman seeks to rile you, leave er' be!"

With hands on hip Kate stood firm, far from intimidated.

"Oh an that would be by your good self then would it!" she retorted.

Leon examined his nails; the terror in the orchard forgotten had been replaced with nonchalance.

"Nay mistress I have neither time nor inclination, but" he hesitated menacingly, "best keep it still all the same!"

Kate hurled the contents of the pail across his path.

Leon bowed low, and stepped delicately through the slime, his fancy boots spattered with filth.

"Merci Madame! Bon premide."

Kate watched him swagger away.

"French pig!" she spat turning on her heels, "ye'll get yur come uppance, mark my words!"

Lurking out of sight in doorway her husband swiped at her, "fer Christ's sake woman that tongue of yours will get us hung, unless e' takes it from e'!"

Kate huffed, "someone as to stand up to the like's of Leon, 'Le Mercenaire!'

Corentyn scuttled beside his master in silence, "go fetch me some ale," Leon demanded, as an after thought he added, nodding at Kate's Inn, "but not from that thieving bitch, get you down to The Arms, an' say it's for me!"

In view and earshot of the workmen he hollered, "and make it quick you little Cornish faery!"

The workmen's laughter rang in Corentyns ears; he kept his head lowered hoping his burning cheeks could not be seen.

The workmen chorused, "Thanks to e' master, this sure be thirsty work! us be parched as mistress Truscott's arse!" a great guffawing filled the afternoon

Leon was a satisfied man, restored to its former glory the little sandstone manor was a sight to behold, the red stone glowed against the greenery and with its new slate roof it was as perfect as when he shared it with Faye.

No longer a figure of fun, the Bishop's favourite was a force to be reckoned with; slowly Leon settled scores, repaying slights with brutality, none dared challenge or criticise his actions.

Now he would vacate his room at the Palace lodging house and move back to his own Manor, parish funds could support his living, the picky Bishop didn't see everything!

At last his energy could go into planning revenge on Ciabhan of Compton Berry, revenge long overdue.

Since Faye's rejection of Leon for her detestable lover, hate had consumed him, It never gave a moments respite, just ate away at his sanity, day by painful day, hour by hour.

Chapter 18
Emma Mackey

Leonora inhaled the air of Pagonston, plant sap and musty earth, tinged with salty sea spray produced a unique scent, the smell of home!

Glad to feel terra firma beneath her feet she didn't care if she never set foot on another boat. Hoisting her little bundle she set off towards the Big Tree, turning left into The Street of Fishers, the pathway was busy with people going about their relentless daily toil, after the peace of the sea Leonora found the noise a little daunting

She patted her salt encrusted hair and turned her nose up at her grubby state, she really was in need of a wash and change, she hoped she didn't see anyone she new, but no sooner had the thought crossed her mind than a familiar voice boomed behind her, "Mistress Leonora? Tis you bain't it?" a lanky man with some effort stood and put down the net he was mending, "Lord child what brings e' this away?" he muttered, "be master Edmund with e'?"

She had only just passed their cottage but simple folk have a knack of feeling anything out of the ordinary! Patiently she answered,

"No Mackey, "Not yet."

"Come on in child," he beckoned with enormous hands, "mother would love to see e' an er's got pot on, you looks a bit peaky to I!"

Leonora let Mackey take the bundle from her shoulder and lead her to the door, his nearness bought the remembered stink of fish guts, and she almost gagged.

A plump red faced woman waddled to greet her, "Oh mercy me look who tis, oh child come here!" Mother Mackey pulled Leonora to her ample bosom, here the fish smell mixed with body odour; Leonora pulled away and straightened her dress.

"Good Lord Child youms thinned down since I last saw e' just skin an bone!" Mother Mackey looked her up and down, "you's still some beauty though," she exclaimed, "the best looking maid in Deb'n if you asks I!" she laughed warmly.

"You be like your mother for sure, an er' was handsomest woman I ever saw."

Leonora felt far from a beauty, in fact she felt downright ugly.

"Oh" she said weakly, "some say I am the image of my Father,"

Mother Mackey paused before spitting contemptuously into the fire, the gobbet landed on a log and sizzled, "nay my sweet lets hope the good Lord keeps Leon's frazzled looks from your angel face, that be one burden you don' need ." Mackey stooped under the doorway, "be brew ready mother?" Mother Mackey wobbled her grey head.

"Aye, I was just telling young missy here how lovely her mother was;

Oh mercy me !" she dabbed at her eyes, "every time I thinks of Faye I
blubbs," she sniffled, "twas a dark deed to be sure."
Mackey scolded, "Stop blubbing, baint the thing to do in front of Faye's
daughter now be it!"
 Wiping her nose on her apron Emma Mackey agreed, "Youms right Son,
ti's in the past now!"
She placed a steaming tankard of fish soup between Leonora's hands,
"Eat! My bird then us'll drink a toast to your good mothers' memory."
The overpowering stink of fish permeated the whole building, a pile of
scallop shells just outside the door buzzed with flies, while a mangy cat
prowled looking for tasty morsels.
Weather beaten Mackey was not as old as he appeared; he and his Mother
spent their time gutting and preparing the daily catch delivered every
morning to their door, hence the name Mackey, Mackerel!
Leonora recalled fish scales clinging to everything when her Mother had
bought her to buy, and the unbearable reek, but it was true they produced
the best fish stew this side of the river Dart.
Leonora chatted happily, these were good people and deserved her
respect, like grandparents they had cared for her, her brother and sister in
their childhood years; she owed them civility.
She told them of the fights with her Father, the rejection that drove her
from Pagonston, back to Plymouth and her Husband.
She described tearfully the devastating fire that destroyed her marital
home and her fruitless searching for Edmund, still missing.
She even mentioned her meeting with Sir Ciabhans squire Alain but
Emma's disgust for everything to do with Compton Berry was obvious.
"T'was nothing to do with me what Faye did, but that there Ciabhan
knew er' was another mans wife! An that's all I'll say!"
Her mouth snapped shut with the speed of a ratters trap.
However Emma did tutt with sympathy and became very angry at
mention of Trey and his obnoxious interest in Leonora.
 "Trey was always a strange un" she said, but you would have the ugly
little bugger tagging along! his Ma was a good friend to Faye though,
would do anything for her."
Leonora recalled her childhood so well.
"I loved Mati and wanted to be kind to her son," she replied.
"no one liked Trey because he was different to the other children, too
grown up, more like a man!"
"oh I member's e' child, a nasty piece of work was Torr! Only obeyed
your father, but your Mother was too trusting to see it!" At mention of her
Father Leonora asked, "And how does my Father? Still wallowing in self
pity? Lost what little he has left?" she spat the question.

"Ahh! Then you must be meaning Leon, the new Church warden, Palace controller and the Bishops favourite."

Leonora's lovely features creased, she looked quizzically at Emma, "my father Leon, church warden? Are we speaking of the same Leon?"

Emma drew her stool closer, "You won't be knowing any of this my sweet, but tis true though, Leon is the Bishops favourite an controls all church business here."

She leant forward as if about to share some dark secret, "rumour as it that wickedness has been done by Leon, that e's a law unto is' self! There's even talk of murder!"

Leonora dropped her head into her hands, "So nothings changed then?" She felt deflated, as if returning was after all a step backwards.

"Nay miss seems e's judge and jury now especially since Watkin was found hanged in his own court, then Oxton Napier cut down on Church ground!"

The same small town gossip thought Leonora, murder at least gave some respite from daily drudgery

Leonora felt suddenly tired.

"Forgive me Emma, I must take my leave, I thought to seek out Kate Truscott, she will give me room and bed."

Emma shuddered, "I wouldn't be too sure of that! Leon's threatened to cut out Kate's tongue! Says if er' can't keep it still he'll remove it for er."

Leonora stifled a grin, imagining her father cutting out Kates tongue; surely even he knew nothing on earth would stop Dame Truscott's gossip once started!

"So you baint goin' to the manor child?" said Emma, "Right andsome tis, now."

For a moment Leonora had second thoughts, the little Manor had once been so lovely, maybe he was a changed man, could Emma be wrong?

"I think not Emma," she thought better of it "father was more than happy to see the back of me."

Mother Mackey nodded wisely,

"You do what you must me bird, you knows your Father best!"

Chapter 19
Kate Truscott

Along the viners' street Leonora walked as dusk was falling, townsfolk settled and candles flickered behind tiny glass panes, some were lit by lanterns hanging outside, and here and there small groups lingered in the fading light.

Tiny green blackberries ripened on lethal brambles filling the gaps between the spattering of cottages that fronted the street, while behind the cottages and hovels, steep slopes of vines twisted down almost to the cottage gates, miniscule clusters of grapes to be, promised a bumper harvest of fruit.

Pagonston would always be home, no matter where she lived, Plymouth was not a million miles away but at times it had seemed so even with Edmund by her side. Once she had dreamt of the world beyond these red shores, but it was becoming clear that here close to the sea in the town in which she was born, was where she would remain, so much so for the Monkey Mans nonsense!

She smiled recalling his words, as she turned towards the Parish Church. Against the white wall of Kate Truscott's Inn a familiar figure relaxed on a stool in the evening's warmth.

Kate gasped on seeing Leonora, "Mother Mary, what in heavens name be you doing here girl? I thought you Plymouth."

Embracing her Leonora replied, "I was!"

As if she were a daughter Kate welcomed Leonora and prepared hot water, she never once asked the reason for Leonora's dishevelled appearance. The seams of her velvet gown were coming adrift, her lovely hair normally so well kept was matted and scraped back plainly; no ribbons or combs sparkled. Kate had known Leonora from a babe, an exquisite child; God only knew what had happened to cause Faye's stunning daughter to look like a vagabond!

Pretty girls were aplenty, the majority ended as slaves of men, their beauty ruined by toil and too much child rearing, occasionally a beauty stood above the rest, Leonora was such a one.

Over the years Kate had grown cynical, tenderly she smiled at Leonora. "You'm can stay here long as you likes me bird!" she said, "tis lovely to have you here again!" Before closing the door on her privacy Kate stole a look over her shoulder, as Leonora stepped from the tatty gown, the green though faded contrasted with the honeyed skin, God in Heaven! If ever a woman deserved to be desired for her beauty it was this young woman.

Kate would have given anything for a daughter like Leonora, The girl deserved more than marriage to the fool from Plymouth, Leon and Faye should have listened Leonora when she tried to tell them, but the words had gone unheeded.

Plenty of landed Knights would have given much to have a lady of her looks on their arm, hadn't her own mother eventually left Leon for one such? Rumour had it that she found perfect happiness with him!

Kate recalled Leonora's similarity to her father, a tomboy inclined to impetuosity, but with maturity she blossomed into the image of Faye, her mother would have been so proud of her daughters' beauty.

the same golden brown hair tumbling over lean shoulders and neat breasts , dark lashes framed eyes, almost identical except for the startling flecks of green, whereas Faye's had been hazel, the colour of autumn countryside; even her choice of jewellery reflected her mother's taste, thought Kate as the amber beads shone like honey in the candlelight.

Kate closed the door and sighed, years had passed since the girl's mother had been so brutally murdered, Faye whose beauty had captivated a Templar Knight, the loyal wife swept from a life of cosy domesticity into his waiting arms, how must great passion feel? At least Faye had experienced such love unlike herself!

Kate's daydreaming was rudely interrupted by her husbands voice cackling like a hag, "you be taking some risk wife aving that girl here, just you wait till the 'Bishops monkey' finds out! Remember his promise!"

"Quiet husband" she snapped back, "It'll take more than a French popinjay to scare Kate Truscott."

Her husband smirked as he replied, "if I remembers right you were panting like a bitch on heat after him at one time, like half the women in Pagons Ton."

"Yes and look who I ended up with! Maybe I should have thrown in my lot with the Frenchman!"

"You were too late woman," said her husband, "for the fair Faye beat you to his bed, didn't she? But she of course was beautiful!"

His words cut, for they were true.

"The girl will see her father when she's good and ready, now move, some of us as work to do." Roughly she pushed her grinning husband out of the way.

"The only tongue you'll be getting from the Frenchman is your own! if he keeps his promise an' cuts it out," he sneered.

His spiteful words echoed in her ears; tears of frustration stung her eyes and reddened cheeks, briskly she made her way to the water pump.

By the morrow, most of Pagonston knew the daughter of Leon had returned, minus her husband!

Leonora broke her fast at Kate's table with a hearty meal,
The dawning of a new day bought with it the dawning of reality,
Life as she had known it was gone, torn apart by the events of last year,
was she a widow or not? Certainly she was without chattels or the
protection that came with marital status.
Claiming home and possibly husband the fire had thrust an impoverished
freedom upon her; a double edged sword if ever, for that freedom had
come at the highest possible price.
Must she rebuild her life, and this time makes no mistakes? Again she
recalled the words of the 'amber man' 'Knights will vie for your hand!'
And smiled at the irony, how often those words would return!
Kate had found a blue linen shift, although old and of a rough weave, the
decorative waist girdle and silver embroidery upon the bodice made it
cling seductively, under a cape it would not show too much flesh.
"To think I could once slip that on and off in a flash sweeting!" Kate said
smiling wistfully; she helped Leonora wash and dress her hair, pulling the
thick locks back with two pretty filigree combs.
When finished Kate admired the transformation, "well Miss Leonora, I
thinks you still be the fairest maid in Devon, never mind Pagonston!"
Adjusting a cloak over Leonora's shoulders she tied the laces across her
breasts, disappointed Leonora pulled it open again but Kate looked under
her lashes warningly, "tis pretty sweeting, but you knows what folk is like
here!"
Leonora frowned but understood exactly what the older woman meant.
"As you wish Kate, now I need some time to think, the sea air is a good
clearer of the mind, I'll decide just when and if I want to see father."
She embraced Kate and headed towards the shore.

White crests topped the waves as an easterly whipped spume above the
turbulent waves, spray dampened her face and unruly wisps of hair, she
tucked them inside the hood and held it tight beneath her chin.
White as fluffy clouds, gulls hung screeching above the sea, smaller black
headed gulls ran back and forth at the waters edge on quick legs, dipping
their beaks into sandy shallows.
Gazing at the horizon, Leonora imagined the lands beyond that hazy line.
Shells littered the sand, shattered fragments rejected by the sea; she
picked up the iridescent pieces of mother of pearl loving the shimmering
colours, mussel shells by the hundreds, blue and black lay beside thick
ridged cockle shells, milky and smooth on the inside. Delicate little
mauve and pink butterfly shells broke easily in two; gathering the
prettiest she tucked them into her cloak.

Above the noisome gulls another sound carried faintly, a human voice amongst the wildness behind her, she scanned the beach and shoreline. Battling against the gusts a man not much bigger than a dot headed in her direction. With dismay she slowly recognised the riders' bow legged gait and wild hair.

Tightly she gathered her cloak about her and hurried on pretending she had not seen, but the voice persisted along with his waving.

"Nollie!" the hated word came clearly, "Nollie! Leonora!" he was not about to give up, of that she was sure!

Finally Leonora stopped and faced her pursuer sullenly as he staggered to a halt. "You know I hate that name!" she said.

Panting heavily Leon stooped and clutched at his chest, coldly she watched his performance, what an actor she thought, the same old Leon! It made no difference whether he was ranting, carousing or dying! The exaggerations were always the same, well let him die here at her feet that would test his acting pretensions to be sure!

While he calmed himself she studied his appearance, how changed he was, the ravages of drink had mottled and reddened his skin, and his eyes once so blue and twinkly were pale and bloodshot; barely a year she'd been gone yet he seemed shorter, and far from impressive, nothing like the swaggering soldier of fortune from her childhood.

Still he was clothed splendidly, far removed from the neglect of last time, though he had gained a paunchy stomach.

Made from the finest wool, his saffron tunic was gathered generously over his girth and cinched with a wide leather belt. Beneath it a sparkling white linen chemise ended in cuffs of extravagant golden embroidery, a long cloak pinned at the shoulder covered both.

Wisely Keeping muscles warm his legs were encased in red hose, over which very sturdy riding boots had been pulled. Clean shaven, only his hair was unkempt and flew wildly across his face as he gathered his breath.

Bored by his performing, she was about to turn her back and walk on when he straightened, fixed her with a bold stare, and smiled craftily,

"Nollie, Leonora, Daughter" he gasped, "Tis one and the same to a father," Wearily she viewed him.

"And what father is so urgent that you pursue me so?"

Arrogant as always Leon couldn't begin to understand the reasons for her irritation; had he not always cared for his Nollie?

"To make peace between us daughter, Is it not about time to forgive?"
Leonora ignored the outstretched hands.

"You have a poor memory father, it is not I who needs forgiving!"
He dropped his hands to his sides surprised at her reaction.

She was still far too proud for her own good! But by God his daughter
was beautiful, even windswept and in a gown that had seen better days,
what a shame her dolt of a husband never appreciated what he had, where
was the milksop? A woman this stunning shouldn't be out of her
husband's sight for a moment!

She kept her hands hidden in the woollen swathes, staring towards the sea.

"Daughter, Leonora," Leon began,

"Fortune smiles on me bringing you home come won't you walk with me
a little? Why be so cold, don't we all make mistakes?"

"And some never learn from them," she replied coldly.

"Oh, Nollie, Nollie, you are still so young," he said.

"No father you are wrong! I am a married woman, and possibly a
widow!" she hissed, "I am no longer your Nollie, Pray don't call me so!"
Leonora walked on putting space between them, returning had been a
mistake, he would never change.

"Too well I recall the times of drunkenness father, the spite and
bitterness, and your all consuming jealousy, I believe you beyond
changing!"

Crafty as an old fox Leon limped pitifully at her side; he knew she
wanted rid of him, convincing her he was a changed man would take
rather more guile than he'd planned.

Over the years he'd relied on an ability to bend the truth, sweet talking
his way from many a situation; his strong daughter however would not be
so easily won over.

Carefully he picked his words, damned if he would apologise just yet!
Leaning a little closer he said, "I have restored the house, the roof no
longer leaks, and the garden your mother loved I've rewalled, sweeting
you would be well pleased with the new pear tree, do you recall the day?"
Angrily she turned halting his empty words,

"Father, do not take me for a fool! I can see right through you, and to use
my mother how dare you! Is there no depth to which you will not sink?"
he tried to avoid the lovely but unforgiving green eyes.

"Don't look so dejected," she added, "your act no longer fools me."
Those eyes reminded him too much of the accursed emerald.

He was disconcerted, all his blustering and talk of the past still failed
to convince Leonora to return to the newly restored manor.

Instead he had another ace up his sleeve, appearing saddened he related
some news recently come to his ears, news that would distress her.
Rumour of Edmund Starts death.

Her emotions for all he knew may have been at boiling point but her
composure never wavered, just those green lights flashed warningly as
she asked just who had borne such news, when Leon refused to disclose
his sauce she replied, "And who I wonder told you that father? Could it
be another schemer like yourself? If it is true how come, I his wife was
not sought out first?" Leonora was loosing her patience.

"I recall Father you cared very little for 'the milksop' as you named
Edmund, why would his death concern you now?"

Leon stamped his feet hard on the wet sand , he was cold, he clasped his
arms tight around his body and pulled his cloak tight, he'd rather be
anywhere than here!

Obviously Leonora was not about to succumb to his charm, and his
tolerance was wavering, "Gods blood daughter, why does it matter so
who does the telling? Is it not enough that the truth be known? And to
whom it matters!"

Leon's face had suffused red and veins throbbed blue at his temple, here
was the same Leon who had thrown his daughter so heartlessly from the
house fighting to control his terrible temper. Dropping his voice he
became persuasive, "sweet daughter , tis true you have reason to hate me,
I admit to doing wrong by you , but am a changed man, let me protect
you against the dangers a young widow faces, wicked men prey on such
as you." Despite the wind turning chill Leonora faced the sea , spray on
her wet cheeks stung, "no Father cajole as much as you will but I have no
desire to return to the manor, I have lodging for as long as I wish it and I
know all about dangerous men!"

Damn that bitch Kate Truscott thought Leon.

"Maybe you could ask the bearer of this news to visit me so that I may
speak with him myself? But let me tell you, I have a fair idea of who this
harbinger of misery may be!" she turned away sharply, "so it bothers me
not!" in Leonora he had created a child in his own mould; he watched her
march away, single minded and stubborn, the cloak wrapped around her
slight body made her seem light, as if the wind at any minute would pick
her up and deposit her back to the safety of dry land. Cursing Leon
tugged at his cape; the wind silenced his blaspheming as he hauled the
damp fabric over frozen neck and shoulders,

Damn and blast the girl's pig headedness.

he had not even got half way to informing her of Sir Ralf's bequest, another way would have to be found quickly , and if she continued to treat him thus it would be extremely difficult.

The justice bearing Ralf's last will and testament were due to arrive in Pagonston any day to inform her of her good fortune, so before they turned up on her door step, if Leon failed to tell her himself she may see it as a deliberate attempt at deception and Leon could miss out on any largesse! His daughter was no nobody's fool!

The castle of Boscombe Valle had been bequeathed to Faye, by way of making amends for what she had suffered at the hands of Halbert, the only condition was that it would only ever pass through Faye to the women of her line, i.e. her daughters; Leonora therefore was the first in line to inherit!

Leon at first felt a sense of betrayal by a man he had served well, a man who denied him the right to inherit, it would seem that for the moment he must eat humble pie, swallow his pride and tell her, but

God forbid the Templar dog should get to her first, the last thing Leon needed was for Leonora to hear of her good fortune from the lips of Ciabhan of Compton berry.

When Leon had seen the unmistakeable seal of his enemy boldly placed at the bottom of the parchment he had nearly choked on his spleen, all he could think of was how his adversary must have crowed on being chosen as chief witness to the last wishes of Sir Ralf of Boscombe Valle!

From the shore any one watching the Father Daughter confrontation would have seen the loser huddled alone and despondent, looking for all the world like a lowly scourer of the shore as he made his way heavy footed along the seas edge, head down and shoulders slumped.

Chapter 20
Boscombe Valle

Trey and Trewin holed up in a rundown castle trusted Leon, they had believed him when he had said, 'keep from sight and leave everything to me...........Trey had no reason to doubt him, his and Leons goals were the same; both hated with a vengeance the same man, neither would rest until the dog of Compton Berry ceased to draw breath.

Trey had been promised the hand of Leonora by her Father, while he schemed to possess for himself the estate of Boscombe Valle.

For now Trey and Trewin would do as told and stay hidden........

****

Boscombe Valle was a small but beautiful Castle come fortified Manor House set deep in the countryside an hour's ride from Pagonston.

Sir Ralf of Boscombe Valle, Leons liege lord had been the last but one of his line, the man to whom Leon owed fealty, and It was from Sir Ralfs estate that Leon had rented the sandstone Manor in Pagonston just after his marriage...for many happy years his and Faye's marital home.

 Ralf an honourable but lonely Knight had grown very fond of the young couple, in particular for the spirited Faye, Leons pretty bride; the couple were like a mirror of his own youth.....and Faye especially had reminded him of his long departed wife.

Of charitable nature and in gratitude for Leons unswerving loyalty Ralf finally agreed to Leons purchase of the tenancy, 'to care for his precious wife and growing family'.

****

Leon guarded a secret, a windfall had come his way, while he planned the best way forward none must learn of his good fortune.

Certainly not the actual benefactress Leonora.............her mother had been left the Castle of Boscombe Valle by Sir Ralf, who had died unaware of Fayes death....... it would pass now to her daughter.

A mere girl, Gods fish! Leon had no intention of letting an opportunity such as this pass him by.

Unfortunately his daughter would soon have to be told for the law required it.............

All Leons Cunning would be needed to possess Boscombe Valle........... for the chance at last to be a man of real means! But how?

Boscombe Valle had featured heavily in Leons life; it had played a major part in the ill fated story of Leon, his wife Faye, and her lover Ciabhan of Compton Berry.

The saga and its tragic outcome had become part of Pagonstons folklore; a scandal ending in murder and the quest for revenge...............

Halbert was Sir Ralfs only child.....his sole heir, arrogant and brutal, devoid of charm and a most unpopular overlord.
Halbert had made no secret of the fact that he waited for his father to die, that he longed to inherit not only the prosperous estate but the freedoms he considered went with it............
The freedom that would give him licence to poach another mans wife.
.....Faye of Pagonston.

Halbert for years no more than a mild irritation for Leon proved far more dangerous when Leon, obliged to serve Sir Ralf, left with him for Normandy, leaving Faye alone; the opportunity Halbert had waited so long for was presented to him seemingly on a plate!
Obsessed by Fayes beauty and his passion for her, Halbert in the dead of night set fire to the Manor, abducted Faye and fled to the safety of his Castle, Boscombe Valle.
There he imprisoned Faye confident that she would be his and knowing Leon remained ignorant of her plight, His passion blinded him to the possibility that anyone else might attempt a rescue.
He had not reckoned on the loyalty of the Templar Knight, Sir Ciabhan of Compton Berry, nor on the courage of Faye's maid Mati.
Fleeing the Manor blaze she and her husband managed to reach the Templar stronghold of Warsmead, knowing that within its walls resided the only man able to help them.
Outraged at such blatant disrespect for a man he had fought with the Templar immediately set out to free the wife of his comrade Leon;
A hasty act of chivalry that would challenge well ordered destinies.

Surprised that any would attempt a rescue Halbert found himself cornered in the very place he felt safest, isolated Boscombe Valle Castle deep in the Devonian countryside. Halberts retainers found themselves quickly overpowered by Ciabhans surprise assault.
Abductor and champion had fought bloodily, ending with the thrust of a Templar blade. Halbert was an ignominious death but no more than deserved, none mourned Halbert, loathsome son of an honourable Knight.
Sir Ralf retained no bitterness towards Ciabhan; but the consequences of the Templars audacious rescue would forever change three lives.

As he Paced back and forth the restrictions imposed on Trey were beginning to irk, "Leon better come up with the goods", he muttered to himself. Treys obsession with Leonora mirrored another obsession, that of Halbert for Faye, years ago.....Boscombe Valle had been silent witness to both, but the irony of his situation would be lost on such an ignoramus as Trey!

As a troubled child growing up in Leon's Manor, tearful adults and their arguments meant little, of course he recalled his fathers rages; when he would shout abuse at his mother, and he could still hear the special curses reserved for the Lady Faye.

Aunt Ida opened his mind well when she had begun her poisonous whispering in his young ears.

"Ow long think e' us'll be ere then?" Trewin hacked at a rabbit carcass, skewering tiny kidneys into his mouth.

Trey spoke from the other end of the trestle; inactivity coupled with concealment had given him a permanent scowl, along with a stubby beard.... reddish it seemed in odd contrast with his straw hair and peculiar wolfs eyes. He dropped the bones he had been chewing on, wiped his hand across his mouth and said, "Can't say."

The weather had turned again, blowy and unseasonably chill, through dark passages a howling made the two men turn, but it was only the wind. Trey lumbered to Trewins side; "tis a miserable hole this!" he belched. Trewin looked up at the man to whom he was tied in service, "bleddy Devon weather," he replied, "Christ! Don it ever end!"

Trey didn't answer but flung his dagger into the trestle where it quivered inches fromTrewins fingers, still sticky from rabbit flesh.

"Bugger me! Master Trey, e' nearly took me fingers that time!"

Trey sneered, "If I wanted they fingers buy I would'n av' missed! You,ms an old maid to be sure!"

Resting his massive hands firmly either side of the dagger he hunched over the table, he seemed to consider his words before speaking.

"Master Leon? I's not too sure of," he said "seems to ave don well for imself though." He waved his hand around the hall, "All this, well as manor in Pagonston! Not bad for a French mercenary, eh boy? seems the proud Leonora is an heiress after all!"

Trewin shook his head, "if e asks I' Master Leon be too clever for is own good, slippery as an eel e' seems ....like all they foreigners! Why us as to be ere' I don know, could be e' thinks us Cornish is fools."

Trey scratched at his stubble,

"You'ms probably right!"

He crossed to the open door, where rain poured from algae covered stonework; it fell like a silver sheet over the low entrance. Beyond the curtain of water, mist coloured the countryside grey, even great oaks seemed as faint misty shapes; Trey shivered as the drips ran under his collar and onto skin.

Hating not being in control, Treys heavy brows creased with uncertainty as he dwelt on Trewins words; it was true he did not trust Leon....the man was different from the humorous Leon he remembered from his childhood, and he thought back to the reception he had received from Leon on arriving unannounced at his door....

Tense and a little anxious Leon had listened while Trey told of the distressing sight he had witnessed on the road..... The sight of the dead Edmund, so distressed in fact that Trey decided to head instead for Pagonston, in the hope Leonora had returned to her father, there they could have told her themselves; a familiar person breaking such dreadful news would be preferable to any callous stranger.

Trey hoped he'd looked concerned as he told of his decision to deviate from his chosen path ......tears had even sprung into his eyes when he said the heartbreaking news was more important to him than avenging his own fathers' death!

Trey had rehearsed his story well, telling how he had met with Leonora in Plymouth, how they had shared memories of the past..........

.Finally Leon appeared to relax even asking Trey to stay awhile, and Trey accepted....so far all had gone according to plan.

As Trey pondered these things, Trewin sidled up, noisily he cleared his throat and hawked into a puddle. As if reading his sullen masters thoughts he asked, "think you Leon believed what you told e' about the girls usband?" Trey nodded, "aye, e' believed that all right ......but e' was lying when e' said e' don know where his daughter is!"

Chewing at his lip Trewin asked, "is that why us is holed up ere' then?" Trey mocked, "You be getting quick Trewin!"

Trey was convinced Leon believed him about Edmunds death, Leonora on the other hand would not have been so easily persuaded, of that Trey was sure! He had worked hard to gain Leon's trust, and for his own end Trey wa prepared to stay in this dreary place.One thing had emerged during Treys time with Leon, Their combined hatred for Ciabhan of Compton Berry.

111

Leon should prove a steadfast ally; and as ally, maybe just maybe he could be persuaded to put forward his daughter….as a bride!

A few times thought Trey, Leon had more than hinted at the prospect. Trey flicked sodden hair from his eyes, "us'll just wait ere patient like, till Master Leon says otherwise.......... it'll take some time to convince that stubborn daughter of his that er' usband baint no more!"

Trewin remembered too well her sharpness of voice on the times Leonora deigned to speak to his master......... and her cold green eyes, like a little lizard.

"Be buggered if I'd try convincing that madam of anything!" he snapped. Just what Trey found so pleasing in the girl was a mystery to him, no more than a maid; yet haughty way above her station….

"Far too free if you asks I," he spat, "Bloody good iding' is what er' needs."

Trey curled his mouth in a dismissive sneer,

"Well I didn't ask e' so shut your mouth!" he growled.

****

Chapter 21
The Newcomer

Mati did not take kindly to the arrival of sister Domenica, the older woman's value to Ciabhan had never been questioned and she enjoyed a special place in the castle hierarchy, second only to old Edwin the castle Seneschal.

Fanciful dreams of hope had faded, she accepted she would never be more than companion to the Master of Compton Berry; her love would forever remain unrequited.

In the day to day running of Compton Berry Mati oversaw anything needing a female hand, births, marriages deaths all were reported by her to Edwin, who logged them for castle records.

Mati enjoyed her life and especially the rare occasions she spent in Ciabhans Company, It mattered not if he were tired or preoccupied; when near his side she was content, however the arrival of another woman was the last thing she desired.

Discontentedly she grumbled to Alain, as she supervised the cleaning of the small room allocated to their visitor.

"Goodness knows why the Master saw fit to bring this young woman here? little more than a child and pretty useless from what I can see! Just Another mouth to feed!" she added spitefully, "and a mouth without voice!"

Before she could utter another word Alain clamped his hand lightly over her mouth. "Enough woman!" he said, "It was not Ciabhan who wanted her here, but me! In truth my lord was very much against it."

Mati pulled his hand away, "Against it?" she spluttered, "then just why is she here?"

Alain smiled, "cease your complaining for a moment and I will tell you?" Leading her to a settle he said, "Mati this is not like you, of what are you frightened? A child, a mute? What threat to you, none could usurp your position, the arrival of this young woman won't change anything?"

Mati hung her head while Alain waited, his sea blue eyes searching her face, after a few moments considering her behaviour she stammered an apology, "What a silly old fool I am! Of course you are right Alain, forgive my stupidity!"

She straightened her apron and fussed with her hair, taking out the ivory pin she loosed then repinned the greying wisps; in those actions remained a flash of the fair Saxon maid she had once been.

She had always reminded Alain of his own sadly departed Mother "No Mati neither silly nor a fool, just old!" he laughed. Her eyes glistened, but seconds later the apples reappeared in her cheeks, she threw back her head and chuckled, a warm reassuring chuckle.

"We're agreed then, enough of this silliness?" said Alain sympathetically, "let us visit young sister Domenica, she needs compassion, if we show a united front Ciabhan will not be looking to blame me again for misguided charity!"

Ciabhan had no reason to meet with the young woman, his views on the subject were clear, she was Alains responsibility, he had not seen her since her arrival, and didn't much want to; besides other things occupied his mind. It had been bought to his attention that of late strangers had been seen at nearby Boscombe Valle, acting suspiciously, a matter for concern in view of the duty that had recently fallen to him.

On his death bed Sir Ralf of Boscombe Valle named Ciabhan as the man he wished to oversee his last will and testament, sure of Ciabhans integrity and honesty.

It was time at last for Sir Ralf's will to be read, Leon's eldest daughter would learn that because of her mother Faye's early death she was now the beneficiary of Sir Ralf's kindness; authorized documents had been sent to the parties concerned and Ciabhan could no longer put off his obligation, however with the pending task he faced a personal dilemma.

Boscombe Valle held very bad memories for him, it opened wounds only recently healed, the thought of meeting with Faye's daughter and possibly Leon would be unpleasant, but Ciabhan had pledged his support to an old and trusting man whose own son had betrayed him, Ciabhan would honour his promise; the document was signed and sealed.

As for his own feelings, they must be put aside; fate it would seem once again had its own ideas.

Maybe because of the coming duty Ciabhans mind seemed of late to be fixated on Leon, if the truth be known he wished now he had killed him, and been done with it!

Nothing else seemed important except the thoughts of murder, day by day they crowded in on him.

In an attempt to cleanse his mind he decided to ride out alone, maybe it would help cure him from the anger raging inside.

Ciabhan had concealed his torment from Alain, the young knight had more on his mind being far more absorbed with the newly arrived sister Domenica; Alain and Mati even now were deep in conversation, discussing how to arrange the room!

Ciabhan was quite disinterested, and bored with feigning concern, while they argued he slipped away unnoticed.

114

in the airless forest he felt content, and let his mind journey back through the jumble of memories; one he recalled was the journey back from Buckfast recently, when he and Alain stopped to water the horses at the Seven Stars Inn, his friend had enquired of the Innkeeper about the well being of a certain young woman, Ciabhan casually asked who the maid may be but Alain had neatly avoided answering, Ciabhan saw little point in pursuing the questioning, however he mused, the young Knights penchant for damsels in distress was becoming a tad wearisome!

Detached he had listened to the Jolly landlords' tale of the mysterious maid's sad return, her plight over her horses and how she finally chose to take passage on a boat bound for Pagonston.

Only when two mysterious strangers were mentioned did Ciabhan become interested, his ears pricked at the Maids fear of them, strangers? Seen recently? He made a mental note to ask questions of his spies. Ciabhan kept a tight rein on his estates and was kept well informed, trespassers were bought to him and a close eye was kept on the machinations of the clergy.

A trusted and loyal network of servants were his informants, verderers in particular were excellent at surveillance and missed nothing, anything slightly amiss was reported back. Discreetly Ciabhan watched over his estate, to some he appeared detached and cold; in reality though the Master of Compton berry remained finely attuned to the every day intrigues about him.

Not for one moment had he stopped believing his adversary Leon was capable still of malice , could that be the reason Leon was so often in his mind, yet again he found himself thinking of Leon.

As his horse plunged on through the undergrowth, Ciabhans blood boiled, why should Leon draw breath while Ciabhan mourned still?

And now to cap his melancholy he had the humiliating task of having to face the man!

Free of coif or helmet Ciabhans hair coiled over his bare neck; limp and damp in the sultry air, loose strands clung to his to his forehead like limpets to a rock. A quilted gambeson fitted snug over a rough flax shift, sleeves rolled to the elbow, though he wore short leather gloves, scratches quickly gathered adding bloody trails to the silver tracery of old wounds, they criss crossed his tanned forearms.

Around his middle a leather belt cinched his waist, without sword, he was armed only with a dagger tucked into a plain leather sheath.

Matching exactly the luminous summer trees, a green and yellow kerchief at his neck absorbed the sweat dripping from his face, unfussy his attire was ideal for a hot day, the only concession to protection was lightweight hose tucked casually into sturdy riding boots.

Without his customary mail, shield, or weaponry, the lord of Compton Berry appeared rather vulnerable, as if mindless of his own well being. Twitching from midge attack the horse shivered glossy black flanks and flicked its tail furiously, the beasts magnificent head shook splaying foam from wide nostrils, neither horse nor rider had a moments respite from the constant insects, Ciabhan flicked irritably at them with a switch, a sure sign of his darkening mood.

When the tangle of brambles resisted and Ciabhan leant over to hack at sapling and thorn, the forests quiet was broken.

Always the green wood had talked to him but today felt somehow different, in this most sacred of places the forests very pulse vibrated, leaves quivered before he passed, on spindly branches they shook though no breeze sighed, fearful of human angst.

Far from the light the forest floor sucked at the stallions' legs, and song birds usually vocal ceased to sing, A whisper more like a long drawn out sigh sucked at the sultry air, like a primeval gasp resonating through ancient pathways, down, down right to the forest floor..... Elements unknown to human kind.

In this magical setting Simple folk could be forgiven for believing in Woodland sprites and nymphs, but for Ciabhan it brought Faye's spirit alive... suddenly in this, their special place she was all around him, she perfumed the air, and teased him from beyond the shadows, her tinkling laughter filled his ears.... her presence was tangible, he reached out...

But in his haste to dismount he stumbled from the stirrup and crashed to the ground. On all fours he tore at the soft moss of her grave, frantic he called her name, desperate for sight of her, but his strength seemed to ebb away, his efforts draining him.

He clawed at the lichen covering her headstone, until words appeared, the words he had inscribed into the limestone; they were still fresh, the words she'd written for him.

Staggering he lunged at invisible adversaries, slicing through the air with his dagger he screamed Faye's name and the forest echoed with his agony, like a man possessed he searched the shade beneath the trees.... God's blood! He could surely hear her, somewhere beneath the towering beech and oak her sighs were calling him.

The green woods heart stopped beating, such anguish had no place within its soul.

Two conflicting emotions tore at Ciabhan wounding him more than any mortal hurt; the love he still bore for Faye, and the hate that burned within him for Leon..... a hate that smouldered for years, slowly consuming him. His need for revenge had simmered, striking when least expected; Avenge his beautiful Faye it seemed he must! If not! Then he had failed her, but hatred in this lovely setting was an unwanted guest, as he sank to his knees exhausted, the forest gathered its son to its heart, wrapping him in a protecting embrace.

Chapter   22
Dark places

"Have you seen Ciabhan?" asked Alain, directing his question at no one in particular but hoping for a reply from someone! Cooks and kitchen boys just looked at him blankly.

Earlier finding Ciabhans chamber empty he'd not been concerned but with the evening meal well advanced and dusk settling he was becoming a little anxious as to where his friend maybe.

Calling for his groom he ran to the stabling, passing under the gate arch he met Mati, "Mati have you seen Ciabhan?" he asked breathless.

"No sir, I thought he was with you," she replied, "after we left Sister Domenica I thought you two had ridden out together."

Alain paused gathering his thoughts, maybe he had forgotten an arrangement; after all he had been busy with the new arrival.

"Think back Mati.....when did you last see him?"

Mati chewed her bottom lip, "I saw him when we were talking, of that I am sure ...but after that I don't know!"

Alain paced back and forth while his groom prepared his mount, "Gods blood, where can he be? It's not like My Lord to venture far without word."

To the guard he shouted, "You and one other prepare to accompany me, arm yourself fully!"

Alain commanded Dickon the Reeve to block and guard all entrances, and exits..."a full watch," he commanded, "everyone on full alert, light all battlement flares, dinner is must wait!"

Alain had some idea where to look in the first instance, there had been times he watched as Ciabhan disappeared into the woods, deep into its heart where paths tangled and played tricks on the follower.

Ciabhan always returned alone, true Alain had helped carry Faye to the secret place, but grief had blinded him to his surroundings, he doubted he could find it again. Only one other, 'The Raven' knew of the glades existence, but he was away in Rome and unaware that it was Faye's final resting place. At this moment Alain would have given anything to have The Raven at his side, he would have known exactly what to do now, Ivan would had have known of his Lords whereabouts.

Mati wrung her hands together and bade Alain take care, Alain didn't know it but Matis thoughts lately had been with The Raven.

"Are there times you wish the Raven was still with us sir?" she said.

Alain looked tenderly at her, "It was his choice to go Mati," he said.

"Be prepared for our late return," softly he added, "don't be alarmed, I am sure there is nothing amiss!"

Just before nightfall, strange shapes scurried over the darkened ground, they dragged Ciabhans limp body into the old hunting lodge. Bent almost double with faces hidden under black hoods the forms seemed inhuman; gnarled, misshapen hands cleared a space for him on the earthen floor. The same veined hands dribbled water tenderly onto his parched lips, before covering him in straw against night's dewy dampness, then in the blackness the figures crouched, watching silently over their charge.
Only the mans laboured breathing and the rustling of night life from the undergrowth made any sound at all, the weak lay quiet in burrows and nests; the forest slept protecting everything within its embrace.
on her beam the barn owl sentinel like, fluffed her feathers and gave a low call before swooping silently down to perch on the slab of carved limestone..........her great eyes missed nothing.

With senses heightened by the importance of their mission, the horsemen kept steady pace with Alain.
Following the track that snaked below the castle walls, they passed the fish ponds and skirted the dark forest on their right, though their eyes grew accustomed to the darkness they still avoided looking into the depths where the trees sighed eerily.
Where the familiar track ended they rode single file along the narrow bridle path, on their left now the larch wood towered steep, blotting out what little light there was on this moonless night.
Brian an experienced castle guard attempted to talk but was quickly sssshhed by Alain who reined his horse to a sudden halt, nearly bumping Thomas the rider in front of him, "What the hell?" Brian grumbled.
Alain signalled for absolute silence.
"There it is again," he said.
The others shook their heads.
"Did you not hear it?" Alain asked, "The faintest whinny."
He cocked his head and listened, furtive rustlings gave away the presence of silent watchers; Alains own mount stamped nervously.
"Yes again," he said, and this time the sound was plain, the high pitched whinny of a restrained but intelligent horse.
Alain pointed to his right where the forest wound up and over steep meadow, dense the dark trees curled towards the faint horizon.
"Methinks yon forest hides something! Stay close swords at the ready!"
With that he turned right and plunged across the small stream. Using the hedge as shelter the group edged towards the hostile forest; thick vegetation made entry difficult. When they finally did break through the world they entered seemed ready to swallow them whole.

The sound Alain had heard was that of a highly trained war horse, looking out for its Master. The lives of Knights depended on trust between themselves and their steeds, both had to be in tune to every move of the other. Alain had been witness to many wondrous examples of the unique bond...from the sound he knew Ciabhans horse close by its master. Leading the horses the three men pressed deeper....although they did not speak the sound of their approach was heard.

Swords at the ready Alain led, unsure of what he may encounter but prepared for anything, again the soft whinny, he needed no more proof that Ciabhan was close by.

Strangely he felt an unseen hand guided him, tangled tracks purple in the night light should have confused him but didn't, only when Brian voiced his concern did Alain notice something rather more sinister was happening.

"Sir" Brian whispered, "is it my imagination or does it lighten somewhat?"

Thomas flicking his eyes nervously responded, "For Christ's sake man, are you trying to scare us to death? It feels like the bowels of hell already!"

"Quiet," Alain rebuked, "look!"

Brian and Thomas could just see where he was pointing..... a clearing had opened ahead of them and from it emanated a light, not warm like a woodsman's fire but bluish like cold starlight, a light never expected after midnight in the depths of a forest.

Transfixed the three men stared ahead, frightened to go forward the slightest rustle made them jump like children playing ghost games; they even shied from each other. Alain, far from superstitious thought logically as he summed up the scene before him, ghosts were a figment of the imagination, they do not exist! There must be an explanation......

"Come forward into the light Alain Rousseau.......let us see you."

A voice like a crackle of lightening sliced the silence sparking panic from the two men, Thomas jumped so badly his horse would have bolted had he not been tightly held, the beasts were terrified, even in the darkness the whites of their eyes showed clearly.

A black shape scuttled into the clearing, resembling some huge broken winged raven it squatted half in and half out of shadow.

"Gods blood!" Stammered Thomas pointing his sword defensively, "what in Gods name is that?"

This time the voice rang out mockingly, "put away your weapon man! .....There is nought to fear here."

"Sheath your swords," Hissed Alain.

"Wisely spoken Monsieur Rousseau, now step forward and see, that for which you search is safe Come."

Alain pushed aside the thorny shrub, and stepped into the glade, his men lingered half in and half out of the shadows.

The 'thing' that talked was not alone; hidden in shade and half light were many more, they melted into the trees, and then flattened like puddles of pitch. Alain felt keen eyes watching his every move.

"You know me?" asked Alain, hoping his voice didn't betray his fear, "how could that be? For I know not of you!"

Sweat trickled from beneath his helmet and dripped into his eyes blurring them, the whole scene surely was a dream; dragging his glove across his face he strained to see, while behind him he heard the uneven breathing of his companions.

"We do not show our faces, we do not exist, but we know all!"

The voice did not sound human!

"Sir" Thomas' voice was urgent, "they are untouchables! Oh merciful God!" he winced, "maybe lepers! Lets leave now before it is too late for us all, or let them eat our blades." Brian muttered agreement, "Satans spawn more like!"

The reply was clear, "Stay your fear man, we are neither! Misshapen and unfortunate yes, it is against the stares of such as you that we keep our faces hidden." A swirl of black and an arm was revealed, resembling a knobbly stick it beckoned, "come, if you wish to see your Master, for it is he you come to collect?"

Alain shrank from the arm, its withered fingers ghastly beckoned again, "Just you Alain Rousseau!"

Alain gawped at the vaulting beeches, the tops disappeared way into the mantle of night, looking up made him giddy and his body seemed to float, he tried to stay focussed.

"You will not find that for which you seek in the sky sir," the creature spoke with barely veiled sarcasm..... Alain was aware of other presences in the shadows, this was obviously their spokesman! He remembered Thomas' fears, maybe their tongues were missing!

The creature touched Alains sleeve and led him to the musty smelling shelter, the shock of a familiar voice made Alain start!

"Well met my young friend, is a man to have no secrets?"

Stepping from the shadows Ciabhan steadied Alain for fear he would fall. "It would seem Hades is not yet ready for me after all!" he said.

Thomas fearful for Alains safety yelled, and the scrape of metal sounded jarring the quiet, "my lord is all well?"

Seconds passed, they had been deserted, had Alain disappeared never to be seen again?

Then came his voice, just a little shaky.

"Nothing to fear friend, there will be four of us leaving."

A soft rain began to fall, a steady plop, plop onto thick foliage. Leaves shivered and bent beneath their weight, the atmosphere all of a sudden felt normal, just a dank and soggy woodland clearing on a miserable night. Had the creatures ever existed? Was this whole experience a dream?

Alain was confused, "My Lord what is this place? Where are we? Why are you here? I feel lost! Were those creatures your companions? Gods blood, we thought them Demons!"

"Demons Alain? I thought you a man of intelligence!

Our God can be cruel, he does not create us all fairly, bear witness to what cruel fate does to some" he looked around him, "those who dwell here prefer to remain unseen, to hide behind cover of darkness."

One hooded figure remained crouching close to a mossy mound, Alain noticed the tablet of stone at one end, now his eyes flicked over the words chipped into its surface and he caught his breath as the truth of the place dawned, the figure began to speak.

"We sirs are guardians of this sacred place, In honour of your Masters benevolence. Others turn away, he does not! He gives us the freedom of his forest, our sanctuary; in return we care for his lady." cracking with emotion the voice struggled, "In the early days a Raven came regularly, roosting every night on the branch that overhung this stone," he gestured to an oak whose lower branches swept the ground. "I know of not one day that ne'er he came, until the day he died." a crackled sob broke from the twisted body, "We found its body upon the Lady's grave, it lays now beneath the oak, we wear black to honour that Raven, and in honour of Our lord of Compton Berry, and his Lady Faye."

Alain glanced at Ciabhan not knowing quite what to expect, but on Ciabhans face was a look of acceptance, a look whose sad eyes said it all; let the past be.

Rain continued, misting the clearing, one of the guardsmen coughed politely, reminding Alain of their presence.

Ciabhan smiled at Alain, "Only one other knows of this place, I wonder, could it be his spirit returns to keep my lady company?"

His words saddened Alain even more, "I will never breathe a word of this night my Lord, and I think," he said nodding in the direction of his companions, "those two would rather forget it completely!"

"They will think this no more than a bad dream," said Ciabhan, "I suspect tonight's experience will keep them well away in the future."

Probably the truth for while the three men conversed in private, Brian swore Demons had brushed past his head and tangled with his legs, when he came to mount his feet could hardly be lifted from the ground!

The rain stopped allowing a little silver moonlight to shine on countryside in full leaf, as a precaution Ciabhan followed a new path, Thomas and Brian doubted they would ever emerge.

Alain knew the truth though, the glade would close behind them, hidden to all but the chosen, he was one of the chosen.

"My wife lies unavenged; Leon may not have shot the arrow that felled her but by God his hatred brought it about! His life should be forfeit! Tis time he paid for his actions"

Taken aback by Ciabhans sudden words Alain reined his horse to a stop, they had just crossed the stream, deeper and faster flowing here than where Alain had crossed before. Mud splattered the riders' clothes, the whites of Ciabhans eyes and his teeth gleamed through the grime, without helmet or protection he resembled a blackamoor.

"My Lord the evil do not escape Gods reckoning, Leon is no exception, he will pay!" replied Alain.

"God drags his feet my friend in calling Leon to account for his crime, and my revenge grows impatient! Forget not that his spite denied me the act of avenging my own wife's murder, for what they did it was I who should have slain both and left them to rot!"

Ciabhans eyes hardened and his jaw set firm, the accusation was clear, he referred to the cutting down of Torrs body.

"I would have celebrated seeing them swing together; you my friend denied me that!" he spat.

Alain doubted Ciabhan would ever forgive him that act of compassion.

For years Ciabhan had appeared to cope with his tragic loss, he had come through the mourning period, and seemed to be emerging slowly from his grief, but had he really, Alain wondered if anger and resentment had instead been festering deep within his soul.

Proof of the depth of Ciabhans resentment came later while tilting with his friend in the courtyard; the exercise was a means of sharpening reflexes, and deemed serious sport. Charged with more energy than usual and on exceptional form, Ciabhan spun the quintain with such force that his lance nearly buckled, those looking on whispered amongst themselves, guessing as to what or whom their master wished was on the receiving end of such a powerful blow.

CHAPTER 23
The Legacy

In the semi darkness of her little cell Sister Domenica listened to the sounds of the castle, birdsong soothed her senses and calmed her nervousness. Since arriving she had made only three attempts to venture beyond the oak door into the unfamiliar world outside.

She smiled timidly at the woman who came regularly to feed and fuss over her; at first the woman had tried to engage Domenica in talk, But still words would not come, Domenica had tried; now when she came the woman just tutted constantly to herself, as if cross about something, Domenica would then turn her face to the wall and feign sleep.

Once when she walked unsteadily along the corridor a young man approached with the woman, he had smiled but Domenica became hot and backed away, the man left quickly and the woman soothed Domenica with soft words and a warm embrace.

From beneath her window the sounds of men's harsh voices would drift up, often there would be laughter but Domenica would hear only menace, any mans voice caused her to shudder uncontrollably and the blood to freeze like ice in her veins.

After Brother Jaime and Brother Justin, the monks who had accompanied her to the Castle of Compton Berry had finished settling her into the little room, she recalled them talking outside the open door.

"I know not if she will ever speak again my son," Brother Jaime's' voice had been serious, "but with patience and kindness, who knows? God willing the future may see the poor girl's speech restored, we can but pray."

A softer slightly accented voice had replied, "be assured Brother, she is in good hands and safe here, my Lord is a benevolent man as you well know, no harm will come to her while at Compton Berry."

Only when she heard Brother Jaime answer croakily had she smiled.

"I know my son I know," he had answered, "Now where is that elusive Master of yours? He promised me some extraordinary Italian red; I'd like to drink my fill before the return ride!"

Nurtured by kindness Domenicas confidence grew, by day in the sanctuary of her room she read the scriptures, seated beneath the gilded cross that hung on the whitewashed wall, and by night she gave herself to prayer, sometimes praying so hard that falling asleep on her knees became normal. Many were the times Mati lifted the crumpled figure from the cold stone floor, placing her gently on the hard pallet.

Mati would mutter to herself, "Oh sweet child, I think God would allow you to pray from your bed once in a while! "You are chilled through." Domenica no longer fought the woman's kindness, rather she sank into the embrace allowing the plump arms to soothe, gradually freed from fear she would even manage a weak smile.

For Doomenica there were however strange flashes of recollection, sometimes a movement or glance from Mati and Domenica would think of another; but she knew not of whom, she was though convinced the memory was a malevolent one! Thankfully as quickly as its blackness descended it would then vanish from her mind; what was it about this gentle woman that seemed so very familiar?

Day by day Matis affection for the girl grew, especially after Alains scolding, guilt had now replaced her jealous feelings by over protectiveness, and she constantly fretted over the girl prompting even Ciabhan to enquire after the girl's well-being, probably more from exasperation than real concern!

"And how fares our young charge, mistress?" he had asked one morning. Taking Mati by surprise, she answered quickly, fearful lest he lose interest.

"The road to recovery is long sir, her mind more than her body has been greatly wounded."

Concern etched Ciabhans face, "damage to the mind causes the deepest hurt, unlike a bloody wound that heals, it cannot be seen!"

Without knowing he did it he placed his hand on his stomach where a dreadful injury had almost cost his life, "The flesh healed Mati, but the mind? I think not."

Mati shuddered, "I recall well that awful time Sir."

An awkward silence followed as they both remembered, "Think you our young sister Domenica will ever talk again Sir? she questioned."

"Who knows?" he replied, "God moves in mysterious ways, memory may force the horror out, then she will speak?"

Mati heard him but wasn't listening, her mind had flicked back to the wound to Ciabhans stomach, as he fought for life, the terrible blood when Faye and Ivan had cut the belt from his waist, its ragged remains lay even now in Faye's sandalwood chest; bloodied and ragged. She was sure Ciabhan still wore some of it, if no longer about his middle then secreted somewhere upon his person, he had been ever reluctant to part with the belt, or the memories it held. Thinking of Ciabhans body caused her heart to flutter; quickly she made a pledge to pray for forgiveness!

"He certainly does," she said, "of that I am sure!" Mati needed no convincing that God moved in mysterious ways.

Her sarcasm was obvious, and Ciabhan frowned , "You would make God accountable for the sins of man Mati?" he chided, "we might not like to face it but some men do take pleasure in abusing women, indeed consider it their right, the spoils of war!"

"No sir, I would not blame God," continued Mati, "but it's hard to accept that a benevolent God would allow an innocent to suffer so, she is little more than a child! Why make men capable of such cruelty?"

Embarrassed that she had spoken so passionately she excused herself quickly and hurried away, leaving Ciabhan bemused, Mati rarely voiced an opinion, preferring to keep her thoughts private and a still tongue in her head. He sighed, not quite understanding the ways of women, and walked on.

Mati had fled to the safety of the curtain wall steps making sure none had seen. She stood hand on breast just inside the dank archway trying to still the heaving and falling of her chest; a sneaky draught lifted her apron and billowed the smock beneath filling her nostrils with the fragrance of freshly laundered cotton. Being so close to Ciabhan, feeling his breath on her face and breathing in his smell often caused such a reaction, but this was excessive; she leant back against the stone glad of the coolness. Outside all was perfectly calm, except for her wild heart; she thought it ready to burst from her breast!

Mati had little time for the male of the species, most were worthless in her experience, worthless! Except for one, Ciabhan! Whom she worshipped! God forbid he should ever discover her secret for her shame would be unbearable, if he did she would have no option but to leave his service. Unlike her own bad choice of a mate Ciabhan had been blessed though somewhat late in life, he had tasted true love, had known passion; for an instant she felt self pity, recalling her disastrous marriage to Torr. How quickly her experiences in the marital bed had put paid to any pretence of love, in truth the stinking mule in the back yard had meant more to his feral nature!

Only the fact that Mati had cherished her mistress Faye stopped the young maid from being consumed by jealousy, she rejoiced when Faye and the handsome Knight found a perfect love, there was no denying fate had made them for each other. Matis well kept secret was for her alone, a dream, a fantasy never to be reality, and she knew it!

By the time Mati knocked at the door of Domenicas room she had composed herself, she smiled as Domenica looked up from her reading. "Come my dear," she said, "let us walk a little, tis time you faced the sun, these walls bring pallor to your cheeks."

Leon's untidy hand scrawled across the parchment, Letter writing one of the last remaining signs of his long forgotten education in manners; it stated simply:

Leonora, dearest daughter, I trust you remain in good health. You are an heiress.

As you cannot find it in your heart to speak or visit me, I must Deliver this news by the written word, for you are the only other aware of this secret.
Simply it is this; you have inherited a substantial gift, you may find It hard to believe, but it is the truth.
The poverty my stupidity reduced you to is ended because of a Generous man.
I do not wish to embarrass you by calling in person at mistress Truscott's, where I hope this will find you, but I am bound by law to inform you of the legacy.

Daughter dear, we must meet, I wait your response.
Your remorseful but ever loving Father.

Leonora had taken delivery of the letter just after breaking her fast with Kate Truscott, it had been delivered by a curly haired and smartly liveried young man who replied politely to her questioning, saying that he represented her Father, Leon of Pagonston.
 The contents of the letter on being read the second time caused Leonora's mouth to drop in disbelief, Kate, curious gasped, "Child, in Gods name don' you tell I tis bad news?"
"Tis no bad news, rather...rather I can't believe what I am reading!" she mumbled, "Here see for yourself!"
Kate couldn't read, "Just tell I what it says me bird?" she gulped.
Leonora still bewildered even after reading for the third time blurted, "It says that I have been left an estate of much value, a bequest!"
"God love us child, tis a jest! Someone plays with you, they as mistook this for fools' day!" chuckled Kate.
"Nay mistress, tis no jester who writes this hand," whispered Leonora, "fool certainly," She added, "For tis my Father!"
Kates husband came into the room, "what's all this then?" he asked.

"Baint you women anything better to do?" he said meanly, "too much excitement for early morn dame!" His eyes dropped to the letter in her hand, "unless tis from the king of England?"

Kate opened her mouth to speak but Leonora interrupted,

"Not quite sir," she said lightly, "but almost as important!"

Shaking his head at the stupidity of womenfolk he stalked through to the back yard.

Barely able to contain their excitement the two women stood shoulder to shoulder while Leonora read the words yet again. Impatiently Kate prodded Leonora, "Do it say who as done this bequesting then? tell I more." She almost jumped with excitement.

The manor lay only minutes from Kate's tavern, snuggled close to the orchard it was one of the few dwellings close to the sea; marshy rough land stretched from manor to the shore, acting as a buffer zone to protect vulnerable pastures. During winter, easterlies would whip up spume and lay it thick on the shore at high tide; sometimes spray would reach as far as the orchard.

She had taken the shortcut, what a playground the apple trees had provided in her childhood. Pushing open the rickety gate she gazed curiously around the yard, in the shade a wizened crone crouched near the pig pen squinting through rheumy eyes, a cockerel strutted proudly and shook his feathers jealously guarding his hens. Just visible beyond the rough sandstone wall that fronted the back garden doves fluttered around the dove cote, their gentle cooing filling the warm still air. The same youth who had delivered the letter pulled open the door at her knock and greeted Leonora with a somewhat exaggerated bow, She stepped into the cobbled screen passage and smiled at the young man as he closed the door behind her, "Master Leon awaits you miss," he said civilly, "This way please," he gestured to the familiar living chamber.

She noticed the cable end of the roof, for so long open to the elements, "Finally repaired," Leon said as she entered and nodded towards the roof, "and not before time, if I say it myself." he thought she may have complimented him and stepped forward as if to embrace her, but seeing no response he stopped and stood aside making room for her to pass.

"I am glad you have come Leonora, it would not have surprised me if you hadn't," he said humbly.

"My letter said I would come, did it not?" Her tone was cool. She believed it just another ploy to win her back; it was Kate who convinced her that replying was no weakness.

"Such news can hardly be ignored," Leonora answered.

"Come sit," her Father said motioning to a carved chair complete with stuffed cushion; as if her comfort mattered!

Wine, two goblets and a selection of sweetmeats on a silver tray were placed at the corner of a scrubbed table. "Refreshments if you need them." he said, then waited for her to sit before arranging himself opposite her, he seemed anxious and reluctant to make eye contact, instead drumming his fingers on the arms of the chair, a habit he always had.

"An improvement since you were last here," he nodded at the ceiling, "everything has been replaced or restored, a costly process."

She could well imagine how hard he would have driven the workers, making sure he had his moneys worth.

"Different certainly from the time last I stood within these walls," she replied.

Leon called the boy hovering by the doorway.

"Wine boy, pour for our guest," he demanded pointing to her goblet.

Leonora put her hand over the cup as the boy prepared to pour, "Not for me thank you." she smiled. Too well she remembered the chaos, the loss of her home, the bitterness of her fathers parting words; it was stamped indelibly on her mind, though nearly a year had passed.

Her father remained silent, gazing at his feet as if not knowing what to say, fingers stopped their drumming and joined prayer like at his lips, she smoothed her skirts over her knees.

"So Father just who is this mysterious benefactor? I find it hard to believe anyone would leave us anything,"

Irritated by the contempt in her voice, he patiently tried to explain, "My life Daughter has been spent in the pay of wealthy men, some wealthy beyond dreams! Many were the gifts I received, but none like this I confess."

Leon's personality contained all that was devious, his very agitation confirmed her thoughts, her patience began to wear thin as he pulled his chair closer; with a soft rustle the boy exited their presence; Leon watched him go before whispering, "Ralf of Boscombe Valle was a benevolent master child, I served him loyally for many years on and off. His only son Halbert was rotten to the core, like an apple gone bad, one that taints all others it touches; it is to Sir Ralf's credit he was aware of his sons' malpractices. Sadly Leonora remembered all too well the name of her mother's abductor, his name when spoken by her Father was spat, Halbert the pig of Boscombe Valle! Strangely he used the same depth of hate when speaking of her rescuer!

She listened, trying to follow her fathers' words. "It transpires that Sir Ralf had left his estate in its entirety to your Mother!"

Leonora's forehead creased," my Mothers' dead, she can't inherit," she stammered, "Oui Cherie that is so, Sir Ralf was at the time unaware of her death," here Leon fumbled his words, as if mentioning Faye disturbed him still.....

"However the shame he felt for his sons deed caused such distress that the old man longed to make amends, he planned his will with much thought, stating clearly that his legacy be handed down only through the female line, you Leonora are the next female in line and therefore the inheritor of your late Mothers windfall; daughter you are a wealthy woman!"

Leonora could still not believe what she was hearing,

"Were there no other sons? daughters?"

Leon shook his head,

"Sir Ralf had no issue save Halbert! May the devil take his soul!"

"And where pray is this document? How do you know all this? are you sure tis not all a cruel jest?"

Leon ran his fingers through his greying hair, "I wish it were," he said, his mind on the Templars imminent visit.

"Sir Ralf so disgusted by his own son's actions against a fellow Knights wife, severed any chance of a male inheriting his estate, the old knight in recompensing us for his sons sins ensured that his sons memory remained tarnished forever."

"But you Father? You served him well I know, why did he not leave the estate to you? I know mother was wronged, but she was your wife, you suffered greatly."

Discomfited by her words Leon could not forget how he left Faye alone, Christ! He could almost hear again the Templars admonishment on the very day she was taken; Leon as always far too cocky ignored him! How different things would have been if he had listened! Too late for regrets now! He examined his fingernails rather than meet his daughters' eyes before adding, "Sir Ralf left me his collection of swords and chain mail." His disappointment could not be disguised.

Leonora's reply was immediate, "A shame then that he chose not to destroy those very symbols of male brutality!"

Leon sighed in exasperation, "Dear Jesus Christ!" his feisty little daughter had become a veritable saint!

Meekly he said, "Methinks the good Knight Sir Ralf never doubted that a female would at least look kindly on her male providers?" He watched her reaction from beneath lowered lids.

"Ah!" Leonora whispered back, "True indeed! A really good Father would think like that." It was then she realised how suddenly she had become valuable to her father, no wonder he was tiptoeing around her, how irksome to learn your estranged daughter was in receipt of such a great gift, and that her father was entitled to not one groat, Leonora grinned, so this is how power feels! "Is the mail of monetary worth Father ?" she asked, "the weaponry must surely be significant, get them valued Father, best not look a gift horse in the mouth!" Words of spite maybe, but what delight she took in his discomfort, time for him to squirm!

"It would have been easy for you to remain silent father, without your letter I would not have known!"

Was she really so naïve? Leon scratched his chin; his daughter was full of surprises.

" Oh but you would have child, surely you know a bequest such as this requires lawful procedure, the documents are at this moment on their way to Boscombe Valle, the formalities must be done in front of sir Ralf's chosen witnesses."

"How long have you known of this Father?"

Here Leon lied, "not long daughter, I tried to tell you that day on the beach, but you were in mood for my news."

From beyond the cob walls a crackle of thunder broke the stillness of the afternoon, Leon pulled his cape from the back of the chair; Leonora watched him fasten the laces, his fingers reminding her of gnarled driftwood as he struggled with the fiddly ties.

"Here let me." she said, the last time she had been so close to him must have been her wedding day embrace, a vivid flash fizzed the room followed quickly by another peal of thunder, the heavens opened; chilly now she pulled her cloak tight around her the deluge drowning her fathers thank you.

"Will you not join us for dinner and stay the night?" Leon was hopeful, and thought he saw a softening in her eyes.

"No!" she said, "I promised Kate I would return, but thank you just the same." Leon called for Corentyn, "escort Mistress Leonora to her place of lodging."

Huddled beneath an oiled leather cover Leonora and Corentyn appeared as some shell like creature, as they trudged through the torrential rain to Kate's Tavern.

Once alone Leon brooded, of all the people who could have been a witness why had Sir Ralf chosen the Templar? Any one else and Leon could have influenced misguided loyalties with his smooth tongue and threats, but the dog of Compton Berry! Gods' fish! He had not a hope in hells chance of bending the truth now!

To add insult to injury Leon was even required to face his arch enemy!

Such humiliation made him shake with rage, he was unaccustomed to feelings of moderation and would as soon slit a throat as waste time on parley! Especially with the Dog Compton Berry, Leon's thoughts would rather be on murder.

He was pacing the room when Corentyn returned; he watched the boy wriggle out of his sodden tunic and scoffed at his bedraggled appearance. "Gods blood boy tis nought but a drop of water, you fuss like a maid!" Corentyn scowled back, "then maybe you should have escorted Miss Leonora yourself? T' would have been proper for a father to do so!" Knowing too well that Leons boot would follow he nimbly stepped aside, backing through the door he declared, "I'll bring fresh cider then master!" Leon glowered after the boy; normally his aim would have been true! Was it a timely reminder of his own slowing reflexes? "Cheeky young whelp" he shouted, "you're too cocky for your own good!"

Corentyn returned with the cider, unfazed by Leons stare he poured a goblet of amber liquid for his master. Leon studied Corentyn closely; "You will accompany me and Miss Leonora to Boscombe Valle", he nodded as if forming a plan, "You shall be her escort and dress accordingly, in velvet and fur Sir, as befits the personal squire of Leon, Custodian of the Bishops Palace."

Illuminating the rooms furnishing and drapes, lightening flashed, in its brilliance Leon's pale eyes glistened as he stared glassily at nothing in particular. Corentyn recognised that far away look, it usually accompanied his masters scheming, what he wondered was the devious brain hatching now? He didn't dwell on it; his only thoughts were of riding to Boscombe Valle with the lovely Leonora, True he would make his Master proud; Leon's squire would carry himself with as much dignity as any Royal Prince of the realm.

Chapter 24
Treachery

Mati could barely contain her excitement, Ciabhan had suggested she accompany him and Alain to Boscombe Valle; she was riding beyond the confines of Compton Berry, thrilled she padded from her small room to the warmth of the kitchens.

Dawning clear and bright, the August day felt slightly chill.

Seasonal storms over the last two weeks had chased away the last humid weather and freshness drifted through the arrow slits, beyond the walls the forest wrapped Compton Berry in a green embrace, like a possessive lover it seemed to want to enter; branches close by swayed like tapestries and crafty ivy had sneaked its way through cracks in the walls. Mati stopped awhile in the gloomy passage and savoured the clean air from one of the arrow slits; with great gulps she drank the air as if from a cup of sparkling water.

A Childs wailing sounded, probably one of Maudie Suttons, tired of waiting while Alain kicked his heels, Maudie had found herself with child after a tumble in the hay with young Tom, Each morning rain or shine she would leave her cottage and, child in tow trudge the narrow woodland track to the castle to collect milk fresh from Matis kitchen.

Ciabhan was already up, Mati watched hidden behind an embrasure as he coaxed his horse from its stall into the bailey, dressed in simple rustic tunic and hose he looked no different from the grooms who tended his horses, only his commanding demeanour placed him as the Master; tenderly he stroked the highly strung destriers flanks and caressed its coat, his voice reached her as he spoke with the young stable boy.

Mati had spent a little more time dressing today, and had covered her efforts with a crisp white pinafore; the soft wool of her russet gown would soil if in contact with kitchen grease, In fact she thought to herself, today I'll instruct Maudie to prepare the first meal, she will be only too pleased to chatter with the other hands, that way Mati would stay presentable, be a credit to her Master.

She very nearly skipped on her way, but feeling a little foolish she stopped and glanced behind fearful should her early morning gaiety be discovered.

Ciabhan had little appetite for food this morning, or if he were honest, for the task he must face, savouring the morning he remembered another such as this, another gilt touched August morning when he had prepared for the tourney on the meadows of Torre Abbey, determined to be the best of the competitors he had put his horse through its paces until every dip and turn, rut and hummock were remembered by rider and beast; it was the day he would see Faye of Pagonston for the second time...The day that would also change his life forever!

In Ciabhans chamber the writing table was strewn with parchment, he had returned from the stables to talk with Alain about his decision, worry lines etched his brow,
"Alain, I am not inclined to meet with Leon today!"
Alain caught his breath surprised at Ciabhans words, he was about to reply but Ciabhan stopped him with a raised hand, "hear me my friend." Ciabhan sighed deeply, placed his hands on the table and hung his head, Alain wondered what had happened.
"Alain," he said finally, "Today I entrust you with a task, a duty that should be mine, I want you to go in my place to Boscombe Valle, hand this letter to the advocate representing Sir Ralf."
He passed the rolled up parchment to Alain, Ciabhans personal seal of a cross and a broadsword stamped in red wax sealed the scroll, another seal swung from the bindings.
"I am not attending today; in my absence you will act as my representative!"
Noticing Alains alarm he added, "This letter explains the entire advocate needs to know, and gives details for my non attendance, it tells the truth my friend!" Ciabahn was quite relaxed but Alain remained serious.
"Why the change of plan, are you unwell?" Alain asked.
"Unwell of mind," replied Ciabahn, "for I vow I would rather run Leon through than set eyes on him! Do you think I will stand by and watch while the keys of Boscombe Valle are handed to the man I hate!"
A young page gathered discarded parchment from the floor, Ciabhan continued speaking. "Cast your mind back a few years Alain, do you not recall a day such as this, the sun shining brittle on a field of combat, those fat mulberries that stained our billowing tents and banners, remember the pennants lined up against the opposition, how they snapped in the easterly?"
Of course! How could he have been so blind! That long ago day of the tourney had birthed just as this one, and he hadn't recognised it! Now he understood why his master baulked at visiting Boscombe Valle, for him the memories remained of a day that had shone as brightly, with no hint of the bloody murder that was to come with the night.
Was it any wonder then that Ciabhan hated the thought of going to Boscombe Valle? It must surely be the last place on earth he would want to be? "My friend I have no stomach to meet with Leon, or his petulant daughter," he said adamantly, "the legal papers are all in order, you simply act in my stead, be assured the advocate will understand.

My resolve is made up."

"Mati will be sorely disappointed," Alain ventured, "she has looked forward to this day."

Ciabhan nodded, "then take her; a day beyond these walls will do her good."

Alain would do as requested; and the prospect of seeing Mistress Leonora again made his stomach leap, though probably her husband would be at her side.

Alain set his young page to polishing metal and leather until they shone, he chose his clothing for the day with care, Blue velvet was favourite for special occasions, French blue contrasted well with black cape and cap, a white ostrich feather complimented all; Not too dressy he felt but elegant enough to mark him as a man of worth, a man capable of being entrusted with great responsibility.

On seeing his transformation Mati clapped her hands together in delight, "Tis long since I saw one so handsome Alain, surely I shall be the envy of every maid in Devon." She had been disappointed on being told Ciabhan would not be riding with them, and tried to hide it by laughing nervously, "one handsome escort is quite enough for me thank you Alain."

In the company of two guards and Alains squire, they set out for Boscombe Valle, taking the direct track that curved alongside the high meadows, Alain pointed out landmarks, "there Mati," he said, "do you see the two oaks atop that meadow? That's where Ciabhan and Ivan flew the falcons; do you remember how he would complain about Bella Donna? How he said the bird was of jealous nature? Many were the gashes to his hands, bestowed on his person by 'the she devil' as he called her!"

Mati followed Alains finger, squinting against the glare she could see the oaks and imagined Ciabhan and Ivan side by side with the falcons, sometimes Faye had accompanied them, with Bella Donna perched upon her cuff she had always looked so lovely, no wonder men loved her! Much to her and Ciabhans amusement Ivan would give the bird a wide berth, and they would laugh together at him, she wiped away a tear and wondered if Alain felt such powerful emotion.

Boscombe Valle was not far but on a track where the sun had baked the mud as hard as rock, beneath the shady overhang deep ruts furrowed the path, Insects hummed amongst the hedgerow and worried the horses, stinging wherever flesh was exposed. Faye had taught Mati how to ride side saddle but today for no reason she chose to ride astride, she bent and plucked a handful of broad leaves, they would be helpful in relieving stings; with spittle she rubbed the leaf on the back of her hand, hoping its medicinal properties would relieve the bites. If she had remembered her riding gloves the discomfort could have been avoided.

Leisurely the little group wound along their way, glimpses of sea glinted in the far distance, until the road narrowed into the shadowy lane that would bring them at last to their destination.

Since passing the high meadows Alain seemed preoccupied, as if lost in thought, occasionally he glanced back to check on her.

****

Sister Domenica had watched Alains party depart, had waved to the excited Mati.

No sooner had they left than another group of riders assembled in the bailey, Four Knights made up the group and she watched as they led their mounts cautiously down the steep path that dropped to the lane below, their sword hilts glinted in the dappled light, as they passed beneath the great oak at the top of the slope. Though his face was half masked and his hair covered by a close fitting helmet there could be no mistaking Ciabhan, and his three companions were vaguely familiar; castle guards seen often about their duty..... But another rider she had not noticed as they gathered and dressed all in black appeared to follow them, staying well behind he seemed more like a shadow, strangely with them but at the same time detached!

Curious she watched until they were gone from view, until undergrowth swallowed the sombre little band; then she turned back to her prayers.

****

Screened by summer's foliage the horsemen cut across the valley. Marshy meadow sucked at hooves but the horses trod cautiously, familiar with the unstable ground, where pasture was hard they pounded confidently but as quietly as possible towards Boscombe Valle.

Even In high summer the valley short cut remained marshy and was little used, even accomplished horsemen were known to struggle with the route, however these experienced riders were unsurpassed in skill, determination, and leadership.

Leonora was surprised on seeing the young Frenchman, especially as she had never expected to see him ever again; her heart beat just a little faster. The great doors into Boscombe Valles Castle were shut, in front of them astride a magnificent chestnut stallion Alain conversed with a portly man dressed in the black robes of a scribe, he seemed not to have noticed her arrival. A little way apart on a palfrey small between two tall guards sat a woman! Leonora tossed her head grandly and quickly loosened the ties at her throat, he must have married!

Alain was attired in a gay blue tunic that was quite the bluest blue she had ever seen, the brightness of the colour seemed somehow inappropriate to this occasion, more suited to a carnival!

As if seeing them for the first time he turned and the white feather in his cap swayed with the movement of his head, Leonora smiled brightly, trying to control the butterflies in her belly, How silly she was, Of course he would accompany the man he loyally served, Ciabhan of Compton Berry; now she really wished she had taken more care with her gown, had not dressed so plainly, especially with another woman present.

As her group advanced towards his a huge wolfhound bounded over, Leonora's timid palfrey shied and she nearly lost control as the horse lurched against the courtyard wall, she struggled with the reins and noticed Alain start towards her, but her Fathers voice stayed him.

"Take control girl tis only a flea bitten hound!" Leon's eyes darted over those gathered in the courtyard, no great committee he noted!

As brash as ever he mocked, "So the dog of Compton Berry is not in attendance; maybe his nerve failed him?"

With the palfrey back under control Leonora hissed, "Do not let your tongue make this day any harder than it already is father!"

"Hard?" he smirked patting the hilt of his sword; "why child this will be easy, do you not see our fancy young friend over there is unarmed?" he nodded at Alain, "Oh the stupity of youth!"

Leonora was not listening for she had recognised the woman; it was Mati, her mother's dearest friend and confidant, not as she had at first thought, Alains wife; her confidence flooded back, "just because you see no sword father does not mean the man is unarmed, it could be that an army is at his back!"

"I think not daughter!" Leon smirked as he ordered her to, "stay where you are!" Commanding Corentyn to guard Leonora, Leon turned his mount towards the motionless advocate, blatantly ignoring Alain.

"I trust the young lady is unhurt Sir?" the advocate asked civilly, "She did well to bring the beast under control, an excellent horsewoman, if I may say!" Leon boastful replied, "Like her father Sir, it would take more than a mangy hound to unseat my daughter; shall we get down to business?"

the advocate cleared his throat and reached into his cloak, so Ciabhan of Compton Berry was right , this brash so called 'Knight' would be difficult

"I have received a letter from Sir Ciabhan detailing the reasons for his absence," said the advocate, "Pray allow me to read his words."

Leon rudely interrupted, "I am not interested in words Sir, I am here to see my daughter claim what is rightfully hers, spare me the lame excuses of a coward! Now just be so kind as to hand over the keys and you can be on your way" Leon smirked over his shoulder as if at an audience, "the roads of Devon are beset by peril after dark!"

The advocate bit his tongue as he withdrew the keys and bent to the small leather chest on his lap, the ignoramus had fewer manners than a donkey, God help his fair daughter.

"For Christ's sake be quick man!" Leon held out his hand, "tis no more than a formality, not the keys to the Vatican!"

Fumbling with the chests lock the advocate glanced at the castle door; still shut he knew what lay behind.

Leonora shifted uncomfortably in the saddle and slyly glanced at Alain who had positioned himself between Leon, the advocate and the door, he didn't return her look, but watched calmly while Leon continued to berate the unfortunate advocate, still trying to explain.

"I really am obliged to read this statement to you sir in the presence of these witnesses" he swept his arm around the assembled group, "I must be allowed to do my legal duty!" the parchment now free of the chest fluttered in his hand. Irritated by such time wasting Leon's patience snapped and he drew his sword, "Gods blood man! Play no more games with me!" he spurred forward and grabbed the reins of the advocates horse and jabbed his sword at the mans neck, "The keys if you please, now!" he demanded, "Or the jugular? The choice is yours!"

Leonora's voice was shrill, "Father please! This is a man of law; let him do his job, for Gods sake! Show some restraint!"

She had half expected some support from the others, but her cry was met with passive indifference; Corentyn alone seemed troubled. Obviously agitated the boys eyes flicked wildly from Leon, back to Alain and the door behind, something was about to happen and he seemed the only one to know! As if stuck fast in tar he was unable to move as the great door flung open.

Leon twisted in the saddle, but Alains sword already pricked his spine, a neat movement from the advocate knocked Leon's sword from his grasp, followed by a sharp blow to his jaw, Leon swayed but stayed upright, his attacker had already backed away; dazed Leon wondered just why had he thought Alain unarmed?

Corentyn had seen the trap unfold but had been powerless to help his master or Leonora, he watched her face suffuse pink as she realised they had been outwitted. In seconds, the whole group so relaxed a moment ago had taken up positions like chessmen on a board, Leon was surrounded.
A hand on her shoulder made Leonora jump, "do not fear child, no one wishes to hurt you!" Mati smiled reassuringly. "Mati, I?" baffled she tried to speak but found her attention turned by further commotion.
The huge door had been flung open and a man hurled through its space, he lay face down in the dirt scrabbling to stand, a tall knight addressed Leon from the doorway, "you are loosing your touch Leon le mercenaire! How unlike you to not see an ambush, hate must be dulling your wits, along with your eyesight!"
Trey grunted like a pig as he tried to stand, in three strides Ciabhan reached him and pushed him again to the floor, grinding his boot into his back, "Behold your friend Leon!"
While Leonora struggled to make sense of what was happening, Leon screamed at the advocate while pointing at Ciabhan, "seize that man, he has broken the terms of his vow, he violates the trust of a fellow knight's last testament, don't just stand there, do your job, take him man!"
When Leon drew breath the advocate spoke, "you alone dishonour a good knight's memory, Leon of Pagonston, will you explain your intention to defraud your own daughter of her inheritance?" he smiled, "the law lords of the land will be most interested."
Shaking herself free of Matis arm Leonora urged her horse to her Fathers side "of what do they speak Father?" she asked, then indicating Trey demanded, "And why is he here?"
She looked around the group of people, "are we not here because of a good mans legacy, has there been a mistake? Tell me father? I will not be disappointed!" Angered by her questions Leon snapped back, "Tis not for a woman to question a man girl, still your tongue!"
Hurt by the young woman's distress Alain jabbed the point of his sword beneath Leon's ribs, "best to tell her man, tell your daughter barely out of mourning who you planned to marry her to!" he nodded to the wheezing Trey. Leon looked away but Treys voice rose, spluttering he pointed accusingly at Leon, "you promised her in marriage, in return for my help in ridding you of ..." A rodent faced man no one had seen scurried to Treys side, "Master?" he gripped Treys arm tightly , "do e' well to remember us were the invited guests of master Leon, if there be a problem it bain't ours, I 's sure the master be able to deal with it!" he squinted craftily at Leon, " come now afore you says somat' you may regret!" Trey moved his ugly head as the skinny man whispered, "Our purpose be better served with a clear head."

"Enough of this!" Ciabhans voice rang clearly, commanding their attention; only the persistent joy of a thrush in full song and Lupos panting refused to stop.

"This man," Ciabhan gestured to the red faced Leon, "has plumbed the depths of dishonesty by attempting to seize for himself the windfall that has fallen by right to his daughter! In the shadow of the dank archway his voice seemed deeper, stunning the restless group into silence.

"to scheme is Leon's way," Ciabhan said above Treys noisy wheezing; he ground his boot even harder, "by promising his daughters hand in marriage to this wretch he knew well that sooner or later her husband would insist she live on his own estate far from Boscombe Valle.... as is a husbands right, Leon of course would have full rein of Boscombe Valle, an arrangement beneficial to only him! I however have no intention of allowing Leon 'le mercenaire' to be my close neighbour!"

Leonora steadying her nervous mount was ashen faced when she confronted her father, "pray tell me this is not true Father, tell me they lie? For I cannot believe you would be so cruel!" her chin trembled as if she would cry and Alain felt pity for her.

By her Fathers squirming in his saddle she guessed Ciabhan of Compton Berry was speaking truth, Leon avoided her accusing eyes, "foolish girl, you know nothing ," he said scornfully, "you've had far too much liberty, made too many mistakes" he looked up defiantly, "I sought only to protect you , give you back some respect!"

His words embarrassed her, with trembling voice she snapped back, "oh, and this is how you seek to protect me is it? With secrecy and deceit! Rather a bizarre way of showing paternal love don't you think Father? Did you really intend to trade me off like a piece of unwanted baggage? Your greed has blinded you to the fact that I am still a married woman!" she held up her hand for all to see the wedding band, "Show me proof he is dead." she spat like a cat protecting her young.

"Oh for sure I know where the rumour of his death comes from now! God's blood father is there no end to your insensitivity? That you put strangers before your own flesh and blood beggars' belief!"

Contemptuously she flounced back to Matis side. Two more guards who'd been waiting out of sight moved towards Leon, Alain dismounted and picked up Leons sword from the ground; for the first time Leon actually looked fearful and held out his hand for the weapon, his eyes begged its return, but Alain shook his head. Leon hawked and spat on the ground, "Ciabhan of Compton Berry, your killers harm me at their peril; our Bishop would not take kindly to seeing one of his own cut down!"

Pushing his mount past the guards he addressed Leonora, "come daughter!" he demanded. She made no attempt to move but sat impassively ignoring him, "come!" he barked, "you have no place here," he raised his hand as if to chastise and Leonora cowered.

With four steps Ciabhan snatched the reins of Leon's horse bringing the beast nearly to its knees, Leon struggled to remain mounted.

"You think too highly of yourself man!" Ciabhan snarled, "You are not worth the wrath of Holy church!"

Dust swirled around the two men, horse foam sprayed Ciabhans head and shoulders as he held on, grit and earth loosed beneath his boots while the horse snorted above him, Leon clawed futilely at Ciabhans hands but could not loosen his enemys grip. Ciabhan charged with fury dragged down ever harder on the harness relishing his superior power, only when convinced Leon was on the verge of yielding did Ciabhan loosen his grip. Only the horses whinnying and Leon's rasping breath could be heard, making sure he was close enough to smell Leon's fear Ciabhan whispered in his ear, "fear not Leon of Pagonston, you'll live! But," and here he paused long enough to savour every second, "I take your daughter! Let's say shall we, that it's for her own; protection?" Leon's mouth opened and closed like a fish gasping for air; humiliated he struggled to retain some dignity, but no words would come

Like a spring Ciabhan opened his palms and released him, Leon hung between saddle and earth, a pathetic spectacle, left dangling behind a screen of debris. Slowly the detritus settled on the fracas, the advocate could no longer suppress a snigger, dishevelled Leon cut a sorry figure but still unable or unwilling to shut his mouth he continued to rant, pointing an accusing finger he croaked, "and you sir, dishonour your profession, your duty is to see the law upheld!" The advocate laughed aloud, "And if you know ought of honour then I am Saint Peter! A full account of what has passed here today will be reported, that is the law, Oh!" he exclaimed waving the parchment at Leon, "the reasons for Sir Ciabhans actions are contained herein; had I been permitted to speak you could have refuted the allegations, however the chance has passed!" Ciabhan, had been examining Leon's sword feeling its weight, and balance, admiring its elaborately studded hilt, then as easily as if it were a child's toy he tossed the weapon to Leon, "a remarkable piece of workmanship Leon" he observed, "the blade just right and honed to perfection, ideal for the kill." Leon caught the weapon in flight and held it triumphantly in both hands poised above Ciabhans head; sunlight flashed along the metal. A muscle twitched in Alains face, the only movement as he held his breath. The two women gasped and Mati clutched her breast,

The thrush stopped in mid song, and for the first time a hidden streams gurgling could be plainly heard.

Suspended in time the moment was as tense as the sword hanging in mid air.

"Go ahead Leon!" Ciabhan growled, daring him to strike...

"Kill me and you will end my torment, let death on speedy wings take me hurry coward! My patience wears thin!" unarmed he faced Leon almost inviting the strike.

Mati buried her head in her hands but Leonora stared, mesmerised, like an ancient Greek tragedy the drama played before her eyes as if for her benefit alone.

Unable to turn away, she should have been willing her father to cut down his sworn enemy while he had the chance; the arrogant Templar had just snatched away her inheritance! But absurdly she trembled for him, in the face of death his bravery awed her, shivers swept the surface of her skin. Detecting movement, she saw a raven bizarrely strut its black body across the battleground, in a blink it had gone!

Her knuckles whitened where the reins stopped her circulation, only her lips mouthed a prayer for his safety. Why must he continue provoking Leon? Was he blind to her fathers' murderous fury? Why did he beg for death? She wanted him to stop; "dear God make him stop please!" she turned to Alain beseeching, but Alain was not God and looked straight ahead, he knew nothing would stop the master of Compton Berry once his mind was made up.

Alain watched the two adversaries like a spring ready to uncoil. Suddenly a flash as the sword sliced downwards, the blades momentum making a strange swishing sound, Mati screamed, Leonora slumped in the saddle, and Alain prepared for the thud of blade on flesh! He knew the blow would be fatal for Ciabhan, his warrior's nerve though was not about to accept his Masters bloody slaughter.

No one present on that hot afternoon would ever remember clearly the next few minutes; on trying to recall what happened it seemed a shroud had been pulled over their collective memory.

Mati opened her eyes just as Trey leap forward, for such a bulky man he was surprisingly light, from being one moment on the floor he was quickly on his feet; as a cat pounces on a mouse he launched himself at Ciabhans back trying to seize his neck as if to throttle, Alain even quicker had lobbed his own weapon towards Ciabhan in a smooth practised movement, sure handed Ciabhan caught the sword twisting to face his new assailant, his back exposed to Leon.

142

But Leon faltered, "Strike man!" Trey screamed, "My fathers' killer! For Christ sakes man what stops thee? Strike!"

Precious seconds passed, Ciabhans blade dented Treys belly, and still he screamed, "Then avenge your own wife coward! Slay the dog."

The words seemed to goad Leon into action, and his sword sliced through the air, downwards to end Ciabhans life!

But instead of ending Ciabhans life the blade cleaved into Treys left shoulder cutting dead his noise and felling him instantly.

Matis noisy wailing revived Leonora, she saw Trey moaning at Ciabhans feet while blood reddened the earth beneath his shoulder and snaked away from his lolling head. Above him like the angel of death loomed her father, in his hand the sword dripped obscenely red.

Like a cornered animal Leon panted, bloodshot eyes flicking over the scene, his assault on Trey was no mistake; Leon had had to think quickly in the tension, hardly time for Trey to learn the truth….. That Leon himself was the killer of Torr.

Given A few seconds more and the Templar and Alain would have restrained Trey; Alain had already been at his masters side.

They would have forced him to admit he had lied, and in front of his daughter and witnesses, this 'tragic accident' gave him the breathing space he needed; he smirked as he leant down over the stricken Trey, "Only madmen leap in front of a drawn blade!"

Ciabhan disgusted smashed his sword into Leon's blade, the blow nearly unseating Leon for the second time, Alain dragged his friend away, "Let the fool be sir! Nothing to be gained from his death". Ciabhan struggled but Alain held fast against the fury convulsing his friend's body.

Leon watched as Trewin frantically tried to staunch the flow of blood from Treys limp body, contemptuously he spat before sneering, "Pathetic fools the pair of them!" Then he turned his venom on Ciabhan, "You have cheated me Ciabhan of Compton Berry," he pointed his sword, "I vow before all the saints I will not rest until I have sent you to the bowels of hell!"

Ciabhan had turned away in disgust from the man he once called friend, he heard only the dull drum of the horse's hooves, thumping the dry ground. Bit by bit dust settled and the song thrush sang, from the hazel trees that bordered the stream his mate replied, their joy clear; even Matis desolate sobbing did not still them. She studied the thin man aiding her whimpering son, lamenting the loss of his young years, their estrangement, and the legacy of hate he had inherited from a bitter and troubled father, he could be dying! She tore at her skirts, dismounted and offered the strips to Trewin, caring not for Ciabhans disgust, but his words cut deep, "He'll live woman; God knows I should finish the fool off!"Mati was befuddled by the goings on, what on earth was her son doing here, and why had he returned ?surely he would have made contact with her, he had lived for a time at Compton Berry, tenderly she held her hand to him, "My son why Boscombe Valle? Did you think there would be no welcome at Compton Berry?"

Bleakly Trewin padded the wound, "looks worse than really tis' lady, don't fret now, nothing you can do 'ere, tis best you go," he nodded to Ciabhans hunched back, "yon Knights patience is nearly done I think!" With difficulty Trey rasped, "I seek the Devil for revenge, not to break bread with him!" Mati saw no affection there, she brushed her fingers across the clammy brow, and with a nod to Trewin stood as one of Ciabhans guards beckoned her. Trewin watched a guard hoist the frail woman her onto the restless mare, he almost felt sorry for her, so sad in the middle of hard faced horsemen; he saw Leon's cold eyed Daughter comfort the older woman as bunched tightly together the riders headed for Compton Berry. Trewin watched them go, he still couldn't imagine what Trey saw in the girl, and from the way she gazed at the Knight Alain she had already made her choice! Trey moaned, his breath coming in agonising bursts, It seemed beyond belief the gentle Mati could have birthed such a brute, and why would Trey think his mother so uncaring, she appeared exactly the opposite; compassionate and tender. Treys shrieks stopped Trewins mind wandering, Leon's sword had sliced clean through quilted leather; shredded skin and blood like sticky treacle oozed from the gash, already Matis strips of skirt were sodden through.

"Shsssh, master" whispered Trewin, "tis' nought." Trey winced, "Liar," he spat, "though I am wounded, take me for no fool!"

Trewin stuffed the rags between skin and tunic, and comforted the stricken man, "you'ms too big and ugly for the devil to be wanting e' now stay tha's moving." Trewin dragged Trey as close to the stream as his strength would allow, he dribbled moisture between Treys bloodied lips doubting his master would survive the night for delirium was upon him, more than water would be needed if Trey was to survive the night. Trewin thought of Treys aunt, the Cornish witch Ida, what he'd give for the ghastly old hag's knowledge of herbal remedies now though. Chill night descended dragging her shroud of indigo, Trewin heaved his patient under spindly hazel, little shield against hostile countryside, in between manic writhing and deadly silence Trey tossed in torment. Trewin never needed prayer, in his eyes he had sinned against none, but this night he prayed to whatever God would listen, he prayed hard to be relieved of his charge, but still he could not creep away, could not abandon the moaning monstrosity that was his companion to the horrors the night would bring.

Chapter 25
Contentment

Leon brooded and planned his revenge, every word of his threat to send the dog of Compton Berry to hell he had meant, sulking he stalked the hall of his manor house like a wounded animal, jumping at the slightest sound. Always within reach was a flagon of cider, his only escape from his failings, and his only comfort.

Corentyn crept about for fear of finding himself on the receiving end of Leon's bad humour; too many blows had found their target recently. The young man with a bright mind and even brighter presence now scuttled like a cockroach in and out of Leon's company before returning to lurk in dark corners, he would take as long as he dare before responding to Leon's yells.

When a flagon smashed he would fill sneakily adding some water, foolishly he believed that by diluting the cider he weakened also his master's temper.

On the Bishops next return his first petitioner was Leon; they strolled in the privacy of the palace grounds, stopping beneath the chamber Leon used when the Bishop was expected.

Short of breath as usual the lardy Bishop paid scant attention between his noisy wheezes as Leon droned on and on with some personal complaint! Draping his robes around his corpulence the Bishop listened as if Leon were a wearisome child. "Leon, my good man this is a matter between yourself and the Templar, I can do nothing to help," studying the bright ruby on his middle finger, he rubbed irritably at the puffy skin risen on either side of the gem, "you of all people should remember the 'fallen' Templar still retains connections in high places," the very highest!"

The Bishops words angered Leon, Gods blood! How could he ever forget? Did not Ciabhans demand for an annulment of Faye's marriage prove the dogs favour! He simmered. The Bishop continued, "For many Sir Ciabhan of Compton Berry remains a champion, the perfect Knight!"

Leon's neck infused red as the pulse in his temple throbbed beneath darkened skin, the thought of his rival as hero almost made him convulse with rage.

"More a thieving dog!" he snapped back, "in league with the County advocate who has himself blatantly disregarded the law, no hero my Lord! But a defrauder! I call on you to see the law upheld."

The Bishops stomach growled reminding him that lunchtime had long passed, now hungry and tired he wished this bothersome brigand would cease whining, but by God he was persistent.

Exasperated the bishop hauled his bulk to a seat and motioned Leon to sit, "Listen my son, there is still a limit to my power! Within Holy Church I have some voice, but outside of those confines I cannot be seen to interfere or favour, I must tread a precarious path of diplomacy, and discretion."

Leon interrupted, "Gods bones man! You are not some piddling minion, but the chosen, the Bishop! Every one listens when you speak,"

His voice faltered as he pleaded, "I beseech you my Lord, just condemn his actions, that should be enough, he cannot be above the law of the land?"

It was time for the Bishop to be firm, "cast your memory back Leon, when all were condemning you it was I who raised you to respectful office, correct me do if I am wrong but wasn't that bending the rules somewhat? Given your troubles at the time?"

True the suspicion surrounding Leon had made the Bishops choice controversial, a brave few voiced their disapproval, but went unheard.

"I picked you in spite of those who questioned my choice, and believe me there were many!"

Leon insisted, even touched the Bishops sleeve, "Just this once? Even the Blackheart would have to take notice of a man of God!"

Exasperated now the Bishop was firm, "You are not listening my son, not even this once can I help you against a Templar...fallen or otherwise! For believe me he follows his own path, you and I are insignificant in comparison, I am as an ant beneath his feet if he so chooses!"

Leaning closer the Bishop whispered behind his podgy hand as if disclosing some great secret, "Tis common knowledge the king has his ear and would be inclined to take the Templars side against the clergy! King Henry makes no secret of his disregard for the Church." Shivering the Bishop pulled his scarlet cloak tighter, "not for you or God above would I cross either man! Now let that be an end to the matter!"

He held out his hand to Leon, "help me up man."

Leon believed the Bishops help would had been forthcoming, he had not considered rejection, stomping alongside the Bishop he attempted to continue the conversation, but the Bishop raised a finger to his lips and shook his head warningly, his watery eyes blank, no longer interested.

At dinner that evening the Bishop cunningly observed to Bertram, "It seems our church warden wearies somewhat of his duties Sir; think you it time to consider another less volatile?"

Bertram nodded.

Bertram nodded, Leon was far too rough around the edges for the refined Parisian and besides he himself was weary of the intrigue that went with being advisor and guardian. True Leon had been ideal for the less pleasant duties, but now he had become an irritant with his intrigues, and his obsession with the lord of Compton Berry was beyond wearisome. Bertram however was planning changes of his own, he pined for his homely wife and family, and longed to retire to the lush countryside of his French estate, he dreamed of living out his days peacefully, of hopefully never setting eyes on the scheming Bishop again.

Achieving his desire was proving far from easy, he sighed long, "and what would you have me do?"

The Bishop regarded Bertram, "find the advocate in question, get letters and reasons for his deviation from duty, apparently there was a letter from the Master of Compton Berry explaining his actions, Leon swears the content of the letter was denied him; personally I would be inclined to believe the former! An advocate is bound by duty, they do not flout the law of the land lightly or without good reason, I am aware also that the deceased lord of Boscombe Valle and The Templar were good friends, Ciabhan of Compton Berry is no fool!"

With a belch the Bishop reached for more beef and popped it into his mouth, "and besides I am curious to know just how the Templar kept Leon from his door!"

"Consider it done," said Bertram, turning away from the Bishops rancid breath, "I will leave for Exeter in the morning."

Leon disgusted by the Bishops inability to assist him began to put his own plans into place; if justice were denied him then he would take the law into his own hands and bend it! Revenge might take time but when ready it would be sweet.

Using his mercenary's skills he scoured the dens frequented by ruffians, and felons, there he found no shortage of cold-blooded souls willing to give their services in return for a few groats from a rich fool.

Eventually he gathered a diverse group of malcontents, fuelled by liqueur and disregard for any but themselves they rode roughshod over the inhabitants of Pagonston; a band of marauders, paid to do Leon's bidding, his adversaries became their own perceived enemy.

No one crossed Leon and went unpunished, No useless Bishop, no Templar dog and no dead old fool who by misguided benevolence had caused this whole sorry charade, Leon would have what he wanted.

147

After returning to Compton Berry both Mati and Leonora remained shaken, Mati stayed inside her room nursed by Domenica, and Leonora in Matis absence clung to Alain, the only familiar figure in her altered state. Finally a visit from Ciabhan coaxed Mati back into the sunshine, but sadness sat upon her normally sprightly self, and for the first time she leant heavily on his arm.

It was hard enough for Leonora to accept being at Compton Berry, once the place she thought of with hate, but now her shelter; so grasping she was now Mistress of Boscombe Valle was almost impossible.

Only Ciabhans patience and the Advocates explanations finally helped her to accept that in her own right and just as Sir Ralf had desired she was the beneficiary through her Mother of the estate of Boscombe Valle, Her Fathers rage or the memories of the dreadful day could not change the fact.

Time and time again they had to describe how it was because of the guilt the old man carried for his son Halberts actions towards Leonora's Mother Faye, sometimes Leonora buried her head in her hands, unable to absorb everything, Alain at her side offered words of reassurance.

From now on, Ciabhan said, Leonora would be under his personal protection, and as the chatelaine of Boscombe Valle she must begin to enjoy the benefits her position afforded, without threat or fear from any. Alain volunteered his services as defender of her person, Ciabhan winked at Mati as he gave consent.

Later as he walked her to her room he bent and whispered, "a romance Mati? Could our gallant Alain have found his hearts desire at last?" Mati smiled back, "destiny again my Lord."

From that moment nothing stopped cupid's mischief, arrows flighted with passion and tipped with desire lodged with exquisite pain firmly through the hearts of Leonora of Pagonston and Alain Rousseau, first Squire, then comrade and now confidant and friend of Ciabhan of Compton Berry,

A love that fate had planned from their very first meeting!

Chapter 26
A Marriage

Tranquil in its sheltered valley Compton Berry emerged unscathed from winter's fury, and as the first cuckoos called from the reed beds Alain and Leonora pledged their troths before the altar in the little chapel above Compton Berrys echoing gate; commissioned by Ciabhan a soft mural had been painted in the corner of the chapel to commemorate their day, and dancing flames from numerous candles illuminated its delicate colours. A priest from the Church of Saint Mary in Totnes Town officiated and in keeping with the couples request the ceremony was kept deliberately simple. Ciabhan stood proudly at Alains right-hand as his friend swore everlasting love to the beauty beside him.

Most of the guests gathered that day in the Chapel cherished their own bittersweet memories of another marriage here so many years before, only Mati sniffled through the exchanges, unable to stifle her sobs, even when Ciabhans back stiffened; she was unable to control her emotions. Plainly for all to see above the neck of his tunic a green and yellow kerchief peeped, Faye's colours, and as surely as night followed day Mati knew that secreted somewhere upon his person would be the remnant of a bloodstained belt. She wiped filmy eyes and tried to focus on the white banner with the blood red cross draped above the altar, still bright the banner was a reminder of Ciabhans own sacrifice. Horrified she noticed moths had feasted on the cloth, that holes dotted the corners, through water clogged eyes she determined to patch the fraying cotton.

When the ceremony was done and the married pair stepped out into the sunshine Matis eyes dried, Ciabhan helped her from the chapel, only unforgiving sunlight on blotchy cheeks as she emerged from its shadows gave a clue to her inner turmoil, but she managed a gay laugh as a young prankster emptied rose petals over her and Ciabhan.

 She greeted everyone affectionately, and then let Sister Domenica guide her to a seat nearby the laden trestles; there she would see all that went on. Age was beginning to take its toll of the devoted and sweet Mati, stiffening limbs made walking an ordeal and fingers once so nimble were gnarled into shapes she barely recognised. Only Sister Domenicas patience as she rubbed and massaged the stiffness away allowed Mati to sew at all, combined with failing eyesight repairing the banner would be a labour of love! Though still voiceless Domenica fussed over Matis comfort and draped a woollen shawl over her shoulders, she brushed the hair from her eyes, tucking most beneath her white cap Domenica made sure a few fair wisps remained to frame her face, just as Mati liked it.....

Then placing herself at Matis side Domenica settled quietly, content to sit and watch she took Matis hand lovingly in her own and held it tight, her face radiant.

Mati felt sorry for the girl but right now was selfishly grateful she did not have to speak, idle chatter bored her of late.

Pipes, timbrels and birdsong vied to be heard as the bright lime leaves of May quivered, chilly the little breeze nipped at bare ankles and raised goose bumps on the breasts of Ladies and rosy maids alike in their summer fineries; silks rippled and garlands bobbed as the gusts flapped bunting and banners.

Mati half watched, half dreamed through heavy lidded eyes, graciously she nodded when accepting respects from guests and occasionally she admonished unruly infants who trampled too close to toes throbbing at the end of puffy ankles, and she remembered, oh how she remembered another day, another wedding, and two equally beautiful lovers! So long ago, everything so long ago now....she closed her eyes seeing all so plainly...........was there nothing more than 'so long ago?'

Mummers capered and minstrels played all the well known ballads in their repertoire, with a face fit to bursting a tiny jester clad in red and yellow hose and tunic scampered among the assembly overwhelming the timid with his antics while reducing others to gales of laughter, snotty nosed babes clung to mothers as they gazed from wide eyes, awed at the monkey like fool.

Mati drifted, slowly the trees and sound and excitement seemed farther and farther away......oh but she still saw Leonora like a star, luminous in the middle of the celebrations, unmindful of the confusion around her she shone, the lovely maiden, Alains bride. With every turn of her body the fine sendal gown shimmered with seed pearls, their little lights dancing upon her honeyed skin, skin as golden and smooth as Devon honey.

Alains arm curled about her waist proclaimed his pride in his young wife, Mati watched her lean forward and smile at the man at his side...a fleeting shy smile as if she'd seen him for the very first time, and was afraid of being over familiar.......

Had it been a trick of the light? But in the time it takes for a leaf to cover the suns light Leonora seemed to become the living image of her Mother, it was as if life once more filled the beautiful body of Faye, life was giving her back. Mati started, making Domenica jump with fright! Concerned she checked the staring trancelike woman. Mati's blood raced through her veins as she realised she had been dozing on the verge of dreaming, do not torture yourself so you silly old fool! She scolded herself silently; let the lovers have their day. She patted Domenicas arm soothingly, "fear not child, tis a dream only!"

She tried but her mind would not be stilled, how could Ciabhan live with such a likeness, a constant reminder of Faye, was he so blind? From where did he draw his strength? Her weary eyes remained mesmerized by the three oblivious individuals, it seemed life in scenes performed around them, Mati rubbed at her eyes as if she could eliminate the image, but the reflections from the past were too powerful.

Mati knew what was to come as she stared unblinking at the trio; about to replay itself was an unforgettable incident that took place so long ago, now it toyed cruelly with her emotions. Spellbound she watched the scene unfold, the gesture of chivalry she had seen before in the courtyard of the Sandstone Manor in Pagonston, an action so guiltless yet so intense Matis breath caught in her throat and Domenica thought she had choked!

Contorted with pain her mouth opened and closed, like a grotesque actors mask.......just as he had bent to take Faye's hand in his on that long ago day breaking Matis heart as he did so ...now Leonora's hand lay in his dark weathered one like the most delicate porcelain; tenderly he raised the fingers to his mouth. Mati knew excitement quickened Leonora's blood, she saw the rush of pink, the second his lips made contact with the back of her hand, a full blush chased the first colouring pink cheeks almost russet.

Mati blinked hard and rubbed again at her eyes, this time when she looked Faye had gone! In her place stood Leonora, a simple bride being complimented by her husband's best man, nothing out of the ordinary! The day was just playing tricks, Mati turned away..........

A sudden bright spark made her turn back, she looked at what she thought she had seen, and the sunlight must be playing games surely? But no! There it was again, an unmistakable flash of green! Mati had seen it just as Leonora let fall her hand after the kiss, after his beard had brushed her skin!

Displayed on the middle finger of her right hand glittered the emerald, Faye's emerald ... .that magnificent jewel given to Faye as timeless proof of his love.

Ciabhan must have made a wedding gift of it to Alains bride, without telling her; Mati felt as if a thousand shards of the splintered emerald had impaled her heart to her very being, she never expected to see the ring anywhere but upon his own finger for ever more, now it adorned the finger of Fayes Daughter. Matis heart was heavy; not from jealousy for she knew he loved her not..........

Handsome in green velvet Alain gazed with undisguised pride at his bride, passion almost tangible emanated from his person, even from this distance Mati felt like an intruder Ciabhan must have felt the same for he took his leave and left the lovers to themselves......

She became aware of a raucous cawing, and her gaze wandered from the lovely couple to where it fell on a familiar visitor of late.

With a flap of its great wings the Raven hopped onto a bendy sapling, bunching its feathers the jet black eyes observed her, turning its head this way and that intelligently seeming to observe her, sunlight filtering down through the leaves pricked at the plumage highlighting its sleek lustre. "Oh tis you again is it!" Mati whispered, as if addressing a familiar friend, and then very quietly.... "if only it really were you!"

Spreading its wings to balance the Raven rested on its little branch warming itself in the meagre sun and watching her.

Then as suddenly as it had arrived the bird cawed once and launched itself into the air, the draught from its wings whispered across her face; thick foliage veiled its flight upwards and out of sight.

Mati knew instinctively that she had been visited, the Ravens departure from her side left her lonely, she liked its company.

Much later in the solitude of the chilly bed chamber she went over the day's experiences and her dark friend.

Jumbled memories past and present filled her aching head until she thought sleep would never come, when it did she welcomed the plunge into sleeps abyss, just before that welcome fall she jolted awake again trembling....at the bottom of the pit in the darkness waited the bird, its vicious beak a weapon on which to be impaled, if its visit had been an Omen! Did it come to warn her, or to offer comfort?

The Raven had shown a total lack of fear, almost human it had watched her knowing she would never harm it, like another 'Raven' in the past she recalled, another Raven fearless and mysterious, human and very much a part of life at Compton Berry, Ivan!

Paralysed by fear she was not brave enough to fetch the wolf skin, it would have to stay in the chest, she tugged her feet snugly beneath folds of night gown, the coverlet tight to her chin, and then hands clasped together beneath the thin cover she prayed especially hard for God to forgive such fanciful ideas

An unexpected late ground frost powdered the castle paths during the early hours, it shivered Matis cold body and caused her steady breath to come in puffs of white moisture; but whether from nightmare terrors or utter fatigue she slept almost the sleep of a baby.

Outside huddled close to her window the Raven plumped its feathers and closed the all seeing black eyes.................

152

Alain and Leonora like Mati were long abed having made their exit at the appropriate time, Ciabhan stayed on after the feasting drinking and making polite talk with guests still able to converse until over indulgence swirled his brain, "rather too much wine I suspect," he chuckled as his cup missed the table top and bounced noisily off the flagstone floor.
His drinking partner a fat Brother from Buck fast nodded sleepily, a dribble of red wine staining his flabby jowls, "Bacchus never fails us in his mischief my son," He mumbled, "but we are above that!"
 Ciabhan staggered to his feet, slapped the brothers back, "as you say Sir, as you say!" then made his way unsteadily through the great hall, outside the night air made him catch his breath it was so crisp, and his boots crunched the frosty grass. On the way to his bed chamber he passed through the deserted Chapel the scent of flowers still lingered, he picked a lily from the floor, amongst wilting spring garlands it lay, waxy head crumpled, the yellow stamen broken; he considered the arum funereal but Faye had loved their stately beauty, it seemed her daughter favoured them too. Still light headed he remembered his observations; sinking to his knees before the altar where a few hours ago Alain and Leonora had taken their vows he crossed himself, and gave thanks for the day. From the Chapel an archway led into a narrow passageway, Ciabhans chamber was situated at the end of the passageway, up a flight of stone steps. Ivan's bed chamber had led down to the left, beneath the Chapel.
 For a second Ciabhan hesitated and half turned as if to go down, a moment's lucidity in his wildly pounding head made him grasp that wine was doing the enticing, tempting him to do something he would regret! Could it be that priests indeed spoke the truth in preaching that over indulgence was the devils instrument?
 He swayed on, his hands feeling along the passage wall, there was no guard tonight in his alcove; Ciabhan missed the first step and cracked his knee on the stone step, he laughed outright, a grown man on al fours! He must look absurd, how Mati would scold if she were to see him stumbling so over familiar ground. She must have retired early; he couldn't remember her leaving the feasting. A new young Paige waited; water to wash and linen cloths ready, when his master appeared slurring his words and knocking into furniture the boy trembled. "Just the water lad," Ciabhan slurred. The boy passed a tankard to his master, Ciabhan downed the liquid and tossed the tankard across the Room, the boy stood open mouthed as Ciabhan collapsed fully clothed on the bed, his legs over the edge, "The boots Lad," he ordered, "take the boots." The page crouched for an hour in the corner of the room clutching water and cloth, when sure his master slept the boy slunk off to his hard pallet beyond the chamber door; Ciabhans snoring continued well into mid morning......................

By the time he joined Mati high on the ramparts, the newly weds were departing, their new home the castle of Boscombe vale awaited; hopefully the enthusiasm of its new young tenants would exorcise its wicked reputation.

Mati looked sideways at Ciabhan and suppressed a smile, a hasty lick of the sponge could not disguise the night's ravages, he wore the same clothes as the night before but had flung an embroidered chamber robe across his shoulders and his feet were slipped into a pair of garish Turkish slippers, she blushed at sight of his bare legs.

"Titter if you must woman!" he said, without making eye contact.

"My Lord," she countered, "I thought for one moment that our Turkish friends had returned!" she teased, but in truth she thought him more handsome than ever.

He looked down at his slipper clad feet and grimaced, "a gaudy gift are they not? I learned quickly not to compliment Hassan's choice of garb!" he laughed. They waved at the little group winding its way up the steep path, appearing then disappearing between the trees; until the flashes of colour were lost to sight, "well may they be happy, they are a perfect match! Alain is a changed man!" He clamped his hands across his eyes, "Gods blood! I've the devil of a head." Without sympathy Mati replied, "I don't have an antidote for over indulgence my Lord! And besides you've let Domenica go, she knew best how to deal with these things!" he scowled back at her, "Alains wife needs young company , and have you not noticed Mati how at ease they are with each other, its strange, almost as if they have met before!...maybe their friendship will speed our young sisters recovery!"

In the cold infirmary Mati sought out and prepared the special herbs for head pain, before touching the pestle and mortar she rubbed her hands to start the circulation in her fingers. She would really Miss Sister Domenica, the girl had a natural ability to heal, she and Mati had worked well together, but it had been agreed that she was better off with the young ones; her herbal knowledge would be of use to them.

Still mute Domenica had remained so since the day she arrived at Compton Berry.

Mati had noticed and considered it as she pottered in what had once been Faye's dispensary, she remembered well the enthusiasm with which Faye and Ivan had put it together, many of the recipes on jars and pots were written in Fayes hand and still legible, her style and flourish unmistakable. Over a marble table a simple oak crucifix hung on the wall where Ivan had mounted it, Mati never failed to polish it or cross herself in front of it.

Chapter 27
Beginning again

In the covered wagon behind waxed leather curtains sister Domenica, travelled, away from prying eyes, beside her a wolfhound puppy curled panting, one of a surprise litter of four fathered by weary old Lupo the castle hound; Ciabhan kept back the only dog of the litter for himself, one of the bitches he gave to Domenica , as thanks for caring for the pups so seriously; 'for her devotion, the bitch would repay her with faithfulness ' he had said. Domenica named the puppy 'Lupina' after her Sire. Noisily Lupina slurped on Domenicas fingers, snaffling at the titbits she fed into its soft mouth.

Leonora poked her head through the curtains, from the musty interior two pairs of luminous eyes greeted her and Domenica smiled a thin smile from behind the puppy's silky fur; Lupina whined.

"Not long now Mimi, our new home is almost in sight," Leonora tickled Lupinas head, "and you my sweet will have the run of the place, such a playground!" She extricated herself from the curtains and untangled her hair; today she had chosen two combs to keep the unruly strands tidy, she took one out tucked more hair into the sharp little teeth and repositioned it, she had done this a hundred times already, a sign of nervousness, though she never realised it. Fashioned from a creamy substance and inlaid with red glass beads the combs glittered in the sunlight, she wore them in honour of Alain from whom they had been a gift in the early days of their courtship; embarrassingly she recalled laughing when told the slides were fashioned from the bones of a giant animal. To Alains chagrin her and Mati laughed outright when he added that these bones stuck out of the animals' cheeks! And nearly reached the ground, Alain called the substance ivoire, and said the 'glass' were red gem stones from the east; much valued and sought after.

From behind, Alain observed every movement his wife made, watched as she adjusted her hair yet again and noted with pleasure the combs. Riding to her side he said, "Let's pray Domenicas speech may return once settled, according to Mati there has been some effort to communicate of late, whatever happened to her was so shocking that her voice just shut down, if she is happy with you my sweet maybe time will bring it back." Leonora tossed her head, patting a few stray hairs back into place she said, "it was you my Lord who gave her sanctuary at Compton Berry, it seems right that she stays close, and I am more than content to have her with us, I understand though Sir Ciabhan was far from happy when asked to take her under his wing?" her eyes clouded, "Would he really have turned his back on her?"

Alain shook his head, "I see Mati has been speaking to you!"
"No husband, not just Mati," Leonora replied, "Sir Ciabhan himself
spoke with frankness on occasions, especially when alone."
Alain took her hand and squeezed it, "Ciabhan has a generous spirit, he
can be reticent and morose but he has his reasons, I knew he would
relent! He is more compassionate than he would like us to believe!"
Leonora lifted her head to the glory through which they rode; once again
a glossy lock escaped the combs claws, May with its promise of new life
felt just like her marriage. A growth spurt had filled the hedgerows,
Primroses and snowy Milk Maids vied for space next to unfurling Devils
in the Pulpit, humble little violets perished beneath trampling hooves,
their beauty short lived. Shadows dappled the pathways, moving
constantly as the party brushed new lime and yellow leaves, Leonora felt
almost fit to burst with pleasure, a pleasure she could never have
imagined. On her finger the emerald glittered, set in gold the stone was
oval, cut in the shape of a leaf, stunning it glowed next to her honey
coloured skin and absorbed springs green. Mesmerised by its depths she
easily imagined darker shapes moving in its centre, memories of the past.
Without foul means or murder, the gem her Father had coveted so
obsessively, constantly insisting it was hers by right, in the end had come
as a gift, a humble and generous gesture from her Mothers' husband,
Alain saw her examining the ring, and smiled, "enjoy it my love, did you
think he would let it grace just any hand? It was destined ever to be yours,
daughter of Faye." His words suddenly made her think of the Monkey
man prophecy, 'Knights and love!' two Knights had bought her thus far,
could he have really seen into the future? Anxious she looked at Alain, he
was all she wanted; she shuddered unable to contemplate life without
him. Alain felt her tense and kissed her fingers to reassure, gently he
pushed her forward as the path narrowed, he loved the way Leonora
relaxed her shoulders when riding, moving languidly from the waist , and
admired her firm muscles when she pulled on the reins; she handled a
horse as competently as any man.
With pleasure he remembered last nights ardour, how hesitant, almost
timid she had been to begin with, then passion spent he watched as
moonlight fell and rose on the dips and crevasses of her nakedness; how
it bathed those spent shoulders in silver blue light, he would selfishly
have watched her all night but for the chambers chill.
A comb worked loose, he smiled at her impatience, as she pushed it back
one handedly. Leonora's strong will did not daunt Alain rather it was a
challenge, another facet of her nature and he loved her for it, if she
remained as strong of will as she was in her passion he would indeed be a

fortunate man, already his belly ached for her, the night could not come soon enough! He had found a mate who matched his passion exactly. Once free of the confined pathway Boscombe Valle appeared at last, Leonora brushed the irritating hair from her face yet again and smiled broadly at Alain, her white teeth gleamed; with barely concealed excitement she reached for her husbands hand, "I have been thinking husband, it would seem I have misjudged Sir Ciabhan, the months spent under his roof have changed my opinion, he and mother were never the immoral or scheming pair I had been led to believe." Surprised Alain asked, "And what pray bought you to that conclusion?"

For a while she gazed at the beautiful castle in front of her as if absorbing its essence, then she said, "Often enough you have said that fate maps our paths, I believe you right, that which is predestined can never be changed by mortal intervention, who would ever have thought of us two being in love? It must be divine planning for I almost feel as if I am treading in my Mothers footsteps!"

Alain lifted her down, "fanciful words my sweet, but who knows? Come, it is you and I from now on!"

A welcome awaited their arrival, verderers, servants, and a small garrison led by a grizzled Knight lined up to meet the new Mistress of Boscombe Valle and her husband.

Leaving the lane behind they rode into the Castle that held so many sad memories, Leonora barely recognised the entrance, so much had been changed. She marvelled at the wide open space, in front of the gatehouse, so different from the last time when she cowered in fear, watching with Mati as her sons blood soaked into the gravelled path. A stone wall now surrounded the, containing it and screening trees had been planted behind the wall, beyond the central Keep, gardens and stone walls stretched, all neatly laid out.

Leonora saw espalier apple and pear trees against the walls, a rose garden, herb borders and even an ornamental pond. Alain had certainly been busy, he had promised to create a palace for her and she adored him for it! "Husband this is beautiful, a dream!" like an excited chid she peered around. The style of building was not unlike Compton Berry, built from the same local limestone; however the façade appeared less forbidding, a fortified manor house rather than a castle, for all its dark past she knew she would love it here. Alain dismissed the watchers and followed his wife, he clutched her arm as excited as she was, "come let me show you our chamber." She giggled as he held her close.

Built around a small inner courtyard, when the gate was closed the house was as efficiently protected as a castle.

"This way my sweet," he said and led her up a flight of steps cut into the thick walls, the climb made her breathless, the steps curved upwards into a short corridor, glassless apertures let in light from the inner courtyard. One more small flight of steps and they reached a large oak door, Alain pushed it inwards to reveal a large chamber built two stories above the gate, six large windows on either side of the room were set with coloured panes, three of the windows looked over the inner courtyard and three faced the front courtyard, and beyond eastwards to rising hills, like Compton Berry the house sat in a valley, though she couldn't see the sea she knew it to lie just over the hills.

Crossing from one side of the sunlit room to the other she was fascinated that in a few steps she could see everything, "I will miss nothing now my love!" she said playfully. Alain laughed and caught her hand, "I'm sure you won't, but this is only the antechamber, come the next chamber is ours alone! Hidden behind a tapestry was another smaller door, Alain tugged the hangings aside, but before entering he placed his hands across her eyes and guided her through, keeping her body close to his.

When he at last he uncovered her eyes, she gasped, "Sweet heaven! what an exquisite room!" she gazed around the bedchamber, a smaller version of the ante chamber she had just passed through, two large windows faced east , unlike the other room these were not stained but were covered for privacy by tapestry hangings; embroidered so cleverly that the light filtered through even though closed, "and this is ours?" She exclaimed. Alain nodded. The room felt of light and airiness, everything seemed touched by gold, when she moved nearer she saw why, golden thread woven throughout the tapestries twinkled with the suns rays, gilding everything in the room.

Dumbstruck she peeped in the huge canopied bed in the middle of the room, she ran her fingers across the bed cover, exotic birds with little mirrored eyes and flowers in vibrant colours adorned its surface fascinated she looked quizzically at Alain. "Silk from the East my love, all worked in such a way as to deflect the light," he said, " here look," he pointed out the tiny mirrors worked into the embroidery, "its these which give the light sparkles see," he swished the bed drapes and lights danced around the walls of the room. "Like woodland sprites on a summer's day!" she laughed. Two huge matching cushions were propped at the bed head, regally two turquoise peacocks gazed from them with mirrored eyes. "I know how much you love light; I planned it as a sanctuary for us, a place of peace, of harmony, a place for love!" He looked at her for approval. His thoughtfulness delighted her but she was lost for words even saddened for she could not believe she was worthy of such excess. Alain leant against the wall happy to watch the woman he loved.

As she wandered the chamber wondering at all the beauty she realised the men in her life had actually pampered her; as a child both parents made sure Leonora and her siblings had every thing they needed, for Leons favourite child that spoiling had made her a little imperious; unaware of it herself, it was a facet of her personality Alain had noticed immediately. When married to Edmund though not wealthy he had indulged her when first married, his hard work bought them a modest home with some social credibility.

During her sojourn at Compton Berry even Sir Ciabhan, whom she treated with caution had insisted his young house guest make use of the best chamber in the castle, once her mothers. She remembered Mati showing her round, how she thought it odd that Sir Ciabhan had remained pacing outside the chamber. For the first few nights she felt strange and sleeping had been uneasy, Alain convinced her to stay there. "Like the emerald Leonora," he had said wisely, "accept it, it is an honour that he would give only to you that you should sleep where once Faye had laid her head. Sensibly she took Alains advice and in time grew to love the room, even the occasional perfume of rose and the sense of her mothers' presence, in fact when the time came to part she left it with reluctance.

A sudden shiver in the warm chamber raised goose bumps on her flesh when she recalled the moment she thanked Sir Ciabhan, she declared it an honour and embraced him, she wasn't quite sure why she felt so embarrassed but she flushed at the memory even now........

Alain bought her back to the present, "well wife, tell me is it to your taste?"
She whirled around to face him, "Husband I am speechless, I am lost for words! I can't believe........."
He interrupted her, "You Leonora lost for words? Praise God a miracle! Then you hate it?" In frustration she raised her hands against his chest, "don't tease so, of course I love it husband!"
Sweeping her into his arms he lifted her feet from the floor, kissing each ear lobe in turn he reminded her of their newly wed passion, recalling wickedly her abandonment. She squealed with embarrassment when he whispered how her desire had known no bounds; swinging her round he hinted at the coming night, how he would once again free her from the fetters of restraint, as well as her clothes! Looking into the green eyes his desire stirred, he felt it now as she pressed her body against his, "you are my heaven on earth wife", he nuzzled her throat, and she whimpered like a captured animal, her arms tightening about him.

Passion enveloped him as he hardened against her skirts, and his hot young blood surged through his veins, hoisting her legs about his waist he carried her to the bed, his hot hands upon the skin of her thighs, the bare flesh just above her fine hose, he felt her grip tighten, and her kisses moisten, he fumbled with the hose and the laces of her bodice as she tried to wriggle free of her gown, felt her eagerness grow, heard her curse the restriction of her gown, thought she might tear it off in her impatience! "And I am the luckiest woman alive," she gasped hoarsely. Slowly enough to heighten her pleasure but with a sense of his own need he peeled down her silky gown until it rustled free of her already spreading thighs, laces , sleeves and petticoats were unceremoniously cast aside until the light streaming through the tapestries bathed the creamy nakedness of Madame Rousseau.

"God in Heaven", she panted, "husband....Take me now!"

The colours of the chamber danced on abandoned flesh as she clung to Alains body matching his thrusting with her own, clawing him to her. Skilfully he caressed his wife's body his fingers probing the hidden delights he knew she craved, she moaned rhythmically broken only by little sobs of pleasure.

Alain ensured that her pleasure lasted as long as she demanded, like a mare in full heat she rode his plunging stallion, tossing her head from side to side as she begged to be filled with new life...his life! "Fill me husband," she rasped as he shuddered to climax, "you are my life forever, fill me up Alain, my love ...fill me to overflowing with new life!"

The Light had faded and the colours by day so bright had dulled, a pale moon peeped through the tapestries.

Alain watched his wife sleeping, oblivious she slept the sleep of the exhausted, her shoulders and breasts uncovered; he ran his tongue along her shoulder and kissed her rosy nipples.

His lips were dry but her body was moist, she smelled of him, no lingering perfume but the smell of animal passion.

She stirred and murmured, he stroked the tousled hair from her forehead........

Quietly he splashed his face with rosewater, and fastened a cloak about his nakedness, then unlocking the door he made his way down to check on the night guard.

Domenica slumbering in the main chamber looked up at him blearily, before closing her eyes again, Lupina bounded to her feet; Alain bent to stroke the puppy, "Your Mistress sleeps," he whispered, "quiet now!"

Chapter 28
Love

Kate Truscott some time after the event delighted in informing Leon of his daughters' marriage and revelled in his discomfort, Leon tried hard to feign disinterest but Kate knew him too well.

"Quite the lady now! Your lovely Leonora," she crowed, on meeting him one afternoon in the narrows behind 'The Coaching House' "A knight for a husband, mistress and chatelaine of a manor, wealth undreamed of and probably with Alain Rousseau's child by now….such a charming and handsome man, quite a catch!" she smiled while turning the knife and just for good measure added, "And under the protection of the Master of Compton Berry no less, it would seem your Daughter at least knows how to forgive!"

Leon scowled, purposely he had avoided the front of the inn but fate had decided to cross his path with hers today he had just left his Church quarters when she wobbled into view, a pail in each hand. God she had some flesh about her now, hard to imagine she had ever been desirable! He hoped the pails contained nothing worse than milk, on last meeting she had thrown foul kitchen slops across his path.

"Mistress, you tell me nothing I do not know already! Pray move aside, so much flesh is disconcerting!"

Kate ignored the insult and stood her ground.

"Hooked herself a Knight your fair maid eh? Just like her Mother, they say history has a way of repeating itself!" Leon felt his blood rise at mention of Faye , but he would not be goaded, he had no inclination to argue, "You will not provoke me woman, good day." He brushed past her ample bosoms; his guess was right she had come from the dairy, the smell of rancid milk hung to her."And if you be going back to the manor, "tell that no good lodger of yours that 'e be not welcome in 'ere no more! Givin' my respectable inn a bad name, 'e an' that rabble of 'is, always an odd un' was Trey!" Leon could have struck the bitch, she had managed to hit a sore point with mention of Trey, for her words were true, he knew too well he must do something soon about the cuckoo in his nest. Trey had far outstayed his welcome. It was Corentyn who had first used the word, making Leon laugh, but 'cuckoo' had stuck. Leon had grown tired of the embarrassing Trey, and angry with himself for taking him on, God knows why he'd promised his daughters hand in marriage, a moment's lack of judgement that he bitterly regretted now. Finding the wounded Trey on his doorstep had disconcerted Leon, how the hell he came to be there was a mystery, appeals for witnesses or the misguided Samaritan who placed him for Leon to find fell on deaf

ears! A mischief maker no doubt, someone aware that Treys presence would make life difficult for Leon, if only he had finished the fool off at Boscombe Valle, instead of wounding him his present problems would have been avoided, Leon had even lied telling Trey he returned later and searched for him in vain, "ask the boy ," he had said pointing to Corentyn , "he knows the truth, there was no sign of you or Trewin.
Corentyn agreed with his master, whether it was right or wrong was not his to question.

Head down and preoccupied Leon walked back to the manor, the cocky swagger gone, and he skulked in the back streets for fear of a woman's tongue! what was it coming to when Leon of Pagons Ton behaved so? He wasn't sure who disgusted him more, himself or the cuckoo!
He mulled over ways he could rid himself of his unwanted guest, so deep in thought that he barely noticed when a herd of squealing pigs nearly ran into him on their way to the orchard, neither did he hear the drover mumble something about, " be 'e ready for these young'uns in thys orchard squire?' he was way past Well Street before he remembered the sows he had ordered!
Suddenly a way out hit him like a lightening strike, an idea. Mistress Truscott who hated him so had just handed him an escape route, a plan began to form, taking root it grew in his devious mind.
Leon himself had only just heard of Leonora's marriage so it would certainly be news to Trey, and he was gullible enough to believe anything the 'superior' Leon said, hence his belief in the marriage.
A plan soon formed in Leon's conniving mind, He would feign surprise and belated rage, enter the house in frenzy, threaten and curse for Christendom! Once realising he had been thwarted Trey would disappear back to Cornwall, to lick his wounds and never be seen this side of the Tamar again; hopefully! If Leon's histrionics should fail then murder might yet be the only option. Leon would need to call on all his acting skills, Trey not the brightest of men should be easy to convince.
In the walled garden Leon spotted Corentyn scattering seed beneath the dovecote, doves fluttered above his head. Leon hid behind the wall thinking to confide his plan to the boy, then decided against it; better he acted alone.
In silence the manor dreamed in its hollow; wood smoke twitched Leon's nostrils, threadlike the bitter vapours curved up and away over thatch, into still air. Adjoining the pig pens were stables, two stalls were empty but Treys mount a friendly old stallion kept for guests because of his placid nature nudged gently at the door latch, his tongue scraping metal

162

against metal made a soft chinking bell like sound, Trey was bound to be nearby; still keeping hidden Leon peeped around the corner, beneath the pear tree hunched over a wooden block Trey was sharpening a dagger blade, he fretted and cursed; since the accident his right arm was virtually useless and he struggled to use his left.

First aware of the commotion was Corentyn; he shot a glance at Trey but didn't bother to speak, Treys morose nature irritated him almost beyond endurance, instead he let the pail drop from his hands and ran to the side gate, only to be confronted by a cursing and spitting mad Leon, he leapt aside as his master crashed through the gate kicking at anything in his path. En masse Doves rose in a flurry of snowy feathers, unseen dogs barked, in turn setting off the ever present gulls.

Almost knocking Corentyn from his feet Leon staggered through the yard, Trey stared slack mouthed at the madman before getting to his feet, for a second Leon thought the fool wouldn't bother! For good measure Leon struck the wall, bloodying his fist before flinging himself past Trey and through the doorway.

"Betrayed, betrayed! A father betrayed my own flesh and blood!" Dramatically he staggered along the cobbles and into the screen gallery falling nearly headlong into the day chamber.

When Corentyn reached him Leon was standing hands spread on the table as if for support, wheezing noisily while spittle ran down his stubbly chin, Corentyn dragged a chair beneath his backside for fear he would collapse. "Master what in Gods name?"

"Talk not to me of God boy, there is no God, No God I tell you!" He paused for effect, Trey lumbered in. "Betrayed! I am a man betrayed by, by my daughter!" he gasped. From lowered lids he saw Treys expression change.

"My promise to you dear boy, our plans, all destroyed by a wilful girl!" Trey stared baffled at the madman in front of him.

"Don't look so puzzled man!" Leon wheezed, "Wedded! That's what the girl has gone and done, got herself wedded!"

"Wedded?" Trey queried. The strange eyes looked shiftily from side to side. "Yes wedded, wedded to, to that, that!" he could barely bring himself to say Alains name, nearly choking he spat the word, "Frenchman, Compton Berry's minion!"

Corentyn smirked from the doorway, so Leon's sparky daughter had got her own back! He felt a sudden admiration for Leon's spirited girl, "One of your own then Master!" he sniped. Leon lashed out, but Corentyn was faster, and Leon missed his target, "one day boy, one day I'm warning you, you'll push me too far!" he growled. Trey hadn't moved, his bulk and still blocked the doorway, "married you say? A husband but? She can't be wed; you said she would agree to our pact!"

"Yes, yes, I know all that but the fact is she's gone and got herself well and truly wedded, and bedded!" Leon snapped spitefully.

Trey looked unconvinced, "an who says er's married?"

Exasperated Leon replied, "Mistress Truscott, that's who!"

Trey cleared his throat and spat, "That sour bitch knows only how to stir up a hornets nest, then watches while fools get stung, 'ers playing with you man!" so the fool doubted him did he? "I know my Daughter Sir," he said, "when her minds made up nothing will stop her, tis typical of Leonora to do such a thing! The same thing happened with the milksop! Too much like her Mother she is, hardly good wife material eh?" He added slyly.

Trey growled, "If tis true then you'm to blame, she should 'ave been reined her instead of making a fool of 'e man! No Father lets female spawn marry where they likes!"

Leon's hackles went up, "And you'd know all about fatherhood! Wouldn't you!" Leon snarled, better you accept it's over man, for t'would seem my wayward daughter has made her choice; rightly or wrongly she is the Frenchman's responsibility now, tis out of my hands!"

Treys peculiar yellow eyes narrowed, too late he realised the promises made by Leon were all lies, marriage to Leonora a hollow promise, too late he realised Leon the schemer would have sworn his very soul to the devil to get what he wanted! For Trey a promise was a promise, Leonora had been her Fathers lure to ensure Trey's loyalty, until he was ready to strike at Ciabhan, now it seemed Leon wanted to change his mind! well the not so clever mercenary had picked the wrong man to double cross this time, Trey would teach him a lesson even if it meant sacrificing Leonora.....she had fled Trey once, she would not do so a second time! And As for her virtue, any she once had was now vanished in the French mans hands, for Trey she was as any cheap harlot!

"it was to kill Ciabhan of Compton Berry that you came to Pagonston in the first place, "Leon snarled, "the dog still lives, so do what you came to do and waste no more time on the whims of a foolish girl, you can return to Cornwall, I must live with the shame!"

Like a miasma tension thickened the air, Leon tried gentle persuasion, "Surely my friend it would be best to return to Cornwall, that way you would not loose face, besides its getting difficult for you to stay much longer, for it has come to my attention that you keep bad company here, townsfolk are whispering that your behaviour is troubling," here Leon tried to sound concerned, " I don't want to see you harmed, however there is a limit to my powers of protection; my standing here depends only on

164

the whim of our Bishop, for your own safety I advise you to leave!" Leon rubbed his chin, and held his hand towards Trey, " but as a gesture of goodwill when the time comes I will still help you get even with your Fathers killer?"

Trey sneered and knocked Leon's hand away, "Don't take me for a fool Leon of Pagonston, an' talk not of my Fathers murderer, I am more than able to deal with 'e." he towered over Leon and fixed him with bitter eyes, " you 'as used me Leon of Pagonston and now want to back out of our bargain....well that be treachery in my eyes, an' I'll not wear it!"

Leon bristled, had he not supported the ungrateful wretch, how dare he talk so, by God he should strike him and been done with it, "boy!" he roared, "I owe you nothing, sometimes plans change...that's the way of it, for such insolence as you show me a lesser man would run you through, forget bargains, just think yourself lucky."

Leon was uneasy, in truth he hated Leonora's errant ways and this deception but he wished no real harm on her, True he was Frustrated at not seizing Boscombe Valle, and yes the desire for revenge on hated Ciabhan burned within him still, But Treys reaction had shaken him, his vicious streak could seriously put Leonora in danger.

Leon wanted rid of him now, how he cursed the faceless Samaritan who thought to dump the barely alive Trey on his doorstep, one day he find the culprit!

"You don' frighten I, little man," he spat at Leon's feet, "I'll be gone by daybreak!" then he turned on his heels and stomped from the room; Leon sniffed, rank body odour tainted the air, Trey Not only resembled a beast of the field but smelled like one too.

He shouted for Corentyn, "hot water boy and plenty of it," he demanded, "The devil how my skin crawls!"

Leonora's whimsies drove the patient Alain nearly to distraction! He indulged her every desire, she in return glowed with youthful health, competing with him for stamina. Gently she would chide, "Pregnancy is no illness husband, here let me help carry that kindling!"

Alain rarely left the confines of Boscombe Valle; his duties at Compton Berry having been discharged with his new role as husband, besides times were peaceful, now he rode or hunted with Ciabhan for pleasure, he still flew falcons and had started a personal quest to find a bird to out fly Bella Donna, still the fastest of the small falcons, and still as vicious as ever! Leonora wanted for nothing, the softest wool from Buckfast, best quality linens and the brightest silken threads, she delighted in her husbands' attention and consideration. Patient and intelligent and immune to self pity Alain was protective in a way no one had ever been to her, she would watch him sleep after passion and listen to his soft snores, she would cradle the unborn child somersaulting in her womb, convinced it was a boy she already named him for his Father.

Tied to the house because her belly made riding uncomfortable Leonora explored, to her delight she discovered an old mulberry tree in a neglected corner of the garden, in the shadow of an ancient barn it bowed under ripening fruit, it must have been loved once though for creaking stakes supported its sagging branches, others had snapped beneath the weight leaving branches to sweep the ground, she kept it to herself like a secret, in moments of solitude she would seek out the magic space beneath its boughs and sit quietly reading romantic verse; she would imagine Alain searching for her and never thinking to look beneath there. She had on occasions seen Ciabhan arrive when he called on Alain, he would take the short cut through the deer pens, she would watch him through the whispering branches, he never saw her or knew she was there. Closing her eyes she felt thousands of years old, as old in spirit as the mulberry tree; here would be the first place she would show her child. With Domenica she gathered herbs for the cooking pots from the kitchen borders, armfuls of sweet grasses, leaves and flowers were hung in the cool creamery to dry. A strong bond had developed between the young women but Domenica remained silent, exclamations only came from her lips. Leonora had tried to tempt the girl with quill and parchment hoping she may be able to communicate by letters, but nothing, either she couldn't write or wouldn't. Occasionally Mati when the weather was warm would ride over from Compton Berry to join them in embroidery, the airy chamber above the gate would ring with their laughter as Mati gossiped; new garments and embroidered linen piled up, Alain declared his child had more clothes than all the babes in Totnes and Pagons ton.

Once in a while Mati would stay the night to watch over Leonora but it was clear she fretted when away too long from Compton Berry and from Ciabhan.

As micklemass approached days shortened, starry nights dazzled the watcher but chilled with dawn's arrival, leaving Septembers damp to mist the panes of the warm bedchamber, little circles of grease dotted clear panes where fingers had rubbed the glass in order to check the weather. Apples reddened on the trees, absorbing every ounce of goodness from a weakening sun, this years harvest appeared good, dotting the fields from dawn to sundown workers prayed for rain to hold off.

Leonora was ignorant of childbirth, village crones mumbled of travail, of dire consequences, And it frightened her, "tis nought to be feared of maid," they would cackle, "Death takes only them what's too old for bearing! Wombs that be past it!" Mati alone spoke words of comfort and truth, "don't listen to them sweeting," she soothed, "sure it do hurt, it hurts like nothing on earth an' you will curse your man, be sure you will, but when you holds that little thing in your arms, the pain, the anguish just goes, now don't worry your sweet head over they old witches, I shall be with e', that's a promise."

In the confines of Boscombe Valle Leonora impatient for the birth grew restless, fine days were spent outside, as much as her belly allowed she joined in gathering nature's bounty, searching out Fat field mushrooms in sheep pastures she cut with care, and never tore them from the ground. Baskets of dark finned fungi were consumed daily, In great flat-bottomed pans they sizzled and spat, black liquid running into chunks of fat pork, weathered labourers packed into the hall and ate greedily.

Hedgerows heavy with Septembers blackberries came under attack from housemaids with babes strapped to their backs, and children at their knees. Oblivious to nettle and stinging insect's child and adult alike plucked the dark fruit from thorny brambles, sucking at blackened fingers; purple pinafores next day fluttered in lines of brilliant white. Stacked in the cool creamery, baskets of berries leaked little blobs of purple over floors from kitchen to store. Jam and apple pie making seemed never ending and the sweet smell of syrup lingered in the sultry air, attracting stinging wasps. Idly watching Mati prepares flour and butter Leonora swatted them. The scene filled her with memories of years ago when she and her Mother would gather first the apples from the orchard in Pagonston and then the blackberries; together they would work in the kitchen preparing autumn delights, such a golden childhood.

"A lucky time to give birth, Christmas!" said Mati up to her elbows in flour, "Blessed the man who like our Lord is birthed at Christmas, t'will be the best gift of all to your husband sweeting."

Leonora giggled, "I do believe he wishes to be born now Mati, he kicks so much!"

Mati shushed her, "Nay child," she said, "tis quiet they go before birth, tis then they fattens an rests up!"

Leonora determined to go to the Michelmas pie fayre in Pagonston, Alain not so inclined gave in reluctantly, with kisses his wife promised it could be her last treat before the birth. He did insist on accompanying them.

So it was that Alain Rousseau found himself the guardian of three excitable women who squealed with pleasure at the sights and sounds of a town celebrating Michelmas, at times he feared young Domenica would swoon with the sheer excitement of it all.

They partook of lunch at Kate Truscott's in the shadow of the Parish Church; they dined on succulent goose and roasted potatoes followed by apple dumplings, all washed down with sweet cider, when fit to burst Leonora sighed, "Husband I am sure you will need two wagons to take me home in!" He laughed, "Then you have only yourself to blame madam! How does your English saying go, eyes bigger than the belly!" Her lovely green eyes studied him, "Some belly!" she giggled patting her stomach to the amusement of her friends.

"Oh tis lovely to see e' again me bird!" said Kate, "you looks so well, an yon husband proper andsome,' ere' lets see what you be avin." Heaving herself from the chair she rummaged for a sewing needle, threading a length of cotton through the eye she held it above Leonora's belly while Mati and Domenica looked unblinking at the needle; despite all their concentration it neither moved from left to right.

Alain tutted in exasperation, "Old wives rubbish! I've some business to attend to, be here before none, I do not wish to return in the dark!" no one spoke as he strode through the door, Kate thought him a little edgy, could it be he had no wish to see Leon? It was possible Leon would be at the bishop's side, he was after in residence.

"My lord worries for my wellbeing," replied Leonora reading Kate's mind, he thinks me fragile of mind, and seeks to protect me but I am strong, just like my mother!" Kate smiled, how very like her mother she was, "strong indeed child, and like your mother far too beautiful, your 'usband knows well the dangers such beauty faces! He be quite right to guard you so, indeed you be blessed to hold Alain Rousseau's heart,"

When lunch had settled, the four women strolled, linking arms with Kate Leonora chattered, she talked of the future her and Alain planned, "I hope for many children," she whispered, "lots of sons for Alain and one daughter at least for me , to name her for my mother."

Kate and Mati exchanged a wry smile, wary guardians of the past both.

The emerald on Leonora's finger glittered so that Kate couldn't help admiring it, "Your Mothers emerald sweeting? Tis rightly yours now, funny when you think how much Leon coveted it!"

"The ring he forced me go to Compton Berry for? Ironic is it not that had I not gone I would never have met Alain, Now I have the ring and a husband, thanks to my Father!" she smiled smugly, "serves him right, he has no one but himself to blame," Kate nodded in agreement.

"Sir Ciabhan himself told me how he gave my Mother this ring as a token of his love on the eve of their wedding, " her eyes misted, "sadly she wore it for such a short time, I let him know I am proud to wear it for her."

Kate stole a glance at her lovely companion, more cynical than loves young passion walking beside her, and without love in her own life Kate had little time for affairs of the heart.

"A generous gift indeed my sweet from a man once so hated, by your father and by yourself if my memory serves well!"

Leonora's expression became pensive, "but I know the whole story now, from his own lips I heard how on the eve of their wedding after presenting my mother with this ring he flung the original into the forest, this is its replacement. After searching long for an emerald, a craftsman cut it to resemble a leaf, see how the facets follow the form of an oak leaf," she raised her hand for Kate to see, " he really loved my mother Kate, it is a story to break your heart!"

"It broke a lot of hearts sweeting!" Kate said sullenly, turning to check on Mati and Domenica. They had stopped to admire the wares of a trinket seller, "Kate I admit I have changed my opinion of Sir Ciabhan, he has been most considerate to me, though he told my Father I was hostage, in truth I was treated as a queen, no malice was directed at me even though my Father had sworn to see him in hell!"

Matis voice joined in, "she is right Kate, "Sir Ciabhan is much maligned by those who know him not, rather he is worthy of the highest regard." Kate's reply was waspish, "Well you of all people should know Mati! seeing as you chose to join his seclusion," She winked at Leonora before adding, "Methinks you jump to his defence a little too hastily Mistress!" Mati reddened as Kate blithely continued, "why if we didn't know better I might even believe you enamoured of our guiltless hero!" she smirked heedless of Matis embarrassment, and just shrugged her shoulders at Leonora's tutting, "It's only joking of course," she threw the words over her shoulder. Kate needed no convincing of Ciabhan of Compton Berry's magnetism, he was the most handsome man she had ever set eyes on, Leon in his youth had been appealing but he paled into insignificance next to Ciabhan; woman would have to be blind to not notice such looks.

169

However she also thought the Lord of Compton Berry proud and ruthless, for her dear friend Faye his attraction had also proved deadly, she dabbed at a tear.

The four women pushed past crowds gathered around painted stalls, they covered their ears as traders shouted their wares loudly , and shyly lowered their eyes when minstrels became over familiar with the love songs and verses. They walked as far as the street of the fishers, greeted Emma Mackey and her son, and turned back gaily to return the same route, strong armed and outspoken Kate protected Leonora and Domenica from over zealous admirers as Mati tutted in the background.

Stopping only to purchase some pepper and pungent yellow spices they sneezed and laughed their way back towards the tavern.

In the church lane that ran past the Bishops Tower and the Parish church; they giggled like girls at a slobbering drunkard as his wife berated and humiliated him.

Masons worked still on the unfinished red stone Church, monotonously they chipped away adding ever more flourishes to the impressive building, "I should think God hisself must be getting impatient! Time that's taking! " Kate quipped; making them all laugh again, their mood was jovial.

Leon stepping from the Bishops garden saw the women approach, unable to avoid them he offered polite greetings, behind him Corentyn jangled keys as he struggled with the gate locks. Leon bowed deeply, "well met ladies, pleasant goes your day I hope?" Seeing their unsmiling faces he teased, "Fear not! For it would seem I am outnumbered!" Kate sneered at such brashness and made to push pass.

"Why the hurry good dame, I offer no threat," he said courteously stepping back and opening his arms to show he was unarmed. "I trust you are enjoying the fayre?" he smiled as his eyes fixed on Leonora, "I am obliged to you all for my daughter appears well chaperoned. " he singled Mati out, " and Mati, how long since our paths last crossed!"

Mati had no wish to be reminded of the terrible day, "In circumstances I would prefer to forget!" she sniffed, "pray now let us pass, we have no time for dilly dallying." Flourishing his cap he bowed exaggeratedly letting them pass, then quick as lightening he stepped in front of Leonora, blocking her way, "Well daughter is there something you wish to tell me?" his eyes dropped to her belly. Leonora shook her head nothing at all father, you can see my happy state of health for yourself, and gossip will have informed you of my marriage." Leon scraped at his chin, "Ah yes, my invite never reached! Tell me why Monsieur Rousseau lacked the courage to ask me for your hand? As is correct!"

Her eyes glittered green like the ring on her finger and anger rose in her throat, frostily she replied, "Pray tell Sir why he should speak to a man full of machinations? Besides the only consent he needed was mine!"
Leon examined his gnarled hands, pulling the fingers until the joints cracked, sighing he said, "don't try those clever words on me girl, widow you say? But Still no corpse, no proof of your husbands actual death."
Leonora frowned, "It is your mind that is addled Father, or does cider make you forget? you yourself bought news of Edmunds death to me? How sure you were of it then! think you I would remarry if not free to do so? Since when did a widow need her fathers' permission to remarry?"
Leon shuffled, while Corentyn rattled impatiently at the stubborn bolt; he saw Domenica looking at him, she coloured bright pink and turned away.
"And forget not," Leonora continued, "that you would have wed me to the brute Trey! You are despicable! Now let me pass for I have nothing more to say to you! My husband waits." Leon followed her glance, then nodded at her belly, "I see Rousseau has more stamina than the 'milksop!" he stood aside, "one more thing Daughter ," he said as she swept past, " The dog of Compton Berry may yet be proven wrong, Justices have been appointed by the Bishop to look at the papers!"
Alain hurrying to Leonora's side acknowledged her Fathers presence with a curt nod of his head, "It grows tardy wife, you have not been kept against your will I trust?" he put a protecting arm round her waist, but his eyes accused Leon. A loud clatter broke the tension all eyes turned to Corentyn, he scrabbled to pick up the dropped keys.
"Damn you boy, tis' only a simple task, must you make such a meal of it?" Leon grumbled.
Leonora leaned heavily into her husbands arm as he guided her away, her friends gasped with disbelief as Leon snarled, "be sure to let me know when my grandson makes his appearance!"
His thick accent seemed more pronounced than ever.

Chapter 29
A Birth

In the early hours of the first Friday in December after a long travail Leonora was safely delivered not of a son but a tiny daughter, the girl possessed a fighting spirit and clung tenaciously to life; according to the crone who passed for midwife, 'T'was being a maid what saved er.'
Mati through long day and fearful night never left Leonora's side, with reassuring words she comforted and encouraged while Domenica prayed for the child's survival as if her life depended on it, if Leonora should loose hers then Domenica would pray for death herself.
Alain shooed from the birthing chamber left his wife's side reluctantly, 'no place for a man!' he'd been told. Through endless hours he paced the freezing corridors and halls, though fires roared in every grate they offered no comfort at all! His blood coursed like ice through throbbing veins, shadows, leaping flames and weak moonlight his only companions as Leonora's cries echoed from the birth chamber and pierced his insides, by God! Facing the infidel had been less nerve-racking; helpless he gnawed his nails nearly to the quick. Domenica searched for him in the freezing chapel and side by side they knelt and prayed , he begged God to take the unborn rather than the mother, while in the throes of childbirth his wife prayed for the exact opposite; such is the way of a woman.
By the time Mati came with news a watery light was breaking through the remnants of darkness, insipid it promised another bleak day, Alain huddled in sleep by the embers of a dying fire twitched, while at his feet Domenicas bitch Lupina stretched and yawned. Mati touched his shoulder, "Alain dearest, fear no more, you have a beautiful daughter." Breathlessly she repeated, "A daughter Alain."
"And Leonora?" he stammered, "my wife? Is she...?"
Mati soothed him, "thank the Lord Leonora is young and strong, she fares well Alain, have no fear! Come see for yourself."
Emotion crumpled his features, bowing his strong shoulders in Matis arms he sobbed like a baby.
Their prayers had been answered, with the safe arrival of the babe their fears were forgotten, they knew themselves blessed. Christmas this year at Boscombe Valle would be the happiest ever, all centred on the tiny child slumbering in a carved oak crib, neither was the significance of a Christmas birth lost on either parent, they watched and fussed over the babe believing her the most perfect thing they had ever seen. As December progressed snow threatened and the land shut down, stock piles of food were used sparingly, and livestock bought inside for their own wellbeing and that of their keepers, warmth was all important.

Determined to be first Ciabhan arrived within hours of the news reaching him, on his heels came winters first snowfall, Alain welcomed him at the gate, their breath coming in streams of vapour as they embraced.
Once inside Ciabhan shook the snow from his cloak and removed a fur lined mantle; snow flakes still nestled in his beard as he was shown into Leonora's chamber, melting they ran from his beard and dampened his neck.
As he kissed Leonora's cheek the sudden coldness of his skin made her shiver, unaware it was so cold she asked, "My Lord, is it so chill outside?"
He wiped his chin on a piece of linen, "aye Madam that it is."
Unfamiliar odours cloyed his nostrils, sweet not unpleasant yet strangely sickly; a new scent, the fragrance of motherhood.
Neither men felt confident enough to hold the infant, both it seemed would rather face the infidel bare handed, smiles passed between Leonora and Mati as the two men clucked over the crib like a couple of mother hens, not until told to move and allow the babe some breathing space did they take their leave.
Delighted at Ciabhans visit Alain lead him to the great hall, there they sat together over mugs of mulled wine, and Alain knew how difficult it must feel for his friend in a place synonymous with treachery so he spoke animatedly of his joy at being a father for the first time.
No mention was made of Faye's imprisonment there by the vile Halbert, no word of his murder or Leon's recent meddling, Ciabhan was quite obviously making an effort for his friend and his wife, a real attempt to bury the demons of the past.
"It pleases me greatly that you visit us", said Alain, "We wanted you to be the first."Ciabhan stretched his legs and sighed, "thank you Alain."
Alain studied his friends' features, no longer were the eyes dulled, rather they gleamed and not because of the fire glow, light sparked deep in their brown depths, even his skin though winter paled glowed with health beneath the surface, and he smiled readily, the corners of his eyes crinkling, humour when it came transformed his face to the vital man of old, the man he had once been. Firelight bounced off the goblet, and danced on the gold chain around his neck making little dots jump upon the skin of his throat and neck. Ciabhan replied, "No force on earth would have kept me from welcoming your little Faye."
Alain frowned, "my Lord what name? How could you," Ciabhan looked up eyes twinkling, "but would you have called her by any other name?"
Alain shook his head, "of course not," he replied, "of course not."
Ciabhan stayed one night before returning over frozen meadow to Compton Berry, before leaving he agreed to be little Faye's Godfather.

You do me a great honour my friend," he smiled.

Christmas Eve bought a blizzard, it swept in from the east depositing little hard lumps of snow on already frozen earth, coastal hills bore the brunt of the storm and soon resembled powdered Mountains, dwellings facing the sea were quickly lost to view, covered by sticky snow.

Compton Berry and Boscombe Valle escaped most of the snow, both sitting in sheltered valleys the blizzard passed over their tops, it remained bitingly cold, leafless trees rattled sounding to the superstitious like skeletons.

Only the brave or the idiotic ventured beyond their own walls, churches normally full cleared quickly of their meagre congregation, even priests reluctantly turned out to hear confession.

Ciabhan battened the hatches and made an effort to join in the festivities, resigned to spending days trapped inside, likewise over at Boscombe Valle Alain and his family settled into the warmth of family life, being unable to travel the few miles to Compton Berry would be a disappointment but not the end of the world.

Any form of Travel was at a standstill, nothing moved along blanketed roads, sounds were muffled and eerie, for the truly destitute life was cruel unless lucky enough to be housed by a religious order or taken in to the estates of compassionate Barons.

Such conditions however failed to keep one determined traveller from Boscombe Valles door; rightly he had guessed their defences would be down.

Frustrated he tugged at the bell beneath the archway trying to raise someone; he supposed the guard were used to the constant clanging of the wretched thing in the wind.

Only after what seemed like hours did a curious guard peep from an arrow slit and notice a shape dark against the whiteness, when certain he yelled for assistance, Leon heard him clatter down the steps, he also heard dogs barking and a sword slide from its scabbard.

William shielded his eyes against the whiteness, a line of footprints led to the wall, just visible and battered by the wind a man huddled while one of the Liam hounds pulled at his cloak, the other growled menacingly, "Keep still man!" William shouted, "Or it'll have yer throat out!" Then he beckoned the stranger forward, something about the stranger made William think suddenly of the angel of death, a loner dressed all in black on holy Christmas Eve in these conditions! William shivered and nearly changed his mind, a simple guard he may have been but the paradox of good and evil, black and white was not lost on him.

the two Liam hounds snaffled at his heels as Leon came forward, wiping his eyes and nose on his cloak he slapped his gauntlet glad hands together "Gods blood man methinks it'd be easier to wake the dead!"

William had no reason to be polite to this brigand, "as you might 'ave been had I not heard that bell!"

He remembered that only today Alain had asked the bell be muffled as its constant swinging in the wind wakened the babe! William wished he'd done it for then this unwelcome visitor may well have frozen to death.

"Well man am I to stand here all night? While you gape like a fish? I'm here to see my daughter the Mistress of Boscombe Valle."

The commotion had bought other guards; William sent one to fetch his master, the two men eyed each other, Leon impatient and William suspicious.

Alain looked where the guard pointed and sighed, Leon was the last person he wished to face. "Wouldn't leave master" William wheezed, "I didn't threaten him as such but thought t'was best to keep him so!"

Contemptuously Leon had turned his back to the sword, and stamped impatiently some feet away, beneath his feet snow had been pounded into a square of muddy ice.

"Real persistent e' was Sir, wouldn't take no for an answer, same cocky old Leon! Tho I's surprised e' ad nerve to show 'is face here abouts!"

Before Alain could speak Leon turned, "ahh, at last Monsieur Rousseau," he shouted from across the courtyard, "God knows I thought to meet my end as a bloke of ice on your doorstep, your guard could do with some manners methinks!" he strolled over.

Alain ignored the sarcasm, William scowled coughing into his beard, and his hands tightened on his sword.

"Well I'm here now!" Alain replied, "And as one supposes even the Devil might sleep on Christmas Eve, pray tell what brings you uninvited to my door?"

Leon bristled, "upstart!" he muttered to himself, "My granddaughter Sir! For I believe t'was a girl, not the son you desired, of course news reached me a little late! For this reason I come now, even through these conditions to welcome the child!" Leon extended his arms and opened his cloak to prove he was unarmed.

"One desires women Sir not sons!" Alain countered, "And I have two now that please me greatly!" He instructed William to lead Leon inside, "none are turned away on Christmas Eve, and you are no exception!"

Leon was divested of his sodden cloak and offered a dry mantle for his shoulders, Alain then led him to the hall where a place was found by the fire, servants curious loitered at their tasks.

Laden with food for the morrow the trestles in the hall croaned, food

175

for the morrow lay on silvered platters covered by great lids, the aroma of fresh bread and spicy puddings infused the atmosphere, and the smell of goose drifted from the kitchens. At either end of the hall fires roared , icy down draughts drew flames upwards and threw smoke inwards, over one fire a cauldron swung, and over the other a line of pheasant sizzled and spat over a lad who crouched miserably turning the spit, his discomfort obvious. Alain stopped a passing house maid and insisted the boy be relieved of his duty, "the birds are done, I have no taste for roasted boy as well! Give him bed and extra cover!"

rubbing his sooty eyes the boy touched his forelock, Alain watched him find a place to lie, and nodded as a woollen cover was found; then he turned his attention to Leon .Time Alain noticed had not been kind to his wife's Father, no longer the suave gallant with a quick repartee and nonchalant air, the once affable French mercenary's petulant mouth and shifty eyes made him resemble more a wilful child thwarted by old age! Alain had served with both Leon and Ciabhan and the comparisons between the two men couldn't be more marked, Ciabhan looks had fared much better, even though he had been touched by great sorrow. His proud bearing and inner strength attracted a respect from men that Leon could never hope to match. Leon sipped wine, gradually his complexion matched the liquid, after years of gulping Devon cider his constitution was unaccustomed to the red wine, unusual Alain mused for a Frenchman to prefer cider.

"Well now Leon," Alain asked, "what really brings my reluctant Father in-Law here? I hope it is not to torment us further with your claims?" Calmed by the nectar of Bacchus Leon slipped lower into the high backed chair, "as I said, to greet my granddaughter, should I be allowed to see her." He swilled dark wine around the goblet, peering into its depths, "quite a drinkable wine" he said, "almost as good as an average French!" "It is French! My wife has an aversion to cider!" Alain replied.

Lupina slunk in and spread full length before the hearth, Oblivious to the ferocious heat she gnawed on a mighty bone, tearing the damp tassels of meat and gristle that clung to the knuckle. Finally irritated by her noisy slobbering Alain shoved her away; from a far corner she guarded the foul object, eyeing the two men malevolently.

"My wife remains fragile," Alain said, "travail left her easily distressed, and tis no secret that her resentment of you runs deep! Maybe this is not the best time." Leon regarded Alain over the rim of his goblet, "My daughter will see me Sir, and the child I raised will not turn her father away!" Alain felt nothing for Leon, any personal regard he once had was long gone, Leon had shown his true colours in his cowardly behaviour towards Faye and Ciabhan, but he was still Leonora's Father, and as such

176

would be shown civility. "Christmas is a time for goodwill to all men" said Alain, "and that includes you Leon, I will ask Leonora if she wishes to receive you!" Alain took his leave and headed towards a flight of stone steps, at the bottom he turned back, "but do not be surprised if she does not!"

The wine, the heat and smoke, and the heady scent of pine made Leon's head swim; he replaced his wine on the table, in an attempt to clear his mind he ran hands through his hair and shook his head, he rose and stalked the room waiting, shadows trailed him like some monstrous twin, draughts made the flames in wall sconces dance; best quality beeswax candles burned slowly, inch by inch towards Christmas day.

Soft snores came from the fire boy and servants who slept nearby, dead to the world from sheer exhaustion they would not have stirred if Jesus Christ himself passed by. A sudden movement reminded Leon he was not alone nor totally trusted! a guard standing at the bottom of the stairway raised his lance to shoulder height barring his way, a look of resignation flicked across leons face; maybe this was a mistake.

A current of air, hardly noticeable shivered his skin and flattened flames that moments before danced upwards; a tapestry twitched and Leon steeled himself for treachery, his hand dropped to the empty scabbard. A smell of rose seemed to enter on the draught and as he looked up his daughter appeared, Babe in arms.

She spoke before he could gather his senses, "I guessed it you Father, even before Alain told me your identity, I knew you would come." She held the child towards him, "here welcome your Granddaughter."

Not sure if she meant him to take the babe he hesitated, "here take her," she said haughtily, "she will not bite; surely you recall how to hold an infant? As you may have guessed her name is Faye."

Leon rubbed his sweaty hands on his tunic before taking the precious bundle. "You tremble so Father, surely not the wine? We do not serve cider here!" she motioned for him to sit.

"Be assured your husband has already told me," he glared.

little Faye cooed contentedly wrapped warmly in her swaddling , every so often a bubble formed at her lips, popping as she screwed her perfect features into a yawn, minute fingers curled around Leon's own as she struggled to focus on the stranger holding her.

Leon mesmerised by the tiny infant, took some minutes to find his voice, "she is a beauty daughter, it is right she be honoured by a visit from her grandfather," as an afterthought he added hastily, "of course I wished to see you also." Unconvinced Leonora exclaimed, "Oh did you?" The babe whimpered, softly to begin with, until for lack of attention the whimper became a full blown howl, discomforted Leon looked at his

177

daughter for guidance, "is she unwell child?" he asked.

"No," Leonora replied, but she does need to eat, I'll take her now,"
Leon handed the little bundle back to her mother, nearly as red faced as
her grandfather she continued to yell. A girl Leon took to be his
daughters maid appeared, "Here" said Leonora, "Faye has made her
Grandfathers acquaintance; it seems she already has an opinion about it!"
Leon made a weak joke, "she'll cry for England with those lungs!"
Slowly Faye's cries turned to sobs in Domenicas arms, before she left
with her charge Leonora kissed the tiny forehead, Leon gently stroked
the silken cheek.

Leonora removed her marten trimmed cloak and adjusted the sleeveless
mantle beneath, settling herself comfortably she waited, hoping that
when her father spoke it would be to offer an apology or beg forgiveness,
he reminded her of a man bowed down by his own stupidity. Alain had
said to go gently with him, that hate had no place near their little Faye!
She agreed to abide by his wishes but they were not her sentiments at all.
"I have brought gifts," he finally croaked, from his tunic he produced a
velvet pouch, "This was yours, I kept it for when you would have a
child!"

The silver rattle was without festive trappings, just slipped into the pouch,
Leonora smiled faintly at the ways of men.

"It was given by my father for your own Christening, he had it made for
his first grandchild, you were ever special."

She turned it over in her hands, envisioning her rough soldier father
keeping the heirloom safe for future children, such sentimentality went
against all he stood for now. "Thank you," she whispered, "it is lovely, I
will treasure it as you so obviously have."

"And this," he dropped a smaller pouch into her hand, "is for you".
Surprised she stammered, "I, I, have nothing for you, I didn't."

"Shh," he whispered putting his finger to his lips, "Will you open it
now?" She wished Alain were by her side, this wasn't as she expected,
she had hoped her coolness would send him on his way, not this, not
gifts! She would rather not open it in front of him, scared that emotion
would weaken her but he looked so crestfallen when she shook her head
that she relented, "if you wish. " From the pouch her mother's golden
torque bangle set with a dark piece of amber fell into her lap, of Saxon
design and very old, she recalled playing with it when young, simple yet
stunning she had never seen another like it, running her finger over the
smooth amber she said, "Mothers bracelet, but there is no need of such a
generous gift."Her Father leant forward and took her wrist, "here let me,"
he said, limply she allowed him to slide the bangle around her wrist, he
turned it so the

amber reflected the firelight, "your Mother loved this piece!" Leonora tried to withdraw her hand at mention of her Mother, but he held it fast, "this was my first gift to your mother, a token of love for amber was ever her favourite!" Leonora's mantle slipped from her shoulder, pulling the folds back up she whispered, "Thank you, it is beautiful."

For the first time Leon noticed the glittering emerald, she knew he had seen it and looked at him defiantly.

He couldn't help himself, "I see you do lack jewels, " as the words tumbled out he was angry with himself, he stood slowly wincing as he straightened his knees, "It is late" he said, " I must keep you no longer Daughter, just one thing before I go, will you forgive my past mistakes? I wish to be part of your life, to watch my granddaughter grow, see strong grandsons? I would do anything! Daughter."

"Anything Father? Anything?" she asked.

Just as an excited child anticipates a treat he nodded, "what is it you would have me do?" he murmured.

She did not hesitate, "make your peace with Ciabhan of Compton Berry!" Leon staggered almost falling back into the chair, unable to believe his ears he muttered, "what?"

"You heard Father, make your peace with Ciabhan of Compton Berry." Leon shook his head violently from side to side, "Too much! You ask too much girl, it is impossible!"

Leonora interrupted indifferent to his protestations, "on the sixth day of January Faye will be Christened, you as her Grandfather should be there, that you will be made welcome is forgiveness! The decision is yours, accept my terms, or be denied future grandchildren!"

Leon smarted at her words, "she is to be christened in the chapel at Compton Berry, Ciabhan has agreed to be her Godfather, and we are honoured." Leon's knuckles whitened as he clenched and unclenched his fists, his stance as usual had a touch of the dramatic about it. "But you well know he is my mortal enemy, his presence no honour, rather the greatest insult you could offer!"

"Stop this foolishness Father! He is no enemy! But once your comrade in arms, a victim himself of cruel fate! You and you alone are guilty of cultivating this hate, even relishing it! I no longer want any part of your quest for revenge!" he tried to explain, wanting her to understand, "you know nothing of which you speak child, " Leonora's eyes glittered, "Oh but I do father, I know it time the past was allowed to lie, make your peace with him or remain a pariah! The choice is yours, think on it." Leon spluttered his puerile objections, but Leonora remained strong, "I mean what I say Father, make your peace with Ciabhan or stay away for ever! Now as you said it is late!"

as she took her leave of him she felt a unexpected pang of guilt, "we are prepared for an extra guest," she said gently, " you are welcome to stay, Father, on such a night tis best to be inside."

If he heard he made no effort to reply, she watched him a little longer, hunched over the back of the chair his mouth worked as if he conversed with an invisible companion, she felt it unlikely that her stubborn Father could change what had become his mission in life!

With a sigh she mounted the chilly stone steps to the warm bed chamber and Alains warm embrace.

Compton Berry last enjoyed such merrymaking at the marriage of Alain and Leonora, the chapel still decked with holly and ivy was readied for a Christening, baskets of pine cones exuded fragrance in the heat from many candles, welcome warmth.

Christmas Day had come and gone with the blizzard, only to be replaced by drizzle and mist, but today at last a south westerly chased away the dreary dampness. It fluttered the finery and feathers of the riders as they rode to welcome the Rousseau's. The procession was colourful, a bright distraction against winter's backdrop, any observer would have seen a happy convivial gathering of friends, meeting for a day of celebration.

Avoiding the flamboyant display of some of his companions Ciabhan dressed simply, beneath a spotless white tabard he wore a blue woollen tunic, a heavy grey hooded cloak covered him to his ankles, black riding boots and gauntlets were of the finest leather, and tied casually at his throat was the ever present green and yellow kerchief. Immaculately groomed his skin glowed from a rigorous cleansing and though his hair hung loosely it had benefited from a trim, likewise his beard and moustache, a generous splash of rose cologne completed his morning ablutions. A hint of rose lingered still on his hair as he bent his lips to Leonora's hand, and embraced Alain, indulgently he smiled at Faye asleep in her mothers arms.

Friends and household servants accompanied Ciabhan, Mati mounted on a palfrey that was gentle enough not to jog her worsening joints was well wrapped against the cold, she rode between Father John, Priest of Saint Mary's and the elderly Seneschal of Compton Berry. For Mati movement had become painful and walking could sometimes be excruciating, Ciabhan assured her he noticed no difference in her abilities, but of course he lied! To make life easier for her Maudie and Tom Sutton had been elevated to senior members of the household; they walked beside Mati with their ever growing brood of boisterous lads.

Also present was Master Dawks, landlord of The Seven Stars tavern, remembering his kindness to her Leonora maintained a relationship with him and Freda, beaming with delight he waddled along resplendent in chamois knee breeches, red hose and a heavy fur lined cloak, topping it all and matching exactly his hose, a red velvet cap dangled an ostrich feather large enough to fan the queen of Sheba! Little Freda skipped beside her portly father like a sprite in a world of dreams.

Leonora scanned the group of people accompanying Ciabhan expectantly, but her Father was nowhere to be seen, though unsurprised by his failure to turn up at Boscombe Valle she at least hoped he might have made his peace with Ciabhan, she reached resignedly for Alains hand, he guessed why, he gave her cold fingers a reassuring squeeze, "Tis his loss my sweet, let it not spoil our day, come our guests await!"

Chapter 30
Missed opportunities

Brushed to perfection the glossy coat of Leon's destrier shone with health, since prime Corentyn had been grooming, he'd buffed harness, halter and saddle, and had just placed the finishing touch of a cover baring Leon's insignia upon the beasts back and rump, determined the horse would match Leon for splendour. Leon looked every inch the proud Grandfather, he'd greased his hair slickly into a tidy knot, and Corentyn had shaved his chin and upper lip closely, a tiny knick had dripped red onto the kerchief at his throat, Corentyn had dabbed astringent on the wound, but guessed rightly that Leon would not study his reflection too closely. Leon's fur cloak with the garish red lining lifted in the strong wind, and Corentyns unruly curls blew wildly nearly obscuring his face, together they admired Corentyns work.

"Shh, steady now, whoa there, you've done a good job Boy," Leon said to his squire as he stroked Nero's soft nose and whispered into the sensitive ears; Nero in return studied its master with intelligent eyes, tossed his head and snorted steam into the chilly air.

Leon was for once contented, not only had he made the decision that would change his life but he was lucky to have a life at all!

Too stubborn to accept his daughters' offer of a bed on Christmas Eve he had returned hours later to Pagons Ton through the worse conditions of the winter, by rights he owed his life to Corentyn who had searched in such conditions for his master, through a blizzard that could easily have killed them both, the experience made Leon's decision for him. today was special for he was accepting Leonora's invite to the christening and would hold an olive branch to his old adversary Ciabhan. For days he'd dithered between yes and no, and his demons had been especially hard to confront when he considered them.... first Ciabhan of Compton Berry had stolen his wife, now he honoured Leonora and his Granddaughter, Alain he placed at his right hand and even the wretched emerald gracing Leonora's finger had been a gift from him, everything once held dear by Leon seemed to have fallen to the Templars; Leon knew he must swallow his pride and pushed the thoughts from his mind. Placing his hands on the pommel and his boot into Corentyns cupped hands he was about to hoist himself into the saddle when something startled the destrier and it shied backwards knocking Leon off balance and tipping Corentyn head forwards. Cursing Corentyn was quick on his feet and fought to steady the highly strung animal, puzzled as to why Leon remained motionless on the floor. "Master?" he placed a hand on Leon's shoulder and pulled it away sharply as a dark trickle of blood snaked from beneath Leon's shoulder, Corentyn spun round expecting to see someone or something but the only sound was the thrumming of an arrow as it quivered against the stall door, the flight feathers red.

His mind raced and panic made him sweat profusely, though he could see Leon's wound was not mortal Leon himself was unconscious; relieved Corentyn exhaled and began to breathe again. Skimming the flesh between shoulder and neck, the arrows flight had scraped through jerkin and skin missing the artery in his neck by a miracle, had Nero not bucked Leon would now be dead! This had been a deliberate attempt on his masters' life. Leon groaned, Corentyn shouted for help, two stable lads rushed over, "get him inside quickly!" he ordered. With Leon slumped between them they stumbled into the house."

"Did you see anyone? Anyone at all near the house?" Corentyn asked, "No sir, us bain't seen no one, no one at all!" trembling they laid Leon on a pallet. "Close all shutters and keep watch outside, let me know of anything strange." The boys nodded and scampered away.
"I will need one of you to run an errand!"

So it was on the day Leon would have ended the hatred that existed between him and Ciabhan, fate decreed otherwise, and his Granddaughters christening day was made memorable by his absence. Incapacitated and bleeding heavily Leon instead lay helpless as a babe, the seeming victim of an assassination attempt.

Corentyn cleansed and bound the wound; the bleeding had been severe and ministering to his reluctant patient difficult! Leon stayed still when the pain was great but when consciousness angered him he thrashed like a flounder! Opium alone relaxed him but under its influence he murmured or called his daughter's name, staring wild eyed he had said quite clearly to Corentyn, "Hurry now boy, I don't wish to keep my granddaughter waiting!"

Corentyn just nodded and Leon fell back onto the pillow in a deep and healing sleep.

Some miles away Leonora strove to keep her feelings to herself, once more her father selfishly put his own woes before the happiness of those he professed to love, he was she concluded a selfish boor who could not change! best for all if he remained forever out of their lives.

A sudden commotion outside the chapel as they gathered at the font made Leonora spin round expectedly, but as the squawking of birds subsided, Lupina slunk panting across the doorway and flopped down in a heap, the cur that had dared to venture just a little too near yelped in the distance.

Alain did not miss his wife's look of distress and placed his hand reassuringly on her back, Ciabhans eyes flicked towards the door then returned to the face of the babe in his arms, he smiled as Father John signed a cross on the little forehead.

Few residents of Pagonston were aware that Leon had been wounded, Corentyn sent for only one person, brave Father Loveday had called the same day; never a favourite of Leon some may think foolish rather than brave!

Since the murders of Oxton and his accomplice Watkin the judge Father Loveday kept a wide berth of the Bishops favourite, his duty however was to care, show concern, it mattered not that his flock be villains, murderers or the devils own spawn.

"Now my son," he enquired cautiously, "what mischief maker has caused you such an injury?" he pulled a stool closer, settled himself at Leon's bed side and made a courageous attempt at conversation, "we will see the culprit caught." Leon however was far from agreeable company; he watched the priest through half closed lids, "I fight my own battles Priest and fear no one, not even Satan!" he said, " So you waste your time and mine with hollow words of justice, must I remind you again of your absence in my hour of need!" Father Loveday coloured above his collar, rose and made the sign of the cross over Leon, "Confession my son is good for the soul, I am ever there for you!" he muttered of divine retribution. Leon hissed, his patience exhausted, "Forget not I am still the Bishops chosen guardian! And appointed church warden, with the Bishop on my side why should I need a Priest?" Laughter rang in Father Lovedays ears as he scuttled from Leon's malevolent presence, always the man unnerved him and he breathed a sigh of relief once outside. Corentyn brooded over his master, Leon was not the most likeable of people, Corentyn himself was having second thoughts about loyalty, but neither did Leon deserve to be felled by a coward's arrow in his own yard? Many had crossed Leon's path to their peril, could it be one had dared fight back, were Leon's days numbered? How many Corentyn wondered would mourn his loss? Then he thought of Leonora, how she'd be unaware of her father's plight, she must be told, for it was her Daughters christening Leon had been about to attend, a decision not taken lightly, Leon had confided to Corentyn; but he intended to offer the hand of peace. Leon must have been thinking himself at that moment for all of a sudden and with a great effort he lifted himself and begged a favour; "would you carry a letter to Leonora at Boscombe Valle?" he croaked.

Corentyn at first refused for fear of leaving Leon alone, "the coward who attacked you could still be close, could even return!"

Leon retorted, "Cowards my friends do not hang around, besides how would they know I live still?"

"The priest knows,"Corentyn replied.

"That fool!" Leon mocked, "Scared of his own shadow, and fearful of losing his own skin, he'll stay quiet!"

Leon had written with great care to his Daughter, mindful of offending he wrote the truth, as he handed the parchment to Corentyn he sneered, "lets hope the hot headed young Madam will not tear my effort unread into shreds!" Eventually Corentyn weakened, especially when Leon said, 'surely it was Leonora's right to know her Father had planned to do the right thing for the sake of his grandchild, not his fault that on the very day of the christening a spineless killer tried to cut him down.

Three loyal servants volunteered to guard Leon, on pain of death, the Bishops certain retribution; Corentyn armed them to the teeth.

Corentyn calculated the journey about two leagues, a ride that compared to his Christmas Eve rescue of Leon would be like child's play! Corentyn at Leon's behest took one of his swords; Corentyn prayed he'd have no occasion to use it for he was barely capable. Thrust into his belt the Sicilian stiletto was far more comforting, Leon had taught him well its merits.

The days since Epiphany had seen dreary dampness replaced by hard frosts, ice encrusted twigs rattled eerily in the wind; icicles hung from barns and animal shelters, for any brave enough to venture out travel was treacherous. Odin trod cautiously over slippery ground, wary hooves slipped on the brittle surface of mud turning cart ruts to slush. Far on the western horizon ribbons of blue grazed the white hills of the moors, once in high summer Corentyn had travelled there, fresh breezes had bought relief from lowland humidity, and he wondered how folk fared up there during winter. An over vivid imagination caused him to shiver, he pulled Leon's best wolf skin cloak tighter. Wood smoke billowed from the thatch of a tavern nestling in the cluster of hovels that made up Marldon, here at the crossroads he would take some refreshment before continuing to Boscombe Valle.

A few shadowy figures huddled in front of a roaring fire, mumbling together none took any notice of the new arrival, Corentyn found a settle as far from the smoke as possible, threw off his cloak and waited for the inn keeper to bring his ale.

"Where be heading Sir? Tis snow on the way so they says," he nodded towards the fire, one of the group had made a coarse joke and a laugh went up, Corentyn smiled, his young features handsome in the fire light, a downdraught started the inn keeper coughing, the laughter stopped, replaced instead with a with a barrage of throat clearing; logs sizzled with spit.

Corentyn answered without elaborating, "I'm for Boscombe Valle sir, an errand, I felt a need to break my journey." Time spent with Leon had taught him extreme caution in company with ears! He added, "A familiar ride for me, tis no burden!" The inn keeper smiled, "Master Alain and his Lady be a good sort, they be the best, an' with a little maid now, may God Bless they all Sir!"

The horizon slowly darkened, a solitary star twinkled where pink became purple, the early herald of thousands as short day prepared for evening. Not another soul had passed as through lanes as quiet as the grave Corentyn approached Boscombe Valle, to while away the time he imagined being the only person left on Gods earth, the thought eventually unsettled him and he spurred Odin on. The cold slowly penetrated his clothing, and he bunched low over Odins neck absorbing the beast's warmth, his breath white in the frosty air mingled with that of the horses own.

Boscombe Valle was not far now, much longer and his already drooping eyes would close on welcome sleep, he supposed the Chatelaine would offer refreshment, his belly groaned making him jump. His mind turned to the lovely daughter of Leon, the Father and Daughters fractured relationship, families he knew did not last forever, and relationships could be strained, his own life had changed once he left his behind on the islands of his birth. With his elder brother he had grown up on the islands sleeping off the toe of mainland Cornwall, but young men seek adventure and he left the safety of his family to travel, first to Cornwall, or Cornvall as Leon insisted, and then into Devon, it had not been as he expected but it was better than dying of boredom on those bleak islands! Suddenly behind him hooves thrummed on sodden earth, twigs cracked and the murmur of low voices jolted him upright and out of his reminiscing; riders were headed his way. Wits numbed by boredom returned in a flash, he'd hardly pass for a homeward bound farm hand, best get out of sight. He guided Odin quickly into a gateway and quieted the beast with soothing strokes, his own thumping heart he fought to control as he lay still as a corpse upon Odin, though well trained he hoped Odin would not give its presence away.

Alain heard the bell a familiar sound, the reason he'd hauled the cumbersome piece all the way from Aquitaine so many years ago, a comforting reminder of his homeland. He looked up from his work, William would answer it, and he always did.

In the forge Reynard was shooing Alains favourite horse, a fine boned stallion, jet black and surprisingly soft eyed, Alain to keep himself busy had been helping, besides he enjoyed the company of the farrier Reynard, like himself a native of Aquitaine, and the reason Alain had taken him into his household.

Alain wondered who on earth would call so late on a winters afternoon puzzled he looked at Reynard, "who in Gods name calls at this hour?" he said. Certainly not Ciabhan, he now used the meadow crossing and would have entered through the deer pens, probably some vagabond wanting charity and a bed for the night, he'd leave William to deal with it, he turned back to the work in hand then stopped again, both men had heard raised voices, "could be William needs assistance," Alain said excusing himself.

From the herb garden Leonora waved at him fluttering her hand airily, he waved back, and blew her a kiss; why on earth was she poking around in the garden now, it was far too chilly and the light was fading fast.

From the shelter of the forge Reynard watched his master quicken his step, on days such as these he was glad he worked with a furnaces heat, he put down his tools and smiled, they were such a happy pair, Alain and his pretty wife; Reynard heard voices again, Leonora turned as if she too heard them......

The kitchen garden at Boscombe valle was bedraggled to say the least, even hardy herbs had fared badly, tough little thyme brown and patchy, flattened itself over broken paving stones, and occasional purple heather brightened dull places; even rosemary that sturdiest of plants still looked decidedly bare of its perfumed spikes. Leonora taking a stroll into the darkening kitchen garden was glad of a little fresh air, the constant burning of fires had dusted halls and chamber with soot and downdraughts made nostrils sting and eyes water.

She breathed deeply of the evening air, a blackbird scurried across her path and up into the laurel hedge, there was no sign of the blue plumbago that had flourished there so beautifully last summer, protected from the winds. Leonora made a mental note to protect the early shoots when they returned; she placed a stick of elder in the ground as reminder of what lived there.

Pulling her hood over her hair she heard the castle bell ring but paid little attention to it, William always took care of callers, lifting her head she sniffed the acrid smoke from where Reynard the blacksmith worked in the forge. Alain too was there, he'd been in the forge all afternoon, she saw him leave and rush along the opposite path, red with heat and glistening with sweat. All he wore were short hose and a leather apron, his arms were blackened and ash streaked, he waved and blew her a kiss, even covered in dirt he was handsome, tonight she would be sure to let him know! He hurried on, no sooner had he gone than she noticed Domenica come into the garden, a man staggered beside her, or did they run playfully together? Leonora smiled then frowned and took a step forward, Domenica hated men! What on earth was she doing? Leonora tried to grasp the bizarre scene when the man crumpled to the ground; she clamped her hand across her mouth as a knife dropped from Domenicas hand, dull metal clattered off muddy slabs. Confusion and understanding battered her senses at the same time, and she thought of Faye, God Almighty what was happening? She started running towards Domenica, it was then she recognised the fallen man, the weasel like features unmistakeable and she panicked. Gathering her skirts she dashed towards the house, Domenica cried out, "the babe, the babe! Leonora heard and her mind worked overtime, the nursery was at the top of the house secure, always secure, a nurse at all times close by, oh! God what if the nurse....? Her eyes flew to the chamber window, it was closed, oh God forbid! Domenica tried to follow but tripped and tumbled over the fallen man, Leonora flew onwards, her head near to bursting as the words "the babe, the babe!" filled it, oddly as she sped beneath the archway she wondered when Domenica had began to talk again, why had she not heard her before, and since when had

Domenica taken to carrying a knife on her person? And there was blood, blood on her pinafore.................

Her life as she knew it and every sane thought ended as she crashed into rock; since when had that been there? from the barrel like chest that blocked her flight she smelled the sickly stench of blood, and in her nostrils the stink of foul breath, dazed she slowly raised her eyes to those of Trey, feral, unnatural; viciously he dragged her head up to face what he looked at, winded and gasping for air she stared with disbelief on the vengeance of a madman.

Corentyn had never heard such a sound in all his life, he cowered in fear, he'd witnessed first hand Leon's cruelty and seen men beg for their lives and die in terror, but this? The scream filled his head, like nothing human. He covered his ears to try to blot out the sound, No hare or foxes' howl sounded so, this was no sudden death scream, rather a terrible torment, a lamentation, as if a heart was being torn from a breast!

Since the two riders passed Corentyn had remained hidden, too frightened to move he had dozed, when sticky eyes finally opened the trees and hedges were draped in nights purple and stars flecked the heavens, the moon stayed unseen.

Dread was a heavy companion and he remained motionless until stiffening arms and numbed legs became unbearable, squirming he slowly teased feeling back into the heavy limbs. Hardly daring to breathe he wriggled upright on Odin's back, Odin snorted and gave a little jump as if he also slept, "quiet Boy." Corentyn hushed. Slowly almost too frightened to move Corentyn listened to the night sounds, it seemed he had two choices, return to Leon and be mocked for a coward, or worse a Cornish faery! Or ride on to Boscombe Valle and see for him what had happened. When his eyes were fully adjusted to the dark he slid cautiously from the saddle, patted Odin's nose and slipped the last lump of sugar into its mouth, then he led the animal to the only tree in the field and tied him securely. An owl flushed from its perch scared Odin as it flew overhead and he shied, frozen to the spot Corentyn prepared for discovery, but except for a nearby fox who barked a warning nothing else stirred. Corentyn had learned stealth, used to being invisible he hugged the hedge like a shadow, though every nerve in his body tingled; melting into the darkness, step by furtive step he approached Boscombe Valle. Of what he was fearful he knew not, only that one thing was certain, evil had occurred this night.

189

Chapter 31
A death

Alain hadn't stood a chance, he had practically run onto Treys blade, one massive strike to the stomach clove leather, flesh and vital organs, Alan staggered a few steps before toppling forward onto his knees, bewildered he looked down at the wound and tried to rise, another blow this time to the back of the head from the sword pommel felled him knocking him senseless, a reflex action lifted his head and opened his mouth but no words came.

Breathing in staccato bursts the brutish figure of Trey loomed, filling the stricken Alains vision, his yellow eyes burned with chilling satisfaction and sweat ran down his face in rivulets, moisture dripped from his bulbous chin.

Through a mist Alain saw the prone body of William his sword flung from him, at Treys feet Alains raked the dirt with his fingers vainly scrabbling for the weapon; casually as a cat toys with a mouse Trey nudged it just beyond reach,

"Well my fine French dandy , " you'll 'ave' company where you's goin', that there cursed Father in law o' yours already be where liars an cheats burn!"

A sound stopped Trey, and he darted forward...suprisingly light thought Alain bizarrely... as Leonora ran blinking from beneath the arch into the yard, Alain heard his wife's little yelp of surprise , he heard scuffling on the gravel and moaned, at the same time his wife screamed; a terrible high pitched howl.

Alain in panic thought her dead when the screaming ceased suddenly, rolling onto his side he kept his knees tight to his belly, he knew the wound must stay clamped. His wifes shrieks started afresh, wild choking sobs as if her throat would burst, "Alain, Alain!" she screamed over and over again.

Frantic for Leonora, for a weapon, all will power deserted him,unable to think clearly he drew sticky hands from his belly and tried to rise, blinding red mist engulfed him and his head seemed to explode,

"Leonora!" he gasped once before his life blood gushed from him and darkened the icy gravel.

Trey loosed Leonora, sending her crashing onto her husband's bloody body.....

190

Reynard had turned back to his work but from the corner of his eye he caught a sudden movement, he was stunned to see mistress Leonora gather her skirts and run from the garden he remembered how slim and brown her legs, And how very unladylike her actions!

He saw also the young nun, she appeared to be wrestling with a man, he was fallen at her feet and she was shouting; the usually silent nun was crying out!

Instinctively he grabbed a length of iron bar, wiped his hands on his apron and started forward, quickly breaking into a run, the fallen man lay crumpled and unmoving, blood stained Dominica's white shift, and a knife glinted on the path.

Before she could understand what was happening Reynard grabbed her from behind, put his hand over her mouth and bundled her towards a door, a key clanked against the wall.

Pushing the struggling girl through he locked the door and threw the bolts. Gently he kept his hand over her mouth, like a frightened rabbit her eyes nearly bulged from her head, on recognising him she ceased struggling; "have no fear," he said kindly, "go to your Mistresses chamber, see to the babe and lock the door, wait there till I come for you Do you understand?" she nodded.

Putting his finger to his lips he motioned her to lead the way, through a maze of corridors they hurried until they reached the private rooms, "here," she pointed at the door.

"Remember what I said," he whispered. Her huge grey eyes blinked once as she disappeared into the room, he heard the bolt scrape home, and the whimper of a child.

Reynard could not tell what was happening he knew only that something was desperately wrong, that the household was under attack. He crept towards the sound of voices; they rose and fell on the draught that shivered the tapestries in the deserted building, the main door must be open. The windows of the long gallery were too high for him to see outside, hopping onto a footstool he peered through a misted window pane and was stunned by what he saw; he clung horrified to the sill. Master Alain was motionless on the ground, beside him on her knees Leonora shuddered violently, though her head was on her chest he knew she sobbed.

Pacing back and forth a bow legged man muttered to himself, agitated he kept looking to the side of the house, as if expecting someone or something.

Life for the simple farrier was black or white, the wife of his master was in jeopardy, beside her a monster prowled, Reynard's duty was to save her, his Master would expect nothing less.

But how? He must think of something! a selection of old weapons hung on the wall of the gallery, a long unwieldy pike, two crossed swords that had seen better days and a dented shield, nothing he could handle with confidence and nothing of more use than the iron bar he carried.

Just visible under a settle in the entrance hall his eyes fell on a garden sickle used for cutting the summer grass, a gardener must have left it while taking a break. He could reach it but what then? Strong as an ox with muscled arms the young blacksmith knew that in his hands the simple tool could be a weapon of death!

Hardly daring to breathe he crouched behind the great door squinting through chinks by the door hinges.

The brute in the yard seemed oblivious to danger from the house, Reynard waited until his back was turned then scrambled neatly for the sickle, two paces and the blade was in his grasp, razor sharp he ran his fingers along the curve! Now for the beast.

Leonora attempted to rise, irritated the beast shouted, "Still yourself bitch unless you wish to join 'e there!" he pointed to Alain, he swung the back of his hand across her face and she fell back, almost immediately she sat upright, defiantly. Reynard thought he would strike again, but instead he bellowed towards the kitchen garden, Reynard must act quickly; the man stopped suddenly in mid step, his back to Reynard.

'now!' like a shadow Reynard detached himself from the doorway and sprinted outside, Trey heard and whirled around but Reynard was already upon him, the sickles blade slashed at Treys side, just under the raised arm , tearing it back Reynard hoped it was through flesh.

Treys arm dropped useless at his side, the sword thudded to the ground, blood oozed from the armhole of his gambeson, slowly he buckled, wheezing. Reynard struck again this time slashing Treys other arm and shoulder; far easier to incapacitate his enemy that attempt an amateurish and messy kill. On his knees Trey flailed about in the snow he bellowed like a bull maddened by jealousy, useless arms hanging limply at his side while his blood darkened the ground. Leonora resisted but Reynard managed to get her through the doorway, Trey fell forward onto his face, Reynard did not wait to see if he moved thereafter.

"Your babe is safe Madam, quite safe!" he assured her gently, she let him prop her on the settle but remained vacant eyed as he slammed the bolts into place, then slowly he coaxed her upstairs to where Domenica waited. "I must secure the house!" Reynard said, "But I will be back! Look to your mistress." Suddenly Leonora seemed to remember what was happening and begged hysterically, "my husband needs help, please don't leave Alain alone! I'm begging you don't leave him alone!"

Domenica held her on to her tightly, while Reynard tried to reassure her, "I will do all I can madam be calm, the child needs you."

As he ran down the stairs he grabbed a small cresset, and lighted all the candles he passed, he scanned the garden from a back window, Domenicas attacker remained exactly where he had fallen, by now Reynard was convinced the two men acted alone, that no others were involved. He hurried to the front of the house; he wondered where all the servants were, until he recalled how when Alain was at home he would give them leave to spend time with their own families. How strange he thought that when most needed, they were probably blissfully unaware of the drama taking place in their midst, sadly he thought of Williams death, Alains right hand man almost certainly had been the first victim!

Now to secure the outer gates, but with three dead or dying in the court yard the prospect terrified Reynard, though the darkness he could plainly see the castle gates and beyond them the black lane; an eerie silence enveloped all, morbidly he wondered if the bodies were as cold as he felt! He must concentrate on protecting the living so he tried to avoid the awful sight, breathed in deeply and made his way to the gates, Trey made a gurgling sound as he passed, Reynard had never felt so alone or vulnerable. As he pulled the rusting gates inwards he remembered Alain mentioning their repair was his next task! He unloosed the securing bolts. A freshening easterly nipped at his ears and little bits of hard snow drifted downwards, though chilled on the inside, his arms and shoulders were wet with perspiration.

Unexpectedly, just as he was beginning to feel less scared the crunch of a footstep on gravel froze the blood in his veins, a shadow even darker than the indigo evening about him fluttered into his vision; Reynard thought of bats and trembled from his feet upwards. Shouldering the gate shut he slammed down the bolts and stepped back distancing himself from the bars and the shadow, his heart thumped so it nearly deafened him. "Who goes there?" Reynard stammered, "A friend sir," the voice said, "I come to Boscombe valle in peace, but evil I fear has beaten me!" he must be able to see the three bodies.

"If you are friend then show yourself!" Reynard snapped.

The stranger stepped from the shadows, the cressets flame lit a young mans fine features, Reynard thought there something faintly familiar about him, " well Sir?" said Reynard. "Sir I admit that I am armed, beneath my cloak is a sword that I am incapable of using, and tucked in my belt is a dagger for protection, look," he removed his cloak and unsheathed the sword, he bent and laid it on the ground, he pulled the stiletto from his belt and placed it next to the sword before rummaging inside his tunic. "For what do you search now?"

193

Reynard demanded. "This," replied the visitor dragging out a parchment scroll, "It is to deliver this letter that my Master sent me, he who insisted on the weapons for my protection." Reynard did not take the letter so he poked it through the bars, a seal dangled from the scroll, "please take it, I am Corentyn, squire to Leon of Pagonston, Mistress Leonora's Father, it is for him that I carry the letter,"Corentyn spoke with difficulty; his teeth chattered so, "Allow me to put my cloak back on Sir, for I think I shall freeze without it!" Reynard nodded and snatched the letter.

Corentyn continued, "Master Leon lies wounded, indeed he was on his way to Boscombe Valle when the attack occurred!"

Of course! Leon's squire, now Reynard recognised the curly haired young man, Reynard could not read words so he pretended to be impressed by Leon's seal. "I and all of Pagonston know there exists bad blood between Father and Daughter, how can I be sure you bear no ill?" he replied. "You don't," said Corentyn, " but I beseech you, fetch Alain Rousseau that I may explain, much longer out here and I will die from the cold!" snow dotted his dark curls and his nose was as bright as a beacon.

Reynard gestured to the carnage around him, "pray look upon my Master Sir, and methinks him beyond reading letters!"

Corentyn gasped the smooth bare shoulders of Alain blueing in the bitter cold.

Reynard reckoned the youth on the verge of collapse, Reynard was by far the bigger and stronger, and still armed with the sickle. Cautiously he eased open the gates wide enough for the spindly youth to squeeze through, and then quickly dropped the bolts behind him. He kicked aside the sword but retrieved the vicious stiletto, a weapon he could handle well, Reynard marched Leon's squire past the fallen and into the house.

Distressed at what he'd seen and too long without his cloak Corentyn crouched numb with shock by the fire, "and Leonora?" he stammered, "Does she know her husbands fate? Must he remain outside?"

Reynard rubbed his chin, "alas she must have seen him struck down, but I think she believes him badly wounded, I could do nothing for him but I could safe guard her and the child! they are upstairs with a servant."

Tapping the stiletto nonchalantly against his thigh Reynard turned the parchment over in his hand.

"A child here?" Corentyn gasped. "Of course, where did you think her child would be?" Reynard retorted, surely he knew she had a child!

"Does Mistress Leonora know you?" he asked Corentyn.

"Yes, I met her on several occasions and she was always gracious."

Reynard handed back the parchment, "then there is a chance she will see you, but do not be surprised if she refuses to read or even take the letter, in this house her fathers name is anathema!"

from behind the chamber door a babes soft mewling could be heard, "Mistress Leonora," said Reynard, "There is one here who would see you, he bears a letter for your eyes only, pray listen to what he has to say."

Corentyn spoke softly, "Madam, I am Corentyn your Fathers Squire, I have a letter for you, in it he explains many things, I beg you read it." he flattened the scroll and pushed it under the door, then they waited nervously for some response.

Leonora picked up the scroll, on seeing her fathers' hand she was tempted to return it unopened, but she broke the seal; her father's scrawling hand for once seemed to bear the truth, she read and re read his words.

From outside the door Corentyn said, "You may remember me, our paths have crossed, I walked you home in the rain once." She did not answer. Reynard grew impatient, precious time was passing; he listened to the creaks and groans of the house. Suddenly she spoke again, "Reynard I have read my Fathers words but I am fearful my husband's attacker is still at large! Are you sure tis safe to open the door?"

Reynard replied, "There is nothing to fear from your husbands assailant, it is Alain who needs us, we need Ciabhan of Compton Berry to help us, but someone must ride to him, open the door for you are needed to help carry your husband inside." iron grated on iron.

She had draped a robe the colour of port wine over her shoulders, it drained her of colour, from vivacious girl and mother she had gained in a short time the appearance of a woman old before her years. Her haunted eyes flickered around the empty outer chamber; satisfied no one hid there she looked towards the windows, knowing Alain lay still outside in the courtyard filled her with pain.

Her eyes were dead, over her shoulder she said, "Domenica keep Faye safe and the door bolted."

Reynard and Corentyn stood aside as she swept past, "Come Sirs," she said, her voice tight with emotion, "Let us bring my husband inside, give him the dignity he deserves."

Ciabhans guard escorted the perspiring Reynard, alone on a small landing he waited while Ciabhan was being woken, moonlight traced a watery finger of blue along the ledge of the hallway window, Reynard had no idea how many hours had passed. Wary of meeting Ciabhan of Compton Berry the blacksmith chewed his nails, as sweat poured from his forehead; beneath an elaborate mirror of blue stones a candle cast a weak light, he stared at his anxious reflection.

Suddenly the door was flung open, Reynard jumped, to find himself facing the renowned Ciabhan of Compton Berry, dishevelled and bleary eyed, behind him Thomas looked on anxiously.

Ciabhan scowled at Reynard, "when?" How? Where were you? The guard? The women? The child?" question after question fired in quick succession.

Ciabhan already dressed and booted held his hand to Thomas who lobbed him a sword, the sound as the sword slid into its scabbard made Reynard's hair stand on end; deftly Ciabhan fastened the baldric over his crumpled tunic.

"you bring grave news indeed," he spat, as the blacksmith stammered forth the night's horrors, a jumble of chilling senseless words, he gibbered like a madman, much more of this and Ciabhans patience would snap and he'd strike the fool! "And Alain?" he demanded, staring hard at Reynard, Thomas at this point stepped between them.

"The guard is alerted and ready." he said sombrely.

Knights bellowed for grooms and arms as the castle exploded in confusion and noise, boots scraped on stone and heavy doors crashed, flares leapt into life. Horses stamped and snorted in the cold air as saddles were hauled onto protesting backs, Compton Berry resembled a battle zone, those already mounted waited edgily for their Master in the bailey. Ciabhan still trying to make sense of Reynard's ramblings listened, while his shaking squire attempted to tie laces and fasten buckles, Ciabhan cursed when the boy fumbled with his mailed gauntlets.

Strangely in all the confusion Ciabhan suddenly recalled another time long ago, a night when two fools had cowered before him in the dark stammering of murder and abduction, those two people were Mati and her moron of a husband Torr, on the night they had sought him out to tell of Faye's abduction, that only he could save her........ Ciabhan stared at the trembling blacksmith; surely history was not about to repeat itself! "I swear Mistress Leonora is unharmed my Lord," Reynard stammered, "but I know not of my Masters fate!" Ciabhans face suffused with blood, and he grabbed Reynard's throat, would have struck him if Thomas had not intervened, "My Lord make haste! For we may yet be too late!" in the rear Reynard stayed well out of Ciabhans sight.

Woken from a fitful sleep Mati peered from an arrow embrasure, the noise was shattering, and the hour was late, stars as huge as queen's jewels twinkled in a black velvet sky, and glistened the snowy ground. She had glimpsed the blackest velvet once, draped around the shoulders of a pompous noble it sparkled with jewels, she had never seen its like again, but tonight the heavens were that very same velvet.

Though impossible to pick out individuals she heard clearly her Lords name hollered by Thomas, nothing but an emergency would raise Ciabhan at this hour, she thought curiously.

Too tired to puzzle over the reasons and too late to try again for sleep she shuffled creakily to the kitchens, as a kitten crawls to the warmth. There the heat would soften her poor old bones, one of Ciabhans hounds slumped down beside her as she settled herself onto a stool, a little fellow with blackened fingers ran to her beckoning, quick as a fox he filled a cup with meat gravy; she drank deeply, resting as the household settled back into sleep.

With her husbands body at last inside she tried to clean it as best she could , she sat with him now though she could see no signs of life. Lost in her own thoughts she started Leonora as riders sounded outside Corentyns face registered pure terror.

"Fear not," she soothed, "tis Reynard returned, God be praised with help!"

On the sight that greeted them there were Stunned exclamations, followed by shouted commands, horses stamped and snorted as riders alighted, jangling harnesses and creaking leather replaced by footsteps and the rasp of steel. The din of locks being hammered open bought peasants shuffling from their hovels, they gathered in little groups whispering curious as to what was happening at the 'big house'

Corentyn nearly jumped from his skin as a loud battering threatened to shear the door from its hinges, he edged nearer Leonora.

Her time alone with Alain was ended, these last hours had passed as a dream, strange noises at times had filled her head , she knew not if they were her own or those of animals, no longer could she tell the difference! There had been one moment when she thought Alain moved, smiled even, and she had prayed harder than ever before, but they were flashes only of her obliterated dreams.

"Go, unlock the door." She bade Corentyn, but he remained rooted to the spot. "no wait!" she added untangling her arms from Alains limp head, "you stay with him."

She recognised Ciabhans voice immediately and unbolted the door, sword held high he resembled the dark warrior angels on church glass, ready to fight evil, he was her salvation but his appearance was truly fearsome! stretchered between two guards Williams body lay on a pallet.

Like vultures on a battlefield shadows moved and watched from beyond the gates, in the courtyard two armed men watched over a writhing figure at their feet.

Though relieved help had arrived Leonora teetered on the verge of hysteria, "My husband is dead!" She sobbed, "We tried, oh My God how we tried to save him," she wailed stumbling after Ciabhan as he brushed pass. At Alains side Ciabhan fluttered his hands over the lifeless body, confidently he felt his neck and wrists, Leonora clutched at her face when he put his mouth to Alains own. She watched him massage Alains chest and place his ear to Alains mouth, all the time feeling with finger tips. Her heart thundered as he ripped the tunic and examined bloody wounds, awed she watched him pound her husband's chest and listen.

Finally he shook his head and she knew him beaten, all she could see through her tears was Alains dark blood, soiling Ciabhans own tabard.

"He should have lived!" Ciabhan whispered, he opened and closed his fists, "An hour and we would have saved him! Thomas!"

Anguished words that made Leonora think he would weep, she knew how men wept for the fallen or a friend, but he remained controlled, though only his body changed.

Limp like a child's rag doll as if life had been sucked from within he shook his head, muttering the same words over and over, "Alain! Good, good Alain; Why? In Gods name why!"

Leonora's own emotion finally overcame her and she broke down wailing like a Saracen, shrieking until fatigue buckled her body and sent her into a faint, before grief had a chance to tear out her soul!

"Two dead Sir." Thomas lowered his voice, "before he died William was able to tell what happened, neither men stood a chance!" he wiped his nose on his cuff and pulled Ciabhan aside, "no need to tell who his murderer be Sir." He nodded in the direction of the yard, "he breathes still!"

Ciabhan covered Alains face, gazing for a second on his friends waxy face, then made the sign of the cross.

"Not for long!" he growled heaving his sword to his shoulder.

Corentyn hovered between awe and dread, and trembled before the Templars icy stare, Reynard more mature nodded in understanding as Ciabhan commanded, "Look to your Mistress!" before striding outside.

Treys chest heaved with each rasp of breath, death he knew approached, let it come quickly he prayed before the Templar took his revenge, but it was not to be, his nemesis would savour triumph after all, the final insult! Trey coughed, blood splashed from his mouth and stuck sticky to his nose and lips, how in Gods name had it not already suffocated him! Two morons watched him still, callously they muttered between themselves heedless of his suffering, Trey heard another join them, any hopes of mercy he may have harboured sank then for he needed no telling who the new arrival was. Immediately cold metal was placed on his jugular, no pin prick this but a heavy deliberate weight! Sweet oblivion was but moments away, he sputtered an agonising, "be quick!"

Ciabhan smiled at Treys terror, he slanted the sword just enough for his victim to feel its weight, to smell and taste its power, to see along the blade on which he would soon perish, " no quickly for you ?" Ciabhan sneered, "Better you go slowly to Hades, in pain to face the devil you serve!"

"Ciabhan prepared his stance, shoulders hunched he gripped the hilt with two hands and his mouth twisted into a grimace ,"in the name of Alain Rousseau, I send you to burn in hells eternal fire!"

Trey moved, but the swords pressure was choking, ineffective fingers made odd clawing movements on the ground; Ciabhan leant upon the sword and bore down, "let this be the last face you see!"

Gristle and bone parted and collapsed. Beneath Ciabhans sword the impaled body convulsed making hilt and blade wobble in the ground, the scene resembled some lonely grave, stuck with a cross and moved by a ghostly hand.

Ciabhan rested gazing grimly upon his work, he watched dark blood bubble through the gaping mouth, reluctant to leave he watched until all movement stopped; silently he prayed the ghastly staring eyes looked already on hell! Never in all his battles had he been inclined to violate the dead, not even in the heat of conflict when bloodlust overrides the soul, but for the first time ever he let himself be dragged away from the odious, foul corpse; a moment longer and he could not have stopped himself from tearing it apart with his bare hands! A break appeared in the scudding clouds, from its cover a fox barked, the snow had ceased but little drifts piled against the walls, where Alain and Williams bodies had lain the ground was clear, Ciabhan burned with all consuming rage. A good knight cut down, a loyal guard murdered; both while trying to protect those they cared for, others dozed by their hearths. Ciabhans eyes cold and dangerous glittered, as harsh as the frozen land around him, they would pay for their inaction, "fire the cottages!" he commanded, Thomas at his side objected, "But sir?" he began, "Do it!" Ciabhan snarled.

The bedchamber remained locked, little Faye slumbered on. From the window Domenica had watched the skirmish in the courtyard, calmly she witnessed Treys death at the Templars hands. Pleasure had actually shivered her flesh with the plunging sword, Trewin she had killed with her own hand.

Finally free of the monsters who'd shattered her young life, she felt nothing fover their deaths; that her gentle nature felt such satisfaction was a revelation. She studied her hands for any sign of the blood that had run down the daggers hilt as it turned in Trewins body; the blood had puddled in her hands and spilt onto the pinafore, it even splashed onto the new winter boots, a gift from Leonora, how gluey it had been! Her gown and boots lay tangled where she had dropped them, her legs felt sticky still beneath the flimsy gown she had thrown on, one of Leonoras. In the wash bowl the water was oily and pink with blood, before touching the baby she had scrubbed and rubbed until her fingers were raw.

Familiar voices sounded from outside and she unbarred the door, Leonora slumped in Thomas' arms seemed only semi conscious, Corentyn and Reynard looked concerned.

"Here," Thomas said, placing Leonora on the bed, "your mistress is unhurt, but sorely shocked!" He motioned to the young men.

"these two will remain with you and guards are below, some hours may pass before our return, but you are safe from harm now."

Thomas was a man of forty and five years maybe, ten of those had been spent in the service of the Lord of Compton Berry, hostility and skirmishes were part of his every day life, but even hardened as he was to injustice he could not help but think how tragic for the beautiful young woman so soon a widow.

He smiled a reassuring gap toothed grin as Domenica closed the door behind him, his thoughts as always he kept to himself.

Under the Lord of Compton Berrys protection the little group would remain safe, and sooner or later come to terms with the tragedy , but this night two good men lost their lives and Thomas fumed, first his comrade Alain, a true and valiant Knight, had perished on the blade of a nithing! And for what? Followed by William, Alains right hand man. By God someone must pay for their deaths, that person could only be Leon of Pagonston the constant thorn in their sides, it was he who bought the two black hearts into their midst; Ciabhan would not allow him to live after this night, he was a marked man.

As the horsemen pounded towards Pagonston Thomas thought back to the vacant eyed young woman on the bed, fortunate for her that she remained ignorant of Ciabhans murderous intent towards her father.

Hours burned away as Leon listened for Corentyns return, impatient he waited to hear his daughters reaction, cider helped ease his pain, he had promised Corentyn to only sip wine but as was usual Leon had succumbed. Hunched along the wall his watchers silently condemned the fool they guarded, Leons eye lids drooped.

Suddenly the door crashed inwards, a violent burst of air stunned the servants into fearful silence but woke Leon instantly.

"Blasted idiot boy !" He cursed, "can you not move without waking the dead?" he fumbled for the sword at his wrist but it clattered to the floor, and spun across the flagstones hitting the wall with a clang.

A voice Leon never wanted to hear again made him recoil in terror, "no boy to bully and beat this time, Leon le mercenaire, but a man come with one intent.........to send you to the devil!"

Leon wide eyed struggled to rise, but Ciabhans sword forced him back onto the bolster, Leon looked into the eyes of his mortal enemy, beads of perspiration glistened on Leon's forehead.

"I've come to finish what your incompetent assassin could not," Ciabhan said tersely, "But before you die you should know what misery you have bought upon your daughter!" he lowered his face to that of Leon, from every pore Leons fear oozed from Leon; Ciabhan sickened forced himself to not retch. "Know you that Alain Rousseau is foully slain, his child left fatherless and his wife a widow?"

Leon's eyes glazed, his head wobbled in denial, sounds bubbled from his throat, forming only gibberish , slackly his lips tried to suck back the foam that dribbled from the corners.

"Yes you pathetic wretch, Leonora's husband murdered and not a year married! What satisfaction you must feel for the hell you've loosed on your own innocent family!"

Ciabhans disgust for the man who had blighted these last years with his hate and desire for revenge was absolute, "You sicken me." Ciabhan flicked the blade, nicking the loose skin beneath Leons chin.

His imminent fate seemed to arouse Leon's spite and his eyes narrowed slyly , "so now you would make her an orphan also?" he croaked, "Widowed and orphaned in one night! Some honour in that Templar!" the effort appeared to drain any remaining energy, he smiled inanely, nervously as if inviting death, even welcoming his end! For the second time this night Ciabhan prepared for a death strike, prepared the blow that would end Leon's useless life, he hoisted the sword to his shoulder. Clear and determined, Ciabhan would never know what caused him to hesitate as he focussed on the dribbling wretch, but disbelief clouded his vision, he wanted to see fear cloud the eyes of one about to die, after all what point if ones enemy did not piss himself with fear!

201

and Leon did not piss himself, rather he stared vacant like from eye sockets that were dark lifeless hollows, No triumph, no fear lit their core, only a brainless acceptance of slaughter ..he would probably die laughing like a lunatic! What pleasure in that?

The signs were obvious to Ciabhan, it was known that sometimes men staring death in the face gave way to insanity, he'd witnessed it on the battlefield after the bladder and bowel had emptied, madness had Leon in its embrace, the brain had shut down, his death blow would be welcomed. Not about to be cheated Ciabahn required at least misery, from his adversary! He lowered his blade.

Deathly pale Leon remained wide eyed, grinning still his mouth had dropped open, the bottom lip quivered as spittle ran down his chin.

"Strike sir! For Gods sake strike" cried Thomas away, "for Alain!" Incredulous he unsheathed his own sword and elbowed Ciabhan out of the way.

"By god if you won't then I will!"

"Stay your weapon man," barked Ciabhan, "look upon his face!" He gripped Thomas' shoulders, "can't you see he already looks on hell? His is a living death, every day reminded of the evil he visited upon his own flesh and blood, why grant him the peace of oblivion? When it is only in living that he will he suffer!"

Fear rose in Leon's throat, the noise filled the room; his right hand opened and closed on an imaginary sword while his left plucked at the coverlet but gathered nothing.

"Thomas this is the dog who swore to kill me and I truly wish him dead, but where is the pleasure in killing one who has already lost his mind, shall I deprive a new widow also of her father?" He glowered at Leon, a pathetic juddering bundle.

"Methinks not my friend!"

Thomas was not as easily convinced, he'd seen plenty of battle and bloodletting but never a man succumb to madness so quickly, more likely this was another ruse by the slimy Frenchman, Ciabhan guessed at his thoughts, "nor will you kill him! Thomas," he growled, slamming his sword back into its scabbard. "Then I hope you are not making a big mistake! My Lord!" he said curtly before stomping from the room.

"Oh! I know I am!" Ciabhan smiled as he wiped a smear of blood from his forehead, he stared at the stain it left on his fingers before wiping it on his tunic. The figure on the bed hunched and drew his knees up to his chin, how small and pathetic he seemed, still the eyes looked back blankly. "Not now Leon of Pagonston," sighed Ciabhan, "Not now, but the day will come when you will beg for my mercy!" he walked from the hall into silence.

202

Unmoving Leon listened to his tormenters footsteps as they echoed along the screen passage; his servants were no more, having fled from fear, now no one was there to relight the candles or fire, and the chill was biting. In a weak voice that sounded more like an early northerly wind through the reed beds he whimpered, crying out for Corentyn!

Some time passed before he realised that he was alone, fear struck at his heart; alone, hated, and now his mind was playing tricks.

Demons he was convinced lurked in the shadows, surely before the night was done they would come for his mortal soul, why he could plainly see them in the corners, could see their vicious blood red teeth waiting to pull him apart! Leon for the first time in his life knew real terror............

Had madness not destroyed his ability to think clearly he would have guessed a lot sooner that Corentyn had chosen to stay with Ciabhan, and his despair would have been total, Ciabhans satisfaction on the other hand however would have been complete...........................

Chapter 32
Safety

Beneath the mulberry tree a little grass remained, elsewhere the earth was brown and patchy, dark in the shadows. Even In this her sanctuary Leonora felt an unearthly chill as she pushed aside branches bare of leaves, there was not the usual comfort or easing of sorrow but rather a harsh lesson reality, life's brutal certainty; Oh, how quickly living becomes death, how soon happiness turns into despair!

She was here because she needed to feel the heart of the ancient tree, beneath its cover at this moment she could die quite happily, let the sodden earth absorb and free her soul, free her from the ache that trailed every waking breath! But with the drawing of her next breath she was disgusted by such selfishness, how could a Mother think such thoughts when her darling daughter lay innocent in her cradle.

Last autumn the tree had borne wonderful black fruit; with relish she had begun to think ahead to this year's crop, had imagined Faye crawling in its shade while she gathered the berries, cruel fate had changed all that! Not long after Faye's birth in December on a clear and frosty morn she had wrapped the babe in the softest lambs wool and carried her to the mulberry tree, Faye's bright little eyes had blinked at the blue sky peeping through the tracery as her mother held her up to the light, a very personal ritual and one Leonora was bound to perform.

Leonora ran her hands over the rough bark, and traced the carved initials 'A' and 'L' with her fingertips; her heart would ever remain beneath these branches though she would never walk here again.

Today her eyes were dry, like a well run out of water; nothing more could be squeezed from the gritty dryness. So many tears had been shed for Alain that her body was parched of moisture, like the deserts she had read of, arid places where nothing grew; like her own body once a passionate, fertile ground, but now dry and barren.

The gentle swish of leaves, a twig snapping beneath cautious tread then halting as if anxious not to alarm her, she sensed who came. "My Lord?" her voice was weak, little more than a whisper, "How?" she was about to say, "How did you know where to find me?" but the energy to care failed her. His reply was curt but kindly, "I knew you would be here, "Come," He held his hand to her, fingers curled. A band of white circled the fourth finger of his left hand where once the emerald on her own hand had sat. She neither took his hand nor raised her head in acknowledgment, patiently he held back the branches waiting, pale sunshine made his white tunic bright though his face was shadowed, she stumbled in the light; only Ciabhans steadying arm at her back saved her from falling.

Compton Berry easily absorbed the sad little group, Ciabhans wealth and power afforded them security and the peace in which to heal.

Reynard and Corentyn in awe of the master of Compton Berry wanted to pledge their lives to his service , he took neither in the heat of the moment, but gave them time to think clearly of their futures . 'Decision making' Ciabhan said could take as long as they wished; both young men however knew exactly whom they wished to serve.

Under Matis motherly wing the two young women and the baby were cared for with tenderness, but Matis own deteriorating health slowly weakened a body and spirit too broken by grief to recover.

She stayed strong for Ciabhan and Leonora but the ordeal of Alains burial took its toll, she loved the young knight as a son.

It was easy to forget because she never spoke of it, that her own son had perished at Boscombe Valle; his name was never mentioned, and not once did she ask what had become of him after his death.

Alain they buried in the small newly built Church a mile from the castle in the tiny hamlet grown around Compton Berry, the new church had been blessed by Father John of Saint Mary's, a wooden palisade protected building and hallowed ground. Isolated in a sea of green the little structure on its mound looked on one side to Totnes, and on the other across open countryside to the Dart estuary and the sea.

'Rather bleak and a long way from Aquitaine' Leonora thought as she watched her beloved husband laid in the cold dark earth.

Her misery was complete as she watched the little spray of holly and ivy tied with one of the pink ribbons he'd bought for Faye, disappearing under shovels of mud. Unable to stop shivering and with her eyes bleared by tears she clutched her cloak beneath her chin, "one day my beloved," she murmured, "we will lie side by side again."

Wind whipped the hood from her head and stuck hair across her eyes, impatiently she pulled it away to gaze again at the hole in the ground, as if frightened to leave him alone; she tried to pull back as Ciabhan steered her away, back to the castles warmth.

Weeks after Alains committal Mati took to her bed.

Gradually she succumbed to the disease consuming her, Domenica nursed her with true devotion greatly pleasing Ciabhan, who though still lost in his own grief hid it well from others, especially Mati. The days passed peacefully for Mati, before her eyes the future of Compton Berry was changing, Leonora's little Faye charmed her and Ciabhan alike, a perfect mix of Alain and her Mother, and named for the woman they both loved. Mati had noticed the obvious affection growing between sweet natured Domenica and the young Corentyn, their coy glances were a delight and she prayed she would live to see another wedding at Compton Berry.

Corentyn was first to pluck up courage and ask Ciabhan for permission to stay at Compton Berry, on bended knee he had begged.

"Get up boy!" Ciabhan had chided, "Stay if you must! But," he paused just long enough for maximum effect rubbing his beard as if doubtful! "One wrong step mind and its back to 'le mercenaire!' now go put your mind to something useful!" Corentyns relief was plain as he tried to kiss Ciabhans hand, pulling it away Ciabhan had said, "I'm your equal boy, no need for that!" then wickedly added, "don't get in the way of Domenicas duties!" Corentyn smiled shyly but answered confidently, "You and her both Sir have my absolute devotion!"

In yielding to the boy's appeal Ciabhan found in Corentyn a loyalty that would last for the rest of their lives.

Winter clung grimly on unwilling to release its grip on the land, slowly the days thawed, turning instead to dampness, it misted the castle walls and crept through every arrow slit and fissure.

Mati never left her room, the same room she had occupied since her arrival at Compton Berry with Faye. Ciabhan had suggested another chamber, larger, more comfortable but Mati clung to the familiar, he did however persuade her to ask for anything she wanted, and insisted the fire in her room was never out. On the days little Faye was bought in and bounced on the bed Mati recalled her own youth, warmed by the sounds of a child her pain seemed less. In peaceful moments she listened to the sounds of the castle, and smiled to herself remembering how Ciabhan used to hurry pass this room in his haste to be with Faye, how his scent lingered at the bottom of the stairs; oh so long ago! Alone in her little room she would often shut out the present, to relive the sweetness of the past.

April's capriciousness was waning as Matis health worsened, a winters cough still wracked her frail body and the lung pain had increased, daily she struggled for breath. Domenica sent for Ciabhan, he remained with Mati. Corentyn and Reynard were despatched to fetch Father John. Mati knew Ciabhan close by the smell of rose, he and Faye's favourite perfume, oh! His face was blurred but the warmth of his breath on her cheek was real, in little sighs it rose and fell. That he should be so close, that her head rested on his chest, that she heard him weep could mean only one thing; she smiled wanly at harsh providence. Every so often she floated above the bed, detached from her human form and looked down on the two of them, his strong body supporting her weak one, she watched her lips move, saw his effort to respond; how light she was a faery child on gossamer wings, in the arms of the man she loved.

Leonora watched Ciabhan gently cradle the ailing Mati, the pair seemed so at ease in each others company that she felt an intruder, an uninvited witness to years of shared memories.

A robin warbled the song strangely at odds with the tragedy unfolding in front of her, Ciabhan motioned for the window to be pushed wide. Leonora crossed the room but Mati seemed disturbed by the movement, and struggled in Ciabhans arms, pointing to Leonora. Rapture lit her features and the years fell away, Leonora's flesh prickled at the transformation.

"My Lord" Mati scolded, "let not Faye see you weep!" his eyes followed where she pointed. "Why how fine my mistress looks, there Sir in the light! Can you see her?" Leonora stood still hardly daring to breathe.

"Yes, Mati I see her," Ciabhan replied.

"Faye beckons Sir!" Matis eyes were wide, "See, and Alain comes also, my dear you must let me go for they call me!"

Leonora stuffed her fist into her mouth to stop from sobbing, while Ciabhan soothed the agitated woman; he kept his face turned away but Leonora knew he wept.

A coughing fit shook Mati, shuddering her woefully thin body, cough after cough convulsed her thin frame until finally she collapsed back, the room filled with rasping, the awful open mouthed grating of approaching death, slowly the noise grew less and less until stopped. As she breathed her last a smile tilted the corners of her mouth; Leonora knew her gone. Wiping first the blood from her mouth, Ciabhan then smoothed Matis brow, closed shut her eyes and made the sign of the cross. Rising from the bedside he crossed to the window as if to fling it wider, but instantly backed away dropping his hands to his side, a look of shock on his face; the robin's song stopped abruptly.

"Gods blood!" he exclaimed, "what the!" From the sill black wings flapped in his face. Leonora recognised the raven. "It is only the raven Sir," she sniffed, "he has been a regular visitor of late."

Ciabhan stammered, "Raven you say, are you sure?"

She nodded, "Yes, Sir, Mati knew it well."

Ciabhan was not given to casual shows of emotion but he appeared somehow cheered by the birds visit, even at such a sad time. "Ivan, of course he'd know! Ivan would come for Mati!" He smiled grimly and turned back to Mati, Father John had crossed her hands upon her breast, now he busied himself with the rituals of death. How Ciabhan envied Mati, she was with Faye and Alain, why! the smile was still upon her lips! "My Lord?" Leonora said wiping her eyes and looking puzzled, "who has come for Mati?" Ciabhan smiled pensively, "Ivan, the raven, he lives still!"

Life's cycle continued, birth, love, death; fate cared nothing for mourning or loss, life marched on regardless!

Mati was laid beside Alain, posies of spring flowers coloured the mounds, and every Sunday morning Leonora carried Faye the league there and back. Others followed Mati into death, old age and chronic ailments succumbed to the harsh winter, death cared not whom it took and the village graveyard became a familiar place for peasantry and the landed alike, a forlorn place of sad greetings and final goodbyes.

Kindly Master Dawks was one of them, Leonora was saddened for his orphaned daughter Freda, but comforted that Mati would be accompanied into the afterlife at least, and by one so jovial. Freda she welcomed to the castle, encouraging her to visit or stay as often as she wished, the girls Father always treated her with respect, now she would repay that kindness by doing the same for his daughter.

Ciabhan retreated into melancholy, the losses of Alain and Mati affected him profoundly and more than he cared to admit, on the occasions he rode about his estate, he cut a lonely figure. However even his sadness buckled with an infant as enchanting as Faye around, he was captivated by Alains little daughter, and would on occasions seek her and Leonora for company.

June arrived in a blaze of days so perfect that all memories of the terrible winter vanished, deep blue days that tumbled by as quickly as Faye seemed to grow, strong minded and straight limbed she thrived, with sea green eyes like her Fathers she was aware of everything, soon outgrowing the wicker crib and baby linen, dear Mati had not failed her for the chest was full to overflowing of the loveliest clothes.

Some even whispered that another Faye had been sent for Compton Berry.

Except for the startling green eyes Leonora looked very like her Mother, inheriting not only her mannerisms but many of her ways also, one of these was a craving at times for solitude. Compton Berry offered a fragile contentment considering all that had passed, but there was no mulberry here to hide under! She kept her sadness to herself

On an afternoon when the castle sweltered she left Faye in the care of Domenica and slipped away, past the great oak and down towards the water sparkling between the trees. The lake shimmered, only the plop of splashing fish and the hum of insects made any sound, it felt as if the world slumbered. The whirr of kingfishers' wings made her start as it darted past, its jewelled colours disappearing in a flash. Gingerly she stepped over the stones that marked the crossing place until she reached the other side; willows dipped their branches where the water lapped at

the bank, parting the fronds she stepped onto dry land and let tranquillity sweep over her, had her mother ever spent time here she wondered, for it was a perfect hideaway. To the left a meadow stretched, at its end a row of tiny cottages nestled, she headed towards them. Underfoot the meadow was springy and water sodden so she slipped through the hedge onto a path that looked rarely used, the woods stretching high to her right were forbidding even in bright sun and she had a weird feeling of being watched. She preferred the meadow full of buttercups that peeped through the gaps of elder and shrubby hazel, the sight lifted her immediately. With the sun on her back she let her shawl fall and tied it low on her hips, she would have lifted her skirts above her knees like a carefree girl, but now twice widowed and a mother it was hardly fitting. The shrieking of buzzards made her look up, against the suns glare two birds probably mates, wheeled in the blue, she watched until giddy. When she lowered her head she noticed the lone horseman, he approached relaxed and indifferent to her presence, intuitively she knew who it was; awkwardness settled on her, or shyness.
Would he think she spied on him?
 Flies buzzed over the horse, its tail swished and the flanks quivered, dust swirled around them both, and the horse tossed its head trying to clear its tender nostrils of dust, somehow she knew from whence he came; the glade deep in the forest where her Mother lay.
Ciabhan squinted, someone stood in his path, he more than likely thought the person a lone villein, he drew close before recognising her, for a moment she thought he would ignore her and ride past! But he smiled on seeing her, Leonora raised her hand shyly.
 Reining in the horse he greeted her, "well met Mistress Leonora, it would seem the sun beckons us both outside, 'tis so bright I fair near rode past you ! Would you have stopped me I wonder?"
 She had seen many depictions of Saints in Byzantine art, here was one in person! His hair shone halo like about his head, mounted he seemed much taller, she heard his words, did he jest, mock even?
"Of course! I would have," she replied haughtily, "you must know I would let none ride over me Sir!"
Brown eyes twinkled in his tanned face, he laid the reins across the horses twitching shoulders, and watched her, then he threw back his head and laughed, not unkindly. "Oh! I know that well Mistress Leonora, but I tease, the heat has addled my brain somewhat!" Though Ciabhan walked with a slight limp, he dismounted like a man half his age, gathering the reins in his right hand he steadied the excitable destrier. "Would you care to ride Mistress, for I am happy to walk?"

Foam sprayed the air as the beast snorted, Leonora stepped back, "I think not sir!"

Still calling the buzzards glided over the tree tops preparing to land.

"Have you ever flown hawks?" Ciabhan asked still watching the birds.

"No Sir though I believe my mother enjoyed the spectacle."

Ciabhan glanced at her, "aye she did Mistress Leonora, we both did."

He was quiet for a while, "So you are familiar with Bella Donna then?"

The birds her parents kept at the manor in Pagonston had been for hunting, and the mews in the orchard out of bounds to children.

the hawks had been flown on special occasions for the entertainment of guests, yes! her Mother had owned a peregrine notorious for its bad temper, even Mati had at times mentioned its infamy.

"I believe Bella Donna a bird of some renown." Leonora replied.

Ciabhans eyebrows shot up, "Renown?" he exclaimed, "The bird is a veritable she devil!"

He recalled some private joke and smiled, "She'd drawn blood so many times that Ivan cowered in her presence!"

Ah! Again mention of the mysterious Ivan; the name was being used often of late.

"You have her still?" she asked, "I should like to meet this harridan!"

The buzzards had fallen silent, and smaller birds twittered once more, Ciabhan appeared not to hear her request, instead he asked an unexpected question, "Would you like to see where your mother lies?"

Unprepared for the change of subject she answered too quickly, "I would," she said, wishing almost immediately that she hadn't.

"Then now is a good as time as any, you will have to ride though."

He remounted then hoisted her up behind him, the beast stamped and dropped its head, Ciabhan leant over the horses ears, "Steady boy, tis but a friend!"

Leonora was an accomplished horsewoman but had never sat on a beast such as this, did she hold its rider, or clutch at whatever she could? Ciabhan had read her thoughts, "Hold onto my belt! he is trained to carry two! in battle it is his duty!" in the heat the forest smelt musty, of animals and dank places beyond daylight, once or twice she thought she saw shapes no more than shadows flitting across their path, she even thought Ciabhan murmured under his breath as if addressing something or someone. When the way was too gloomy she turned her face into his back. Confident the destrier plunged forward, not once did Ciabhan command or pull hard on the reins, the horse knew where he was headed. She did think it dreadfully lonely; never would she have left Alain in such a place! Did this man perhaps have a darker side to his nature she wondered? was he after all a jealous man possessive of his wife even in death? a chill crept over her clammy skin.

With a whinny of triumph the horse suddenly thrust from darkness into a place of light, a clearing so bright that Leonora blinked in disbelief that such a wondrous place existed! Open mouthed she gazed at the clearing and was still open mouthed when Ciabahn reined the horse to a stand still. Birdsong filled the air, where a moment ago all had been silent; from the vaulting green a myriad different songs filled the forest.

Ciabhan waited at her stirrup, so awestruck was she that she hadn't even been aware of him dismounting, "Leonora," he said, "we are here."

She dismounted and straightened her clothes covering careful to cover the scratches on her legs, still she remained wide eyed.

"Is it not beautiful?" he asked, "a fitting place for Faye?"

Way above her head the arching green canopy took her breath away, "Oh yes! "She exclaimed, "It's the most beautiful place I have ever seen, like a dream!" She followed Ciabhan across the clearing to what seemed a mossy bank, "Faye said exactly the same when she first saw this place." The mound was so covered in moss that it resembled velvet; his strong hands caressed the velvet. "Not quite her favourite green," he smiled, but in August it pales, and becomes the green she loved, more the colour of lichen." He moved to an upright stone at the head of the grave. "These are her words."

Leonora watched him closely, watched his every expression and movement, he wiped the writing with his sleeve. Chiselled neatly, the verse was a simple poem of love; he read aloud the words with no embarrassment, moving words from his dead love...her Mother.

Bluebells nodded beneath the tall beeches; wading amongst them Leonora picked an armful and laid them on the mound.

As she stood Leonora said, "Mother would encourage us to pick spring flowers for those too ill to leave their beds, 'Let us spring to them,' She would say." Ciabhan smiled at the memory and pointed to the overgrown lodge, "just inside the entrance, "there," he said, "roosts a barn owl, every year she raises another clutch successfully, the first time Faye and I saw her she nearly scared us both to death! And our love had barely begun!"

Leonora tried to envisage them together, but as always her thoughts turned to her own loss, "Alain told of a secret place, do others know of it?" Ciabhan was quiet for a while.

"Alain of course I chose to help me lay her to rest here, Ivan our comrade knew also of this place, whether he is aware of my wife's fate! I know not!"

"Alain said he had written to him some years ago," she said.

He smiled, "I suspected as much."

With his head bowed in private thought or prayer, he walked to the edge

211

of the clearing and disappeared.

Not at all afraid Leonora knelt at the mound and prayed for her mothers' soul, she begged her Mothers forgiveness for ever doubting her integrity, and then mouthed her respect for her Mothers strength of heart, she signed the cross and rose just as Ciabhan reappeared.

Cupping his hands for her to mount he said, "So you too are now aware of this place Leonora."

Grasping the pommel she glanced back over her shoulder,"yes," she said but s so alone."

"Believe me Leonora she is not alone!" he replied, "Do you think I would leave her unwatched? Trust me Leonora she is not alone."

The glade closed in on itself, this time she was convinced shadows moved.

As they approached the lake Leonora was walking by Ciabhans side, again she spotted the kingfisher, this time perched on a low branch, she pointed excitedly and together they watched as it plopped into the water and emerged with a tiny fish.

At ease in his company Leonora asked questions and though reticent at times he answered her, even though certain subjects may have been painful. They talked of Faye and Leon; of his fondness for Alain and the mysterious 'Ivan' and she discovered that nothing more than his fondness for black had earned Ivan the nickname 'the raven' and of course his hair as black as ravens wing! Slowly she began to understand how fate had turned and twisted their destinies.

A sty marked the beginning of the woodland path that led up to the castle, shaded and hazardous it was strewn with boulders and her feet soon suffered but she refused to ride insisting that she preferred to walk. When they came to the ancient oak Ciabhan pointed to the initials 'C' and 'F' no fancy heart or elaboration, plain and simple their proclamation stood a little apart from the rest. Seeing them emerge from the shadows a groom ran to take the sweating horse, Ciabahn fluttered a green and yellow kerchief across his forehead shiny with perspiration, "Gods Bones that's some climb!" he gasped.Neither Leonora's scratches nor her stubbornness escaped his notice, nodding at her feet he said, "I hope neither those cuts nor such obstinacy will stop you from joining me at dinner tonight Leonora?" he knew she preferred to dine less formally at the lower trestle, but not one to ignore a challenge she countered, "It would be my pleasure." When sure he was out of sight she removed her sandals and limped across the grass, her stubborn streak must have been part of her father she mused as the softness acted like a salve on throbbing feet as promised she took her place at table that evening, a trencher already marked her place, fayes high backed chair remained as always vacant, with Ciabhan on one side and Leonora to the other.

Domenica raised her brows quizzically on seeing Leonora at the high table, Leonora shrugged her shoulders back and smiled enigmatically. Ciabahn spoke to her across the empty chair, "It seems we have a romance in the making," he neither whispered nor spoke so they might be embarrassed but made a discreet gesture in the direction of Corentyn and Domenica.

Leonora had known all along of the growing bond between the young couple, it had taken seed on the terrible night Alain was killed, she smiled back, "so I believe, tis no secret sir."

Ciabhan raised his glass to the couple, "then we will do all we can for them." Domenica flushed pink from neck to forehead as his gaze fell on her. "It appears another suffers a malady of the heart Mistress!" he said turning to Leonora, "I see master Reynard cannot take his eyes from you! Pray do him the honour of a smile!" Reynard quickly averted his eyes, only then did Leonora realise why the Farrier was always so close by. Truly shocked she snapped, "I am but six months a widow Sir, tis an affront to Alains memory to suggest that any might express interest so soon in his widow!"

Ciabhan shrugged, "then my apologies Mistress for I meant no offence, you are but young still and men will be men, no harm in being aware of it!" As an afterthought he added, "Alain would not have wanted you to become as a nun!"

She let her cup be refilled; his callousness was at odds with the man she had spent the afternoon with.

"You did not find another so soon?" she replied. Stinging words that she regretted immediately for she knew they would wound. Dabbing her mouth she made to stand, but he reached out to stay her, placing his hand over hers. He was not angry but his eyes were sad, dull like moorland peat, he forced her to meet his, and when he spoke it was with a heaviness of heart. "No other woman on Gods earth compared to your Mother, not one could match her beauty or spirit," he glanced at the empty chair, "Forget not when you judge that time was no friend of ours, age was ever our enemy! Youth and its chance had passed!" Each word filled with passion, "remember that Faye was the love I held in my arms but for the blinking of an eye, but in my heart forever." His fingers tightened around hers and she thought he would surely crush them. Someone called his name. "That it could only have been different," he whispered, " I ache to join her." He withdrew his hand and turned away, she flinched.

Humbled she looked about the hall at her dining companions, hoping none had noticed; guilt overwhelmed her, the crowded hall had suddenly become lonely, and she felt totally out of place. She observed uncouth men at arms and their coarser sergeants spluttering through the meal laughing as if none had a care in the world.

Unmindful of the smokey downdraughts Ciabahn conversed with his Reeve, Richard, or Dickon as he was known; nodding his head wisely Ciabahn stabbed at a chunk of beef fallen from his trencher.

Alger the aged Norman armourer whose job it was to teach Reynard the ways of the Master struggled to keep the young mans attention, while vain Knights emboldened by wine boasted ever louder of their dubious exploits.

Corentyn huddling beside Domenica listened patiently as she struggled to make herself understood above the clamour, rarely did he take his eyes from her face.

Reynard still cast furtive glances when he thought Leonora wasn't looking; and Maudie Sutton's own blatant interest in the farrier went seemingly ignored by her husband until finally exasperated by her brazenness he cowed her with a withering stare!

Mother of God! Mused Leonora this place is a veritable hive of desire! She swallowed the gritty dregs of wine and felt a movement at her elbow, 'Winnie' Faye's nursemaid tugged at Leonora's sleeve, "tis the Babe Mistress" she stammered, "Er' be restless and awful hot! Tis best you come!" the girl looked terrified.

grateful of a reason to leave the table Leonora soothed her, "don't fret so child, of course I'll come."

Taking her leave of the diners Leonora hurried to Faye, Winnie at her side muttered but Leonora was not listening.

Little Faye was so pale she resembled a faded rose, one whose petals were wilting , way past their best, glassy little eyes gazed at her Mother and the child began to whimper. Pulling the sheet down Leonora felt behind Faye's neck where the linen was soaked through, Winnie pulled the covers back up; Leonora gently pushed her aside.

"The babe is far too hot; the poor little mite is nearly roasted!" she said. Winnie gasped as Leonora removed all the swaddling and linen, in seconds she had stripped the little bare. "Open wide the window!" she ordered. Night breezes soon freshened the room and the child, in front of the open window Leonora stood until the child cooled and calmed.

"Remember it does no good to wrap a babe so tight Win, 'tis better the child moves, now fetch clean linen for the crib then my dear bring Miss Domenica to me." Leonora smiled kindly, for Win trembled as if about

to weep, "its not your fault child, you were not to know," she comforted ,
"but remember, in summer months no swaddling!" Win nodded and
scampered from the chamber.

Scent wafted from the land, some blossom gave their best perfume in the
hours of darkness, from below hidden in shrubbery a nightingale sang its
little heart out, surely the most heavenly sound on a summer night,
a serenade for her and Faye alone, melancholy suddenly threatened as
Leonora recalled her mother, if only she were here, could be with them
both.

A rustle at the door bought her back to the present, without looking
around she said, "Domenica It is nothing to con.......!"

She stopped mid sentence as a powerful scent of rose filled her nostrils,
she whirled round half expecting to see a ghost, her Mother adored roses!
Framed in the doorway Ciabhan stood awkwardly.

"By God you scared me sir!" she breathed "I thought it a......!"

He finished the sentence, "A ghost?" he answered, "one visits here, but
you would be blessed to see her!"

He indicated Faye, "how does the child? Nothing serious I pray?"

Leonora shook her head, "no Sir, the night was a little too warm and
Winnie rather too enthusiastic in her care!"

He frowned, "she can be replaced a mature woman maybe?" Leonora
smiled, "No need for that, Winnie suits us well."

Faye's large eyes fixed on her mothers as Leonora crossed to him, now
seemed a good time to apologise for her earlier unkindness, the babe
turned her head back to the window as if not wanting to leave the
nightingale's song.

"Sir, about tonight!" she stammered, "I did not..."

Without taking his eyes from Faye he said, "It is forgotten, think no more
on it." Leonora changed the subject, "Thank You for your concern for
Faye, but as you see she appears better already." Ciabhan seemed
unconvinced.

"It would be more than I could bear if harm came to her," he countered.

To Leonora it was out of character that this commanding Knight, at times
so harsh could be so touched by a babe in arms! Was this tiny speck of
humanity now his Achilles heel? Could such a passionate man care so
much for a mere babe, and a girl child at that! "But you are her
Godfather, she said, "since Alains death you are the most important man
in my Childs life Ciabhan, 'tis natural you should care!" For the first time
she addressed him in the familiar and her cheeks coloured, he seemed not
to notice. "Were that I her father!" he muttered, an innocent remark,
intuitively Leonora knew what was meant and far from offended,

"We know not what the future brings Sir," she replied.

Barely audible he answered, "Fatherhood was never meant to be, my life was controlled by a higher destiny...but this child" ...he never finished the sentence. Domenica and Winnie burst through the door, Winnie in her rush stumbled full into his arms, "less haste Mistress," he scolded, "methinks your charge not about to go anywhere!" He indicated the sleeping Faye and grinned." Winnie flushed pink.

"Your help has arrived Leonora, I'll take my leave," Winnie received what she thought was a withering look and flinched as he strode past.

Domenica was already showing her selection of herbs to Leonora when he appeared again in the doorway, Winnie nearly jumped from her skin. "I meant to ask," He said awkwardly, "allowing the babe fairs well, would you care to watch Bella Donna fly she is well overdue for exercise?" Leonora hesitated, "thank you sir but I would be ill at ease in the company of so many men."

He nodded but seemed slightly deflated, "I planned only a small party, myself, the falconer and of course a chaperone for yourself!"

Soft as down Faye's breath came in little huffs, her colour a healthy pink.

"Then I would be pleased to accompany you Sir, providing your Godchild allows!"

This time he bade them all a courteous goodnight, "but of course" he said.

chapter 33
A Future

1189 year saw the death of Henry II, his son the impressive Richard Duke
of Normandy and Aquitaine, inherited his throne.

Henry an energetic and wise king would be mourned at least by the
population, rather less so by his widow Eleanor and his remaining sons,
the lionhearted Richard and devious John.

Richard for some time had harboured desires for a third crusade, and his
plans would not be altered by Henrys demise, Henry very likely would
have joined his Son and Philip Augustus of France in their mission, but
fate in the guise of death intervened.

All over England and France monies were raised and petitions sent out
for those brave and steadfast enough to join Richard and his then friend
on their crusade, for the glory of securing once and for all the golden city
of Jerusalem for Christendom.

The south of England sometimes seemed forgotten by the rest of the
country, loyal to the monarchy it was a relatively peaceful quarter in a
land of change.

Compton Berry slumbered in its valley, occasionally a Baron jealous or
bored by inactivity would rattle his weapons like a child having a tantrum
but nothing intimidated the Master of Compton Berry, his fiefdom
remained orderly and his villeins free.

However news of the king's passing away bought many visitors to the
gates of Compton Berry, daily saw the arrival of past comrades, Barons,
Knights, nobility even the occasional prince and all with their mesnies,
each expected hospitality and entertainment; Maudies feet rarely touched
the ground she was so busy.

Without exception every guest had but one question on his lips, each
beseeched some on bended knee, that the Lord of Compton Berry do
them the honour of joining their great last crusade......

In the sheltered world she had grown accustomed to Leonora at first
showed little interest in the gossip that filtered like summer sunlight
through windows, she had quite enough to occupy her days, men's talk of
war meant nothing. Tittle Tattle and rumour was carried by Maudie or
Tom, sometimes by Corentyn now he worked closely with Ciabhan, she
had listened when Corentyn confided that the thought of ever leaving
Domenica filled him with dread, in reassuring him she chose to ignore
her own concerns.

Reality only hit on the day she accompanied Maudie and Tom into Totnes for supplies, there she saw for herself the excitement caused by news of a fresh crusade, this was no idle gossip but fact!

Crowded with excitable travellers and sad eyed women the landing stage seemed fit to burst with bodies, alongside the usual wool cargo the jetty was piled high with warlike equipment and supplies, animals yelped or snorted and stamped in holding pens.

While Thomas disappeared into the tavern Maudie and Leonora plonked themselves at a trestle, Maudie wiped at the ale stains with the sleeve of her gown. "Maudie?" Leonora asked, "what actually is happening, what does all this mean, will it affect Compton Berry?"

Maudie scraped her auburn curls back beneath her cap, "Well crusade bain't good news ever!" she said, "not for us women anyhow, that's for sure! Different for men of course, and for the Master tis expected he'll go." She screwed her eyes against the glare looking for Tom, just inside the tavern door he appeared deep in conversation with a well dressed man, light bounced off a glass full of amber liquid.

"Course tis only what I's heard around the castle." Maudie added.

A coldness swept suddenly over Leonora, "you mean Ciabhan will go? surely he is needed here!"

Maudie a little shocked by Leonora's use of the familiar sniffed, "An who by Miss? Yon castle will run itself, us'll see to that, makes no difference whether Master be there or not!" when Tom appeared with drinks she scolded, "an about time too! I saw e'eyeing up them hussies!"

Tom rolled his eyes.

Maudie drank deeply and smacked her lips together, "Mistress here wants to know if Master Ciabhan be going to them crusades, what thinks you Tom me dear!"

Tom put down his empty glass, "Don e' ask I maid, Master be more like to tell her anyways!" With that he sloped off back to the tavern, raucous laughter followed soon after. "Will Tom have to go Maudie?" Leonora questioned. "I doubt it miss, e's no fighter my Tom, an e's of more use to Dickon, no matter to I though if he do go!" she smiled with fake coyness and smoothed her apron over ample breasts; Leonora remembered the lustful looks Maudie had given Reynard in the dining hall. Warmed by the sun the women enjoyed watching the crowds, more than once Maudies head swivelled at some handsome young knights' squire, quickly she'd look to see if Tom had noticed. Maudie made no secret of her wayward nature, in fact she revelled in her sexuality, Leonora's own needs were of late becoming apparent but she knew well that it was her widows demureness and modesty that earned her the admiration of Compton Berry; but how she missed the loving of a truly good man!

An elderly couple hand in hand asked if they could sit at the trestle, Maudie more than happy to gossip chatted away happily to the Dame while her husband wandered into the tavern.

Uninterested in their conversation Leonora sat facing the sun with her chin resting in her hand and her eyes closed, her mind drifted.......

The atmosphere of change at the castle could no longer be denied, she realised it already affected her personally, for only this morning Ciabhan had sent word that he was unable to join her in flying the hawks, the depth of her disappointment surprised her.

Maudies voice droned on softly, and the lapping of water at the jetty soothed the senses as much as the ale had, lulled and relaxed Leonora tried to remember when her fascination for the hawks and for Ciabhan had first began; surely it was on the night her darling little Faye lay so unwell, the night he called to enquire after the child's well being.......?

Before leaving the room he had asked Leonora if she would care to join him on the morrow to witness her mothers' notorious peregrine fly. Readily she agreed.

The pleasure of that day meant for the first time since Alains death she actually looked forward to something and it became a regular occurrence for her Bella Donna and Ciabhan. Of late though he had excused himself often from her company, saying only when asked, 'Castle duties my dear!" She forced herself to recall their first meeting in the mews.........

Hunched like old men in a queue the birds waited patiently on their stands, Brian the falconer busy adjusting little leather hoods and tying jesses took no notice when she entered, but the birds swivelled their heads in unison.

Ciabhan there already looked up and greeted her arrival, "Here put this on," he said passing a hide gauntlet, "their enthusiasm may result in blood!" he laughed. Had been a wise move for more than one snatched at her fingers, there were ten birds three were peregrines; she tried to guess which might be Bella Donna. Confidently Ciabhan moved along the row introducing each individual, he calmed with little clicks of the tongue as he stroked their breast feathers, "And which one of these would you say is the 'she devil," he asked dryly.

A bird smaller than the rest with beautiful clear markings fluffed its feathers in expectation and turned its huge eyes on Ciabhan as he approached her; almost adoringly! Opening and closing her lethal beak the 'she devil' made little mewling sounds, all the while watching her 'Master.' The falconer straightened as they halted by Bella Donna, looking up from the hawk on his wrist; Leonora supposed he wanted to see Bella Donna's reaction to the visitor!

A bored flicker of curiosity was all Bella Donna deigned to give Leonora, along with a warning hiss. "That's her," Leonora whispered a little too eagerly.

Irritated by the unknown Bella Donna gazed malevolently at Leonora. "She likes you!" chuckled Ciabhan, "as I knew she would!" His eyes luminous in the gloom held her gaze, but it was hard to believe the bird liked her at all, surely he jested! The falconers voice broke in, "aye Miss that she does." Ciabhan lifted the bird onto Leonora's arm, Bella Donna stalked the gauntlet leisurely stretching her talons, she let Ciabhan stroke her breast, even raised her head so beneath her beak could be caressed," believe me Leonora ," he said, "she likes you."

Unsure Leonora muttered beneath her breath, "She doesn't look as if she does!"

Now stroke her," he encouraged; he took the fingers of her free hand, "like this." Against the birds soft breast he rubbed Leonora's finger tips, she feared the bird may strike but Bella Donna seemed content to worry at the frayed leather, not aggressively but as if giving warning.

"She knows exactly who you are!" Ciabhan whispered, "She is yours now." He took his own bird, a goshawk from Brian's arm, "now are we ready Madam!" the three of them exited the mews, where Ciabhan had been standing lingered the faintest perfume of rose..

That introduction to her mothers' peregrine saw a bonding between mistress and bird, which in its turn developed into a closeness between Leonora and Ciabhan. for him it was a chance to renew the sport he so enjoyed with Faye; for Leonora it became a new and challenging interest; that it was spent by the side of such a knowledgeable companion made it all the more pleasurable. Little by little her heartache eased.......

A chill breeze shivered her arms and raised the fine hairs, Maudie no longer chatting had gone.........it reminded her of the high meadows when the wind would rush through the valley and tug at her hair and cloak, with Bella Donna clinging to her sleeve and Ciabhan at her side Leonora felt true exhilaration, It was there that the presence of Alain and her mother could be felt most. If she strained her eyes she could almost see them there, watching together from the shade of the sentinel oak. Was that why, she wondered that Ciabhan looked so often to the ancient tree? So many of his memories were in those fields, his dreams and future hopes; surely their very image must be stamped on the landscape of those wild meadows.

She was still lost in thought when Thomas touched her shoulder, "be e' ready to go miss?" he said. She had intended to purchase trinkets for Faye and maybe a small token of appreciation for Ciabhan, for his patience and kindness, but time had flown by and Thomas was obviously impatient to be on his way, in a billow of skirts he was shoving Maudie onto the cart, with a slap to her considerable rear he joked, "youm's getting a right arse on you maid!" Maudie wriggled her hips suggestively, "An you should know!" she giggled.

Perhaps next time Leonora thought but maybe there would be no next time if he was leaving! But there again he probably had cloak pins a plenty.

Once on their way the women sang while Tom whistled, quite unmindful of the carts bumping. Maudie looked at the supplies behind her, "Ave' e' got all that master asked for?" she said

"Aye woman." Tom replied, "But that thieving Percy drives an ard bargain, 'e sure as anything baint up to any good, but I ad e' in the end." Pleased with himself he sniggered smugly.

Turning off at hangman's cross towards Compton Berry they quieted, all knew Leon had strung Torr up here for the beasts and birds to feed on, and all knew Leonora estranged from her Father, so to save any embarrassment they fell silent until the gallows had been passed.

"I hope you was fair Tom," said Maudie breaking the silence, "you knows the Master be 'ard on bullying, Lord I be parched." She ran her tongue over dry lips, "Do I miss Mati's lemon water!"

Low on the horizon dark clouds massed and a gust of oven like wind nearly took off Maudies cap, thunder growled like an angry beast. "Rains a coming Tom," Maudie observed, clasping her cap tightly.

"Master Ciabhan plans on flying the hawks, e' asked Tom to make ready for the morrow," she hesitated, "be e' goin with im Miss?" Maudie stole a sideways look at her companion, Leonora feigned not to hear but her cheeks still flushed pink and it had nothing to do with the oppressive heat.

The cart rumbled under the archway and jerked to a standstill just as the first plops of rain pattered into the dust, two of Maudies brood ran to greet her, reedy little voices nearly drowned by thunder claps, she grabbed their hands and disappeared to the kitchen. The rain was welcome relief from days of humidity, Leonora lingered awhile in the open-air enjoying the warm rain upon her skin.

She watched as Tom backed the horses and cart into the storeroom, startled by the storm they shied and bucked nearly shedding the whole load, Reynard hurried to his aid from the forge, within minutes the load was safely inside and intact.

As the rain turned cold she shivered and stepped back into the covered stair well that led up to the curtain wall, the deafening claps of thunder drowned all other sound as it reverberated around the hollow space.

Neither Ciabhan nor Corentyn rushing down the steps knew of another presence until they ploughed into her, knocking Leonora's feet clean from under her. Corentyns warning cry was too late as he grabbed at thin air but the force of the collision had caused her to fall striking her face and cheek against the wall. Ciabhan hindered by full riding gear narrowly avoided trampling her as she slid to the ground, his sharp spurs ended inches from her face.

"What in Gods name does she here?" he groaned, "go fetch the nun."

Stunned, Leonora opened her eyes and blinked, her head was agony and she thought she was dying, she tried to speak.

Lightening lit Ciabhans anxious face, "Don't speak," he said, "You are winded, stay still and let me see the damage," he turned her face towards what little light there was and wiped the blood with the hem of his tunic, when she saw the blood her face crumpled as if she would cry.

"Tis but a graze madam, a deep one but you'll live!"

He rested back on his haunches and sighed, "though you'll not be in the saddle for a day or two, and no hawking! Now let's get you to the infirmary."

He picked her up as if she were but a child and carried her to the infirmary, "I'll leave you in Domenicas good hands Mistress, she'll make sure you rest, I'll speak with you in a day or two."

Taking Domenica to one side, he spoke in hushed tones while adjusting his riding cloak, the leathered storm hood he pulled tight over his head and made a few changes to belt and baldric, and then he beckoned to Corentyn, "come lad," he said, "time runs on, tis only a few hours to compline."

Leonora had a wretched night; her head ached and pounded in spite of Domenicas administrations, and swaying trees so close made her think of demons writhing beyond the window, though Domenica slept in the room next to the infirmary Leonora was still nervous. Domenica suggested it better she stay the night here where help was at hand as a knock to the head could sometimes become worse later on, but Leonora hated the idea of being away from Faye, and objected, but Domenica would have none of it, finally a reluctant compromise was reached.

once during the night she woke in panic, fearing her head would explode, and her body felt as if it had had been jolted and bent beyond its limits. Some foul tasting liquid had been left but Leonora had thrown it from the window in disgust, too late realising her mistake! For her agony she would have taken poison! She slipped from bed and limped to the half open door, ferocious wind whipped the trees to frenzy but the rain and thunder had ceased, distant lightening flickered through the forest like an expiring candle flame, slowly her fuzzy brain cleared except for a strange tinkling sound, it took a few moments for her to realise that it came from outside and was not in her head. From an arrow slit she looked out over the castle walls, dawn would soon arise for its half light played on the green sweeping against the lower walls. She pulled her hair from her eyes and winced, it had stuck against the bloody graze, she heard the horsemen before she saw them, a group of maybe six? She couldn't be sure. Bunched together they rode beneath the entrance arch. Above the winds howling she had heard the jangling of harness and spurs; a sputtering flare showed clearly Ciabhans face.

She passed the hour until dawn in fitful sleep and woke surprisingly refreshed to bright sunshine and a familiar gurgling, beside the bed Domenica stood smiling down at her, in her arms Faye pulled playfully at her hair. Maudie bustled in with a jug of warmed milk and honey, thick chunks of bread and butter nestled beneath white linen, "Get this down thys neck, there's plenty enough for you and little un," she said, "can't believe you 'ad that do' yesterday Miss, Lord, I thought master would 'ave my an Toms guts!"

Leonora looked puzzled, "but why would he?"

"For leaving you alone of course!" Maudie replied.

Leonora couldn't understand what Maudie meant.

"But you didn't leave me alone?"

Maudie heaved a sigh, "Oh tis nothing miss, t'was a jest only!"

She cooed to Faye wriggling in Domenicas arms, "come on me bird try some of this, it'll make e' a strong little maid." Faye sucked at the spoon with relish.

"I, s just heard," Maudie said, "Master is definitely goin' on crusade, e reckons to be away in less than the week, Tom as just told that to I."

Leonora resting against the cushions swallowed hard, Maudie looked at her in alarm, "careful miss, don't want e' to choke now do us?"

She looked at Leonora with shiny blue eyes, "he's taking Reynard Miss!"

Leonora wasn't sure what to say, "And why wouldn't he?" she said bemused, "Reynard is an excellent farrier and loyal, in fact he is indispensable to Ciabhan."

"I don't know them big words miss, but I know Reynard makes I laugh." she said patting her belly. The gesture wasn't lost on Leonora; had Reynard yielded to the wantons charms after all! She wondered.

"And Ciabhan told you this?" Leonora asked.

Maudie exasperated sighed, "no Miss, t'were Tom what told I, but Master Ciabhan had told 'e this morning, my Tom will be left ere' as help for Dickon." Domenica still holding Faye was not listening, Leonora raised her eyebrows quizzically sliding her eyes in the girls direction, Maudie understood immediately, "No miss", Maudie answered, "'e aint' going, that I knows for sure! Master Ciabhan baint' that cruel!"

Domenica needed Corentyn at this point in her recovery, to have sent him away would have been cruel indeed, and Leonora smiled back at Maudie with relief, Domenica remained oblivious of their unspoken concerns. With a wink Maudie whispered, "'es a good sort at heart, now I best be gone, Tom don' want me out of 'is sight lately, and I's much to do."

So that was it! Leonora's saviour, for that's what he'd been for her was leaving. By his own admission Ciabhan was no longer a young man, she did not want him to leave when there was a chance she may never see him again, would he find the time to speak with her? Could she change his mind? There was more chance of the sun falling to the earth!

"Come Domenica," she said, "I need the peace and quiet of my own solar!"

The curtain wall was far less sinister by day and Leonora smiled at the nights fears, beyond the arrow slits the forest no longer roared but swayed almost seductively, she felt embarrassed by the word 'seductive' it conjured images of desire; how had it found a place in her barren mind? The chapel door was ajar; Domenica put a warning finger to her lips, Leonora frowned, "Master Ciabhan, since before Prime has been alone there, he did not bother even to break his fast."

Leonora whispered back, "Is something amiss?"

Domenica shrugged her shoulders, "I know not but half the night he has been at prayer!" Leonora recalled the night's late riders.

Cautious of the steps they turned into the stairwell; water ran down the walls and puddled the steps Leonora clung to the iron rail.

The bailey was filled with people; Dickon was giving concise orders, explaining patiently Ciabhans wishes. Even Compton Berry's seneschal the ancient Edwin was present, grey as an old goat he watched the proceedings quietly sitting behind a trestle he scratched on a parchment and kept to himself. To volunteer for crusade was a significant moment in an individuals life and worthy of support, even the normally superior verderers listened respectfully, while a group of sergeants huddled by the stables stayed their squabbling long enough to note the instructions of the man under whose banner they would ride.

Last nights rain had left everything freshened, ramparts glistened in the sun as drips plopped from sodden thatch, underfoot the grass was slippery and paths muddy where the earth was churned to mire. The commotion and riot of colours made little Faye's eyes nearly pop from her head, she squirmed in Winnies arms opening and closing her little fists in greeting to every ahh! And ooh! Leonora glanced back at the chapel, and imagined him in prayer, on such a fine morning the chapel would be flooded with amber light.

Leonora retreated to her chamber feeling more than a little sorry for herself, only Faye's antics kept her from despair.

Dangling on her mothers lap Faye amused herself with the shiny green ring, fascinated she pulled her mothers finger this way and that, even sucking on the stone, Leonora feared for the delicate skin and pulled her hand away to stop her from harming her tender little mouth.

Leonora admired the emerald in the light, in its green heart fissures criss crossed the quartz, why she could even see her own reflection! What a story this ring could tell! She watched Faye playing with it and wondered if it would one day adorn her own finger.

Beneath the window ledge her mothers sandalwood chest remained still, the fragrance of sandalwood permeated the chamber. Leonora rested the babe against it and supported her chubby arms, she beamed at the sturdy child as she stamped her feet on the silk rug, Faye gurgled with pleasure; the new game had detracted her attention from the ring.

Leonora traced the unusual teardrop shapes carved into the chest it seemed to tell a story; a maiden pursued by a handsome horseman, richly attired his hair flowed like a mane and a magnificent moustache curled about his cheeks. The chest must be old for in places the delicately carved flower vines were almost worn flat, Mati said it had been carried all the way from the east as a gift for her mother, Faye rattled the metal lock with curious fingers, Mati also had said that it contained everything treasured by her mother; that Ciabhan kept the key safe at all times.

The urgency that gripped the castle descended without warning on Leonora, with Ciabhan about to depart she realised she had never really thanked him properly for his support during the terrible months since Alains murder. angry with herself she couldn't imagine why on earth she hadn't purchased something on that day in Totnes? Or found time to make something, how shallow and selfish she had become of late taking everything as if her right! What if he never came to say goodbye? For he didn't have to! then would never know how much she owed him; The idea that he might not come was unbearable.

God in Heaven where had these feelings come from? It must be the blow to her head, could it have unhinged her mind, but of course it had! Unknown as yet the truth smouldering deep inside her steadied itself, for the revelation when it came would be almost too shocking for her to countenance.

With the sound of departures daily in her ears she languished alone, Domenica and Maudies skills were needed; only young Winnie escaped extra tasks.

On the day Ciabhan finally did call Leonora barely recognised him, he looked no different from the servants loading the supply panniers.A chamois tunic open at the neck was girdled about the waist with a simple leather thong, loose moleskin hose were tucked into suede boots laced in the Saxon manner, and his hair was scraped tightly back into a tail. Dark smudges beneath his eyes gave away his exhaustion but still the fragrance of musk rose clung to him, unlike the unwashed many.

"My apologies Leonora," he begged, spreading his hands before him. She pretended not to care and replied, "For what Sir?"

He shrugged his shoulders. "How mends the wound? May I look?" he asked before stepping closer.

"But of course," she answered, turning her head for him to see better. Gently he felt the skin tutting with concern as he did so and making her uneasy, "Is it so bad?" she asked, "will it leave a mark?"

He stood back and observed her, "It heals cleanly, you have nothing to fear," he smiled indulgently, "Your beauty is intact!"

Leonora felt her skin prickle and knew her colour rose, by chance Faye started to whimper and he moved to the cradle, in contrast to the pristine linen his fingers seemed dark, Faye must have tried to suck at them for he withdrew them quickly, "no, no my sweetling, these are no teat!"

He turned back to Leonora she hoped her blush had disappeared, in truth she suspected he would never even have noticed.

"There are things you need to know Leonora," he said seriously, "can we talk, for I fear time runs on."

Leonora gestured for Winnie to take Faye; the maid gave a timid smile and scuttled away.

Standing in front of the open window, Ciabhan looked down at the chest, "it seems I terrify that girl," he said distractedly.

"I think you do sir! Pray tell when do you leave?"

He looked up, "when all is completed, the baggage has already gone." before she could stop herself she blurted out, "I understand the journey hazardous, must you go?" Her voice had risen slightly reminding him of the time she first visited Compton Berry, she must have noticed too for she lowered her voice before saying, "I fear for your safety!"

her words seemed to take him by surprise, he stroked his beard, "And why would you fear for me Leonora, it's what men do! You must not distress yourself."

She felt a little foolish but continued, "It's just that I never thought of you leaving! Others maybe but you..."

He put his finger to his lips silencing her protests, "my dear, you must know that even Alain would have made the same choice! With no hesitation."

226

No! she thought, here he was wrong, Alain would never have left her! of
that she was certain! She must have seemed sad for he changed his
manner, "do not distress yourself on my account Leonora, this journey I
have undertaken more than once, and God has always been on my side!"
he motioned her to sit, "you and Faye will lack for nothing, provision has
been made for all your needs, there is however something you should
know." He put his hands together and placed them on his chin, as if in
thought. "It has been bought to my notice that your Father is to join us, he
rides under the Bishops banner, he seeks absolution for the strife he has
caused."
His next words showed a great generosity of spirit, "if it so pleases you,"
he said gravely, "I will personally take responsibility for his safety!"
he waited patiently for her reply.
"Yes do so," she said humbly.
"Then so be it." he promised.
Here was a man prepared to defend his mortal enemy, the man who
would have killed him willingly; Ciabhan seemed satisfied by her answer.
"Here," he said, taking a key from around his neck, "the key to your
mothers' chest, everything therein is now yours believe me you will need
the heart of an ox not to be moved by her honesty, promise me you will
guard well her memory."
 He stood but made no attempt to leave, then awkwardly he said,
"Boscombe Valle, your home, do you wish to return there?" unprepared
for the question she snapped back, "Have you forgotten Alain? Murdered
on its soil! "Never ask me if I would return there!"
Gently he said, "I understand your distress, but a decision must be made
before I leave. You are welcome to live or remain here as long as you
wish, but Alain worked hard to increase Boscombe Valles productivity, it
is too valuable to neglect."
Upset by the subject Leonora thought she would crack, "then do as you
wish with it!
Women! They would try the patience of a saint! Ciabhan wanted no
female tears and besides he'd noticed the green flash of anger in her
eyes; they so resembled her mothers that he nearly choked on the sudden
rush of sorrow, Gods Blood! The sooner he was away the better!
"Many are the Orders that would be grateful for extra help!" he
responded.
Ashamed of her loss of control she said calmly, "My Lord it goes without
saying that I trust in your excellent judgment, please do what you
consider is best, I will be content by your decision."
The sound of raised voices rose from the bailey, " methinks tis time I
left!" he grimaced not unkindly, "do remember that Edwin my seneschal,

though he may appear ancient to you is here to help, he minds my lawful wishes; should I not return," he paused, reluctant to say what he must, "it can be said no other way.... you and the child inherit Compton Berry, exactly as my wife would have done!"

Leonora's emotions threatened to give way, "your generosity is overwhelming Sir! I am undeserving of such kindness, all this time under your roof and I have given nothing in return!"

His response surprised her, "And what would you give me Mistress, Some trinket, of what worth is that to me?" She looked at the emerald, it flashed on honeyed skin, and so was this another meaningless bauble then?

He guessed rightly her thoughts. "No!" he said quickly, "not that! Not the ring; you misunderstand!"

The emeralds green almost matched the anger in her eyes of a moment ago.

"I gave this ring to your mother, it represented our undying for each other, that it sits now upon the finger of her daughter and is worn in Faye's memory is enough!"

He gestured towards the empty crib, "know Leonora, that although fate has denied me Fatherhood, you and Alain have already given back something of what destiny stole," it was then she understood, "behold your priceless gift Madam!"

He seemed fatigued, "I need nothing more!"

With good timing Maudie appeared, hands on widening hips she almost filled the doorway, "Sir, youm's wanted below! Reynard keeps asking for you!" She watched the two of them curiously; Leonora fumed, surely it was obvious that Ciabhan was speaking with her! But Maudie remained still, like a rock, immovable!

Good God thought Leonora she looked to be again with child! Had her blatant desire for Reynard already been rewarded with his seed?

Maybe it was Leonora's imagination but Maudie even appeared to scowl at Ciabhan, but of course if he were taking Reynard away she would hate him!

Ciabhan muttered something about 'being away then,' then with no more than a cursory nod left the room, Maudie waddling after him asked loudly, "'Tis tomorrow you leave then for sure Sir?" his reply filled Leonora with horror, his voice echoed back along the passageway, through the open door and lodged in her heart; "aye mistress," he said, "tomorrow for sure!" That was it then, he would be away for God knew how long! her foolish objections had fallen on deaf ears, and Maudies interruption had stopped further conversation. Angry, frustrated and unable to vent her anger it exploded inwardly shivering every nerve ending and filling her body with a terrible ecstasy. He needed nothing, he had said so quite plainly; it was she whose mind was possessed by desire! The truth though long in coming had finally dawned, she clutched at a chair for fear her legs would buckle.

Why even now the devil cavorted on her minds fertile ground teasing with thoughts of lust; where for six months she had been emotionally barren.

What started as admiration and respect for her protector had turned to obsession without her realising, now the obsession was become a dangerous hunger and she was clearly no longer in control of rational thinking.

Of course a new life! The one thing within her power to give; surely the ultimate gift!

And the principled Lord of Compton Berry? Why it was plain he would never accept willingly what she offered, female guile would have to be used! Imagining his horror merely heightened her desire, made her belly quiver with a thousand butterflies!

Now her irritation with Maudie had turned to gratitude, for Maudie Suttons proud wantonness had merely served to show Leonora's own simmering passion.

The soft little cheek quivered but her thumb never left her mouth as Leonora kissed her daughters forehead, she would slumber the whole night.Leonora checked that the little glass bird could be seen, always on the window sill its colours delighted Faye, beside it a night light burned steadily. Winnie only came into the chamber at night if her mistress called, Leonora had been adamant from Faye's birth that she alone cared for her child, night and day, not some serving maid no matter how well the intention!

Into the passageway Leonora padded barefoot past Winnies curtained alcove, from the wall slit she saw a thread of cobalt low on the horizon, the only break from all enveloping blackness, at ground level it disappeared completely; unobserved she stepped into the bailey.

She'd heard men speak of pitch, a sticky black substance that when boiled scalded everything it touched; could this night be as black as pitch for it seemed darker than any other she remembered. No stars glimmered and the moon was in hiding, she breathed a sigh of relief, but shuddered at the thought of divine guidance! Domenicas little cell and the infirmary were in darkness, what if her pure friend should see her now? A flash of shame crossed Leonoras mind, unheeded it fled..

She headed towards the gleam of the chapel candle, a beacon it shone like blood through the stained glass, the only glimmer of light in this blackest of nights! She pulled her cloak tight, lessening her shadow as she climbed the steps of her accident.

Squeaking like a trapped mouse the door could have been an alarm, loud enough to wake the whole castle, half in and half out she hesitated her mind working overtime for an excuse, but not even a bird stirred.

Fizzing n the sudden draught, the altar candle flickered across Ciabhans Templar Standard , bathing it in amber light. Leonora was surprised at how warm the floor was as she crossed the chapel and turned into the gallery never looking to the left where Ivan's living quarters hremained unchanged.

Hewn into the gallery wall close to the stairwell was a niche for a watchman, happily his wife was tonights priority.

Would Leonora's path have altered if she'd known of her mothers own guilty secret? When a moment's passion had lost her an adored friend and very nearly destroyed Ciabhan?

What if she had instead chosen to open the chest and read her mothers words, would she still have followed her desire or would self control have won the day?

But almost in a mirror of her Mothers folly, as a moth to the light and certain death Leonora never wavered; drawn only to his magnetic flame onward she fluttered light as a dandelion seed ever upwards.

230

Coolness licked at her legs and feet, while the low throb in her belly near overwhelmed her, once she stumbled but the ache only intensified at thought of un-fulfilment!

She tapped lightly and waited, at the door, no more than a few seconds passed but it was an eternity, she heard a rustle like tapestry being pulled aside just before the door opened, She had not expected his squire. Well schooled the boy brushed pass without looking at the female caller his Master's bed companions were of no interest to him.

Leonora slipped inside the chamber, with a dull thud the door closed behind her and the hanging dropped into place, through her lightweight cloak she felt the prickle of coarse wool, and in her breast her heart beat with the fury of a drum.

"Mistress Leonora?" Ciabhan had questioned sleepily; in the dimpsy light his eyes were luminous, " And what pray Mistress brings you here at this ungodly hour?"

Winnie scrubbed furiously at the mysterious foot prints, so dainty were they that five muddy toes could be seen perfectly. She knelt back and wiped her hands on her apron at Leonora's waking sigh, "God luv us Miss, this floors a mess, goodness knows where these came from!" she swept her arm over the floor.

"Where's Faye" asked Leonora, the crib was empty, Winnie coloured. "You was sleeping like the dead Miss, the little one was crying so that Miss Domenica came an took er' theys gone to see Master Ciabhan leave."

Leonora flew out of bed, mud on the hem of her night gown matched that of the floor, Winnie frowned. In seconds Leonora reached the ramparts, she looked down onto an unbelievable scene.

It was as if the whole of Devon's nobility was gathered at Compton Berry, confusion, sound and dust tightened her throat even up here she struggled to breath. She watched as gaily apparelled Knights on brightly adorned steeds conversed and clasped hands beneath banners and standards, in every colour imaginable, in restless groups they waited, as if for orders. Amongst the sea of bodies squires and servants ran hither and thither, fetching, carrying and avoiding blows, along the walls young maids and wives with babes in arms wrung their hands and dabbed at eyes.

Directly beneath the wall where she stood Reynard mounted on a fine beast wrestled its head to obedience before reaching down to clasp Corentyns outstretched hand, Domenica with Faye tight in her arms looked on, gently she placed her arm around Maudies shoulders as the older girl wept,Tom waiting his turn to shake Reynard's hand eyed his wife suspiciously!

Though Leonora peered hard at the crowds Ciabhan was nowhere to be seen.

From behind her a grating on the steps made her turn, red faced and perspiring he looked over warm in heavy riding attire, he wiped his forehead with the green and yellow kerchief.

"Gods blood Mistress as if it weren't hot enough in all this paraphernalia, I'm expected to climb to the top of the castle to take my leave of you!" he re knotted the kerchief at his throat.

She laughed nervously, he looked far too handsome for grumpy words. "Well may you laugh Mistress, for..." unheeding of what he was about to say she interrupted.

"You look splendid Sir, but I'm compelled to ask again, is there nothing that would make you change your mind?" though his next words were cruel she knew he did not mean them so. He looked at her knowingly.

232

"You must know by now Leonora," he said, "there is nothing that would keep me from my duty." Her heart sank even though she had expected nothing more.

It thumped again wildly when he reached down, took her hand and raised her fingers to his mouth, "But," he added, "remember there is everything to bring me back!"

His eyes glittered, hard, black and deep they were not the eyes of last nights lover, but those of a man already at war!

Turning on his heels he was gone, the clatter of his boots faded but the scent of musk rose lingered, its essence taken up by the warmth of the great stones hung in the dusty air.

A horn blast rallied the companies, the sound ran through her as smoothly as a blade, it was followed by a great cheer that battered her senses, as Ciabhan stepped out into the mass she could barely see him so veiled were her eyes by tears.

Tom and Dickon escorted him to his restless destrier, Ciabhan embraced them both before turning to Corentyn, with particular warmth he took the young mans forearm and said a few words, then bending to his master's stirrup Corentyn helped him mount.

With raised arm Ciabhan acknowledged the massed greetings, a clarion blast sent up a great cheer, then whirling their mounts towards the steep path the riders departed leaving behind them a din of snorting horse, yelping hounds and the muttered curses of a hundred battle thirsty Knights.

Leonora could watch no longer, she sank to the ground ripping her back on the stone parapet but beyond caring.

Only Reynard looked back briefly but the glare from the sun obscured everything and anyone that may have been watching from the high ramparts.

233

The incoming tide filled the barques' sails with an invigorating easterly that pushed the sturdy craft briskly up river, alone on the prow the dark skinned man looked once on the horizon he was leaving behind and turned his eyes landward, three times now he'd made the journey up river to Totnes, this would be his last.

With eyes so dark they were almost black he noted every hill that sloped to the river, glimpses of red soil made his stomach leap with childlike expectation as he anticipated his journeys end. He cut an exotic figure, even though dressed conservatively in black, maybe it was his decorative hide boots, for they looked strangely at odds with such simple garb. The breeze tugged at his cloak and billowed it around his slender form, tightly he clasped the lapis lazuli brooch pinning his cloak, his other hand rested on the handrail, he seemed impervious to the rock and lurch of wood on water, occasionally he gathered the folds of his cloak around him as if cold, but for a man who'd been at sea for weeks he looked surprisingly fit, with glossy hair and a healthy skin he could easily have just sailed around the headland!

Hair, as black as raven wing except for a little grey at the temples whipped across his eyes in straight black strands.

When not on the brooch his fingers tightened on the sword hilt tucked discreetly beneath his cloak, to a watcher he would seem to be reassuring himself it was still in place. As the channel narrowed and the reed banks closed in, the familiar scent of damp soil and foliage reached his nostrils, and he breathed deeply, shortly the river would widen again and Totnes would be in sight, terra firma would be beneath his feet and his senses would be free of salt and sea. Now his journey was nearly ended he allowed himself to think again on the circumstances that had finally bought him back; his reluctance to believe the words; 'Faye dead!'

How he had wept on reading Alains letter. The words short and brutal had been honest! Years had passed but he wept still; an accident the words had blurred.

'To our comrade, Ivan Dei Romani Scuri, Brother in Arms, and dearest friend. 'it is with great sadness that I tell you Faye of Compton Berry has died, the result of an accident, all that could be done was done, we are all utterly bereft at our loss, this my friend is surely fates cruellest blow!"

The letter begged his prayers for Faye's soul and for Ciabhan in his grief. It ended, 'As we remember you also in our prayers. It was signed simply; Your friend, Alain Rousseau.

Ivan shuddered and pulled his cloak around him for the hundredth time, after reading the words he had no recollection of the darkness or himself falling, only a faint recall of the brilliant murals in the painted room suddenly dulling; much later he had woken on the floor, a mess of blood and tears beneath his face.

'Faye dead!' Faye the adored wife of his great friend Ciabhan, so soon a widower, the friend Ivan had cuckolded! The words imprinted on his minds eye and stayed, haunting his every waking moment.

Rome that sunny happy city of his youth, the city he'd spoken so often of to Faye surprisingly had offered no spiritual comfort at all; with vain hopes of easing his pain he fled its painted Churches. He sought exotic places where, if not happiness he might find some distraction; but he soon realised that a heart so broken needed more than a pretty face or stunning sunsets.

Cyprus that glittering island of Aphrodite, women as lovely as the legendary goddess herself served only to remind of loves bitter sweetness, a short sojourn only.

Byzantine and its wonders fared a little better, providing him with an understanding of beliefs different to his own, Islam he found fascinating, it led to him questioning his own reasons for crusade. Constantinople also reunited him with his Turkish friends, two Christian Turks who'd fought with both Ciabhan and Ivan in Acre, settled now with families; they shared Ivan's grief for the Lord of Compton Berry, the man they had followed to England. They begged their Christian Brother to remain with them but in the end had to reluctantly let him go. Ivan had vowed never again to set foot in Palestine, the land that had bound him and Ciabhan together in war, honour and suffering, true to his word he kept away, and instead sailed on orange scented breezes to Sicily. As Palestine's landscape had been harsh, so the island of Sicily was beguiling, and as seductive as a beautiful woman.

The Templar Fortress that had offered shelter on his previous visit remained a sanctuary; he was alone now but some monks remembered him still. Ivan stalked the ramparts and watched eagles circling overhead, their plaintive cries thinning the higher they soared. Sometimes he sat quietly reading while lizards basked on the baked earth.

In the shadow of mighty walls he cooled his body from the ferocious sun, and wandered through fragrant groves of citrus, beneath canopies of glossy leaves he lay on the ground studying the blue patchwork above; as once beneath English willows he'd relaxed by the lake with Faye at Compton Berry. Then they had talked of his childhood and the countryside beyond Rome's walls, fascinated she had listened, her hazel eyes reflecting all the colours of the lake. Oh such cruel memories!

It was during the sultry heat of a Sicilian afternoon, when the chirping of crickets nearly deafened the listener that he experienced what he could only think of as a "calling." Just as a thunderbolt may strike without warning from a clear sky, he saw his future stretch before him, though drowsy with heat he knew England! The country he never expected to see again, nothing he tried would erase the image, rather it beckoned all the more! That land that kept its charms veiled in mist and rain; as effectively as a chaste maid might protect her virginity.

England! The country that had granted such happiness, and then as if in a fit of pique withdrew it bestowing even greater sorrow!

The visions persisted; not leaving Ivan free for a second!

A light sea mist chased the barque as it ploughed on; since leaving Devon's shores all those years ago Ivan had squashed any desire to return. If he had stayed would Faye be alive now? The thought tormented him and he pushed it from his mind. He recalled instead the love between Faye and Ciabhan, a supreme love written in their fortunes; he had had to leave for he had no place in its future.

The 'calling' affected Ivan deeply, more and more he believed that Faye's untimely death was compelling fate to beckon him home, he supposed even that destiny maybe had not yet finished with him after all!

He felt for the crucifix around his neck, felt for its comfort.

"Not long now sir," the captains gravelly voice broke Ivan's dreaming, "one more bend an' our journeys done, can't take me some real ale soon enough, an' one o they ripe wenches what serves it up! What say you sir?" the captain winked, Ivan smiled, the crossing had been incident free, quite an achievement given the nature of sex starved seamen.

"You've earned all the wenching you can do Fonzi, and this," he tossed a purse of silver to the grinning captain who caught it with iron hands, he counted the coins with relish, "Very generous Sir, enough for all the wenches in Totnes! And more!" He thrust forward his privates in a vulgar gesture as he bowled along the deck, a couple of lads idled on deck and he cuffed one of them, "Off your arse's an get packing for the fine gentleman!" when they sniggered he snarled back, "any filth upon they bales and your feet will not even touch dry land!"

a few curious stares followed Ivan as he strode down the gang plank, but most were too absorbed by their own business to really notice the dark skinned stranger, as far as they were concerned he was just another visiting foreigner, probably off to the Brothers at Buckfast; the townsfolk of Totnes were well used to the bizarre! Serving wenches

236

stopped their duties as he passed boldly they watched some with dropped jaws, other women more discreetly eyed the handsome stranger from lowered lids.

Handsome men were rare of late, for the call to crusade had left the land barren of eligible young men! Ivan's extraordinary looks and spear straight bearing would always invite interest.

A young monk with a scroll of parchment tucked under his arm idled on the bridge, he noticed him immediately, there could be no mistaking Brother Ivan Dei Romani Scuri! Discreetly he followed as the traveller headed to the Seven Stars Tavern, when Ivan stopped Erasmus approached, At the tug on his sleeve Ivan turned to face the young Brother.

"You do not recognise me Brother," stammered Erasmus, "it was you Brother Ivan who taught me to read Latin, I'm Brother Erasmus now.

Ivan grinned broadly, "Of course," he said grasping the young mans outstretched hand and looking him up and down, "but I remember only a timid youth."

Erasmus beamed, "I knew it was you Brother, even with the passing years I would have known my mentor, you haven't changed at all, but I never thought to see you hereabouts again!"

Ivan smiled, "My friend I never expected to be here again!"

He was genuinely pleased to see the young man and explained, "I must make arrangements for lodging, will you not wait awhile so we can talk further?" Ivan looked little different than when he used to visit Buckfast in the company of the Lord of Compton Berry or with The Lady Faye, just more mature and rather important!

"Brother", Erasmus said, "before you decide, we have space a plenty at the Brothers town lodging, be assured the priests and Brothers would be honoured to receive you."

Ivan hesitated, "Brother Erasmus I am no longer in the employ of Church or Abbey, it may be better if I lodge here."

Brother Erasmus answered, "that will make no difference at all, I know they will be honoured to have you."

Ivan smiled at the enthusiastic young Brother, "Then I will be honoured to accept," he replied.

Muddy on even good days, the hill leading to the Church of St Mary's was sticky with ordure, before them a pair of oxen ploughed through the rubbish pulling a cartload of wool bales, bound tightly in calico the vendor had made sure the cargo was well protected, Ivan and Erasmus picked their way through the filth looking for an opportunity to slide past the lumbering oxen, each time a gap opened the drover would yell, causing the oxen to lurch sideways in a fresh spray of sludge, townsfolk

brave enough to venture into this mire resembled some strange breed of
brown and white cattle themselves, Cattle probably being the cleaner!
to preserve their garments both men hoisted their tunics as high as was
respectable, Ivan lamented the destruction of his fashionable Italian
boots, and cursed more his naivety regarding the English weather! How
many pairs of boots had he ruined courtesy of these shores, would he
never learn!

Conversation was impossible until they turned into the walkway that
wound around the church grounds, not until they found a seat outside the
Guildhall did they speak; with weary legs outstretched in the sun they
watched the mud dry.

"By all the saints," Ivan's breath was laboured, "methinks these legs
have become mud!" They laughed at their appearance.

Wiping the mud from his face Ivan closed his eyes, how often had he
passed these seats and sat for a while, placed for the convenience of those
waiting to be admitted to the Guildhall he recalled all the old grumblers
waiting to air grievances. Sometimes when Ciabhan had acted as
mediator in one of the chambers Ivan had waited thus for him.

He let the sun warm his face, he could have dozed but Erasmus
interrupted, "Sir, do you recall the time you bought a Lady to meet our
Priest? And a group of young acolytes had to be shooed from the Church
because of curiosity?" Ivan nodded.

"Well," continued Erasmus, "I was one of those boys, And never have I
forgotten old Father Georges' outrage or the way his flesh wobbled when
he walked, if I I remember right I think you wanted to laugh too!"

A frown creased Ivan's forehead, Erasmus thought he'd angered him.
Throughout his long journey Ivan had tried to push away the past
especially when thoughts of Faye and Ciabhan had become unbearable,
now innocently his companion had opened painful wounds.

Ivan sighed deeply and replied, "Oh indeed my friend, I remember as if it
were yesterday, I just wish I didn't!" Erasmus studied the features of the
man beside him, beneath fine brows almond eyes were so clear that the
whites emphasized the blackness of the pupils, they were like deep dark
water and just as fathomless! The corners were crinkled showing he'd
not lost any of his humour, but smudges of blue beneath showed a lack
of sleep. Those eyes dominated a striking face, blemish free, so unlike
Erasmus' own pocked skin, when Ivan smiled Erasmus noted that not one
blackened tooth existed amongst the brilliant white, how he wondered
could that be! Erasmus knew something of this man's history, that he'd
trained for a Templar Knight, and was skilled in the art of combat,
probably he had killed! If so did he smile when taking a life? How would
his foe have reacted facing such radiance at the end of a sword!

Erasmus tried to picture him fighting alongside the Lord of Compton Berry; they must have resembled story book Knights! For Ivan was almost as legendary as Ciabhan himself!

For the first time Erasmus realised just why he'd been named 'the raven,' for such gloss and blackness only existed on that bird's wing! The inky waterfall was broken only by a few greying strands at his temple.

Neither had age thickened Ivan's girth, still wiry he walked with a lithe grace from the hip, no clumsy stomping or rolling with bandy rider's gait, all his movements were elegant; though there was nothing feminine about him, rather he resembled a sleek cat stalking its prey.

Brother Erasmus was as much in awe of his guest now as ever he had been, and couldn't wait to introduce him to the Brothers at the lodging house, "Tis nearly none, most will be at prayer," he said, "our kitchen has a reputation for the most flavoursome stews, beggars reside on our steps in hope of being fed, unlike some we do not see them as an inconvenience."

Ivan stood and motioned the young monk to lead the way.

In the shadow of the squat Saxon fort a curve of thatched dwellings faced the sandstone heights of St Mary's, these housed the dormitories where visitors were accommodated, the first floor reserved for guests while priests and monks slept on the ground floor. The fort was a watch tower and served as deterrent to attacks, no one could remember the last attack or when the red and white standard of England had not fluttered at its staff. Ivan gazed upwards fascinated still by the structure, the walls were in shadow and seemed to loom over the cottages giving a false feeling of being larger than it really was, at its base green grass gently sloped away. Shielding his eyes to better see the fortress Ivan accidentally bumped a pedestrian nearly unfooting the fellow, the man cursed and spat at Ivan's feet, only Erasmus' apologies prevented a scene, but the man still muttered of filthy foreigners! "I fear I have been too long at sea my friend", Ivan mumbled. As they passed St Mary's the chanting of Monks rose and fell, and bells clanged; a familiar sound long missed, Ivan stopped to listen. Doves and pigeons flapped upwards in flurries of feathers only to return cooing moments later. "I hope you do not miss a service because of me Brother?" said Ivan. Erasmus nodded to a low door on the right, "its only practice." he pointed," through there Sir." Ivan stepped into a low room heavy with wood smoke, tiny windows allowed in just enough light, trestles stretched from end to end, Two men in white aprons conversed while a boy sulkily stirred whatever bubbled in a huge cauldron suspended over the fire.One of the men said something to his companion and beckoned, "Come on in Sir, the Brothers are at service but you are most welcome, we turn no one away!"

the boy jumped to his feet, grabbed a trencher and placed it on the trestle nearest the fire, a steaming chunk of boiled beef was ladled quickly onto his bread. "eat your fill man, looks like you could do with something inside you!" one of the men said, he looked at Ivan with little piggy eyes, "not from around these parts are you?"

Ivan shook his head, "No, I am not."

The cook called to his assistant for refreshment, "wine or ale Sir?"

Ivan stuck to wine; it was a long time since English ale had passed his lips.

"Visitors are few hereabouts since crusade started," said the cook, "most Barons have gone off to do their bit, now its only the priests and the odd traveller we serve , and of the beggars!" He studied Ivan's sombre attire, "you looks a bit like a Man of God yourself."

Ivan wiped his mouth, "No Sir I am not a priest! I am visiting old friends, I hope the beef they serve is half this good!"

The cook beamed he would have asked more questions but someone else came in and he scurried away.

Ivan finished to eat, graciously thanked the cook and stepped back into fading sunlight, the cook watched him go sure he'd seen that face before.

"Tell me Erasmus how fares My Lord of Compton Berry?" Ivan had finally had the opportunity to ask as they sat together in the dormitory, "it has been too many years!"

Not once had it occurred to him that Ciabhan would not have been resident at Compton Berry.

"Brother, you have not heard? Ciabhan of Compton Berry is in the Holy Land, on crusade. Replied Erasmus."

The goblet in Ivan's hand clattered to the floor, wine like blood snaked across the cobbles. "The Holy Land? You must be mistaken Brother!" he gasped, "Ciabhan hated it there!"

Erasmus looked at the floor, swallowed hard and continued, "These two years he has been gone, it is said King Richard asked in person for Compton Berry's Knight."

Of course Ivan was aware England's new King had called for another crusade, but Ciabhan like himself never wished to set foot there again; in his own words, 'never again!'

"God in heaven!" Ivan slammed his right fist into his left, "dear God, tell me I dream!" He paced the room. "And Alain?" he said, "The Knight Alain Rousseau, is he with him?" Erasmus hunched his shoulders wishing he were elsewhere. "But of course," Ivan continued, "of course he would be at Ciabhans side." Erasmus could not believe Ivan knew nothing of the French knights' death, why had this task fallen to him?

"Sir" he interrupted as Ivan paced, "Alain Rousseau is dead!"

Ivan stopped in mid step, he clutched at the edge of a trestle, knuckles white they matched his blood drained face.

"Two years past sir," Erasmus whispered, "cut down on his own land in front of his wife!" Ivan remained still, his features hidden behind a curtain of hair; Erasmus avoided looking at his face but knew he wept.

"and not a year wed," he continued, " his tiny daughter left fatherless, his wife so soon a widow!"

Ivan stared through the tiny window, he glimpsed the happy outside world; crimson like blood streaked the evening sky.

"A wife? you say, a child?" Erasmus nodded.

"Monsieur Rousseau married the Lady Faye's daughter; the child is Faye's Granddaughter. The widow and her child remain at Compton Berry, under Ciabhans protection.

Stunned Ivan struggled to understand his Gods cruelty, and to contain his rising anger.

Alain married to a daughter of Faye? He recalled she had borne two daughters, and a son to Leon.

"Who would hate one as good as Alain Rousseau? And in Gods name for what reason?" he asked Erasmus, he in turn just shook his head.

"Yet Ciabhan still left for crusade?" Ivan said in disbelief.

"Isn't that what Knights do Sir, do they have a choice! I am so sad to be the bearer of such news; in truth I believed you knew, that it was the reason you had returned!"

Ivan straightened and pushed the hair from his eyes; he dragged his fingers across his forehead and massaged the crease between his brows, he felt drained, "it's no fault of yours."

Then as if expecting Erasmus could offer an explanation he said pleadingly, "But why does God test my very soul so!"

Ivan woke in the early hours on the floor of St Mary's; he'd no idea if he'd been there all night, a day or maybe a hundred years!

The Chill from the cold floor had seeped into his bones and set him shaking violently, not wishing to wake he desired only sleep, it at least numbed his pain and blocked reality if only for a while, however a force quite beyond his control made him haul himself to his feet; he looked around blankly.

The young monk, who had sat all night watching over him, placed a cloak about his shoulders and without a word shepherded him gently to a place of safety.

241

Chapter 35
A Homecoming

Brother Jaime's' emaciated body lay unmoving beneath a threadbare coverlet, his mind was alert, Jaime pondered often on why God let his body fail him yet kept his intellect intact! He would much have preferred to hop out of bed and join his fellow Brothers at prayer, instead his body slowly deteriorated while his mind worked overtime!

With watery eyes he looked on the glossy head of the man hunched at his bedside; he stroked the shiny hair, was it for this he was made to linger? If so he must do his best for God and for the desolate man beside him.

"My son, do not question why! know only that it is your destiny to return to Compton Berry!"

Ivan's reply was barely audible, "but for what, only strangers dwell there now! Those dear to me are no more, Faye, Alain, Mati; even Ciabhan has left, and a chatelaine who is a stranger to me! No Brother Jaime no purpose whatsoever can be served by my return, it will only open wounds afresh." Ivan heaved himself to his feet, "Tis best I leave!"

Jaime took his hand, "that chatelaine is the widow of Alain Rousseau, the daughter of Faye, to come all this way and not pay your respects would be ill mannered! Would you turn your back on her, Ciabhan did not!" Of course the old man was right.

"I fear the pain of memory," Ivan replied weakly.

"I know how you feel my Son, I know!" said Jaime. He pointed to a framed embroidery on a shelf next to a pile of scrolls, the letter 'J' had been delicately worked in fine silks, entwined with vines and fat purple grapes; woven into the border were the colours of Jaime's native Spain. "A gift from the lovely Faye of Compton Berry," he croaked, "by her own hand, a gift, she said for my patience in teaching her about healing plants; I prefer to remember her alive," he whispered.

"Your departure tormented her, but Ciabhan was ever strong and accepted fates whim, he never doubted that Faye's heart lay with him." For a moment there was an awkward silence between the two men, something in the old mans tone made Ivan think that he knew of their secret, "She was very fond of you Brother."

Jaime's rheumy eyes twinkled. "Ah!" he grinned, "For certain the pretty minx was fond of me, but it was ever the two of you she loved!" Had Ivan imagined it or did the old monk stress 'the two of you?' Jaime sighed, "God made us men fools for beauty my son, tis no sin to desire it! he patted Ivan's hand, "God understands our weaknesses, you are not alone!" smiling he added, "do not turn your back on Faye's daughter or Compton Berry, they expect you."

"Then tell me brother," Ivan said dismissively, "Is it also written that Ciabhan and I will meet again?"

Jaime blew out his cheeks, smiled secretly and raised his eyes to the heavens; "I am a humble monk my son, not Merlin! Just remember that You have more reason than most to know that fate and her handmaiden Destiny are capricious! They alone guide those who tread their tangled paths!"

Crafty old Brother Jaime did indeed have his way, for two days after their talk Ivan found himself making his way out of Totnes town.

Nothing daunted the sturdy little mare Ivan had purchased, swaying under his meagre possessions she plodded on confidently. Other than the curious looks he'd become accustomed to Ivan encountered no problems, fellow travellers either acknowledged him politely or passed by silently; the mare instinctively headed in the direction of Compton Berry.

Ivan lingered at the spot where the road forked and remembered Faye and their stand off, he recalled the day as if it were yesterday, even the lark song was the same.

Distant hills shimmered and danced in the midday haze, he had quite forgotten how lovely Devon was, surely he mused paradise itself was no match for an English summer! Hedgerows had yet to be cut back and in places he had to duck, dry earth soon dusted his boots red.

Surrounded by such beauty he quite forgot the horror of gallows gate, on perfumed breezes the taint of corruption reached his nostrils, he covered his mouth and nose against deaths stink. Crows black as night rose flapping from his path like skittish demons cawing displeasure at the intrusion. Ivan tried but was unable to ignore the remains of the poor wretch whose remains dangled obscenely, God only knew what the birds squabbled over, and what offence wondered Ivan had the pitiful creature been guilty of? And convicted by whom? No such one he recalled had ever hung there at Ciabhans behest; he demanded no such vile revenge! It seemed brutal England was still an unforgiving place.

Ivan's heart beat just a little faster as the gate lodge came in sight, a hawking party of four people, three with birds exited and turned left towards the high meadows, though some distance away they saluted him courteously, the last rider glanced behind him and slowed as if to stop, then changing his mind spurred forward to rejoin the two women. The female in the lead balanced a small falcon on her wrist, her companion appeared to cling unsurely to the reins of her mount while a lively hound bounded beside like a guard, only the one rider had looked back and soon all were out of sight.

243

Instead of turning into the castle entrance a sudden change of mind made Ivan follow the riders, the castle of Compton Berry was hidden in the valley but the crashing of axes and men's voices competed with the drumming of woodpeckers. In the familiar surroundings Ivan felt a great spirituality envelope him, so powerfully was the feeling that it nearly crushed him breathless!

He halted at a peregrines call, above a small copse she hovered, the neat head ever watching swivelled first to her left then the right, Ivan would have known Bella Donna anywhere, and his heart lurched; did she remember him? Softly, as he used to do he whistled, curious to see who called so familiarly she dropped lower, she knew him! Remembered his fear! While she watched him suspiciously Ivan wondered who was brave enough to fly her! A high pitched whistle from the valley momentarily confused the bird; another whistle and she swooped out of sight.

Bent by the prevailing westerlies the old oak still cast its shadow, how often had he and Ciabhan sheltered in its shade?

Ivan tethered this mount and walked across the scorched meadow grass, brittle it crunched beneath his feet. The hawking party were grouped at the bottom of the hill, their whistles and calls carried clearly on the breeze, slipping the cloak from his shoulders he untied the laces of his tunic and leant back against the oak, utter peace washed over him. Beneath that silent tree the spirits of the past beguiled him, whispering of lost pleasures, why! Their voices could still be heard! Faintly they spoke to him; surely he had never been gone!

The distant sea slipped hazily into sky and horizon.

Leonora seeing movement underneath the oak had asked who watched them; Dickons reply that her eyes were playing tricks didn't convince her. "Dickon," she persisted, " I surely saw someone, methinks him there still," her eyes were good, she shielded them from the sun, clearly she saw the figure of a man in the shadows, "There Dickon see! I am not mistaken," she shouted. Her temple throbbed, her heart thumped, could it be? Was it Ciabhan? She should have known better than to let her hopes rise for Dickons next words dashed them, "Nay mistress, tis not the Master but..." He recalled the stranger, something about the way he sat his horse; Leonora already halfway up the field did not look back.

She reached the oak just as Ivan stepped from its shade.

Instantly she knew who the olive skinned man standing before her was! Ivan Dei Romani Scuri, somehow it was appropriate that here in the high meadows she should set eyes on the legendary Raven for the first time.

Not once had he taken his eyes from the young woman, the tinkling of little bells fastened at her wrists accompanied every move as she spurred her horse up the hill, before she reined to a halt he knew exactly who she was, how she would talk and walk, and whose eyes would stare back at him; more than that he knew she knew him!

He seized the halter rein and stroked the sweating horses' nose, crouched on her Mistresses' gauntlet Bella Donna eyed him malevolently, Ivan gave her a wide berth.With a goshawk flapping on his wrist Dickon still laboured up the hill; Corentyn, Domenica and the hound followed as if they had not a care in the world.

Her skin bore no idle woman's pallor, it glowed with health as if an outside life were usual, and her clothes were sensible, she wore a chamois tabard over a simple long sleeved shift, and though the day was warm her shoulders were protected from the sun by an amber scarf, the breeze whipped light brown hair about her face making the matching amber drops in her ears dance; frequently she pulled the fluttering scarf about her. Uncoifed and wearing only earrings and a ring the young woman was Faye personified, except for her eyes! Faye's had been as soft as the moist hazel woods, eyes that had bewitched him. Those that watched him now were certainly beautiful! Almost too beautiful to be real; but their depths hid a brittleness, a suspicion!" good-naturedly Ivan let her scrutinise him and whilst she did so he watched her back. White teeth gleamed as she held her head to one side as if better to observe him, her half smile could not mask the hint of petulance, it marred what would otherwise have been a perfect mouth. Beneath tidy brows and fluttering lashes the beautiful green eyes regarded him boldly, maybe if he were closer he'd see a little hazel therein, but mostly he was reminded of water lily leaves floating on deep dark pools, they matched almost exactly the emerald gleaming on her outstretched hand.

"So Ivan Dei Romani Scuri," she said in the voice he already knew, "it seems we are after all destined to meet." He smiled his enigmatic smile, "that is presuming I speak with Madame Rousseau!" he said. Her persona altered briefly and the lovely eyes dulled as she answered, "Indeed Sir I am Leonora, widow of Alain Rousseau, though nearly two years have passed since my dear husband was lost to me; as alas are others!"

She guessed he was about to ask after Ciabhan, "I pray nightly for my Lord Ciabhans safety, she said, "however in truth I have received no word of him." Ivan responded, "I pray for him too, Mistress." She studied him a little longer, handsome with a lively intelligence he was in reality far from mysterious, and certainly nothing like the sinister raven he'd been named after! She fancied Alain and Matis descriptions a little exaggerated to say the least! In Alains own words this man had been his true comrade and mentor, on the other hand however some whispered that he'd been the lover of her mother, and the betrayer of his friend Ciabhan! It was common knowledge Leon hated him!

"And you presumably," she said, "are the 'raven!"

He grinned, "Was! Mistress, now I suspect many other names may describe me, however names were the least of my worries!"

His confidence was impressive, at last another man she could trust. Dickon reached them at last grinning from ear to ear; he greeted Ivan with genuine warmth.

Leonora dismounted keeping Bella Donna balanced on her forearm, "well Sir," she smiled mischievously at Ivan, "You are more comely by far, and I for one would be loath to compare you to that hideous creature!" Ivan bowed his head in mock gratitude.

Such hair! Thought Leonora as it fell around his face; Ravens wing! That was it, Ravens wing! Small wonder his name had been 'the Raven!'

She offered him her hand, "Will you walk with me sir, for there is much I would know?"

Chapter 36
Understanding

The moment Ivan rounded the elm and gazed once more on Compton Berry he realised that no matter where in the world he may travel, this small corner of Devon would always pull him back, whether he wanted to be here did not matter: destiny's decision was final!

Looking as if he might roast yet still wrapped in wolfskin Edwin shuffled over, no introduction was needed, "Ah! At last you are arrived my boy," he said, and "I see you have made the acquaintance of Lady Leonora." Ivan grinned, "Yes, we are acquainted," he looked at Leonora but she had turned at the sound of a child's voice.

"It's good to be here my friend," he said embracing the old man. Maudie sauntered across the sward, a boy of two years or so straddled her hip and a little girl not much older pulled excitedly at her hand, seeing the stranger her face lit and her lips parted coquettishly, "Good as gold he's been," she said not taking her eyes from Ivan, "both of they as been angels; good Lord Miss!" She exclaimed on seeing Leonora's grubby dress and boots, "looks like you 'as been doing a jig in Devon's dust!" She winked shamelessly at Ivan, he laughed back, "Not quite Mistress, but we did walk most of the way." A groom had already lifted the girl up behind Leonora, she snuggled into her Mothers waist, but Maudie still holding the babe for Leonora to take could hardly tear her eyes from the handsome stranger, only the impatient edge to Leonora's voice as she waited to take the babe snapped her from her trance! "Thank you Maudie," she said, "I'll take him now." Leonora placed him across the horse's neck and hooked his chubby fingers around the reins, as the groom led them away she beamed at Ivan, "I look forward to seeing you at dinner Sir," the child observed him through huge innocent eyes; Ciabhans eyes!

Ivan wasn't sure whether it was the shock of seeing the boy or Leonora's own dazzling smile, but suddenly he was floundering in a void of disbelief; transfixed by the child in Leonora's arms he hadn't heard Edwin until he repeated himself, "Sir, will you take of some refreshment?" Ivan shook his head, "no, no, Edwin I can wait." Ciabhan, a child? With Leonora? How? Of course! How foolish of him! What man could resist such a smile? Edwin replied, "As you wish; the Master made it clear before leaving that everything be readied for your return, Ciabhan plans as well for the unexpected as he does the expected!" Edwin guessed at Ivan's turmoil, and added, "Except this time the unexpected has caught him out!" he paused, "the image of his father is he not? Yet Ciabhan has no idea he has sired a son! Ivan remained silent.

"Come," said Edwin, "give me your arm; these legs are not what they used to be."

The household remembered 'the Raven' and greeted him respectfully, whispers of 'The ravens back' travelled faster than fire consumed the heretic! The two men made their way to the little chapel, Ivan's chapel! his place of sanctuary.

Candles sputtered on a stand," all for Ciabhan," said Edwin, but this special one," he pointed to the light flickering beneath Ciabhans banner, "has not been allowed to go out from the day he left." Edwin crossed himself, before indicating the passage way and Ivan's room.

"Ciabhan left specific orders ," he said, "that everything remained just as you left it," then with a sense of relief he added, "I have now discharged that duty," he smiled, "Compton Berry has waited long for your return." Ivan decided against asking how his return was expected with such certainty. Edwin took Ivan's hand as a Father would a Sons,, and fixed him with wise eyes, "God allows these things to happen my son; it is not for us to understand! But nothing he does is without reason!" Ivan prostrated himself before the little altar, the altar at which he had presided over Faye and Ciabhans nuptials, when he'd Honoured the promise he'd made to his friend; it was the last duty he had done at Compton Berry, for by dawn he had left.

Ivan stayed prone until his mind calmed; he knew not what game destiny played, only that it clearly desired something of him! Could it be to protect the little son of his friend? If so he would do it willingly and without Judgment; let destiny? Fate! Do with him what it would!

Below the chapel Ivan's room remained as he left it all those years ago, he ran his finger along the chipped table, he remembered the wood splintering as the table crashed to the floor during his fight with Torr, and how Ciabhan so charitable of mind chose still to save his friends life even knowing the truth of his deceit; how Ivan was humbled!

Above the pallet his crucifix remained, the colours only slightly faded, the tapestry of Saint George still covered the arrow slit, he recalled how the wind whistled through it on wintry nights; he tweaked aside the hanging, shadows had lengthened darkening the green, only the tops of the forest remained bright in the last rays of a weakening sun; it was maybe two hours to compline?

A tap on his open door made him turn, "hot water Sir." A sturdy lad placed a tub on the floor while two others filled it with steaming water. "Mistress Leonora asked this be sent for you," said Tom, "us'll be eating within the hour." He put down a small vial of oil and left, the distinctive smell of patchouli filled the room, the scent of another time!

Chapter 37
The holy land 1192

Flames danced in the night sky playing tricks on the minds of men and making them think of demons as sparks flew high into the darkness. Huddled together for warmth in night's bitter cold, warriors talked of campaign, of battles won and lost, of expectations and of doubts.

The camp moved like a sleeping beast turning and grunting in its slumber, the stink that permeated camp life was always the same, horse ordure and horse flesh, burning wood, pitch, the unwashed; and never far away the reek of foul middens. Pervading all the stench of blood hung ever present; the tented town wallowed in it! If one managed to avoid a stay in either infirmary or the surgical tent one would believe God was truly on his side! Bloody and agonizing treatment procedures more often took life than saved it; field surgery denied dignity even for those in the final moments of life.

After the surrender of Acre Ciabhan opted to share the same hardships as his men. Well-regarded by high and low; Christian and Muslim, the Lord of Compton Berry required no special favours from either the French or his own King Richard.

So frequent were the sounds of death and suffering that the living moving mass of the army were immured to its horrors; Ciabhan was one such. He listened to the sounds of the camp as he cleaned his hands and forearms; with the blunted edge of his dagger he dragged at the grime, what he would have given to feel water on his body! No matter how hard he may try the reek of blood could not be erased, it cloyed at his nostrils and tainted his skin, the idea of a scented bath invaded his thoughts, a fleeting aberration only for guilt quickly overcame him as he watched his fellow crusaders.

He observed the mixed group under his command! Die hard warriors and the usual mix of crusaders with their own causes, religious zealots, Christians swept along by fear of change, old Knights forever seeking glory in vain causes! And young Knights ready to die for God; thinking to keep him Christian!

The bravest of all were possibly the Pilgrims for in their quest to reach the golden city of Jerusalem they met with the harsh reality of bloodshed, and heat, of life in the brutal battle camps; they learned quickly that absolution came at a cost!

Excluding pilgrims Ciabhans unit were mostly regular fighters familiar with the art of combat; all that is except for one, Reynard! Alains young farrier showed no combatant skills whatsoever, he was and would remain a simple but excellent shoer of horse; if he lived he would one day be a first rate armourer. When Reynard fell victim to fever Ciabhan used his contacts and acquired at considerable cost the best Saracen physician to save his young squire from an untimely death; the incident caused Ciabhan for the first time to question whether it mattered at all who claimed Jerusalem for their own, Christian or Muslim! Worse still, did he care!

He wiped the dagger and rested his head against the rock.

For many of the crusading armies their work was complete with Acres capture, their duty to Richard discharged. Ciabhans thoughts lately turned more and more to home, who was he to play God with the lives of others? He watched Reynard thoughtfully as he rubbed oil into the harness and saddle, had the time come to reassess his motives?

Ciabhan maintained still his striking looks, a little more aged and much more cynical! a cut had laid open the flesh on his cheek, but the healthy tissue had healed well, a scar resembling a silver thread ran from the corner of his eye to mid cheek, a small dimple had been created which made him a appear to smile, when he did not; it had been suggested in jest that the wound even enhanced his handsomeness!

Ciabhan had never in his wildest dreams expected to be in these lands again, last time had been to do penance for the sin of loving Faye; for breaking his strict Templar vows.

But denying his love for Faye had proved impossible; badly wounded and against Ivan's better judgement Ciabhan insisted on returning to England, adamant that he would die only on Devon soil, however fate had other ideas; and the tale of Faye and Ciabhan was born!

On finding himself again on Muslim soil Ciabhan claimed this tour of duty his last , that only duty for King and country had bought him, in fact it was for penance, self punishment for sin; what that sin may have been he kept to himself.

Reynard noticed Ciabhan watching him and smiled, Ciabhan returned the young mans smile, of a sudden he was struck by the fact that he did not want to end his life here, in some desert grave marked only by a pile of dusty stones. He closed his eyes and saw clearly the glade of tall green beeches, heard the soft drip of summer rain; in everlasting sleep his Faye waited for him there; fate would not cheat his heart again!

A grating Breton accent cut through Ciabhans thoughts, as if to tear him maliciously from them, Ciabhan knew the voice too well and opened his eyes.

"My bones ache from lack of action, the accursed night damp rots me!" Ciabhan wasn't angry at the interruption, rather he was glad, his head needed to be clear, a walk would help, and he had decisions to make! He grasped the extended hand and heaved himself to his feet, "Aye, too idle for too long," he answered, "methinks tis time to go!" Leon was a head shorter than Ciabhan; reverently he looked up to the taller man.

His right eyelid drooped permanently giving him a sinister look as he strained to see out of what remained, the left eye, red from over compensating watered heavily as he constantly wiped at it, only a gap toothed grin when he laughed saved him from being the grotesque, a reminder of what had once been handsome features.

None of this however affected his ability to fight like a cornered lion! The mercenary lived on in him.

"You mean, England! Back to England?" Leon gibbered like a fool and repeated, "England?"

Ciabhan mused on how inspired his letter to the Bishop had been. "Yes, man England; maybe see the grand daughter you mention so often?" Leon stopped gibbering, instead his face twitched with anticipation, "you would let me see her?" he said.

Ciabhans letter had asked the Bishop to allow Leon of Pagonston to accompany him on crusade, by keeping Leon his enemy close, Compton Berry and those within it remained safe, intelligent thinking had removed the danger. Using his influence Ciabhan saw Leon coerced into taking up the cause of the true cross and placed by the Bishop under his sole command! Leon imagined the decision his own! And never recalled doing any wrong, but believed the Bishop when he said he must atone for his evil doings; all that really mattered was that his path to heaven be obstacle free!

"You would let me see her?" he said again, trying to suppress a hopeful grin. Certain things triggered Leon's malady of the brain, mostly he was a genial comrade and fellow crusader until one of his mists descended, then he would become violent and rage, imagining insult where there was none, cursing he would berate himself sometimes tearing at his person until drawing blood; as if the conflict were with his own soul, cruelly he'd become known as 'Leon the insane'

"That's right, Faye your grandchild!" repeated Ciabhan.

For Leon's good conduct Ciabhan had resolved to reunite him one day with his estranged daughter, Leonora; for it seemed time had finally tempered the fool. The irony was not lost on Ciabhan that it was he who remained tormented while his old adversary seemed at last contrite!

"Ah oui, Little Faye! Named for her lovely Grandmother."
Leon laughed quietly to himself.
And why does the fool laugh? Ciabhan thought frowning; did lunacy
cause some misguided humour at mention of Faye, just where does his
damaged brain wander?
"Something amusing my friend?" said Ciabhan, with a patience he did
not altogether feel!
Leon regarded him lopsidedly and raked his stubbly chin.
"Named for the faeries she was, destined never to be one mans woman!"

Neither man had ever mentioned Faye; both held memories far too
painful, so the name of the woman they both loved had stayed unspoken;
until now. Ciabhan guarded well his rising anger at Leon's dismissive
words.
"You shared children! I was left with memories only!"
Leon still studied Ciabhan, his head tilted on the side to better see him,
whether he envied his companions looks or even noticed, one could not
tell.
Lifting his felt cap Leon scratched furiously at his scalp, wispy grey
locks came away in his fingers, in disgust he examined the hairs, "blasted
lice!" he cursed; a stream of expletives followed before he became still
enough to continue talking.
When finally calm his reply was not that of a madman! But profound,
with not a shred of ill feeling,
"You alone hold the most precious memories my friend; never forget it
was for your love that she died."
Time stopped for Ciabhan, his arms turned to lead, limply they hung at
his side, the beating of his heart slowed and threatened to stop altogether
as he recalled the lifeless body of his wife in his arms, dead from the
arrow in her breast.

In the already oppressive heat of an August dawn, Ciabhan, Leon and
Reynard sailed from the shores of Haifa on the first stage of their long
journey home..

Chapter 38
Compton Berry

From beyond the open window a nightjars persistent grating woke her, lifting her head from the mans chest she watched as he slept, watched his steady breathing rise and fall, and watched his eyelids flutter, his mouth moved as if in silent conversation.

He stirred to free his hand trapped beneath her, he did not wake just turned and sighed deeply, when she raised her body a chill swept her naked shoulders.

Her heart beat fast in her breast while the throb in her head felt as the pounding of hooves on unyielding earth........

When the nightjars' voice became a troublesome she slipped from the bed and crossed to the window, kneeling on the sandalwood chest she pulled the latticework frame shut; careful not to move the little glass bird in its place on the ledge.

'Soon' she thought, 'I will read what lies within the chest.'

Across the Turkish rug she padded back to bed and slid shivering into the warmth of his arms, he stirred then and turned to her opening his eyes fleetingly, content she was beside him he nuzzled her throat, and smoothed the hair from her face; sliding her leg over his thigh she pressed her body closer...............

Safe in the painted chamber two children slumbered, no sounds from outside disturbed their innocent dreams, a night light cast a steady glow on downy cheeks.

Little Faye Alana breathed softly on her back beneath a canopy of muslin embellished with tiny silver stars, her glossy lashes curled onto ivory skin.

Beside her in a sturdy crib befitting his status, flushed from a day spent in the autumn sun, her brothers' eyes flickered beneath closed lids, dark curls clung to his damp forehead.

Ciabhans little hands still gripped the wooden sword made especially for him by Dickon, these past golden weeks it had never left his side;
He resembled a miniature knight ready for battle........................

FINE